DAUGHTERS OF KA

The return of the
Turquoise Goddess

Other books by Debangelique Thompson

Daughters of Ka – The Hunt for the Turquoise Figurine
(Book 1 in the Daughters of Ka series)

DAUGHTERS OF KA - THE RETURN OF THE TURQUOISE GODDESS

Debangelique Thompson

Cover art and graphic designs by Natalie Lourens and
Wesley John Visser of Spider Inked Tattoos and Piercing.

For L'Oreal and Anais, my own beloved Daughters of Ka and for Oscar, my own valiant protector.

1

THE GUARDIANS OF THE WATCHTOWERS

Across the arid expanse of the Great Desert to the impenetrable swamplands of the Al Suud, home to the much-feared and mythical Ninki Nanka, all who heard the gut-wrenching cries of pain of the majestic avatar of Aten, as it spiralled uncontrollably through the air, knew instinctively that the forces of evil were gaining strength.

The bright full moon and the fiery sun competed for dominion in the afternoon sky. It was a sight often beheld by the people of Ka and one that foreshadowed a time of chaos and despair, when the powers of the two most potent Gods would visibly be at odds and many innocent souls from all the many kingdoms across Ka, would be caught in the middle of an age-old feud which existed between Aten and Luna.

The capture of Aten's falcon was no coincidence. It was a meticulously planned operation which Luna had to execute if she was to succeed in her plan of revenge. Luna had often seen Aten's falcon fly over her Mountain Island fortress. She could feel its asphyxiating presence as it hovered in the skies above her. She had always resented the audacity of Aten at sending his feathered spy to watch her every movement. She had long since planned the capture of Aten's winged protector and with it the destruction of the Eye of Wedjat. The falcon was symbolic of the vast blue heavens; with its right eye representing the sun and its left eye representing the moon. It was an outward manifestation of Aten's power, which Luna was determined to control, if she was ever going to be rid of Aten.

That day the powers of the wind and the air, that constantly blew over the Dead Lands, had been driven by Luna into a violent and frenzied whirlwind, which caught the falcon off guard. Unable to resist being drawn into a confused vortex of air and wind and despite its powerful wings and its total supremacy over the skies, the falcon had been rendered defenceless and unable to resist the dark forces of Luna's moon magic as it had been pulled

1

into her icy grip. Luna watched as the stunned falcon fell into the azure waters of the volcanic crater. Its turbulent descent had by no means caused its death, since Luna needed it to be alive if she was to capture its powers for herself, but the fall had rendered it momentarily dazed and unconscious.

Luna reached into the waters and grabbed the falcon by its legs. It did not react to her touch. The weight of its limp body felt heavier than Luna had imagined. Seeing it race through the skies at sunrise, it had always appeared as a large and powerful God-like figure, but in Luna's hands, it seemed ordinary; a creature of mere flesh and bones. Luna heaved a sigh of relief and satisfaction, since the first step in her plan to gain control over the first of the four great Elementals was complete. The capture and imminent sacrifice of the falcon meant that Luna would control the forces of the east. No longer would they be able to bring light, enlightenment and the promise of new beginnings. Rebirth would never again triumph over death.

Luna rarely ventured beyond the protection of her icy realm, but she had had no choice to do so, especially if she was ever to achieve her evil ends. She had to capture the falcon, the Gelada baboon, the black snake and the bull, which were all symbols of the Elementals. She knew that her presence was no longer a welcome sight to the peoples who inhabited the Dead Lands or any other kingdom of Ka and thus her operations to capture the Elementals had been executed with stealth and precision. Of late, she had always expected the same reaction from everyone that she had encountered across Ka. She knew people both hated and feared her. Any vestiges of love and admiration that they had once felt for her, had long since disappeared. Their feelings of love towards her had been replaced with feelings of hate, which they harboured in their hearts and in their minds.

Luna's cold and malice-filled heart could however, still recognise the difference between love and hate, but she was beyond the point of caring how people around her felt about her or about how she behaved. She had convinced herself that the opinions of others mattered little. The lives of the mere mortals of Ka were dispensable to Luna. The cancer of revenge had taken seed in her heart and had, over the years, spread through her body like an all-consuming fever. She lived and breathed to exact her revenge against Aten.

Initially, Luna had surmised that if she thwarted the mission of the Daughters of Ka and prevented them from reuniting the pieces of the Turquoise Figurine, it would have been enough to bring Aten to his knees, but she had underestimated the tenacity and strength of the sisters. It had been Fera's fearlessness; shown in the way that she had risked her own life and limb to save Candace and her sisters, Feur's intelligence and diplomacy; evident in how she had negotiated with Ezana and in how she had convinced Candace to enter into the war against the Beja and finally Boise's courage in how she had fought off the iron-like jaws of the Eloko, which had proven insurmountable obstacles for Luna's plot of revenge. She admitted that she had underestimated them and the steadfastness of their male companions, who remained tirelessly devoted to their female charges and to their mission.

Luna had also miscalculated the abilities and resilience of the men and women of Ka. She had fully expected Candace's anger at Kerma to kill all vestiges of love and forgiveness in her heart, but that had not happened. She had expected Dahlak's jealousy and covetous love for Candace to cloud his judgement and prevent him from co-operating with and working alongside Kerma, but it had not. Her failed manipulation and mind control over Ta-Seti and the weakness displayed by both Ta-Seti and Al Aziz, whose minds and judgement, clouded by their deep-seeded need for revenge, had proven bitter disappointments to Luna. The evil of the Eloko had also proved a mere bump in the path of Mwari and his charges.

Luna chastised herself for not judging the hearts and minds of the men and women of Ka better. She resolved never to trust mere mortals again, especially those who were too greedy or too petty to be visionary. Luna understood with greater clarity than ever before, that if she was to overcome the sisters' steely determination and fearless courage, she would have to call upon the powers of the Guardians of the Watchtowers to be with her in her quest to destroy Aten.

Thus, under a full moon and deep below the cool waters of Mountain Island, Luna, dressed in a dark blue robe, decided to invoke a magic circle and assemble the Wheel of the Four Winds. The wheel was merely a cross with a circle around it, constructed of small brown pebbles sourced from the shores of the Emerald Lake, but it represented the great powers held by the four winds.

Luna walked towards the four cages positioned in a row in her icy lair. The inhabitants looked at her with anger and mistrust. First, she removed the black rock snake. She had captured it as it had slithered its venom-filled body across the dry and dusty earth of the Danakil. It represented the winds of the north. Just as the snake could shed it skin to reveal a transformed exterior, so too could the north winds bring the power of renewal, the power of night and clarity of decision. Luna was all too acutely aware that she would need to constantly reinvent her powers and make clear decisions if she was to succeed in her revenge against Aten. Luna placed the snake in the centre of the circle and callously chopped off its head.

She then turned her attention to the male Gelada baboon, which appeared half asleep, still under the influence of Luna's powerful moon magic. Luna looked carefully at the large creature with its course hair; dark face with pale eyelids and long, heavy cape of hair on its back and bright red patch of skin on its chest. Its appearance was distinctive and striking.

Gelada baboons were much sought after in certain parts of Ka and they were revered by the Axumite peoples. Luna had found it immensely challenging to journey through the high grasslands and deep gorges of the Gulf of Zula to locate such a mythical creature. Her labour had been rewarded when she had easily snared a large male baboon in one of her expert hunter's nets. The energetic, clever and sharp-witted Gelada represented the south winds, the essence of life-blood and vibrancy, which Luna knew she would need in order to rejuvenate and replenish her powers. Luna sacrificed the life of the baboon with one swift slit of its throat, so that its warm life-giving blood spilled onto the floor at her feet.

Luna then looked at the majestic bull, snorting and angry in its cage. Such creatures were sacred in the Great City of Catal Huyuk. She had not contemplated even attempting to trap such a large and potentially vicious creature. Instead, she had capitalised on the evil of men to do her bidding for her and in particular, a poor family who lived in the plateau of the Great Mound of the Great City, who had been more than willing to steal the wayward creature and travel many miles to bring it to Luna, in exchange for a small fortune in gold, silver and copper coins. Fortunately, there still existed those within the realms of Ka, whose hearts and minds could be turned at the mere promise of wealth.

Luna had been relieved when the bull had arrived, for it represented the power of the winds of the west; potent and strong. Of all the Elementals, Luna could benefit most by the potency and consolidation of strength brought to life by the west winds. The bull met with the same fate as the Gelada. Luna was swift in her movements. For most people, it would have been no easy task to sacrifice living creatures, but Luna set aside any scruples that she may have had and reminded herself that the times in which she found herself were indeed desperate and that her actions were necessary for her survival, albeit brutal and cruel in the opinion of many across Ka.

Lastly, Luna turned her attention to the falcon, the feathered companion of her nemesis. She expected that bringing its life to an end would have been as simple a task as it had been with the other symbols of the Elementals, but she had bitterly underestimated the strength and tenacity of the winged creature. As Luna removed it from its cage, it seemed to revive from the effects of her moon magic. Its wings beat ferociously. Luna realised that the powerful medicinal herbs, which she had used on it, were wearing off. The last thing Luna wanted was for it to regain consciousness. Without giving it a further thought, Luna held its head to the floor and with one violent gouge with

5

her sharp nails to its right eye, she removed its eyeball. The falcon reacted instantaneously and violently to its assault by pecking at Luna's hands and forearms. Instinctively, Luna loosened her grip of the bird. As she did, it managed to stand to its feet and then, despite being in obvious pain, it took to flight. It circled Luna's icy lair and flew into many objects, for its injury had impaired its vision. Eventually, it found the opening through the curtain of water and exited into the open air grotto.

It seemed as though the falcon's struggle for freedom and escape lasted an eternity, but in reality, it took only a few minutes for the falcon to find safe harbour in the blue skies above Mountain Island, once more. Luna felt cheated. The ultimate prize would have been to end its life along with the lives of the other Elementals, but on that occasion, she had not succeeded. The falcon would live another day and Luna would get yet another opportunity to capture it.

Luna made a mental note that when she did, she would not let it escape again. Despite her failure in ending the life of the falcon, Luna had fortunately succeeded in blinding it. That act was significant in of itself, for the destruction of the Eye of Wedjat meant that Aten's power would be weakened, since the eye of the falcon represented the all-seeing eye of Aten. The destruction of the Eye of Wedjat meant that the balance and order in the universe would be upset and imbalance would then, at long last, bring chaos.

Luna, stood before the Wheel of the Four Winds, closed her eyes and moved in a circular motion, as she chanted;

"I call upon the Guardians of the East to be my messenger from the spirit world and give me knowledge and wisdom."

She held the Eye of Wedjat in the palm of her hand and squeezed it tightly in her grip, so that blood and tissue oozed between her fingers and trickled down to fall on the pebbles to the east of the circle. She continued;

"I call upon the Guardians of the South to sharpen my intellect so that I may outwit my enemies." She poured the blood of the Gelada monkey into the circle.

"I call upon the Guardians of the West to make me strong and powerful to defeat and destroy my enemies." The blood from the bull was similarly poured by Luna to the west of the circle.

"Lastly, I call upon the Guardians of the North to give me the strength of will and clarity of intention to see my plans come to fruition."

Luna took the body of the snake and wrung the blood from its lifeless body so that it too, fell onto the pebbles positioned to the north of the circle. When the sacrifices and chanting to the Guardians of the Four Winds was complete, Luna ended her incantation with the words, "Let the blessings of power be upon me."

Luna felt an intense sense of achievement. It had been years since she had felt so powerful. The last time that she had felt the life force of her powers curse through her veins so potently, was the time when she had learnt that the Turquoise Figurine had been smashed to pieces. The Elementals had then been thrown out of sync and her powers had multiplied. Luna had then succeeded in capturing the powers of the Four Winds for herself. She had then been able to wield the power of the air and the wind to blow destruction all across Ka. At a mere touch of her hand, ravaging fires brought hopelessness and despair. The waters across Ka, whether they were found in the seas, lakes or even the rivers, had flooded the earth to decimate feelings of perseverance and focus of the peoples of Ka. The violent waters and harsh rains had always driven and strengthened Luna's sixth sense and heightened her spiritual and psychic abilities.

She knew then that she would need to be at her most powerful and perceptive if she was to thwart the mission to reunite the pieces of the Turquoise Figurine. Luna felt emboldened and empowered to execute of rest of her evil plans. She was adamant, that come what may, she would not fail, since she had the forces of evil moon magic behind her and she controlled the powerful Guardians of the Four Winds.

***

At dawn on the second day that Mwari and his party had journeyed up the Great Sky River, they were greeted by the

7

appearance of the Morning Star, as it flashed swiftly across the pale dawn sky.

"Did you see that?" shouted Fera excitedly, as she pointed towards it. "It must be Aten riding across the sky on his steed, with its copper coloured mane!"

Although Fera had told her sisters about her adventures into the Al Suud and in particular, about the appearance of Aten on his magical horse, only Jadon and Gideon could really appreciate the magnificence of Aten's power. The sight of Aten riding towards them at dawn, resplendent in the light of a new day, had been a sight which Fera would never forget and one which she had found hard to explain or even to truly convey its magnificence to her sisters in words that would do it justice.

"No, that is the Heliacal Rising." replied Mwari.

Everyone looked shocked to hear Mwari speak. He had sat in silence for most of their journey up river, since they had departed Meroe.

"What's that?" asked Boise.

"It's the Morning star. It makes its first appearance in the sky just before the sun rises. It heralds the time of the summer solstice and the beginning of the season of inundation."

Everyone half expected Mwari to continue, but he stopped and looked away. Daniel continued,

"The season of inundation marks the beginning of the rainy season." remarked Daniel to Boise. "It is a time when the moon tugs at the seas and rivers to create tides. The Great Sky River will flood soon. The waters will then bring plenteousness and sustenance. Farmlands will be nourished for the year ahead."

Daniel looked around him at the farmlands that bordered the banks of the Great Sky River. He continued to explain,

"These shores of the Great Sky River would ordinarily have greeted us with colourful and vibrant scenes of agrarian activity, but with the onset of the rainy season, they are now abandoned. At any other time of the year, the farmers along the banks of the Great Sky River, would usually have been planting and cultivating their crops in the rich fertile soil, but now the rains have forced many away from their lands towards the metropoli of Axum or Meroe, where much work can be found; either building the great pyramids and temples, mending tools or simply looking after animals."

Daniel was always a fountain of information, both useful and useless. On that occasion, everyone in the boat listened half-heartedly to Daniel as he told of the lives of those who made their homes and their livelihoods along the banks of the Great Sky River.

With the rain beating down on their faces and soaking their bodies as they made their way up river, everyone's thoughts seemed to drift. Nena remembered the last images of Ezana as he had stood resolutely on the quay in Meroe. The boat journey had afforded her the opportunity to consider her feelings. She questioned whether she had indeed made the right decision for herself. Her whole life had been centred on her family and their well-being. She had never dared make a decision without first consulting her family. Admittedly, she had been tempted by Ezana's marriage proposal. He had promised her a life of luxury and splendour that she had always dreamt of and told her that she would want for nothing. Although he had expressed appreciation for her appearance and for the fact that he would be proud for her to stand by his side, he had never once expressed his love for her.

Nena had initially resented her sisters' harsh words to her and their warnings against Ezana's motives, but time had taught Nena much about the things that she wanted and needed in her life. She knew then that a life without deep and abiding love; a love which was not vain, nor motivated by self-gain, would be doomed to failure. Despite being offered a life with all the trappings of wealth, Nena had finally realised that her place was with her family. Romantic love would come and go and one day, when she met the person who would consider her as more than just the sum of her outer features, she would know, and her decision to marry such a man would not have to be a trade-off between her love for him and the love for her family. She would not have to sacrifice one love for the other. She could have both and be blissfully happy.

Fera sat watching Mwari, as he sat at the helm of the boat. She recalled the cautionary words of Aten when he had told her, Jadon and Gibeon to travel by day and avoid the Great Sky River. Dahlak had echoed the same words of caution. Fera felt disconcerted and dissatisfied that Mwari had nevertheless, elected to travel to Abydos by river and moreover, during the day. It was a though he was totally ignoring the wisdom of Aten's advice.

Fera's first impression of Mwari had been that he was headstrong and domineering and that he had always wanted to be in control of every situation, but after the events in Meroe, she had reconsidered such conclusions. All her life, Fera had become extremely irritated by people who thought that they knew better and failed to heed the good advice of others, but the events of late had taught her otherwise.

She had accepted that she was powerless to change Mwari's decisions, for after all, he had been appointed by the Holy Mother Goddess to lead their mission. His decisions were final, irrespective of what she or any of the others may have thought, but she saw qualities to be admired in Mwari's character and in his deeds. In the short time that Fera had known Mwari, she had realised that he was a very focussed and driven man, but that he was also an honourable man, one whom she felt that she could trust.

She was, however, not sure what exact emotions drove him, for he remained very guarded, almost secretive. He very rarely spoke to the men, unless it was to bark instructions at them, which he expected to be carried out with meticulous precision and unwavering loyalty, or unless it was to converse with Boise. Their friendship, if one could call it that, seemed to have strengthened as the days had passed.

The exact foundation of such friendship perplexed Fera. She could not imagine what an elderly soldier, hardened by life and war, would find in common with a young, impressionable girl, like Boise. Fera knew beyond a shadow of a doubt that there were no romantic ties between them.

The attention and kindness shown by Mwari to Boise was more that of a father towards a daughter. Fera wondered what her own father would have thought about Mwari. She concluded that he probably would have liked him. He most certainly would have applauded his dedication to the protection of Shoa's daughters. Mwari had proved himself to be a strong and trustworthy leader and it was that quality which grew Fera's estimations of Mwari in leaps and bounds.

Fera also realised that many of her initial opinions of the others in their party had changed. She had at their first meeting, liked the brothers Harim and Hasshub, but their conduct in Roha-Lalibela had left much to be desired. She was disappointed and sad that they had not met her high expectations. Daniel, on the other hand, had left Fera feeling slightly ashamed of how she had jumped to conclusions, without giving him the benefit of the doubt. He had ably come to their rescue on many occasions. If he had not been able to appease the suspicions of the Royal legion at Lalibela, they would probably all have been apprehended before she had had the chance to find the first piece of the Turquoise Figurine. Boise and Feur had both sung his praises for his valiant conduct in fighting off the Eloko and Fera so wished that she could have been there. The idea of raising her sword or even her dagger against the ravenous Eloko would have been thrilling. At least, she had got a taste of battle in Meroe. Feur disturbed Fera's reflections,

"You look deep in thought."

"I was just thinking about everything that has happened. It feels as though we have lived a lifetime of experiences in such a short time." replied Fera.

Feur smiled and nodded in agreement. She felt optimistic about their future prospects. They had overcome such great obstacles in Lalibela and in Meroe, but Feur could not for the life of her shake off the overwhelming feelings of dread which she felt. The unexpected and the unknown made her shudder.

Fera and Feur both watched Boise and Daniel as they sat huddled in the boat, in deep conversation. An intimate closeness between them was clearly evident. Fera had decided that there was no purpose in refusing to acknowledge the friendship and love that had developed between them. She knew that if she continued to denounce their relationship, the ties between Boise and Daniel would only have grown stronger. Eventually, Boise would have been forced to make a decision between the love for her family and the love for Daniel. Fera feared that Boise may have chosen her new found love above her family's wishes and that decision would devastate Fera's parents. Fera would not allow that to happen. She loved her parents and her sisters deeply, albeit that she did not always see eye to eye with her mother or Nena. It was that love for her family which motivated Fera to stay strong and to boldly face whatever situations they found themselves in, no matter how trying or unpredictable.

It was not long before the soft rain started to fall more heavily. The sounds of the rain and the waters of the Great Sky River, as it lapped against the sides of the boat, rocked Fera and her sisters to sleep that night. They felt relatively safe, for they knew that Mwari and the men kept watch over them as they slept. No-one would ever have imagined that that night would be the last night for many days to come, that the sisters and their protectors would be safe and all together in the same place. The scenes of utter chaos that the sisters were awoken by in the early hours of the next day, when the cloak of night still deceptively hid the sun from the day, would remain etched in the minds of Mwari and his party forever.

Mwari had as usual, assigned very specific duties to the men, who remained highly vigilant as they made their way towards Abydos. Daniel vowed that he would never disappoint himself or Mwari again as he had done in the forests of Meroe, when he had failed so abysmally at guarding and protecting Feur and Boise. That night, Daniel sat upright and alert in the boat and stared into the night sky, with only a full moon casting eerie shadows over the deep waters of the Great Sky River. The rain fell more heavily as the night wore on. The darkness and the incessant rains made visibility difficult. Daniel noticed an up-serge in the winds, which blew more and more ferociously. The waters beat more forcefully against the sides of the boat. He stared out in the darkness beyond. He strained his eyes to see more clearly, for he thought he saw movement in the distance. He waited and focussed on a spot on the horizon and noticed that the water seemed to lift into the air. The sight, in the dead of night, was alarming.

He was hesitant to wake up Mwari and the others, just in case what he saw turned out to be nothing significant. At first, he imagined that tiredness was playing tricks with his mind and he questioned if what he saw was in fact real or not, but when the movement occurred again, he sat bolt upright. The sight that played out before his eyes, proved totally puzzling. He saw the violent wind whipping the waters into a turbulent frenzy, so much so, that the water was lifted from the surface of the river into a funnel-shaped spout which rotated, around and around and moved faster and faster as it rotated. It looked as though it not only carried water in its violent grip but some other objects, which Daniel could not ascertain the nature of.

The water spout appeared to be moving in the direction of the boat. Daniel became deeply concerned and feared that the boat would be capsized. If that eventuality arose, he surmised that it would have been better if everyone was awake and fully cognisant to face whatever dangers would come their way. Daniel would have preferred to get Mwari's attention quietly and then slowly alert the girls, but there was no time. The force of the winds and waters, as they churned within the water spout, hit the boat with such great velocity that Daniel, panicked and horrified, simply screamed,

"Wake up! Wake up!"

Mwari was the first to react. He was a light sleeper. Years of being a professional soldier had necessitated him sleeping with one eye open. That night was no different. When he saw the water spout, he instinctively grabbed the rope which lay in the boat. He screamed at the top of his voice,

"Fera, wake up your sisters."

Fera was startled to be awoken by Mwari. The look in his eyes and the tone of his voice sent shivers down her spine. She immediately, without understanding the reason for Mwari's urgent pleas for them to wake up, set on the task of alerting her sisters.

"Take this rope and tie it around you and your sisters. Your waists will do. If this boat tips, at least you will stay together. Men, equalise the weight of the boat. We need to do everything to keep it from capsizing."

Jadon and Gibeon then moved to the port side of the boat. Mwari, Asaph and Daniel sat on the starboard side of the boat.

"Start rowing. We need to fight against being pulled under." added Mwari.

Their frantic efforts at rowing seemed to steady the boat, despite the violent winds and driving rain which would not abate. Just as they had steadied the boat by rowing desperately against the current and the bashing waves, more and more turbulent waters seemed to rush over the edges of the boat.

"Girls, scoop out the water. This boat must not sink!" shouted Mwari.

Fera looked around the boat frantically for some vessel that could be used to hold water. Her mind raced with many thoughts, all of which were muddled. She thought of using her shoe to scoop water, but then realised that it would not hold liquid, at least not sufficient quantities. They were left with no choice but to use their hands. She began to cup as much water as she could from the boat. Her sisters followed suit, but as much water as they removed, more was carried by the erratic winds and dumped into the boat.

The men joined in. Their sole task was to keep the boat afloat. Just as their efforts seemed to be paying dividends, another calamity seemed to befall them. It was Nena's screams of pain that alerted Mwari to the fact that something sinister was afoot. Wind and relentless rain was abruptly replaced with hard objects, which seemed to be carried by the water spout towards them. The objects which fell from the skies, were hard and cold and fell from all directions. Everyone was pummelled by the unknown objects, which rained down mercilessly on their heads.

There was no-where to turn. The boat, which they had struggled to keep afloat amid the downpour of heavy rain, was at risk of being sunk by the sheer weight of the onslaught. Asaph looked down at his feet, his arms held protectively over his head to avoid being injured. It suddenly dawned on him what the falling objects were. He exclaimed with shock,

"They are frozen fish. Look Mwari!"

Asaph handed a frozen fish to Mwari. It was encased in solid ice. More and more frozen fish rained down around them.

"The boat will never withstand the weight of these. Look over there, the boat's got a hole in it. More water is seeping through the hull." observed Mwari.

"We need to evacuate!" added Daniel.

"We cannot. The currents are too strong. Even the best swimmer will not survive." shouted Jadon. The wind, rain and falling fish made it difficult to talk to each other, much less to plan their escape. "Besides we are too far from the shore. We will never make it."

"Does everyone know how to swim?" enquired Mwari.

The sisters, who sat huddled together, trying in vain to shelter their heads and faces from the falling objects, replied that they could swim. It was one skill that their father had insisted that they had learnt at a very young age and Fera was glad of it. Daniel, Jadon and Gibeon replied that they could also swim. That only left Asaph, who remained silent. Mwari turned to Asaph and said,

"We do not have a choice. We need to get out of this boat or we will go down with it. The river is not that deep. Trust me, you can make it. Gibeon, you look out for Jadon and Daniel, you help Asaph to the shore."

There was no time for the men to wallow in embarrassment or self-pity. Their lives and the lives of the sisters were at stake. Asaph hated the idea of having to rely on the other men. He had always thought of himself as tough and capable. Jadon turned to Asaph, who seemed to have been rendered paralysed by fear at the thought of having to swim to shore,

"You can do this. We all can do this."

"I cannot. You know what lurks beneath those waters, don't you?"

On hearing Asaph's words and understanding that he was referring to the feared Ninki Nanka, Fera regretted the fact that she had told her sisters and Asaph about her journey into the Al Suud.

"I cannot get out the boat. You all swim ahead. Perhaps if you go first, I can muster up the courage to follow." added Asaph.

To Mwari, it really was a most incongruous sight. Asaph was the most muscular and strongest of all the men. He had experienced no difficulty in dealing with the frightful Eloko. He had fought ably alongside Candace's deformed army, yet he was afraid of swimming a short distance. Granted, Mwari understood that the vicious creatures lurking within the waters of the Great Sky River, were a major obstacle for Asaph, but Mwari had vowed that he would let nothing get in the way of the completion of their mission, least of all a violent storm. Mwari tried to be patient and reassuring towards Asaph, but found the task very difficult. When it became abundantly clear that Asaph would not budge, Mwari instructed,

"We will go ahead. You watch and see how we manage. Everything will be fine."

Mwari hoped that Asaph would be able to find the courage that he needed to follow them, but witnessing how Asaph was clutching desperately to the sides of the boat, all hope seemed doubtful.

The men lowered the sisters first, one by one into the turbulent waters. The rain and frozen creatures continued to pelt down over their heads. Nena gasped, as her body sank beneath the cold waters. She clung to the boat while her sisters were similarly dropped into the river. Once they were all submerged, they swam as quickly as they could towards the shore.

"Stay close. Kick. Do not allow the currents to pull you under. Fight the waters." shouted Fera to her sisters.

It was a mammoth task for Fera and her sisters to keep afloat, all tied together with the same piece of rope. At times, Nena, who was the weakest swimmer amongst her sisters, struggled bitterly to keep her head above the relentless waves, which only seemed to grow bigger and more fearsome, since they had been left vulnerable to the power of the Great Sky River, outside of the relative protection of the boat. Boise and Fera took turns to keep Nena from being overcome by the waters. Nena cried, screamed and swallowed copious amounts of water throughout the entire ordeal.

"Hang on to me and stay calm, will you, or you are going to pull us all down with you?" shouted Boise at Nena.

Boise found herself doing the exact thing that Fera had always been accused of, but shouting at Nena on that occasion would be the only thing that would save all their lives. Fera never imagined that a river could be so unpredictable and threatening. Her thoughts drifted back to her beloved Catal Huyuk. She remembered her afternoon frolics in the Charshamba River. She had never once felt scared when she swam beneath its refreshing swells. Its depths had always been a source of intrigue and excitement. Its waters had always provided her with a measure of escape from the monotony of her life. Although she had never once caught a glimpse of the mystical Goddess Imanje, she had never wanted to stop diving deeper and deeper below the river's surface to discover its hidden mysteries and secrets.

Fera's experience that night, as she was violently pushed and pulled by the waters of the Great Sky River, proved vastly different to her childhood memories of swimming in the Charshamba River. The waters of the Great Sky River frightened her. She feared what lurked within their dark depths. She knew that they would never survive an attack from the Ninki Nanka. How she wished that Mwari had not chosen the route to Abydos via the Great Sky River. The reality was, that Aten's warnings had all but been ignored by Mwari and his party, much to their own peril.

After endless minutes of kicking, screaming and being engulfed by dark waters, Fera reached the shores of the Great Sky River. She felt relieved to feel the hard earth under her feet. She mustered as much strength as she could to pull her sisters from the waters.

"Pull, Boise! Pull Nena!"

Feur was the last to be pulled to safety. Choking and gasping for air, she lay almost breathless on the smooth sand.

"Are you alright Feur?" enquired Boise with concern, for she knew that Feur's wound from the Eloko attack had just recently knitted. Boise hoped that it had not re-opened. The murky waters of the river contained all forms of bacteria which could prove dangerous to a freshly healed wound, but fortuitously, Feur's arm was well on the mend.

It was not long after the sisters had arrived ashore that the men started to make landfall. First Mwari, then Daniel, then Jadon and lastly Gibeon, reached the shoreline.

"Where's Asaph?" asked Fera.

"He's still aboard the boat. He refused to come. We tried to pull him in with us, but he is so much stronger than us." lamented Jadon.

"How will he get off the boat? The rains and winds do not seem to be abating. In fact, they seem to be getting worse." asked Fera.

"We tried to get him to come with us, believe me!" added Gibeon.

Fera did not doubt that the men had done everything possible to coax or even coerce Asaph to shore. If one thing was certain, it was that Asaph was stubborn. Fera thought then, that perhaps it was a family trait, since both her father and herself, if the truth had been told, had streaks of intense stubbornness within them.

As they discussed Asaph's predicament, the storm took a turn for the worse. Where at first the sky was simply black and menacing with rain and later filled with icy creatures which fell down on them, suddenly, dark clouds punctuated with sharp streaks of light, could be seen. Each bolt of lightning was preceded by loud thunderous roars.

"The Gods of Thunder and Lightning are fighting again. Remember what father used to tell us?" commented Boise recounting the tales of their childhood.

"This is no innocent spat. Something sinister is happening. Such violent storms are not prevalent in these parts. It is as though all the forces of nature have been awoken from their slumber to direct their wrath and vengeance on us all tonight." said Daniel.

Although no-one dared mouth her name for fear that simply talking about her would strengthen her powers over them, they all secretly suspected that Luna was behind their watery ordeal. Mwari surveyed their surroundings for possible places to take shelter from the storm.

"Take cover under that scrub over there!" shouted Mwari, as another bolt of lightning struck. Everyone obeyed, except Fera.

"I cannot abandon Asaph. He is family. We must wait for him."

"We are not going to leave him, but we cannot get struck by lightning. We would not be of any use to him then, would we?" asked Mwari in an authoritative tone as he stood before Fera.

After thinking on it for several seconds, Fera reluctantly obeyed and moved to where the others stood, huddled beneath some low-growing scrub. The vegetation around them had changed from lush growth to semi-arid scrub. There were few places that one could take shelter, but they made do, the best that they could. Everyone stared resolutely out to where the boat drifted on the raging waters. As the waves swelled and crashed against the boat, Fera could see the boat appear and disappear behind the waves. Every bolt of lightning shone momentary streaks of light over the river causing the boat to suddenly appear then disappear from sight. Every time lightning struck, a scared and bedraggled Asaph could be seen clutching hopelessly to the boat. It was apparent that he was unable to move. Perhaps fear of drowning or simply fear itself, had overcome him. Mwari and the men shouted in his direction, begging him to swim ashore, but Asaph would not heed their calls.

As they remained huddled under the scrub, Boise looked to the sky. Her father had always told her that during a violent storm, loud thunder usually preceded the lightning bolts. His age-old wisdom was proving true that night. Thunderous roars and vicious streaks of light illuminated the night sky. Daniel looked up into the heavens. Although the dark night sky was still interrupted by vicious streaks of lightning, the rain, quite suddenly and inexplicably, abated. It was as though someone had magically clicked their fingers and made the rain stop and the humidity rise. It was a truly unexpected phenomenon to observe.

"Perhaps the storm is moving over." commented Daniel. Mwari looked less than convinced.

"I doubt it. Something is amiss here. Just a few minutes ago, it was pouring with rain. Now the air has turned from cool and wet to humid and dry. The lightning and thunder have increased in their intensity." replied Mwari.

"This storm reminds me of those days when we found ourselves in the Great Desert to the west of Ka. Do you remember Jadon? We so wished and prayed for rain, yet none fell. One would look to the horizon, which looked as though a rain storm was approaching since the clouds appeared ominous with wispy and grey streaks at their bases, but to our great disappointment, little rain ever fell." reminisced Gibeon about the good old days when he and Jadon had travelled across the length and breadth of Ka as soldiers for hire. There were many ruthless and power-hungry leaders across Ka who had always welcomed any able-bodied man to join the rank and file of their large armies. Gibeon and Jadon had fought in many protracted and bloody wars, advancing the greed of other men. From the very beginning of the Holy Mother Goddess' mission, it was that fact which had bonded Jadon and Gibeon with Mwari. They knew little detail of his life or the places that he had been to or the wars that he had fought in, but they surmised that their life paths had much in common with Mwari's. The way of life of a soldier was never a mystery to anyone who consciously chose it, but for most, such decision was never as simple as it would originally have seemed. Jadon and Gibeon had exercised free will in agreeing to join and fight in one army after another, but they had quickly found that after having joined, all semblance of free will had been lost, since a soldier had to obey the instructions of his commanders, sometimes blindly and other times with the full knowledge that his actions would be contrary to his own moral code. A soldier had to go where the action would be, despite often not knowing the outcome, but all the time hoping against hope that he would live long enough to share in a victory and the spoils of war that came with a crushing defeat of the enemy.

Jadon and Gibeon had initially wondered whether they had crossed swords with Mwari before, whether unbeknownst to either of them, Mwari had stood on one side of the battlefield, while they had stood on the other. They would never have known, since they could not specifically recall the countless unknown faces that they had faced in battle. They had learnt to become immune to the consequences of their actions. It was better to avoid the eyes of the men, whose lives would inevitably have to be brutally extinguished at their hands. Jadon actively encouraged himself not to dwell on the past. Their present circumstances offered more than enough food for thought. Jadon contributed to Mwari's assessment of their situation.

"Back then, we called it a Virga, a dry thunderstorm. It is perhaps the cruellest of storms. It can drive good men to insanity. The warm air only brings greater humidity. The dry air then strangles the moisture in the air allowing no rain to fall." added Jadon.

"What causes a Virga?" asked Boise.

"No-one really knows. Nature is a mystery." replied Mwari.

Boise waited for Mwari to expand on his reply, but he did not. Instead, his mind seemed to drift to some far off place, leaving Boise at a loss for words. Mwari knew that some natural phenomena were beyond the comprehension of mortal men. As a child, the natural world and how it worked had been an endless source of fascination for his young mind. He had asked his father on many occasions how rain knew when to fall just when the farmers had planted their crops and why winds blew so ferociously at certain times and then were deathly silent at other times. His father had been a wise man with a treasure chest of knowledge about the wonders of nature.

Growing up, Mwari had lived through many dry thunderstorms and thus he was able to recognise the true nature on the storm that circled the angry skies above them. His thoughts were cast back to the days when he had stood on the red earth of his father's maize fields. Back then, they had always dry planted the maize seeds just before the rains fell. Often rain clouds would circle from the east. Everyone who would see them had hoped that rain would come, but they had, more often than not, been disappointed, when the sun broke through the angry clouds to shine once again. Blistering heat would then wilt newly sown seeds.

As a young boy, Mwari had resented the searing sun and the dry winds which blew across the lands of his birth. To him, they did nothing but tease and dupe the earth into believing that rains would come. The continued prosperity and survival of his people had depended on the arrival of the rain. Although as a boy, Mwari had felt that the wind and the rains had held his people hostage, he nevertheless, always had a very healthy respect for the natural world, a respect which had been sown in the seeds of his youth. His father had always taught him to be respectful of the earth and the forces of nature. His father had always told him,

"We do not own the land, my son, the land owns us. We are its custodians for future generations. The land lives. It cannot be possessed. We cannot control the forces of nature."

"But, we can Father! We can bring the rain. The Rain Queen can bring the rain." Mwari had often reminded his father, who in turn, had smiled warmly at the headstrong and precocious notions of his eldest son.

"Yes, my boy, she is most certainly powerful enough to bring rain to our lands."

Mwari had been raised with a strong belief in the powers of the Rain Queen. She had ruled the Balobedu Kingdom and as a powerful magician, she had brought rains to her friends and drought to her enemies. People from neighbouring tribes had always brought their daughters, cattle and other gifts to her to appease her tempestuous nature. Mwari recalled how his own people had tried, sometimes in vain, other times with great success, to control the forces of nature. The elders in his kingdom had observed the Mukwerere ceremony, at which they had asked the ancestors for rain. Mwari and the other children had been chased away by the female elders as they had brewed beer for the ceremony. Only those women, who had no longer slept with men, were allowed to perform such sacred task. The pots of beer had then been placed at the base of the muchakata tree, which was so sacred to Mwari's people that no-one had ever been allowed to be cut it down.

The tribe's spirit medium or Svikiro, as she was known, had then danced around the tree. Mwari felt as though he could still hear the soft clanging of the trinkets tied around her ankles, as her feet had tramped the dusty red earth of his homeland. He could still picture the image of the Svikiro as she had danced to bring the rains, with her black cloth draped around her waist and her head adorned with her headdress of feathers, sourced from the Great Fish Eagle, which was the divine messenger of the Gods. Spirit mediums believed that Fish Eagle feathers in the Svikiro's headdress held great mystical powers, since all objects had spirit, even those obtained from the dead, since the dead lived in a parallel world to the living.

Thoughts of his past and his childhood flashed through Mwari's mind and happily drowned out the chaos of the moment in which he then found himself.

"Mwari, are you listening to me? What must we do? Should we wait out the storm? What about Asaph? Surely we cannot leave him at the mercy of the river?"

Boise was intent on bringing Mwari back to reality. It seemed, of late, that he often drifted away to some far-off place. It was disconcerting for not only Boise, but for the others as well. They looked to Mwari for guidance and support. If he was unable to provide that, then they feared what might happen to them.

Mwari suddenly remembered where he was. His reminiscences had left him with an overwhelming feeling that the worst of the storm was not yet over. He feared that Luna was not quite yet finished with them that night. Her powers reminded him of the great powers of the Rain Queen of his youth, yet Luna's powers were infinitely more powerful, sinister and unpredictable. The teachings of his youth and his father's words had put him on guard. His mind searched for meaning, trying to make sense of the events which unfolded around them.

Suddenly, the rains and winds no longer posed the most serious threat to their survival. From the corner of his eye, Mwari spied of a large black mass moving swiftly towards them. At first, he could not distinguish what it was, but as it came closer and closer, he realised that he was looking at a massive flock of birds.

Ordinarily, birds which flew in great numbers, would just fly overhead, unhindered and undeterred by the human activity below them. They went about their business and humans went about theirs. Mwari sensed with impending dread that the birds which he saw flying towards them, were not intent on flying past them at all. It appeared as though the birds were flying directly in their direction, as though they intended to attack them. He was convinced that their evil presence had been conjured up by Luna. Mwari pointed to the sky and shouted,

"Take cover! Those birds are heading directly for us!"

Everyone looked at the mass of black rooster-like birds flying at them. Before anyone could react to Mwari's instructions, the birds dove down and attacked them. There was no place to hide from the attack, which was vicious and swift. The birds pecked at everyone's arms and faces. The sisters crouched low to the ground and wrapped their arms around their heads to protect their faces from the vicious claws which had reached out from the skies to attack them. Mwari and the men instinctively drew their swords. They swiped and jabbed at the birds, but their attempts at warding off the avian attack proved futile, since the birds were pitch black and were difficult to see clearly at night.

It was only when the bolts of lightning illuminated the sky, that the men got clearer views of their attackers. That afforded them the opportunity to stab their targets with a modest measure of precision and success, but unfortunately for the men, as the bolts of lightning struck, the birds became more vicious and even more persistent in their attempts to claw and peck at their human victims. It was as though the lightning was inciting the birds to become more rancorous. The men soon realised that no amount of fighting off the birds with their sticks and knives would deter their advances. The birds seemed impervious to all the men's futile attempts to ward them off.

"What are they?" shouted Boise in a frightened tone.

"They look like lightning birds or Impundulu, as my people refer to them. The lightning has brought them. I have seen many such creatures back home. They are the personification of evil. My people believe that the lightning bird is the evil fiend of a witch. Such a bird is passed down from mother to daughter. First, the bird does the evil bidding of the witch and then continues its legacy of evil when the daughter of such a witch carries on her mother's trade." replied Mwari.

It was the first time that anyone had got a glimpse into Mwari's background. The sisters were shocked by Mwari's revelations.

"How do we get rid of them?" asked Feur.

"They will not die. To puncture the heart of an impundulu is futile. They will simply rise from the dead. There is only one way that they can be stopped."

Mwari paused for a moment, resulting in the onset of impatience in Fera. It seemed so surreal to Fera to be trying to have a serious conversation with Mwari amidst the onslaught of sadistic birds above them.

"Well, what is it?" asked Fera impatiently.

"They must be burned. Their dead black souls cannot then return to the living world through the flames of fire."

"That's all good and well, but how will we catch them?" asked Nena, who continued to keep a vigilant eye on the birds as they tried to peck at her arms and head.

As Mwari told the girls of the need to kill the birds, his mind had already been calculating how he could practically bring an end to the impundulu.

"We won't have to. Find everything that can be burned; clothes, scrub and wood, in fact, anything that you can lay your hands on. We will light a large fire. The impundulu are attracted to fire like moths to a flame. Once they fly too close, the flames will engulf them. Trapped in the grip of fire, they will have no way of escaping."

Everyone scrambled around their close vicinity to pick up small pieces of wood and scrub. The task was made significantly more difficult by the continual pecking and clawing from the ravenous birds. All the collected items were then hurriedly thrown in a large pile which was lit by Mwari's expert hands. Many a cold night under the stars had necessitated Mwari acquiring the skill of making fire, so he easily lit the flame. Within minutes the flames grew bigger and bigger.

"Add more things that will burn. We must let the fire burn as big and as bright as we can get it." instructed Mwari.

The surrounding vegetation was sparse and the little that they could retrieve was waterlogged, so the sisters were left with no choice but to throw some of their outer garments on the fire. Anything superfluous was cast into the flames. When the flames grew higher into the night sky, everyone took cover at a distance from the fire. Just as Mwari had predicted, the impundulu were instantly attracted to the fire. They flew recklessly towards it in their droves. Hundreds of birds careered towards the flames, their ear-shattering screeches could be heard as they caught fire and their feathered, black bodies withered in the heat of the scorching flames. It was a shocking sight, especially for Boise who treasured all living things. Mwari saw the terror in her eyes and tried to comfort her,

"They are not living creatures, Boise. Their immortality comes from great evil. They feed off the blood of humans. We needed to kill them otherwise our lives would have been in danger. They would not have stopped until we were all dead. You understand?"

Boise felt strangely calmer upon hearing Mwari's words. She respected Mwari greatly. He had saved them several times during their mission. She was grateful for his presence. She reached out and touched his hand as a show of the depth of her admiration and esteem for him. He smiled at the gesture.

When the skies had cleared of the demonic presence of the impundulu and the violent bolts of lightning, which had preceded their arrival, had disappeared, everyone breathed a sigh of momentary relief, which was short-lived when they remembered that they still had to face the problem of how to get Asaph to shore. The unfortunate man still clung desperately to the boat, which remained trapped in the treacherous waters of the Great Sky River.

Mwari was mindful that the urgency to get Asaph safely ashore, was apparent. The rickety boat had withstood such an onslaught, first from the deluge of waters gushing into it and then from the weight of the frozen fish which had torpedoed down from the sky. It was a miracle that it still floated upright and that Asaph had not been driven out of it by the vicious pecks of the impundulu. When the boat came into view, but looked empty. Asaph was no-where to be seen.

"Asaph, are you okay?" shouted Jadon.

It took a few moments, but slowly Asaph's fear-filled eyes and tear-stained face sheepishly appeared. Obviously, he had taken cover in the boat during the attack of birds.

"It is all over now, the rain seems to have abated. The waters look calmer. If we all made it to shore, so can you." shouted Gibeon.

"You are not afraid are you? A big man like you, scared of a little water." teased Jadon.

Daniel quickly figured out that Jadon and Gibeon's strategy was to tease and ridicule Asaph out of the boat. If they poked at his pride enough, perhaps he would get angry enough to save himself. Fera joined in,

"Are you like one of those measly and cowardly city boys back home? What would my father say about your lack of courage? You were chosen to accompany us on this mission because my father thought you courageous and brave. The way you are acting now is neither courageous nor brave. You will never live this down, you know. When everyone back home knows that you cowered away in fear, you will be ridiculed forever." egged on Fera.

Asaph thought for a while on his possible courses of action. Fera was right after all. He would always be seen as a coward if he had failed to swim to shore. He rationalised with himself. He knew that if he stayed in the boat, he would eventually have landed up in the water anyway, since the boat had taken on too much water already and would probably have sunk. He also knew that Mwari would eventually lose all patience with him and the party would then just have left him there. What would he then have done? He was big in size, but he knew very little about the world outside Catal Huyuk. How would he have defended himself against all the unknown creatures that seemed to be popping out to attack them? If the truth be told, he was afraid to go it alone.

After wrangling with his own fears, Asaph eventually decided to bite the bullet. He cautiously swung his legs over the side of the boat and with a deep inhalation of warm air, he fell into the water with a loud splash. He gripped the side of the boat. Everyone on shore was relieved that Asaph had seen the light. Mwari silently prayed to Allah for giving him the patience to allow the men to encourage Asaph to shore, albeit that their particular brand of encouragement had taken the form of shameless bullying.

"Grab onto the rope Asaph. We can then pull you ashore." shouted Daniel.

"I can't see any rope. Where is it?" said Asaph.

"It is there to your left. Just grab it. For heaven's sake Asaph, open your eyes will you." shouted Fera.

She felt herself becoming agitated. They had struggled long enough with Asaph. If it had not been for him, they might have been able to move deeper inland, away from the river and the dangers that it brought. Fera, however, reminded herself to be more generous, since Asaph had after all risked his life to save Boise and Feur from the Eloko's clutches. Once good turn deserved another, she thought and after all, he was family.

At first, Asaph experienced great difficulty in locating the rope. Admittedly, closing his eyes afforded him a measure to cope with the extreme anxiety which he felt, but it greatly hindered his efforts. He rationalised however, that if he could not see the water and whatever lurked within in, perhaps he would be safer. He grudgingly opened his eyes. The water rushed around him in frenzied swirls. He grabbed the rope.

"I've got it. Pull me in." he said with a mouth full of water.

Asaph started to move through the water as those on shore pulled him towards safety. The shore seemed to be getting closer and closer. He felt calmer. Unexpectedly, he felt something touch his leg. It was more of a brush, really, as though some cold, rough object had grazed his skin. He felt his skin burn. Asaph chose not to think about the possible cause of his momentary pain. He focussed on the goal at hand, which was to get to safety as soon as possible.

The men continued to pull him towards shore. Asaph felt another brush past his leg. He then felt a violent tug and was pulled under the water. He gasped to catch his breath. His lungs burned for lack of oxygen. He wondered how long a man could survive under water. He made a conscious decision to close his eyes once again. He did not want the last thing he saw to be the fiendish eyes of the Ninki Nanka.

He felt his body sinking deeper and deeper into the strangely welcoming embrace of the river. The air in his lungs was spent. He felt as though his mind and body were drifting off to a calm and wondrous place. In his mind's eye, he saw images of his beloved mother. It was as though she was right there with him, her hand outstretched towards him, beckoning him towards her. He wanted to go to her. She had always been his pillar of strength. It felt so instinctively natural for him to seek solace in her warm embrace. Anywhere that she was, had always been a safe and warm place for him to be.

After what seemed an eternity, he felt a thud as his feet touched the river bed. His mind was pricked back into reality. He panicked for a moment when he realised where he was. He was startled that he had reached the bottom of the river so quickly, for he had always believed that the Great Sky River was extremely deep. He involuntarily opened his eyes. Darkness enveloped him. He could see nothing. Suddenly, the blackness became filled with iridescent colours and brilliant greens and blues which flashed before his eyes. He thought for a brief moment that the face of a woman appeared to him, but then he thought differently. He remembered the face of his mother.

Starved for oxygen and driven by fear and panic, he thought that his mind was playing tricks on him. The beautiful face appeared again, that time it came into his vision more clearly. It was the face of a young woman. She had brilliant white eyes which shone like pearls. Her small waist and large breasts enticed his masculine senses. He had no experience of women to speak of and the alluring creature which floated magically before him, offering herself to him enticingly and seductively, proved to be irresistible.

His mind fought to propel himself towards the light and the air above, but his body was lulled into submission by the seductive creature before him. She did not touch him nor hold him within the water's embrace, but he felt hopelessly trapped, bereft of independent will and volition to fight his way to the surface. He felt the passionate kiss of her lips on his and the push of her voluptuous breasts against his chest. He wanted to stay with her, be her slave.

His peaceful idyll was interrupted by a tug at his arm. The touch was not from his new found love. It was rough and desperate. He felt another pull, then another and then he felt his body being pulled upwards through the waters to the surface. The mesmerizing darkness became dotted with light. He felt anxious and desolate at the thought of parting from the magical woman, but he was left with no choice but to leave her. The decision was not his to make. The last thought to cross Asaph's mind was a feeling of immense despair.

Having brought Asaph's limp body to the surface, Jadon and Gibeon made their way to the shore. It had been an exhausting ordeal. They had not imagined Asaph to be so heavy. It was like something had been holding him, as though his body had been weighed down with several bags of stones, making it heavy and burdensome to pull to the surface. But, fortunately, they had persevered until Asaph was safe on land.

"Is he alive?" asked Nena, who thought that Asaph's body looked weak and lifeless.

Mwari knelt beside the wet and bedraggled body. He listened for any signs of breathing. There were none. If Asaph was to be saved, Mwari would have to react quickly. With all his might, Mwari clenched his fist and brought it down firmly on Asaph's chest in the hope that the force would jolt his heart to beat once again. He cleared his airways and turned his face sideways so that any water collected in his lungs and throat could escape. Asaph's lips had turned blue. His skin felt cold to the touch. Mwari repeated his life-saving manoeuvre.

The sisters stood close by, silently and fearfully dreading the eventuality that their minds had already recognised. Asaph was family. He had always been there for them. Throughout their childhood, he had assumed the role of their protector, his unusually large and bulky frame, had offered protection against the teasing and taunts of the Great City's bullies. Mwari's loud thumps to Asaph's chest were heard over and over again. He looked like a mad-man possessed. It was Daniel, who decided to step in,

"Enough, Mwari, he is gone. He was under the water too long. You have done all you could. Leave the poor man be!"

Daniel could see that the incessant blows to the body of their dead relative was a disturbing sight for the sisters. Nena, Boise and Feur were sobbing loudly. Fera stood in shocked silence. Mwari's continued his relentless thumps. The face before him was no longer that of Asaph. He once again saw the small brown eyes that had always tormented him.

"I must save him. He cannot die. I cannot bear it if he died. If it wasn't for me, he would be alive. I killed him." sobbed Mwari.

Everyone who stood nearby was perplexed by Mwari's reaction. They failed to understand his words. He seemed confused.

"He drowned Mwari. You did not kill him." added Jadon.

"I stopped too late to save him. I believed them when they told me that I was right. Oh, God, I killed him!" Mwari was shouting and cursing at the top of his lungs. It was the first time that Daniel thought that Mwari could harm others, if not himself.

"He seems to have completely lost control of his senses." shouted Daniel.

Mwari's ramblings made no sense and he was frightening everyone around him. Daniel decided to take drastic measures to stop Mwari. He hated the idea, but he was left with no choice. With all the force that he could muster, he hit Mwari over the head with the handle of his sword. Mwari slumped over unconscious. The sisters gasped in horror.

"Was that really necessary?" asked Jadon.

"You and I both know that if we had tried to pull Mwari away from Asaph's body or simply punched him and if we had not knocked him out with the first blow, Mwari would simply have struggled and fought us off. He is stronger than he looks and you both know it." replied Daniel. Jadon and Gibeon nodded in agreement.

Mwari may have been older than them all, but he was surely fiercer than all the men combined. Mwari's body was dragged away from Asaph and left propped up against some scrub. With Mwari subdued, Daniel turned his attention to the sisters. He reassured them that all was well. He embraced Boise tenderly.

"Nothing will ever be well again! Asaph is dead. He would not have died, had we never agreed to leave the Great City on this mission. Who else is going to die? You? Me? All of us?" shouted Fera.

Daniel knew that he had only recently established a truce of sorts with Fera. If he treated her heavy-handedly then, he risked doing great damage to their relationship. For Boise's sake, he reigned himself in,

"Fera, you must calm yourself. Nothing is going to happen to us. No-one else is going to die. No-one could ever have foreseen what happened here tonight, not even the Holy Mother Goddess herself. It was an accident. Asaph could have been saved. He chose to stay behind in the boat. We all tried to coax him ashore. You know that everyone here did everything in their power to rescue him, but it was not to be."

"You don't know for sure who will live and who will die, so don't go pretending otherwise. You lord your education over us all. There are many things that you do not know; many things that you will never know. Asaph was a wonderful friend. He did not deserve to die like that, alone and scared."

Daniel had no words to reply, for he knew Fera was right. He himself questioned how events could have turned so catastrophic. Fate was a cruel mistress and unpredictable at the best of times. Life and death were questions that were shrouded in mystery. Daniel suspected though that it was not the hand of fate which had dealt them a death-blow that night, but a force far more powerful and exacting than fate or death could ever have been.

When Fera started to sob uncontrollably, Daniel stepped aside. There were others there whose place it was to comfort her. The sight of Fera crying was a rarity, if ever seen by her sisters. Fera was the strong one amongst them, the shoulder that they could always lean on. The tables were then turned. They would be there for Fera. Boise, Nena and Feur embraced their sister tenderly. That night, the sisters' tears for Asaph, their clumsy, oaf-like protector with a heart of gold, who was their constant childhood companion and their tears to console the ache in their hearts for their parents and their beloved Catal Huyuk, could be heard by the men as they sat silently and in shock around the campfire.

2

HELIACAL RISING

The following morning, a brilliant sunrise heralded a day filled with promise and one, which was far removed from the devastation of the night before. The tumbled and weather-beaten landscape around them remained the only vestige of the violent storm that had ravaged the area.

"You would not know that the Great Sky River so savagely took a life, would you? Just look at it now, so calm and tranquil? It looks so beautiful." remarked Fera sardonically as she surveyed the river. Feur placed her arm on Fera's hand.

"We will never forget him. His spirit will no doubt be with us as we journey on." said Feur reassuringly.

"I know he will. We will probably need every bit of help that we can get." replied Fera.

"Especially with the cooking!" added Boise, with a glimmer of a smile on her face.

Boise and Nena had attempted to make breakfast that morning. They had decided that it would be a fitting tribute to Asaph if they had made a meal, but their attempts had left inedible burnt offerings on a plate, which to their own surprise, everyone had eaten, not so much since they were ravenous, but more so, out of respect for Asaph and as a nod to his culinary skills.

Fera understood what her sisters were trying to do. She knew that they were intent on getting her to focus on the positive things, such as on life, on love and on laughter. It would be difficult for her, but Fera was determined to go on and not to let the death of Asaph be for nothing. If they failed in reuniting the pieces of the Turquoise Figurine, then Asaph's death would have been for nought.

When she had awoken that morning, Fera had decided that failure would be intolerable. She committed herself, with steely determination, to the fact that they would forge ahead and succeed, no matter what. Daniel was also eager to leave the events of the previous day behind them.

"We need to get going. The road to Abydos is long. See if the boat is salvageable. Perhaps we can mend it." said Daniel.

"I am not putting a foot inside that boat. I refuse to travel by river. After what happened last night, surely you cannot expect us to journey up river. Aten told us not to travel by river, did he not? And did anyone listen to him? No!" shouted Fera.

"We do not have a choice, Fera. Travelling by water is the quickest and the ....." Jadon wanted to mouth the words 'safest way to travel' but, he stopped himself. He remembered Asaph and did not say another word.

"Well then, how will we get to Abydos. You know that the Great Sky River flows directly through Abydos. It makes sense." asked Jadon.

"It does not. Nothing makes sense anymore!" echoed Fera.

A few minutes of frenetic arguing ensued with Fera denouncing the plans of Daniel, Jadon and Gibeon to travel by river. Feur tried to get them to speak calmly and rationally, but the discussion became more and more heated.

"You are not my keeper. You are not our keepers. The decision is not yours. We will decide for ourselves." shouted Fera, looking at her sisters and expecting them to take her side in the argument and agree to travel by land.

Boise, Nena and Feur were torn by the decision. Both choices frightened them. The proposition of travelling by land, as Fera had wanted to do, seemed viable given the violent storm of the night before and since it was the season of inundation, further storms would be inevitable. Daniel's proposition of travelling by water, however, seemed the best alternative, but such choice would have been wholly and utterly outweighed by the velocity of Fera's wrath if they did not side with her.

The sisters knew deep down that Daniel's plan was the most sound. The river held dangers, but the road to Abydos was totally unknown to them. There could have been a strong likelihood that they would have encountered far greater dangers if they travelled by foot, more so than if they had continued by boat. Torn between a rock and a hard place, they remained silent, hoping that Fera's stubbornness would relent.

"If we put this to a vote, there would be six in favour of travelling by boat." remarked Daniel.

"Obviously sums are not a skill that you have mastered." quipped Fera. I do not know what is more condescending, the fact that you, as a man, think that you have the right to decide for my sisters what they should do or worst yet, that you have the temerity to presume that my sisters will side with you. My sisters will follow me. I am the eldest and I know what is best for them."

"Do you really, Fera?" asked Daniel. "Your sisters have minds of their own."

Fera wanted to lash out with a harsh retort, but the look on her sisters' faces, left her speechless. She did not have to ask their opinion, for it was displayed on their faces. She felt like screaming out and calling them traitors. How could they betray her like that? Was there no honour amongst sisters? Fera felt defeated. Her own sisters had turned on her. She just wanted to run; to get as far away from them as she could. The death of Asaph had dealt her a hard blow. She felt as though every fibre of her being was exhausted, yet angry and confused. Unable to deal with the situation, she turned and ran along the shoreline. She really did not know where she was going. All she knew was that she needed to be alone. Daniel tried to follow her, but Boise caught his arm,

"Leave her be. She has always assumed the role of our protector. We have always let her take the lead and make decisions for us. It must be a tough realisation for her that we can look after ourselves now, that we can make our own decisions and stand alone."

"We will talk to her." added Feur wisely.

They found Fera a few hundred metres up river. She was sitting on the banks tossing stones into the river. Each stone cast into the water, caused a rippled pattern on the surface. Boise, Nena and Feur walked to where Fera was and sat beside her, in silence, allowing her to vent her anger and her frustration with every stone which she tossed into the water. It was Feur who spoke first. Just as Fera was about to pick up another stone, Feur caught her hand. She opened her palm to reveal a smooth stone at its centre. Feur continued,

"Sisterhood is like this; you know? This rock has been fashioned over thousands of years to form a solid mass. No matter where it is thrown; no matter where it lands, it remains strong, unbreakable. We are sisters. Our bond of sisterhood will always remain strong and unbreakable, no matter where we land. And we will, in all likelihood, land in different places and be fashioned by different events in our lives, but we will always remain strong. Fera, we love and respect you as our elder sister, but you must allow us to go out into the world and make our own decisions."

"I only want what is best for you."

"We know, but we also know what is best for us. We have the right, just as you do, to make our own decisions. You must respect that. You will always be our big sister. But stand next to us, not in front of us. If we stand side by side as equals, we can only get stronger, more formidable." Feur smiled, as did Nena and Boise. Fera understood Feur's words.

"I am sure that the men will not want to mess with you again after that display of anger and shouting. Gibeon looked positively afraid of you Fera." added Nena.

The sisters hugged and smiled. Fera realised that her sisters had grown up, seemingly overnight. Their journey was changing them all, perhaps her most of all and definitely, for the better. It had most assuredly had a profound effect on Fera and she was glad of it.

"Now, let's get back and see if Mwari is awake, shall we? said Boise. After his less than gentle bash on the head, Mwari had slept soundly through the night. "Perhaps he will have the answer we seek."

On their way back towards camp, Boise admired the rugged terrain around her. Even a violent storm could not decimate all of nature's beauty, she thought. Whilst picking some small water flowers, which she intended to place on Asaph's freshly dug grave, she noticed something strange laying at the river's edge. At first, she assumed it was a piece of driftwood carried ashore. It was conceivable that all manner of debris could have found their way ashore after the storm of the night before, but the object moved and then moved again. Boise felt convinced that it was most definitely not a piece of wood. It looked like some kind of creature. Perhaps it had been wounded. She ran to where it lay. To her amazement, she discovered that it was a bird.

"Look here!" she shouted towards her sisters. They all hurried up the rear. "It's an injured bird."

"Be careful Boise. It may peck you. Aren't injured creatures likely to peck at you?" cautioned Nena, who knew nothing about wildlife.

"It won't peck at me. Shh, little one, I will not hurt you." reassured Boise, as she carefully leaned over to pick up the injured creature.

"It's a falcon. I recognise its features from the books in the library of the Great Temple." said Feur, proud to have identified the creature.

"Its head seems to be injured. Look, there's a gash over here. All this dried blood. It must have been injured a while ago." added Fera. Boise closely inspected the wound and was shocked by what she saw.

"Its eye is missing. It must have flown into something and got its eye caught, perhaps on a branch?" surmised Boise in horror. She could not bear cruelty or injury to animals.

"Perhaps the storm swept it way off its course. The storm could have pulled it out of the skies. The winds, lightning and thunder last night were ferocious enough to capsize our boat, so anything could have happened to this defenceless creature." said Nena.

Despite, whatever calamity had befallen the injured bird, Boise set about immediately to clean its wound. She relied on the trusted medicinal herbs of her mother. The bird did not resist her efforts nor peck at her, not even once. Fera found it most strange. The little she knew of falcons, she would have thought them to be wild birds, unreceptive to human touch. It proved a total puzzlement to Fera that a wild creature would allow a stranger to handle it, but then again, Boise had the touch of a healer. Over the years, she had brought many an injured creature home with her, most of them had been wild and to Fera's best recollection, none of them had even once attacked Boise.

As Fera watched Boise handle the falcon tenderly and compassionately, she looked more closely at the bird. For some strange reason it struck her as looking familiar, as though she had seen it before. The only place that she had seen a wild falcon had been in the Al Suud, as it had flown overhead Aten as he had ridden in on his beautiful steed. Fera had not seen the falcon at close range, so she would have been unable to determine whether the injured falcon was indeed Aten's. After all, why would Aten's falcon have been flying so far north and so far away from Aten? Fera understood that Aten would never have been separated from his falcon. Unable to tell one bird from another and unable to ascertain with any degree of certainty whether the bird belonged to Aten, Fera quickly dismissed the notion and turned her attention to the day ahead. They had to resume their journey as soon as possible.

"I'll name him Haru." said Boise. "It means the 'one who is above, the distant one'. It seems appropriate, don't you think. I'll get you healthy again. You'll soon fly, Haru, you can be sure of that." said Boise lovingly.

Her sisters were not sure if Boise was talking to them or to the bird. As usual, when an injured creature was in her midst, Boise's attention was single-mindedly fixed on the creature and she forgot all about her human companions. It was an admirable, yet annoying trait which her sisters had learnt to live with.

***

When Mwari awoke, with a mighty bump on his head to match his equally severe headache, he overheard Jadon and Gibeon talking. The sisters were no-where to be seen.

"I would never have expected that he would have lost it like that. It was a though he was somewhere else, talking about some other person. I don't even think that it was Asaph's death that sent him to that dark place." said Jadon.

"Well, I hope he is over it. We need his guidance. He cannot react like that again. The girls were frightened out of their wits." replied Gibeon.

Mwari regretted his behaviour. He had spent years running away from the images that haunted his dreams and his every waking moment, but when he came face to face with death, he struggled to suppress the ghosts from his past. He reckoned that he had two choices, wallow in self-pity and risk their mission or put aside the events of the day before and pretend that they had never happened. If anyone raised the issue, he would tackle it head on, but he doubted whether he could explain his reaction to Asaph's death. His party would not understand, unless he told them the whole story and that he did not want to do. Even if he could, he would not know where to start. So, Mwari decided that silence was best and he chose the latter course of action.

When the men realised that he had awoken, they too opted to pretend that nothing had happened between them. Men found it easy to keep a stiff upper lip and not to discuss things that dwelt in the past. The sisters, however, tackled Mwari head, on when they returned to the campsite.

"What came over you last night Mwari? We were so scared and so worried for you?" asked Boise, being the only one of the sisters who felt comfortable enough to interrogate Mwari outright.

"I apologise profusely for my behaviour. I feel ashamed at causing you distress. Please forgive me. It will not happen again."

Mwari thought that the sisters would have been satisfied with his response, but Fera was not. She sensed that there was more behind his apology. Her curiosity was piqued, but the sisters sensed that he did not want to discuss the matter further. They had seen Mwari lose his temper and did not want to risk a further incident if they pestered him and besides, they had been taught not to pry into other people's business. Their mother had always told them that if a person had something to say, they would say it. Sticking one's nose where it was unwanted would just cause unnecessary disruption, so Fera let the matter rest. Perhaps one day Mwari would open up to them. Fera just hoped that whatever secrets Mwari was hiding, that they would not impact on them or on their mission.

It was ultimately decided to travel to Abydos by land. Fera was the only elated one amongst them. The men remarked to Mwari that they thought it a bad idea, but they knew that once Mwari's mind was made up, there was no turning back.

"We will travel by day along the banks of the Great Sky River, that way we can be assured of staying on course. Abydos, lies about six and a half miles west of the Great Sky River. We will rest by night."

Mwari's instructions were obeyed. The terrain was not difficult to navigate on foot, unlike the rugged outcrops of the Great Mountain which they had crossed, despite cold and icy winds and unlike the deep ravines of the Gulf of Zula. Their movements were however laboured by the intense heat. The season of inundation not only brought with it heavy rains but also searing seasonal heat and energy-draining humidity.

"Keep yourselves hydrated. Drink often from the Great Sky River." cautioned Mwari. "Unfortunately we find ourselves travelling through the most intense heat of the dog days."

"The dog days! That sounds rather peculiar," remarked Feur. "What do you mean?"

"Intense heat prevails in this part of the world for forty days. Summer is then at its cruellest. I have travelled through the Great Desert on many occasions and the dog days most certainly present an unbearable challenge. Legend has told that it can become so hot, that people can become sick with fever. Some animals are said to turn vigorous and strong, so strong that they gain supernatural powers. They have been known to attack people, even kill them. Other animals simply wither and die, so intense is the heat."

"Now you are just teasing us, Mwari." replied Fera.

"I do not believe that any creatures in Ka could be evil. Nature is not evil." said Boise.

"Perhaps not by design, but evil is a dark force which lurks everywhere and can corrupt anything." added Mwari.

Everyone knew that Mwari was right. They had seen the forces of nature; the winds, the rains, the lightning and the thunder used for very dark ends indeed. Asaph's death was a testament to how the power of nature, if yielded for an evil purpose, could result in evil ends.

The travelling on foot indeed proved burdensome, but the party journeyed on, stopping to rest whenever they could and to take refreshment and sustenance from the cool waters of the Great Sky River. The bright spot amidst the heat was when they set up camp at night. It was then that they could not only rest in the cool evenings, but also sit around the camp fires and listen to stories. Daniel always had a great tale to tell. His travels proved an endless source of interest, more to him than to anyone else, but it was Mwari who proved to be the best storyteller amongst them. The sisters were enraptured by his ancient and heroic tales of war. It was during one such tale that they learnt the history of the great City of Abydos.

"So Abydos is actually an ancient funery site?" asked Feur.

"Yes, it is the home of the God of the Underworld. His name is Khnemu-utem-ankh."

"That's a bit of a tongue twister. Thank heavens, we don't have such long and complex names." added Jadon.

"I suppose a great king deserves a great name. He is after all the Giver of Life. He holds the secret to immortality."

"I don't know if I would want to live forever." remarked Fera. "It just doesn't seem right. Things have a beginning and an end. That's the cycle of life."

"I would love to live forever, but I'd want to stay young. I could not imagine being old and then living forever. If I am going to die, I can die old. One does not have to be a good looking corpse, but to live for all eternity and not be looking one's best, now that would be cruel punishment indeed, don't you think?" commented Nena. Everyone laughed. Of course Nena would be fixated on her appearance.

"You will be pleased to know, Nena, that Khnemu died when he was young. People say that he passed into the Land of Light as a young man, beautiful and strapping."

Nena did indeed look satisfied by such revelation.

"Tell us about Khnemu." enquired Feur, ever curious.

"Well," replied Mwari, "He was a great King. He taught his people how to be civilised, how to cultivate the earth and how to improve the fruits of the earth. He gave them laws to regulate their conduct and instructed them on how to obediently follow the Gods. His kingdom became so peaceful and prosperous that he decided to share his great knowledge with neighbouring kingdoms. He set out on a Great journey. In his absence, he left his brother Ast to rule his kingdom in his stead."

"Oh no, that was his first bad decision. We all know how brothers can betray each other." interjected Fera. Everyone knew that she was referring to Ezana and Ta-Seti.

"Not all brothers betray each other Fera. But as Fate would have it, in this case, your suspicions are correct. His brother did betray him. When Khnemu returned from his travels, Ast did not want to give up the throne. He was so jealous of Khnemu that he plotted and conspired with seventy-two other people in the royal court to kill Khnemu. Their plan was to build a chest of elaborate gold and ivory and to offer it as a prize to any man who could fit into it. All the men in the kingdom tried to squeeze their bulky frames into the chest, but no-one succeeded. Since the chest was purposefully built to fit the frame of a small man and in particular one man, being Khnemu, every man who lay in it could not fit. Eventually, Khnemu decided to give lying in the chest a try."

"And surprise, surprise, he fitted perfectly!" said Jadon.

"He did at that. Once Khnemu was in the chest, Ast shut the lid and locked him in. He then threw the chest into the Great Sky River. Khnemu eventually died and passed into the Land of Light."

"How tragic!" said Feur.

"What a terrible way to die. I cannot imagine being suffocated in a box and then probably drowning." said Nena.

Nena knew that she had touched a raw nerve, almost before the words had slipped past her lips. But it was too late. With one insensitive comment, she had brought back the sad memory of Asaph and his tragic death.

"Oh, please forgive me. Fera, I did not think."

It was a fact that Nena never gave a moment's thought before she said things, so Fera brushed it aside and asked Mwari to continue with his story, since that was the best way to forget. Mwari continued,

"Khnemu's wife was left utterly distraught by his death. She decided to embark on a journey to find his remains. He deserved a proper burial. She searched for many years. Eventually, she found the chest. It had come to rest in the great Kingdom of Byblos. It had become lodged in the branches of a large tree, whose branches had grown around the chest. It had transpired that the King of Byblos had ordered the tree to be felled and the wood to be used to build the roof of his palace. He found the chest and coveted it as a prized possession. Khnemu's wife attempted to barter with the King for the return of the chest, but he would not budge until a time came when his only son had fallen deathly ill. Khnemu's wife saw her chance to get the chest back and so she offered to nurse the child back to health in return for the chest. The child lived and the chest was returned to Khnemu's wife, much to the anger and contempt of Ast. He would not tolerate that the mortal remains of his once powerful brother were returned to the kingdom to be honoured by his people, so Ast stole the chest once again. This time he scattered the dismembered body parts of Khnemu in different places, hoping that they would never be found again. But Khnemu's wife loved her late husband more than life itself and so she relentlessly searched for his body parts. Luckily, she found them and to prevent them from being stolen again, she buried them in different burial sanctuaries within the great Temple at Abydos, which was built to honour Khnemu. People to this day pilgrimage to Abydos to pray to Khnemu and leave offerings for him, like intricate ivory carvings and glazed pottery and tiles."

Everyone who listened to Mwari loved a good story, but his particular story had left them feeling as though it was too close for comfort. Had Mwari told them the story as an encouragement or as a caution? Just like Khnemu's wife, they too had embarked on a great journey. Would they succeed like she had? Who was plotting and conspiring against them? That night, sleep should have brought rest and peace to Mwari's party, but instead it left feelings of fear and doubt in the minds of the courageous travellers.

It had been a particular fear of Daniel that travelling by foot across the western border of the Great Desert, would bring their party face to face with the many dangerous desert tribes who roamed its plains, especially Al Aziz and his men, who had escaped being caught by Ezana and Jalu. But for several days, Mwari's party traversed the scorching sands of the Great Desert, quite alone. There was not a soul in sight. On the eve of the third day of travel, quite unexpectedly and fortuitously, they came across the small village of Dongola. They were warmly received by the locals who invited them to join their feast in celebration of the Goddess of War, Sekmet.

Jadon and Gibeon were all too keen to join the jovial festival of intoxication where, as the locals told them, the flooding of the Great Sky River was celebrated. The festival provided an opportunity to relax and unwind from the tumultuous events of late. The death of Asaph and being at the mercy of the Elementals, convinced Mwari to loosen his reign a little on the sisters and his men. What harm could there have been in letting them have a little merriment? Dancing and singing with the locals might have been the most appropriate way to heal weary bodies and minds, thought Mwari. And thus, the invitations to dance, eat and drink with the locals were readily and gratefully accepted by all.

Watching her sisters dancing around a large campfire, Feur sat alongside Mwari, as one of the local elders told them of the origins of the festival,

"Today we celebrate Sekmet, the sister of Hathor." he said. "They had rather a tempestuous relationship. I suppose, like all sisters do."

Feur understood his words. There was always something that she and her sisters fought about, especially Fera and Nena.

"Sekmet wanted to destroy Hathor and all who were loyal to Hathor. She stopped at nothing. Her bloodlust was insatiable. Not even a war between Hathor and Sekmet could quell her desire for victory over Hathor. Thousands of innocent victims were left in her trail. Hathor sought peace and so she devised a plan to trick Sekmet. Hathor poured beer coloured with red ochre powder into the Great Sky River. The waters turned red, so red in fact, that the water looked like blood. Sekmet, driven mad by her all-consuming lust for blood, mistook the waters for blood and drank and drank, until she became so drunk that she was unable to wage war against Hathor and so the killing and slaughter of thousands of innocents stopped. Hathor had achieved peace, albeit through clever trickery."

"That was ingenious of her." said Feur.

"Yes, wasn't it? Today, my people remain the peace-loving descendants of Hathor. There are many desert tribes who still invoke the dark powers of Sekmet. My people neither seek out nor encourage war and so each year we appease the blood lust of Sekmet. We cannot very well flood the Great Sky River with red-coloured beer since that would be a waste of good beer, but we most certainly do take every precaution against war by honouring Sekmet. We drink in her name, thus preventing her blood lust and anger from rising once again and bringing war and destruction to our lands." Both Mwari and Feur shared the sentiments of one of their kind hosts.

A long night of heavy drinking had left all the local men and a good number of the local women passed out drunk by early the next morning. Mwari and his female charges had gone to bed, not intoxicated by the beer, which flowed plentifully in the village, but satisfied and happy to have witnessed the sights of hope and joy which they saw around them. It was a far cry from the last few days which had swamped their senses in sadness and despair.

Mwari's rest was short-lived, however. He was suddenly, in the early hours of the morning, awoken by a cacophony of blood-curdling screams. He was not sure if they were human or animal in origin. In the daze of sleep, he initially struggled to get his bearings, but he quickly collected his thoughts and realised that the village was under attack. As he looked all around him, he saw tent after tent enveloped in fire. Bodies lay strewn all over the ground. Some locals ran for their lives, screaming and wailing as they ran. His mind tried to process clear thoughts. What manner of enemy had attacked the village? Was it the Beja under Al Aziz's leadership, come back to execute one last, desperate attempt at revenge for the Beja defeat in Meroe?

Mwari looked around him. He saw no Beja warriors, no camels and no Emela-Ntouka. All, he saw, to his great horror, were hundreds of painted dogs, viciously and ravenously devouring human flesh as they trawled through the village. He imagined himself to still be asleep, for the sight that he witnessed, seemed impossible to believe. Tent after tent was ruthlessly attacked and set alight by the dogs that appeared to breathe fire.

Realising that their canine attackers were nearing the tent in which his female charges lay sleeping, Mwari made a hurried dash towards the sisters' location. The tent seemed unscathed, as yet, from an attack by the fire-breathing dogs, but they were getting closer and closer. Mwari was a hundred metres away from rescuing the girls, when he found himself encircled by a pack of dogs. Their red eyes stared out malevolently from behind their snarling teeth. White saliva drooled ominously from their mouths. There was no doubt in Mwari's mind that he had come face to face with the rabid dogs that had been told of in the tales of the desert tribes with whom he had occasionally sought food and lodging during his many travels across the Great Desert.

Mwari's heart pounded. He recalled the tales of how insatiably menacing and evil the rabid dogs of the Al Suud were. Legend had told that during the dog days, they sought the company of Sirius and his evil dwarf companion. Ordinarily, the dogs roamed the grasslands of the Al Suud, but the intense heat of the Great Desert had been known to drive them mad, a madness harnessed by Sirius for his own evil ends. They would then roam the grasslands of the Al Suud and the sandy plains and dunes of the Great Desert to wreak havoc on the local inhabitants. Packs of rabid blood-thirsty dogs would attack and kill gratuitously at the beck and call of their evil puppet master. The season of the inundation, which brought rains aplenty could never quell their thirst. All the rains and the swollen waters of the Great Sky River did, was to drive the dogs more and more mad.

Mwari had never seen the mad dogs of the Al Suud. He had only ever heard of them through magical campfire tales and thus he hardly believed them to be real. That morning, he had received a rude awakening to their actual existence. He stood back, daring not a movement or the blink of an eye as the dogs edged closer towards him.

"Mwari!"

He heard the voices of Jadon and Gibeon as they appeared from their tent. Obviously the effects of their liquor-filled night had dimmed their senses, for they too had only reacted to the noise and screaming when the attack was well under way.

"Stay where you are. Do not make any sudden movements. They will attack at the slightest chance. Even the smell of fear will draw them in. Move back very slowly and get me my sword. We will need to get past them if we are to save the women." instructed Mwari.

The men did as they were told. Jadon threw Mwari his sword. Together, they fought off as many dogs as they could, all the time dodging strands of fire being thrown from the mouths of the dogs. As the men stabbed and killed their vicious attackers, more and more packs took their place. Mwari was becoming increasingly concerned for the well-being and safety of the women. No matter how hard they tried, they could not reach them. Ferocious packs of fire-breathing dogs stood between them and four helpless girls.

***

It had not been the deathly screams of village people around her that had awoken Fera that morning, but the immense pressure of being strangled. She had felt a body climb on top of her and then cold hands reach around her neck and squeeze the air from her lungs. When she had realised what was happening, she had opened her eyes to look straight into the black, vacuous eyes of her unknown attacker.

Instinctively, she had immediately tried to fight off her attacker. She flailed around on her sleeping mat, kicking, slapping and trying anything to push her attacker's hands of death from her throat. She stabbed her fingernails into the flesh of her attacker. Still, the relentless and asphyxiating strength of her attacker prevailed. She could not scream. After several minutes of fighting, her body grew tired. She felt herself slipping away. Her vision was disappearing, going into the blackness.

Suddenly, she heard a yelp. To her, it sounded like the cry of a wild animal that had become injured. Her attacker loosened his vice-like grip. She opened her eyes. Feur was on top of the attacker, struggling to pull him away from Fera, but Feur was too weak and was thrown across the tent, to fall with a loud thud on the floor.

Out of the corner of her haze-filled vision, Fera saw Nena and Boise at the opposite side of the tent, huddled in the corner in fear. Fera saw her attacker rummaging through their belongings. It was obvious that he was looking for something. But what, she wondered? They had so few belongings with them. Not having found what he was obviously looking for, the attacker walked over to where Boise and Nena stood. He slapped Nena through the face. Blood spattered from the corner of her mouth.

"Where is it? If you do not tell me, I will kill you both?" Boise was too afraid to answer. She had no idea what the stranger wanted.

"You will talk, one way or the other. I'll see to that." Their attacker sneered as he issued his threat.

"I do not know what you speak of. Who are you? What do you want? asked Boise hesitatingly.

"Do not play games, girl. One of you has it. I want it. What do I have to do to get it? The attacker had moved so close to Boise's face that she could smell his foul breath. Nena fainted.

"I do not know what you want. We have nothing of value."

Boise knew full well that her words were not the truth. She knew that Fera had the scarab, given to her by Candace, hidden in her cloak lining. It was the safest place for it, together with the first piece of the Turquoise Figurine. Nena could never have been trusted to keep it safe and neither would it have been safe with Boise, who had been known to lose things.

Boise tried not to look in the direction of Fera, who was lying lifeless on the other side of the tent. Their attacker caught a brief glimpse of Boise's eyes as she momentarily looked Fera's way.

"So, she has it, does she? I thought so."

As the man turned towards Fera, Boise eyed her escape and tried to run. Perhaps she could get help? Perhaps Mwari was in their vicinity?

Before she could move an inch, a vicious, snarling, saliva-drooling creature growled at her feet. She jumped back, startled and afraid.

"I would not move if I were you! They hunger for blood and flesh, particularly that of a young victim such as yourself." Boise gasped.

She knew that Fera would be utterly defenceless against a further attack. Feur and Nena lay unconscious and thus were not in a position to rescue Fera. Boise realised that she was Fera's only hope. The man oozed desperation and violence from his every pore. Boise became acutely aware that he would stop at nothing to get what he was looking for. If Fera regained consciousness while her searched her person, she would definitely try to fight him off again. He would kill her. Boise had no choice, but to risk the wrath of the terrifying dog which guarded her so closely.

She slowly reached up to her neck and removed her amulet. She clasped it slowly in her hand and threw it in the opposite direction to where Fera lay. She had hoped that the dog would chase after it, since that was instinctively how dogs behaved, she surmised. She intended to then move in the opposite direction. Her hopes were dashed, however, since the ravenous creature anticipated her move and instead of moving away from her, it pounced on her. Its jaws ripped savagely into her flesh. Her skin burnt as though it was on fire. She yelled out in pain. She fought heroically to rid herself of the rabid attack.

During her attack, strangely, Boise found herself questioning how it was that of late she had always found herself being attacked by vicious creatures. Their journey thus far had led her into the clutches of the Eloko. She had only been saved by the unremitting fortitude of her sister, but it dawned on her that there was no-one there to save her from the vile jaws of the rabid dog. She closed her eyes to cope with the excruciating pain of her flesh being ripped from her bones. She just wanted the pain to be over. She thought of home and her animals. She thought of Zeb, Fera's docile dog, who had never and would never have harmed a soul. She felt strangely calm thinking of distant memories.

An audible yelp drew her attention sharply back to reality. Daniel was there. He had lodged the blade of his knife squarely in the centre of the dog's brain. It was dead. Daniel pushed its foul-smelling body from Boise. Boise's body was shaking uncontrollably. She felt the life-blood draining from her body.

"Stay awake my love! I'll get you help." said Daniel reassuringly. Boise felt her energy draining from her body, all she wanted to do was to close her eyes and sleep.

"No Boise, stay with me. You must not give up. We have fought too long and hard to be together." pleaded Daniel.

Boise wanted to stay with Daniel with every fibre of her being, but waves of pain and tiredness flowed over her.

She remembered the ripples on the surface of the Great Sky River, as Fera had tossed her smooth pebbles into it. She felt peaceful and serene. She saw her sisters beside her. They smiled at her. Boise lost consciousness.

Daniel looked around the room. Inside, he felt as though he was dying. He screamed for help. All he saw were the lifeless bodies of the woman around him. Their unknown assailant had fled the scene of his crime, much to Daniel's chagrin. Daniel then turned his attention to getting help.

"Nena, Feur, wake up for heaven's sake, wake up. Please! Boise needs your help. She has been badly attacked!"

Feur fought her way through the pain she felt at having been brutally slapped across her head. She could not see clearly. Her vision appeared hazy. She was not sure if her eye was swollen shut or if it was filled with blood. She reached up to touch her face and her eye. Her hand was covered with blood as she withdrew it. Nena lay close to her, seemingly unharmed, for Feur saw no obvious signs of injury. Feur crawled towards Nena and shook her.

"Nena, wake up. Boise needs our help."

Nena regained consciousness and she and Feur made their way towards Boise. They were shocked at the sight of Boise. Her arm and shoulder were badly injured. The rabid dog had sunk its venomous teeth deep into Boise's flesh. Red blood oozed everywhere.

"Apply pressure to the wound, Nena." instructed Feur. "I'll find some cloth to bind it. Daniel, check on Fera."

Before Daniel could reluctantly draw himself away from his beloved, Mwari and the men appeared in the tent. Mwari moved swiftly to Boise's aid. Jadon set on the task of reviving Fera. His persistence paid dividend. Fera's attack had been brutal in its severity, but it had not taken her to a point beyond life. The momentary lack of oxygen had rendered her unconscious, but when Jadon's soothing voice had brought her back from her dark abyss, there were no other signs of her ordeal, other than some nasty bruises to her neck and shoulders, the outward evidence of the heinous malice of her attacker.

Fera, initially found it difficult to breathe and to talk, but she responded to Jadon's question as to whether she was alright,

"I feel so dizzy. My throat is very dry."

Gibeon leapt to fetch her some water. He gently held the cup whilst she drank, since Fera's hands shook uncontrollably.

"You would feel like that. You almost had the life wrung out of you by that loathsome creature."

"I didn't see him coming. Those villainous black eyes will haunt my every waking moment. I shall never sleep soundly again. Who was he?" asked Fera. Mwari interjected.

"That fiend was most likely Sirius. He has been known to roam the swamplands, commanding the loyalty of tens, if not hundreds of packs of painted dogs. Usually, they are harmless, but this incessant heat has driven them mad." said Mwari.

"Mad! I think that is an understatement. They were breathing fire. Have you seen the death and devastation that they have left in their wake? The entire village has been destroyed and for what purpose?" asked Jadon.

"I can't say what motivated our particular attack. Many local inhabitants across the Al Suud and along the Great Sky River's western border have cowered in fear for many years at the appearance of the morning star, for they know it heralds the summer solstice and with that comes the increased likelihood of pillaging and murder at the hands of Sirius and his rabid dogs, as they maraud their way across Ka."

"This Sirius was searching for something." piped in Nena. He slapped Feur when she refused to tell him anything." added Nena.

Mwari felt perplexed. Obviously the amulets which the girls wore around their necks had some value, but surely not so great a value that Sirius would be driven insane to get his hands on them?

"We have no time to dwell on that now. We must get Boise some help." said Mwari.

Mwari knew that time was against them. He knew that just one bite from a rabid dog could be lethal and Boise had been bitten most savagely. Mwari feared for the life of the young woman whom he had come to care so deeply about.

Feur bound Boise's wounds as best she could and applied a poultice of herbs, which she had hoped would prove strong enough to draw the poison from Boise's body. Feur ardently wished that he mother was there with her.

"This is only a temporary measure. It may not work and then what will we do? Does the village have a medicine man or woman? Perhaps they will know better. Surely they have treated such wounds in the past?"

Feur was rambling, but she could not help it. She feared for Boise. Jadon and Gibeon heeded Feur's call for further help and went in search of someone in the village, or what was left of it after the attack. They hoped to find anyone who would be able to offer some expert guidance on how to treat Boise's wounds.

"It will work. It has too." echoed Daniel defiantly. Boise's healing herbs had worked their magic on Feur before and so, he fervently hoped that they would work once again.

No-one had the will power to argue or labour the point of whether they would. If there was ever a time for positive thinking, it was then. Feur turned her attention to Fera's wounds. She similarly applied some soothing herbs in the hope that they would reduce the swelling and bruising to Fera's neck.

"What about your eye? You need to treat that gash." mouthed Fera hoarsely.

"Never mind that, it looks worse than it actually is."

"I'll look at it." volunteered Nena.

As Fera watched Nena wash and care for Feur's wound, she was struck by a tidal wave of emotion. It was not like her to cry. She had always considered crying to be a sign of weakness. Fera was not sure if it was the love, compassion and deep relief that she felt, given the fact that they had lived through yet another ordeal or if it was the days of pent up emotions after the death of Asaph and the aftermath of the storm, but she could not prevent herself from crying.

Her sobs were loud and deeply touching to all who heard them, most of all Mwari, who felt more and more guilt for dragging the sisters on the journey. He rationalised that he could never have foreseen what dangers would await them, but he nevertheless felt helpless to prevent the dangers that they had continually been subjected to. Mwari moved close to Fera to offer her a modicum of comfort. Such gesture was equally foreign for him. His heart had been closed off for many years from human emotion. It was safer that way. But he felt more and more as though his four fearless charges had caused a window in his heart and soul to re-open.

Sadly, the medicine man had met the same fate as countless other villagers. He too had been ravaged by the jaws of the rabid dogs. Jadon and Gibeon feared having to tell Daniel such news. They knew that a man, driven mad by fear and angst over the woman he loved, could react highly emotionally. The reaction on Daniel's face made his emotions very clear to them. He looked like a caged animal, driven mad by his own limitations and shortcomings at being unable to help Boise.

"The villagers told us that if we want to help Boise, we must make haste to Abydos. Its Temples are a place of considerable power and healing. They said that the priests there will know how to heal her." relayed Jadon.

Daniel knew better than anyone that Temples, especially those at Abydos, held great meaning. Their very architecture, metric proportions, symbols with which they were associated and even the materials from which they were constructed, like sandstone, basalt, white and black granite and unbaked brick, symbolised Mother Nature's powerful elements. Sandstone often represented the earth, strong and firm, upon which a temple's foundations would be founded. The basalt and white or black granite represented fire and the unbaked bricks made from the mud of the Great Sky River, symbolised water.

"Well, in that case, we do not have a choice. We must depart now. There is no time to waste. We will not stop until we get there." replied Daniel, in a desperate and impatient tone of voice.

Everyone set about collecting their meagre belongings. Boise's cold and already clammy body was carefully placed on a tarpaulin suspended between some branches and she was wrapped up in as many blankets as they could find to prevent her from suffering the ill effects of shock, severe pain and fever.

As they walked swiftly towards Abydos, Daniel found himself deep in thought. He had tried desperately not to focus on Boise's deteriorating condition. Her face looked more and more pale and beads of fever ran from her brow. It was clear that the medicinal herbs which had been applied by Feur had done nothing to stem the tide of the poison from the dog's bite which seemed to be taking hold of Boise's body. It was not the loss of blood which caused everyone to fear, but rather the fever which coursed through Boise's veins. To keep himself from focussing on Boise's worsening condition, Daniel chose rather to busy his mind with inconsequential thoughts. He recalled the lessons given to him by one of the elderly priests in the library of the Great Temple back in Catal Huyuk. He had, with great enthusiasm, told how the Temples of old had been constructed. Daniel had learned that a King would perform a ceremony called the 'Stretching of the Cord'. He would use a divine Instrument of Knowing, which was a turquoise crystal tied to the end of a piece of string, to demarcate the area where the Temple would be built.

Another ceremony, known as the 'Setting out the Four sides of the enclosure' would commence with the digging of the first furrow, which was dug four times. The first brick laid would also be prepared four times. That would symbolise the unification of heaven and earth. The designated Temple enclosure would then be purified four times. Once the construction of the Temple was complete, the 'Festival of Entering' would be held.

That was a time when ordinary people would be allowed to enter the Temple for the first time. The Temple would then finally be named during the 'Handing over of the Temple to its Lord' ceremony. It was not only during the construction of a Temple that such a ceremony would be held. Every year, in celebration of a Temple's existence and power, various rituals and ceremonies would be repeated. Daniel had always understood the importance of ritual and ceremony. He had been raised on the power that both could yield.

As Daniel had expected, the L-shaped sandstone structure of the largest Temple at Abydos, the Temple of Seti, made for an awe-inspiring welcome to Mwari's party, as they drearily entered the Temple precinct, which consisted of nine or ten Temples built on the edge of the Great Desert. Fera, Nena and Feur felt relieved to have eventually arrived. Their overnight journey had proven to be exhausting, but none of them had been concerned by their own physical limitations or injuries. Getting help for Boise was all that mattered to them.

As they approached the Temple of Seti, they saw a number of priests, who went about their daily tasks of cleaning and praying. Mwari's enquiries for help were initially met with suspicion. The presence of all manner of strangers to the Temple precinct was commonplace, but Mwari and his party's dishevelled and exhausted appearance must have taken the priests by surprise. But, despite their initial reticence, within no time at all, their fervent pleas for help to see the Master of the Secrets of the House of Life, were heard, when one of the young Temple priests bade them entry into the Temple of Seti. He was adamant that only two of their number could enter. There was no arguing amongst Mwari and his party. The men were too tired and Fera and Nena both felt that their efforts would have been better spent watching over Boise.

Feur and Daniel were after all, the most capable of appreciating and understanding their surroundings, since both had spent copious hours in the Great Temple reading about the mysteries of Temple Life. They both knew that the Temple of Seti was incomparable with any of the Temples that they may have entered or even have learned about in the many ancient scrolls, which they had read and which had remained hidden in the depths of the great library, but, at least they were better prepared and hopefully better equipped than the others for whatever lay before them as they walked through the large carved wooden doors of the Temple.

As the heavy doors were closed behind them, Daniel and Feur found themselves in a vast courtyard with a flagstone floor which looked like ripples of water, since the stones had been laid in an irregular pattern. Feur felt slightly disconcerted, as though she was walking on water. The walls surrounding the courtyard were decorated with murals of great Kings of Old as they had vanquished their enemies. Off the courtyard, they were led into a great room with high ceilings. The walls and ceilings in the first hall were adorned with every bright colour imaginable. The air was warm and balmy and scented with the fragrance of myrrh. Feur and Daniel followed the priest in silence. Their surroundings were intimidating, yet humbling. As they exited the first hall, into what appeared to be a smaller, darker place than the first hall, since only shards of light came in through the door, the priest spoke to them, for only the second time since they had first met him. The unexpected whisper of the priest's voice, the shadows of light on the stone floors and the ghostly appearance of images of a falcon head, lion head and lotus flower which decorated the walls, made for an eerie experience. Feur felt herself shudder as though a donkey had walked over her grave.

"We will now enter into the third hall. This place holds the most sacred place within the Temple. It is called the House of Eternity. It is the resting place of the great God of the Underworld." whispered the priest.

As they passed by the seven inner sanctuaries which led off the main passage of the third hall, the priest stopped before each door of the seven sanctuaries and quietly mouthed the name of each room. His voice was barely audible and all Feur and Daniel heard mentioned, was the name of one of the sanctuaries. It was called the 'Gallery of the Kings', so named after the Great King of Abydos and his predecessors.

Eventually, they stopped at the entrance to the House of Eternity. They were told to wait, while the priest announced their presence to the High Priest. Feur felt immense anticipation at the thought of meeting the most senior of all the priests at Abydos. She had only ever met the Great Prophet back home. She imagined that the High Priest at Abydos was held in as high a regard as the Great Prophet was to worshippers and men of the cloth, back home. It was not long before an elderly priest, with a shaven head and dressed in pure-white linen robes, with a leopard skin draped over his shoulder, appeared.

"I am Ptah, the Master of the Secrets of the Hall of Life."

It was not his soothing and gentle voice that attracted Feur first, but the three falcon plumes which were tied to a chain around his neck. Feur remembered that the number of plumes worn by a priest denoted the hierarchy of their importance. Ptah continued,

"I believe you seek an audience with our Lord Khnemu. I am afraid that it will not be possible at this time."

"Please, I beg you. My sister will die. Time is running out for her. We cannot save her alone. We need your help!" beseeched Feur.

"If we cannot see the great Lord, are you not able to at least see her then? Are the priests not able to help in some way? The villagers at Dongola said that the priests at Abydos could help us to heal Boise. Were they wrong?" The desperation in Daniel's voice was palpable.

"I realise the predicament in which you find yourself, but a priest of this holy order can only heal a person with the authority and permission of the great Lord himself. I, myself, am only a teacher and mentor to my fellow priests. I do not possess any healing powers."

All her pent up worry and fear found release as Feur burst into tears. Ptah took pity of the innocent-looking girl before him and replied,

"Very well, bring the girl to me. I shall judge the urgency of the situation."

Daniel wasted no time in retrieving the lifeless body of Boise and placing her on the altar in the third hall. Ptah examined Boise closely. After a few minutes of thorough and silent observation, Ptah summoned another of the priests. Feur and Daniel were introduced to the Prophet Kheri-Heb.

"This is my brother. He is The Possessor of the Book of Healing."

The newcomer was dressed similarly to Ptah, with the exception that only two falcon plumes hung around his neck. The Prophet acknowledged their presence, but said nothing, not even a word to Ptah. Feur was eager to ask whether Kheri-Heb would be able to heal Boise, but she was quickly silenced by the young priest who had first escorted them into the Temple. He drew his index finger to his mouth, as though suggesting that she should remain silent. He whispered to Feur,

"It is best that all healing be done in a peaceful environment."

It proved to be an excruciating few minutes whilst they all stood by and watched as Kheri-Heb carefully scrutinised Boise's wounds. Intermittently, he shook his head, as though he could not believe what he was seeing. His facial expressions perturbed Daniel and Feur, who could not make head or tail of his conclusions. Surprisingly, when he eventually spoke, his voice was deep and matter of fact,

"When was this girl bitten?"

"Yesterday morning. The village, where we had stopped to rest, was attacked by several packs of rabid dogs." replied Daniel.

Kheri-Heb summoned the young priest to hand him the book which was placed near the altar. He paged through its contents to settle on a page which read, 'spell to heal dog bites'. He lit a bushel of sage leaves. As their medicinal fragrance wafted through the air, he chanted,

"Giver of Life, extract the venom from the flesh and veins of this young girl. Rabid dog, remove your venomous saliva from her body or I shall summon the God of the Underworld, who dwells within the inner sanctum of the House of Eternity, to vanquish you."

Kheri-Heb repeated the chant over and over again, at least four times, by Feur's count. Between each chant, the Prophet waited for some event to occur, perhaps for the powerful incantation to magically arouse Boise from her feverish sleep, but no reaction came. Feur grew more and more worried, for it seemed as though the spell was not working. After several chants, Kheri-Heb announced,

"This girl is slipping into the Realm of Light. It has been too many hours since she was bitten and the poisonous venom has taken hold of her life. She is now at death's door. Whether he will let her in, is beyond my comprehension. That question is for another to answer."

"No, she can't be dying!" shouted Daniel. "Please do something. Is there nothing else that you can do to save her?"

"Her eyes are changing. The veil of death is upon her." It was as though Kheri-Heb had already resigned himself to Boise's fate. Feur would not give up. She threw herself on the ground at the Prophet's feet,

"I beg you to save my sister. I will do anything, give anything, to let her live. Tell me what I must do?"

Kheri-Heb reached down. He gently took hold of Feur's forearms and looked deep into her eyes.

"There is only one amongst us who can save her."

He looked in the direction of Ptah who had stood to one side, silently observing the events as they had unfolded.

They spoke no words, yet Daniel understood their exchange. It was obvious that Kheri-Heb had asked Ptah to relent on his initial refusal to allow Boise to be brought before Lord Khnemu.

Feur and Daniel both heaved a sigh of relief when Ptah invited them to follow him. He moved silently towards the innermost sanctuary within the third hall, known as the House of Eternity. Feur followed him. Daniel drew up the rear carrying Boise in his arms. They walked through a doorway which led down a staircase into a subterranean Temple. Fire torches dotted the walls of the sanctum. All Feur could see was a large room, its roof was supported by ten black granite columns and at its centre, stood an island-like platform surrounded by water. The torch-lights flickered on the surface of the water, which remained calm and motionless. The air carried the smell of damp and wetness. Feur likened it to the smell in the air after it had rained.

"We will leave Boise here. Lay her body in the sanctum and leave." instructed Kheri-Heb.

Feur and Daniel felt uneasy leaving Boise in such a dank and eerie place, but they did as they were told and reluctantly turned around and walked out of the sanctuary, leaving heavy wooden doors to close softly behind them. Feur sat next to Daniel, in silence and with baited breath, as they waited in the third hall, not being able to comprehend the nature of events which were unfolding on the other side of the door.

**

The last thought which had crossed Boise's conscious mind had been of her family and her beloved Catal Huyuk. Since then, she had drifted in and out of consciousness. She had heard muffled voices, their exact impart, had been completely lost on her muddled mind. She had felt pain, warmth and cold. All she sensed around her then silence and darkness. She knew that her spirit was not conscious. It was as though her mind and soul had transcended the mortal realm. She thought that she heard someone call her name.

"Boise, Boise!", someone called out through the cold darkness. She opened her eyes. She could see nothing, although she was acutely aware of the confines of the sanctuary. In a sleep-like trance, she saw herself step across the water which surrounded the platform in the centre of the Temple. She felt amazed at being able to walk on the surface of the water. Her steps were light and left no ripples in their wake. The water's surface remained calm and serene and the ceiling of the sanctuary burned fiercely.

Boise imagined that she was in hell, stuck between the dark abyss of the cool underground lake and the fires which raged above her, which although they looked as though they burned red-hot, they exuded absolutely no heat and no light. Her heart froze for an instant. As a child, she had been taught of the existence of the underworld. She had constantly been reminded by her parents that it was a place where a naughty child would be cast away to, if she had been disobedient and unkind. She wondered if she now found herself in such a place and whether she had indeed upset the Great Spirit. She racked her brain to think of a reason for her to be sent there.

In spite of the darkness, her vision became clear. She saw a man sitting on the island, which was surrounded by water. He appeared tall and young. He carried a crook and flail. She felt drawn to him and his words,

"I am Khnemu, Lord of the Underworld. I am an Eternity and an Everlastingness. I was destroyed and dismembered, but I am still. You have found me Boise, for I am here."

Boise felt confused. The stranger she saw, knew her name and yet she had just met him.

"Are you ready, Daughter of Ka to pass into the Realm of Light?" he asked.

Boise hesitated for a moment. Her spirit and her body were tired and weary. They craved rest, but her mind could not escape the notion that she had some unfinished business to attend to. She had never imagined that she would face death at a young age. She had dreamt of growing old with the man she loved. She wanted children and a home. She would have felt cheated of a life of love and laughter with her family if she had answered yes to the question posed to her by the all-powerful God of the Underworld.

"I can see you struggle with this decision. You are in two minds. I shall make the decision for you." replied Khnemu.

Boise felt as though her mind was racing through her thoughts. She wanted to choose life, but the grip of death weighed down her body and her mind. She wanted to shout out that she had much life yet to live, but she could not find the words. The decision as to whether she lived or died was not hers to make. Khnemu's voice sounded through the darkness,

"You are a child of the earth. You have much to accomplish before you pass into my Kingdom. The Scales of Life have been consulted, on whether you should be granted permission to enter into the afterlife and their response is no. There will come a time when our paths will cross again. A time when death will welcome you favourably, but now is not that time."

Boise felt strong hands lift her body towards the flaming ceilings and transport her across the waters. She heard a voice whisper into her ear,

"You have travelled far, but you have further yet to travel. Although your body is cold, rigid and death-like, your mind is awake and vital. You will return in both mind and body to complete your purpose on earth."

Boise felt her hand being opened and an object being placed in her palm. Her fingers were closed around the object. The voice whispered again,

"Give this to Hathor. She will recognise it and know what to do with it. She will heal your body and give you what you most need. You must fulfil this purpose before you come to me again. We shall meet again."

The voice in the darkness fell silent. Boise felt strangely calm and at peace.

As the doors opened to reveal the luminescent torch light which caressed the calm waters, Feur and Daniel rushed into the room. They found Boise's body in the same position in which they had left it. Her skin was deathly pale in colour and icy-cold to the touch. Her arms were folded across her chest. Her hands secretly clasped the gift from Khnemu. The expression on her face appeared tranquil and serene. Daniel carried her body out into the third hall and placed Boise on the altar once again.

"She is still unconscious. Has she been healed? It does not look as though she has been healed." said Feur frantically. "The Lord of the Underworld has not saved her life."

"Alas, he has not taken her life. It is not his place to save her life. Lord Khnemu determines whether a person must pass into the afterlife. The fact that she is still with us now is proof that it is not written in the Book of Life that she be given over to death at this time. The Lord of the Underworld has not given her the gift of death. She has more life yet to live, but that life will not be found within these walls. The gift of life is to be found elsewhere. You will have to seek out the healing powers of the Goddess of the Stars. Travel to Dendera and find her there." instructed Ptah.

"What about Boise?" Will her condition not worsen? How will we keep her alive until then? Will we reach this Dendera in time? asked Feur.

She had so many unanswered questions. As though oblivious to her doubts, Kheri-Heb handed Feur a pound of garlic and some herbs and said,

"Mix these together and apply to her bites every day. They will prevent the poison from claiming your sister's life, but you must hurry. Although our great Lord Khnemu has prophesied that she will live, you must not anger him. He has her fate in the palm of his hand. If you disobey him, he can change her fate as quickly as he has decided it."

Daniel had no intention of disobeying Lord Khnemu, for if there was one thing that Daniel knew for certain, it was that the will of the Gods needed to be respected and obeyed, without question.

Mwari and the others were relieved when Feur walked out of the Temple precinct. It had been several hours of anxious waiting, not knowing whether Boise would be saved by the priests of Abydos or not. Their relief turned to dread and fear when Daniel, carrying a still lifeless body of Boise, emerged from the Temple. Fera and Nena ran to Daniel.

They observed Boise. Her body felt cold. It was as though the life was slowly draining from her. They realised that there was no improvement in her condition. Feur updated them as to the events that had transpired in the Temple.

"So, the bottom line is that no-one in there could save Boise?" concluded Nena impatiently.

"And now, we have to leave again to seek help elsewhere. This is slowly becoming an annoying fact of our life. We keep chasing the impossible. We never seem to get ahead. This mission is slowly draining the life out of us. It surely did that to Asaph and now Boise clutches to life by the slimmest of threads. I do not know how much more of this I can take." Nena felt exasperated.

"We have no choice in the matter. Boise's life depends on us getting her timeously to Dendera. Time waits for no man." replied Jadon.

Mwari paused and thought deeply about Jadon's words. He was right. They needed to capitalise on time. If they all took Boise to Dendera, it might thwart the success of their mission to retrieve the other six pieces of the Turquoise Figurine. Mwari was resolute. They had to make up some time. He wondered whether there might be some way that they could kill two birds with one stone; one being to take Boise to Dendera to seek out the healing treatments of the Priestesses of Hathor and the other, being to reach Bandiagara, more sooner than later. Mwari addressed the others,

"The decision to go to Dendera, it seems, is unequivocal. Fate has intervened in that, but we are running out of time. We still have a mission to complete, irrespective of the unforeseen obstacles that have been thrown in our way. We need to reach Ife soon for the seventh day of the seventh month draws near. I propose that Daniel; you take Boise on to Dendera. Once she has been healed, you can travel to meet us at the Pearl of the Desert."

"Are you proposing that we separate? asked Jadon.

"I am. If we split up, we can accomplish more in the time that is available to us." The men seemed receptive to the idea.

"I'm listening." said Gibeon.

"Well, if Jadon, Gibeon and myself travel on to Bandiagara, we can locate and secure the piece of the Turquoise Figurine there. Whilst we do that, Daniel will have travelled to Dendera, found help for Boise and then re-joined us further along the route."

"Who will we travel with?" enquired Nena, referring to herself and her sisters.

"I thought it best that Nena and Feur travel with you Daniel. They can take care of Boise, since after all she needs constant attention, with the application of those herbs which the Prophet Kheri-Heb gave to you. Fera, you can decide if you want to accompany them, but I consider it a wise idea if you travelled with me."

"Why, are you afraid that I will get up to mischief?" retorted Fera.

"Quite frankly, yes, I am. Besides, I may need you. This is your mission after all. You are one of the Daughters of Ka, not I." Fera considered Mwari's words for a moment and then replied,

"Mwari, have you forgotten that you were chosen by the Holy Mother Goddess to guide and protect us. You now want to separate myself and my sisters. How will you then keep your promise?"

"You are absolutely right. But circumstances have changed since I made that promise. There are two compelling reasons why my proposal is the best way forward. One, the time of our reckoning is fast approaching. If we fail in our mission, the consequences could be catastrophic for all of us and for Ka. Two, well, I was wrong. There isn't a better reason. No matter what happens, we must push forward."

"I don't care about this mission. We need to decide now who goes with me to Dendera. Boise's life hangs in the balance. You may want to debate the best strategy for the success of our mission, but I have neither the time nor the patience for this. I am leaving for Dendera, with or without you."

Daniel uttered these words resolutely and adamantly. It was clear that his main priority was Boise's health.

"I agree. I am going to Dendera." decided Nena emphatically. Feur concurred.

"Alright, I will go with you and the men." resolved Fera to Mwari.

"So, it is decided then. We shall meet at the Pearl of the Desert."

"That is where Aten lives." said Fera.

Fera realised that it was no co-incidence that Mwari had elected such destination for their rendezvous. She wondered whether Mwari suspected something which no-one else knew. Heaven only knew how greatly they had benefitted from the guiding hand of Aten on so many occasions during their journey and no doubt, they would probably have needed his help again? Travelling to Aten's home in the Great Desert would be one way to assure them of the presence of his powerful protection.

And so, with the decision made to travel on to their next destinations separately, the sisters bid each other a bitter-sweet farewell.

"At least I know where you will be this time." said Feur to Fera. "When we were separated at Lalibela, the worst part of it was not knowing whether you were alive and well." Fera hugged Feur and Nena and said,

"Look after yourselves. Get to Dendera as quickly as you possibly can. I have every faith that Boise will be healed there. I will see you all very soon." said Fera. For the third time in so many days, Fera found herself hugging and crying with her sisters.

"This is becoming an all too familiar sight. Mother and Father would be surprised at our behaviour." teased Nena.

Fera and Feur looked confused and so Nena emphasized,

"Since we have lately always been at each other's throats!"

"Would they really? Is this not how sisters should behave, after all? Laugh and cry and share experiences together. If we cannot do all those things with each other, then who can we do them with? I feel as though this mission has brought us back to the closeness that we once shared as children." added Feur. Fera reached into her cloak and took out the scarab amulet which Candace had quickly thrust into her hand as they had departed Meroe. She pushed it into Feur's hand.

"Take this. Candace once told me that it symbolised life and protection. May it keep you all safe and sound!"

Fera watched as Daniel and her three sisters disappeared into the sunset. Daniel did not want to waste any time and so it was decided that they would travel through the night to reach Dendera by daybreak. Fera was saddened by the fact that the destinies of herself and her sisters seemed to once again be drifting in opposite directions. Her sisters were headed for Dendera and the healing hands of the Goddess Hathor. Fera's destiny, lay in the impenetrable terrain of the Great Desert and the countless unknown dangers which lay in wait for them there, lurking behind its great dunes and hidden in its dusty winds. Fera shivered at the thought of it. She convinced herself that all would end well, but the reality of it was, that no-one, least of all she, knew for sure, just how their mission would end. Would they succeed in re-uniting the pieces of the Turquoise Figurine and would she and her sisters ever be reunited again? The answers were in Fate's hand.

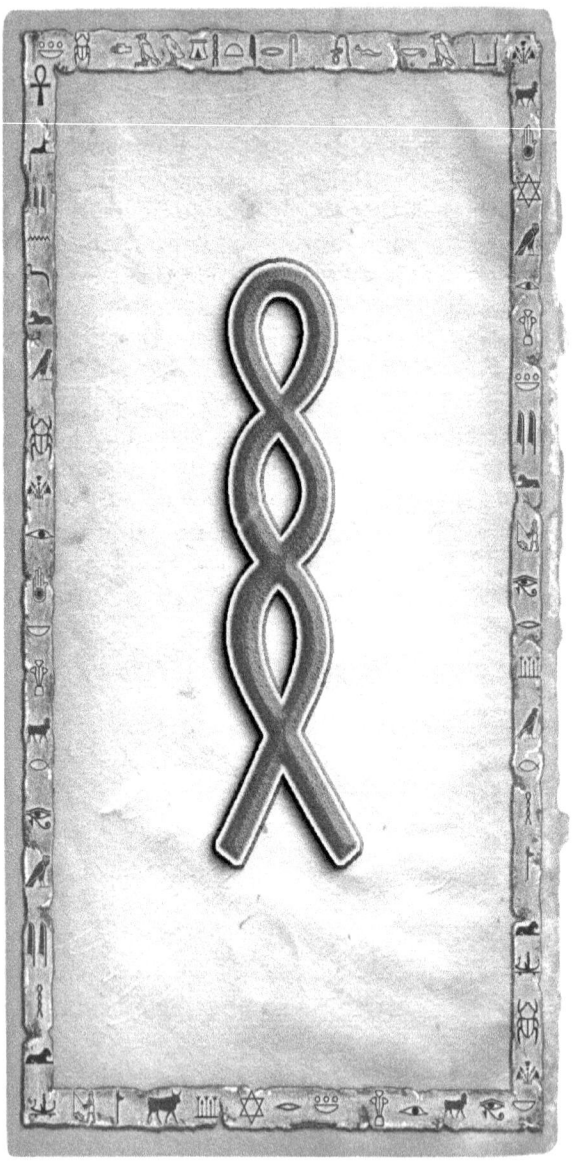

3

WINDS AS THICK AS BLOOD

The women who stood watch on the rooftops of the Old Town kept a vigilant eye over the vast golden sands, which stretched out towards the horizon for as far as the eye could see. The sands and dunes of the Great Desert were constant intruders into the ancient city, as were the ruthless raiders of the slave caravans, which criss-crossed the Great Desert in pursuit of human flesh.

The Pearl of the Desert was an important stop for traders and adventurers alike. It held the largest water source for hundreds of miles between Abydos and Bandiagara and since water was a most valuable commodity, next to the trade in slaves, the Pearl of the Desert was a popular pit stop en route across the desert.

Like many, inevitably drawn to the majestic landscapes of the Great Desert, Aten also made his home in the ancient desert city with its many buildings, strategically clustered in tightly arranged circles, so as to protect its inhabitants from the harsh desert winds. All the buildings of the Old Town were painted luminescent white so as to reflect the vibrant rays of the desert sun.

Everyone who passed through the ancient city knew that it was the domain of Aten. Many sought refuge behind the city's fortified walls and Aten's protection. Few could enter the city limits without their presence being announced. The female lookouts, who stood day and night on the rooftops of the many double-storied houses which made up the city, were the city's first line of defence. The other was Aten's second sight, should he ever have needed their help.

Only women were allowed to roam the rooftops of the city. It was their domain to socialise, but most of all, it provided an effective look-out point to scout possible intruders to the city. The women's abilities to quickly recognise intruders was only out-matched by Aten himself, who as everyone knew, had all-seeing powers. He saw that which took place within the city's limits, as well as that which transpired beyond it, before most others. Locals and visitors alike, slept easy knowing that Aten was their constant protector.

As Aten walked out onto the rooftop above his home that morning, he looked up. The skies were a clear and brilliant blue. There was only one thing that was out of place and that was the moon. A still pale, but nevertheless perfectly formed sphere, hung ominously in the sky overhead. Aten knew that Luna's powers were getting stronger, since her presence was becoming visible even during daylight hours. It was, as though, Luna was so near, that Aten could feel her presence; so close, that he could speak to her as though she stood next to him. His words carried through time and space towards her icy lair,

"You have no powers here, Luna. The heat and vibrant sun will destroy your evil. I know what you are trying to do, what you have done. You can unleash your powers through water and rains which carry nothing but death and destruction, but the power of the sun will diminish its potency. I shall overcome your evil and so will the Daughters of Ka. You greatly underestimate their strength. You may be conjuring up your evil tricks to stop them, but they will triumph. Good will ultimately conquer evil and you will be defeated. Know this, every obstacle you put in their way, will be thwarted by me. I will shadow your every move and do everything within my powers to protect them. You may have elicited the powers of the Elementals, but I have many loyal allies, who will stand by me, against you and your tyranny. They will guard and guide all travellers who venture through my domain."

Aten knew, beyond a shadow of a doubt, that Luna was relentless. Her need for revenge against him and her desperation to stop the sisters from succeeding in their mission, knew no bounds. But, that made Aten more steadfast than ever before to destroy Luna. He would use all his powers and invoke any spell which would bring Luna to her knees. Thus, Aten set about casting a spell to ensure the safety of Fera and her sisters as they travelled to meet their respective destinies.

He took a piece of white cord. He laid it down on the ground in a circular shape, with the two loose ends opening to the east. He placed a bright yellow stone in the centre of the circle. He painted a blue triangle on the stone and held it up to the skies as he chanted,

"All powerful Sun, which looks over us all and guides us towards the light of day, guard and guide the Daughters of Ka on their journey, so that they may once more return to me and to each other."

Aten repeated his words several times, all the while staring into the dazzling sunlight. He felt a warm, dusty wind against his face. It had blown up from nowhere, as though it had been conjured out of nothing. Although, only a wisp of air then, it would gain strength. Aten instinctively knew that it was Luna's response to his spell. She would never give up. Aten continued his chant, until eventually, when he became momentarily blinded by the sun's rays and felt the immense power of the sun as it travelled through his being, he stopped his chanting.

"May the Light guide and protect you all., Daughters of Ka."

As Aten said these words, the innocent, young faces of Fera and her sisters danced across his mind's eye. Through time and space and with all the power that he could muster, he willed his good wishes and blessings towards them.

***

Fera and the men had joined a camel train of merchants en route to the west. Mwari had recommended that crossing the Great Desert in numbers was not only the safest way to cross the desert, but also the quickest.

Since saying goodbye to her sisters, Fera had felt a range of emotions. The deeper that they had ventured into the Great Desert, Fera had felt her emotions transition from sadness to determination. If there was one truth which rang home to Fera, it was that the harsh desert conditions forced one to forget self-pity and regret. The intense heat created by the scorching sun, which shone perpetually in the bluest of skies and the almost non-existent rainfall, made one acutely aware that one's life hung precariously in the balance, every hour of every day.

Mwari and the men had crossed the Great Desert on many occasions before, so they knew what to expect and had acclimatised themselves to its severe conditions quite easily. Fera never became envious of anything, but as she drudged through the terrain of the desert, she wished that she had possessed the apparent optimism of the men, who took the hardships that they were faced with, in their stride.

She wished that she had the tenacity and stubbornness of the dromedary camels, which the merchants rode. The creatures were singularly endowed beasts of burden who were un-phased by the burning sands underfoot and the searing heat beating down on their humped backs.

They had travelled across a varied terrain. At first, the semi-arid savannah of the Sahel was not much of a physical challenge for Fera. She found that, despite being on foot, she could easily keep up with the men. She considered complaining about the fact that Mwari and his party were not offered camels to ride, but then she thought twice about it. The merchants, although amenable to Mwari and his party travelling with them, remained unapproachable, especially to the women.

Fera realised from very early on that she found herself in a man's territory. Not many women, if any for that matter, made their living as merchants trading through the vast expanse which was the Great Desert. The merchants probably left their many wives back home and lived a solitary and somewhat nomadic existence. The only time that the presence of women would be encountered in the desert would most likely have been in the small, remote villages dotted sporadically across the desert and even then, the numbers of such women would have been limited.

For any woman, however, there were distinct dangers if one travelled with the desert merchants. Mwari had warned Fera of these on the night that they had first joined the camel train,

"Keep to yourself. Keep your face down and your head covered with your qob for your own protection. Many of these men might find your presence threatening. Others may feel that you are invading their space. There is only so much protection that Jadon, Gibeon and I can offer you. If we are outnumbered and over-powered, they will be able to get to you. This is the domain of the slave raiders. You are a young and beautiful woman, a great prize to be traded and bartered with."

Fera looked visibly shocked. Mwari's words left shivers to run down her spine. Instinctively, she wrapped her djellabas, her long, loose dress-like outer robe, with its hood called a qob, around her body and over her head.

"Don't look at me like that, Fera. You understand me well. This is a dangerous place, for you, more than most. So, heed my advice."

Just as their journey through the semi-arid savannah landscape had ended, so had their entry into the rocky Hamada of the Great Desert begun. The stone plateaux of the desert could sometimes present itself as high arid mountains, reaching thousands of feet in height, whilst, at other times, it could appear as deep depressions, salt flats or even high steppelands. The Great Desert made for a diverse landscape.

Fera found herself continually surprised and fascinated by nature. She had seen the worst and the best that it had to offer as they had journeyed across the arid desolation of the Dead Lands, through the breath-taking splendour of the deep ravines of the Gulf of Zula and the watery splendour of the Al Suud and lastly, into the vastness that was the Great Desert. She was thankful, though, that the leader of the camel train had elected to cross the Great Desert where the terrain was less impenetrable.

Mwari was grateful that their crossing would completely obviate the need to travel through the mountainous areas of the Great Desert. He remembered a time, many moons back, when he had fought in the army of the Great Sultan Mohammad of Almohad, who had sought to firstly dominate and secondly unite the various warring tribes which had made their homes in the mountains and steppelands of the Great Desert. Mwari often felt as though such times of old were a lifetime away from his present circumstances, but the appearance of a familiar image or a familiar place would awaken his memory and the events of his past life would surge to the forefront of his mind once again. Such memories unsettled him. Not all his past memories were good. Most of the time, he actively sought to repress them, especially those of his family.

Travelling with the merchant train brought a modicum of comfort to Mwari and his party. The merchants were generous enough to provide them with a tent to shield them from the elements. They also shared in their meals, which although rudimentary, were hearty and sufficient. The commands of the leader of the camel train; a tall, stern-looking man with a huge scar across his face, stretching from the corner of his mouth to his ear, were considered sacrosanct.

Jadon and Gibeon would have traded their war stories for his, but the commander never engaged in conversation long enough to warrant enquiries of that nature and besides, they feared that he might bite their heads off, literally, if they had dared the impertinence of asking how he had come by his scar. They imagined that it was the remnant of some war-weary heroics. Fera thought otherwise,

"I think a woman did that, perhaps a betrayed wife or a jilted lover?" Fera laughed inwardly, since she was beginning to romanticize things like Nena always had.

"A woman would never get so close so as to do that to me. If it happened as you say it did, Fera, she must have been rather skilled with a knife." bragged Jadon.

"Any women could disarm any man." bragged Fera.

Jadon disagreed strongly with Fera's contentions. Always up for the challenge, Fera relished the idea of trouncing Jadon's preconceived notions about women and their fighting abilities or lack thereof.

As she sat next to Jadon in their tent during a brief moment taken by the caravan to rest, temporarily sheltered from the harsh midday sun, Fera saw the ideal opportunity to teach Jadon a lesson. She tilted her head to one side, licked her lips and batted her eyes seductively. She leaned in towards him, her breasts just pushing slightly against his forearm. She whispered something into his ear. His body language told Fera that his whole attention was devoted to her. He giggled at her words. Her hand moved seductively from his shoulder and her graceful fingers lingered on his chest, though not touching his skin. His attention was undividedly hers. She might not have been practised in the art of flirting and seduction, not like Nena at any rate, but she had seen as a girl how the young boys of Catal Huyuk had been turned giddy and malleable when beautiful girls had flouted their feminine wiles. With Jadon totally under her spell and with one swift manoeuvre, Fera grabbed Jadon's knife which was tucked into his belt at his waist and deftly drew it towards his throat.

"See, it's easy and you never even saw it coming. Where would you like it? A cut across here or one across there?" asked Fera, as she carefully traced the tip of the knife across Jadon's throat and then from his mouth to his ear lobe, all the time holding his head back by his long jet-black hair.

"That's not fair! You tricked me."

"Did I?" Fera smiled broadly and laughed out loud. Her laugh was warm and rich-toned.

Mwari closed his eyes and enjoyed the sound of it. He tried to remember the last time that he had heard a woman laugh with the kind of laugh that made a man's heart leap; the kind of laugh that made a man know that such laughter was directed at him and him alone. He realised with overwhelming despair that the last time he had experienced such a moment was when he had married the love of his life.

They had married young. They had been so in love, even from the first time that he had seen her. She was slender and graceful, but it had been her eyes, which had entranced him from the moment that she had looked at him. He still saw those eyes in his sleep, begging and pleading with him. Even when he woke up with beads of cold sweat running down his face and chest, it was those beautiful wide eyes that would castigate him. He could never escape them.

Fera's laughed abated. She planted a big kiss on Jadon's cheek, the kind of kiss bestowed by a sister to a brother. Gibeon rolled with laughter on the warm desert sands. He knew how his best friend hated being outsmarted, especially by a young snip of a girl. He thought it good that someone, even a woman, could bring Jadon down to size. Mwari words changed the tone of their jovial bantering,

"I have spoken with the caravan leader. From tomorrow, we shall not be travelling by day any longer. The heat is proving unbearable. It will be far safer to travel by night." Mwari took one look at Fera's reaction. He knew exactly what she was thinking.

"Yes, I know what Aten said; we should travel by day, but Fera, we cannot. We are travelling at the hospitality and might I add, the mercy of others. I have learned in life to pick my battles and this is most definitely not a time to fall out of favour with our hosts."

Fera was not happy, but she was convinced by Mwari's reasoning, for after all the skies were cloudless and offered no respite from the searing sun. The winds blew dry and dusty and every bit of moisture simply evaporated from the air. Just as the perspiration rolled down Fera's face and neck, the dry wind would steal any vestiges of moisture from her body. It was as though the forces of the sun and the moon were raging a fierce battle in the summer skies and all who trod the scorched sands of the Great Desert, were easy pickings in their feud.

They braved the searing heat and stinging winds of the day, by resting in their tents and travelled by night under moonlit and star-filled skies. In the late afternoon hours on their third day of travel through the Great Desert, the winds blew incessantly and harshly, whipping up sands, which stung any exposed flesh. Fera had been grateful for Mwari's advice that she wrap herself up in a heavy and large cloak, which in fact had been Mwari's own cloak in days gone by. Such garment protected her, not only from the wind and sand, but also from the chill of the cooler desert nights. The Desert proved to be a mysterious adversary, with its hot days juxtaposed against its cooler nights. On that day, instead of packing up and heading out at dusk on their continued journey, Mwari and his party were told that they would need to rest for a little longer where they had stopped, since a storm was approaching. Mwari had sensed that the winds which blew around them, seemed more forceful than before.

"How do you know?" asked Gibeon of one of the merchants.

"The habboob always starts like this. Look to the horizon over there?"

The merchant pointed to a large bank of grey clouds, which hung ominously in front of them. It was an unusual sight for Gibeon and the others, since they had for their journey thus far, just experienced clear blue skies during the day and ever clearer skies at night.

"You will need stay in your tents during the storm. Whatever you do, do not venture out. You will get lost."

"What do you mean, get lost?" asked Jadon.

"He means that the winds will become as thick as blood with the dust and sand which they carry with them. I have seen such sandstorms before. You would not even be able to see your own hand if you held it directly in front of your own face. If the sand does not blind you, it will surely suffocate you." added Mwari.

He had become trapped in such a severe sand storm once before. It had happened during his journey south, on his way home, from fighting in the war of the Great Sultan Mohammad. An habboob had blown in from nowhere. The dust storm had not only left dozens of men and horses dead in its wake, but it had wreaked havoc for many inhabitants along the Great Sky River. The dry wind of the dust storm had not only stripped the soil of all moisture and nutrient rich particles which were coveted by the nomadic farmers, but it had also left behind it a legacy of death for many years after that given that it had turned, once fertile farmlands into wastelands, in the blink of an eye.

Later that afternoon, ferocious winds, just as the trade merchant had prophesied, blew in from the east. At first, the winds brought with them a soft, almost dry rain. Before long, the winds appeared to change direction and they blew in from the opposite side of the Great Desert. The rains brought cold air, which hit the ground violently, blowing dry loose sand up from the desert floor. That created a great wall of sediment, which moved swiftly towards them at a high speed. Fera and the others felt as though they were in the midst of one of Nature's violent temper tantrums, as though the elements were raging against each other and all who stood in their path, making survival an uncertainty.

By the time that they had seen the formation of the wall of dust, the merchants had sought cover in their tents, which were firmly pegged into the sand with large metal pegs. Even the camels were tied together and their eyes were covered with rags, so as to protect them from the vicious sandstorm.

Fera took cover with the men as they weathered the storm. The winds raged outside their tent. Mwari noticed that the metal pegs which held the tent to the ground, were starting to lift from the ground, so strong were the gusts of winds which blew.

"The tent will not hold. These harmattan winds are too strong. If it blows away, you must grab onto any solid surface that you can. Avoid being carried away by the winds." cautioned Mwari to Fera and the men.

Fera wondered what on earth Mwari had meant by any solid surface, since in a desert there were none. Mwari's words were not even cold when the tent was torn off its pegs, leaving Mwari and his party exposed to the elements. Fera panicked. She did not know how to react. Sand blew everywhere. It filled her nose and her eyes.

Through her heavily obscured vision, Fera saw the most horrifying sight that she had ever witnessed in her life. A wall of dark dust, as wide as her eyes could see, rolled towards them from the east. With it, thick sand churned and rolled; to totally envelope her and the men. They had no time to run and no place to hide. She coughed, since breathing was made incredibly difficult. She almost lost her balance and then a voice shouted at her from deep within the sand trap,"Fera! Take hold of my hand! Hurry!"

It was Jadon. He grabbed Fera's cloak and pulled her towards him. Together they fought their way towards the camels, who lay huddled nearby in a large group. They crouched next to the beasts of burden and covered themselves with their cloaks. Staying protected and shielded from the storm by the large frames of the camels, was Jadon and Fera's main priority. Even the foul and pungent smell, which exuded from every inch of the camels' bodies, was not enough to get them to budge from their positions.

Fera could not talk, for when she wanted to say something to Jadon, her mouth filled with dry, coarse dust. Fera wondered where Mwari and Gibeon were. Had they also sought safety near the camels? The dust blew relentlessly. Fera found it impossible to breathe. If she closed her mouth and breathed only through her nose, it was just as bad as when she chose to block her nose and breathe in through her mouth. For some inexplicable reason, the sands conjured images in Fera's mind of being mummified and placed in the burial tombs of Meroe. She imagined the process, as explained to them by Daniel, of a corpse being voided of its organs and blood and then being filled with medicinal herbs, except that in Fera's imaginings, the victims were not yet dead. Their mouths, eyes and ears were stuffed against their owners will. Fera had to stop herself from thinking such bizarre thoughts. Thankfully, Mwari and Gibeon crawled across the sands to join them. The light rains soon turned heavier.

"We need to move away from here. These rains will bring a mud slide and we are too exposed. We need to get to higher ground." shouted Mwari.

"What higher ground? There are no rocky outcrops here to shelter us." said Gibeon.

"No! but there are those dunes over there! We will have to make a run for it. Let's hold hands and make our way there. The dunes will shelter us." Jadon and Gibeon were less than convinced.

"What if we get lost? What we see at one moment can disappear under a wall of sand in another. It's too risky." added Jadon.

"Well you stay here then, we're going."

With those last words, Mwari abruptly pulled Fera to her feet and dragged her into the sandstorm. The wind stung Fera's cheeks and burnt her eyes, but she had no choice. Mwari was determined to reach the safety of the dunes. Fera fell into the sand.

"Leave me. Go. I can't do this."

"Not over my dead body! Get up and stop whining." Mwari was deliberately harsh with Fera.

He heard her scream for him to stop hurting her arms, but he did not care, he ignored everything around him. He remained focussed on one thing and that was to save Fera. He would not lose Fera or allow their mission to be thwarted, if he could help it. Mwari tried to drag Fera by her arms. She fell again. That time, instead of falling into sand, she fell face first into what appeared to be mud. The rains had become so heavy that the sand had swollen to form mud.

"Get up or you will get stuck. I may then not be able to pull you out." shouted Mwari once again at Fera. Mwari pulled and pulled at Fera's body, but his efforts yielded no change in her position. Fera was well and truly stuck.

"I can't move my legs." shouted Fera.

Fera struggled to save herself. She tried to find some surface in the sand upon which to leverage her weight, but her every effort made her sink further and further into the mud. The rains continued to fall. Fera felt hopeless. Mwari was soon joined by Jadon and Gibeon. They too heaved and pulled to try to extricate Fera from the muddy grip of the desert sand. Even with their combined masculine strength and effort, nothing seemed to be working. Fera felt herself sinking. She became afraid. In sheer desperation, she screamed out into the sky to the one person whom she knew would help her. Aten had answered her pleas for help once before. She fervently believed that he would rescue her again.

Time stood still as Fera waited for Aten's help, all the time struggling to keep herself from sinking further into the mud. The rains that continued to fall overhead and the winds that surged, acted in a frenzied unison to sweep large masses of mud and water across the desert floor. There appeared to be a river of mud and water rushing towards the place where Fera remained trapped. The men continued hopelessly to dig Fera out of the mud. Fera choked and coughed. She swallowed huge amounts of muddy water. She felt nauseous and dizzy. In her dazed-like state, Fera imagined that she saw strange images dance before her eyes. It was as though the figure of a woman; a beautiful woman, dressed in a deep blue cloak, which draped from her head to the desert floor, stood on the horizon, edging on the winds. Her hollow voice grew louder and louder and was carried by the winds across the desert.

Fera thought that her voice resembled the sounds of the wind as it blew through the trees near the Kara'in caves and the forests that bordered the Charshamba River. Only, the winds which blew across the desert, blew with a thousand times greater velocity and volume than the winds she had recalled in her childhood memory.

The woman's cape bellowed and flapped in the winds. The woman chanted words which Fera could not clearly make out, for they were said in a strange tongue which Fera had never heard spoken before. Fera became afraid. She imagined that she had to be hallucinating or at death's door, for the water and air choked her lungs. She fought tirelessly for survival as she sank deeper and deeper into the bowels of the Great Desert. She heard Mwari and the men's voices, as they demanded that she keep fighting and that she keep her head above the surface.

Mwari racked his brain for some solution to their dilemma and became desperately despondent when he realised that there was no way out. They were indeed caught in the midst of great evil. He knew that nature on its own would never have been capable of such destruction. The harmattan winds were known to be extremely hot, dry and dusty, but the winds which then engulfed them, carried with them the smell of evil and malice, as though some other-worldly being was manipulating nature for their own evil ends.

Mwari remembered the words written in the letter that he had received from the Holy Prophet. It was beyond doubt. The storm could only have been the handy work of Luna. The hauntingly mysterious, yet treacherously evil apparition which had appeared in the skies and churned the winds into a violent frenzy, had to have been sent by Luna. Mwari feared that they would all meet their untimely death in the storm. He prayed silently for death to be quick and merciful. Just as he felt all hope dwindle, he heard another sound echo above the winds. The voice spoke,

"I am the Mistress of the Dunes and you are not welcome in my domain. Leave at once! I will not allow you and your Mistress to do your evil bidding here. Be gone!"

Mwari looked around to see the origin of the clearly audible voice. He saw nothing. Where did the voice come from? Whom was it addressing?

In response to the invisible warning, he heard the sound of laughing, the kind of guttural and mocking laugh made by a person, driven mad. The winds, rain and mud amassed around them unabatedly. Suddenly, the dunes which Mwari had been running towards, appeared to churn into a funnel-like shape in the sky. Mwari looked disbelievingly at the scene as it played out before him. It was as though every inch of sand from the dunes was on the move. The sand was magically thrown across the desert landscape to deposit in the place where Mwari and his party were. It was as if the dunes were moving to protect them with their sandy embrace. The sand piled up higher and higher around them until the violent winds no longer touched their skin and the muddy waters no longer swept across their path.

"The dunes are shielding us from the storm!" shouted out Jadon.

"Quick, let's pull Fera from the mud." instructed Mwari.

The men gave one last, exhausted tug and pulled Fera to the surface. They all sat huddled together, as the last vestiges of the storm played out in the dark skies. The sand from the dunes formed a barrier of sorts, holding back the winds and the rains. It was not long before the rains magically and mysteriously ceased and the dunes lay peaceful once again.

The image of a woman formed from within the dunes. Jadon and Gibeon had seen many beautiful women in their time and during their travels through Ka, but the woman who lay on the dunes before them, was by far the most beautiful woman that they had ever laid their eyes on. She gave the appearance of being naked, but in reality her entire body was fashioned from of the golden grains of sand which made up the dunes. Her body, golden-hued and glistening, was lithe and slender. Her arms and legs were graceful. Her hair was a tumultuous mane of sandy curls that cascaded down her shoulders across her voluptuous bosoms and down towards the sandy surface where the curls blended seamlessly into the dunes themselves. Jadon and Gibeon stood with their mouths agape. Her voice and golden eyes enraptured them,

"Fear no longer, for you are now safe. Travel through my domain in peace and safety." reassured the beautiful woman.

As quickly as she had appeared, she had then disappeared, her sandy body sinking away and becoming one with the dunes. Fera and the men lay on the desert floor, exhausted and incredulous. It was Gibeon who spoke first,

"Did you see that? I don't know what you all saw, but I am sure that we just witnessed something mystical. I would never have believed it if I hadn't seen it with my own eyes. It was unbelievable!"

Everyone simply nodded their heads in agreement. They were too tired to speak. They questioned whether anyone would have believed them if they had ever been asked to recall the events of that night, for they could scarcely believe it themselves.

Fera did not remember how she had managed to fall asleep that night. She was soaked through with rain and mud. Even the shock of their experience and the cold night air could not prevent her eyes from falling shut. Sheer physical exhaustion over-whelmed every fibre of her being, so much so, that when she awoke the following morning, she felt quite shocked and relieved to have lived through the night and to have escaped the grip of the violent storm. She was alive and so were the men. The warm sun beat down on her face. Her body was covered in dry mud. Her skin felt as though it was cracked and dry.

"You look a right state." remarked Gibeon.

Fera's hair was glued to her face with mud and her once beautiful and olive-hued complexion had turned brown in colour. She was barely recognisable as herself.

"I wouldn't talk if I were you."

Gibeon and Jadon looked no better. Their hands and faces were caked with dry mud. Mwari's skin was as black as night and thus a coat of mud on his cheeks made no real difference to his skin colour, other than to lighten its shade.

The merchants eventually found Mwari and his party. Mwari was glad to see that they had come through the storm unscathed. Their only casualty was the loss of two of their camels who had sadly perished. The merchants were evidently quite used to the unpredictable nature of the desert.

From past experience, Mwari knew that the inhabitants of the Great Desert were deeply traditional, their beliefs embedded in thousands of years of ritual and superstition. He did not need to talk of the previous night's occurrences. The merchants had probably encountered similar, if not worse events than those which Mwari and his party had had the misfortune of living through. Consequently, not another word was spoken amongst them of the mysterious women that had magically appeared to them all. It was best that they resumed their journey to the Pearl of the Desert as soon as possible.

They never managed to depart as planned, for just as the merchants were readying the camels and collecting what meagre belongings they still possessed, which had miraculously not been carried away in the strong winds, they saw a party of masked slave raiders in the distance.

They were moving towards them at a fast pace. Mwari recognised them immediately. They were the Garramantes, a particularly vicious tribe of desert dwellers who roamed the Great Desert to attack nomadic farmers and to threaten, rob and ultimately close down markets where people bought and sold goods. It was in that way that they maintained total control over commercial life in the desert. But, it was their trade in human flesh which made them most feared. They stole women and children at will, to sell across the length and breadth of Ka. They had appeared from out of nowhere, the trail of dust left behind their hundreds of horses, barely distinguishable from the sand, mud and dust left in the wake of the storm. Jadon was quick to read Mwari's reaction to their sudden appearance.

"We must get Fera out of sight." said Jadon.

Mwari looked at Fera intently. She did not look herself. Any vestiges of her femininity had been lost in the storm. With little time to spare before the masked riders were upon them, Mwari took out his knife. He walked over to Fera and grabbed her hair as though he intended to cut it. Fera realised with horror what Mwari was about to do.

"No! I will not allow you to cut my hair. I will kill anyone who touches me."

"If you don't do this, those men over there," said Mwari as he pointed in the distance, "they will recognise that you are a woman. They will do far worse things to you than cut your hair."

"I don't care. You cannot do this."

"Well, what do you propose and be quick about it. You have literally minutes to conceal your gender." Fera's mind raced with confused thoughts; none coherent, all frenzied.

"I'll tie it back. Surely if I stay back and hide behind my cloak, they will not recognise me? I look a fright anyway. Behind this mud and grime, who will know that I am a woman? I won't make a sound."

Fera tied back her hair with a strip of cloth torn off the bottom of her cloak.

"For your sake, I hope that that will be enough!" said Mwari.

Before Mwari could think up another plan of action, they were surrounded by the masked riders. They circled the merchants and Mwari and his party. Their stallions were large and lean. The horses appeared to be thoroughbreds, no doubt pillaged from some or other rich travellers who had crossed the Great Desert, thought Jadon. They galloped around and around their newly-found captives, all the time shouting and screaming in a language which Fera did not understand. She felt quite afraid and became dizzy watching the horses gallop in circles around them.

After their show of victory and bravado, the majority of the masked men positioned themselves, still mounted, in a circle around their captives. Most of the men remained saddled on their mounts, but a small group of men chose to dismount. They were led by a particularly large rider and were all clad in black. It was obvious that the large rider was their leader. He spoke in a deep voice. Fera listened as Mwari translated the man's words to Jadon and Gibeon. Mwari's voice was barely a whisper, but Fera strained her ears to listen. The masked man said,

"I am Fezzan, leader of the Garramantes. You are trespassing on my land. For your crime, you will all be taken as my slaves."

The merchant, who had graciously allowed Mwari and his party to join his camel train, courageously stepped forward and spoke out,

"We are simply merchants travelling to the west. We meant no harm. We have travelled this route many times before. We were not aware that we passed onto your lands."

The man called Fezzan walked up to the merchant. He held out his hand. For a fleeting moment it looked to Fera as though he was walking towards the merchant; to perhaps shake his hand and introduce himself, but to Fera's horror and disgust, the masked man never intended any action which could be construed as civility. Instead, he reached for his scabbard and deftly removed his knife and plunged its curved blade into the soft flesh of the merchant's belly. The merchant keeled over. Only one hollow grown managed to escape his lips before he fell into the sand, dead. Red blood oozed from his wound and left a rivulet of blood in the sand. Mwari pushed Fera behind him. That way, he thought that perhaps he could stifle her gasp and keep hidden her presence from the ever-vigilant eyes of the masked horde which stood watch over them. Fezzan looked over to Mwari. His eyes glistened from beneath his black mask.

"Do you also have something to say?" asked Fezzan of the boy behind Mwari.

"I... No. My son is young and it was the first time that he has seen a man killed. It took him by surprise" Fera cowered in Mwari's large and protective shadow.

"Let your son come forward. It is truly a glorious day, is it not, for a father to see the making of his son into a man, is momentous? The experience of death is one event that will put hair on a man's chest. As for the other... well that is far more enjoyable."

The hordes of men started laughing. Their vulgarity had not escaped Mwari, Jadon and Gibeon, who hoped that Fezzan's last comment had totally escaped Fera's comprehension. It seemed as though it had, for Fera did not react to it.

"I said bring your son here." commanded Fezzan, that time his behaviour was far more domineering.

Mwari felt ambivalent. If he did as he was commanded, he would risk Fera's identity being revealed. He would place Fera in huge peril. If he refused, he risked all their lives. Mwari stood defiant. He glared into the eyes of Fezzan. The two men stared each other down, neither one looking away. It was Fezzan's hearty laugh which ended the standoff.

"We'll make a man of him yet. You had better get him ready for what lies ahead. When we reach my tunnels, he will have his shyness beaten out of him. It is no place for weaklings or those who cower behind their fathers, like sad, little boys. Hard work will get him out of his shell."

Fezzan took the matter no further, but Mwari understood clearly that it was not the end of anything. Fezzan was clearly not a man to be trifled with or disobeyed. Mwari sighed silently with relief. He knew that he had dodged a situation which could easily have ended catastrophically for them all. Fezzan turned his wrath elsewhere.

"All of you, hear me well. You are now the property of Fezzan of the Garramantes. You will be taken to my Kingdom at Tamazgha. If you resist, we will kill you. You have no choice, but to submit to my authority."

Fezzan paused. He then walked slowly towards his captives as they stood huddled in a mass. He looked closely at their faces. He stared into their fearful eyes. He could smell their fear. He liked the feeling of being in total control and being feared.

Fera watched his every move. She had never seen such a man as Fezzan before. Mentally, she compared him to the men she knew. He was taller than Mwari and she had once thought Mwari to be the tallest man that she had ever seen. He had broad shoulders. His frame appeared large, but she could not be quite sure of his exact size since his large black cloak hid his physique from view. His hands were large. His skin was not as dark as Mwari's, but it nevertheless appeared darkly tanned under the desert sun. His voice was very deep and intensely masculine. His mannerisms were course and vulgar and he appeared to relish violence. He represented every character trait that Fera abhorred. She felt convinced that she did not like him. She questioned herself as to why her opinion of him even mattered. She did not immediately know the answer.

Mwari, Jadon, Gibeon and Fera and the remaining merchants were tied together, much like a herd of goats would have been, to prevent them from straying from the flock. They were relentlessly marched towards the desert kingdom of Garama in the Land of Tamazgha. Every step they walked, took them further away from their mission and from the likelihood that they would meet up with Daniel and the sisters once again.

It was evident that the Garramantes neither liked nor trusted the merchants who traded across the Great Desert, since it was the merchants who bore most of the violent wrath of the masked hordes as they travelled.

The Garramantes saw the merchants as traitors, men who had made gold and the pursuit of wealth their gods. The merchants, in reality, were nothing more than competitors, but the Garramantes detested anyone who got in the way of their activities. The goods that the merchants were carrying west had been greedily pillaged and divided between the masked men. The merchants had been stripped down to their undergarments. Their skins blistered and festered under the harsh desert sun. Their bodies turned black and blue with the endless beatings that they received at the hands of their captors.

Mwari and his party tried to keep a low profile. They ate when they were allowed to. They marched when they were ordered to. Mwari stayed close to Fera and tried as best as he could to shield her from prying eyes. The most challenging times were when Fera had to answer a call of nature. Jadon and Gibeon took turns with Mwari, watching over Fera. Fera, in turn, kept deathly silent, never venturing to speak, even to Mwari. She marched alongside the men, like a ghostly figure. Her feet became sore and blistered, but she silently bore the pain.

They stopped intermittently at various encampments along their desert route. They were nothing more than a number of rough tents erected in a way to keep the desert sands and winds out and the food provisions, camels, horses and the spoils from pillaging, safe. It was clear that the Garramantes policed the desert with stealth and precision. Their encampments were strategically placed in a bid to maximise their pillaging activities. Their numbers not only found rest and food there, but they could also use such encampments as their desert bases from which they could launch their fresh raids and pillages.

The valuable trade routes across the desert offered them ample opportunities to steal goods from camel trains moving west, but to also sell those very same stolen wares, whether they were handicrafts, salt, gold or food. Everything had a price and the Garramantes were known by everyone across the length and breadth of the Sea of Sand, to skilfully extract value from any item which they sold.

Fera learnt quickly just how cruel the Garramantes were. She saw things which both equally horrified and terrified her whilst being held their captive, but it was the Garramantes' treatment of their slaves which made her cry inwardly as she slept each night. Women and children were prized possessions for the slave raiders, but they were not treated as such. Their treatment of their slaves earned the Garramantes their reputation of being uncivilised barbarians. Children were whipped and women were abused. Fera heard their screams cry out in the dead of night. At such times, she thanked the Great Spirit for Mwari's foresight in keeping her identity a secret. Their pretence had gone well beyond the fact that she was supposed to be Mwari's young son. They had led their cruel guards to believe that she was mute as well; that way, they would never have had to explain her inability to speak to anyone.

After Fera had witnessed the abuse towards the slaves, she understood more than ever, the need for her to remain silent and anonymous. Her life depended on it. At least, Fera could still silently be a part of Mwari and the men's plot to escape. At night, when the guards were otherwise occupied and Mwari and his party were behind lock and key at one of the desert encampments en route to Garama, they secretly discussed their plans.

"It will be impossible to leave until we reach the Wadi Ajal, where the Garramantes live." whispered Mwari.

"How do you know where they live?" asked Gibeon.

"I have been there before. The Garramantes live on a one-hundred-mile chain of oases in the Great Desert. Their commercial centre is located at Garama.

It will most likely be there that they will sell their pillaged goods."

"And the slaves?" added Jadon. Mwari nodded, evidencing that slaves would similarly meet their fates in Garama.

"If we keep our heads down and stay alive until then, we might stand a chance. Out here we have no-one to assist us. In Garama, we may find a sympathetic ear. I have made many friends and perhaps equally as many enemies during my life, but hopefully I will encounter the former in Garama. I still have some gold coins given to us by Ezana. Perhaps they will come in handy if we need to buy our way out of this misadventure."

"That's a polite way of putting it." replied Jadon.

He hoped that Mwari had the coins well hidden, but then realised that he must have done so, since the coins had not been found when the slave raiders had searched them. Mwari had in fact protested deeply when they had grabbed Fera and wanted to search her body. He had convinced them that his son was nothing more than an imbecile; hit on the head as an infant and rendered mute and that he would never have trusted him with anything of value, since he would just have lost it or given it away. He had told them that that was exactly what the stupid boy had done; gone and given all their money to some poor beggar on the road. To show his fatherly consternation and disapproval at his son's behaviour, Mwari had slapped the boy over the head and when he had fallen to the ground, he had kicked him in the behind. The guards lived according to violence and cruelty and when they saw it being practised by others, they relished it. Consequently, they let Fera be and never searched her person. Thus, the coins and the first piece of the Turquoise Figurine had remained hidden in the lining of her cloak.

Mwari was greatly relieved by it all, but Fera was livid that she had been slapped and kicked, even if Mwari had only tapped her softly and made his actions look thoroughly convincing, to say the least. He had clearly read Fera's emotions. If she had been able to speak, she would have stabbed him with her dagger, which remained fastened to her thigh. Mwari reckoned that it was worth risking Fera's anger if it meant that her person remained safe and no-one discovered that she was in fact a woman.

They arrived in Garama on the early eve of the second day after their capture by the slave raiders. They had entered a large compound, consisting of many buildings. Mwari and his party were little prepared for the events that lay in stall for them there. The slaves, of whom Mwari and the others counted themselves a part of, were immediately sorted so that they could be herded towards the tunnels, which flanked the valley that was the Wadi Ajal. Fera had no time to appreciate her surroundings, which were green and lush in sharp contrast to the brown, dry and never-ending expanse of the Great Desert.

The slaves were lined up in the heat of the afternoon sun. They stood motionless and awaited their fate. If they were fortunate enough to be bought, perhaps they could remain in the centre of Garama, but if they were deemed suitable to work in the tunnels or foggaras as they were locally known, which stretched far into the mountains in the pursuit of the mine fossil water from the limestone layer beneath the desert sand, which the Garramantes desperately needed in order to sustain their continued life on the wadi, then they would be doomed. Only the strongest of the slaves were chosen for such work, since the Garramantes needed strong slaves to keep the tunnels maintained. Faced with the prospect that they could be separated from each other, Mwari searched his mind for possible solutions to their dilemma. He whispered to Jadon and Gibeon,

"Do what you must, but pretend to be sickly. Cough, keel over, moan! Do anything. They must believe that you are not strong enough to work the tunnels."

The men tried to do as Mwari had suggested, but despite their best efforts, they were still chosen. When the slave raider set eyes on Mwari and Fera, there was little that Mwari could do to convince him otherwise, for Mwari looked neither frail nor physically impaired.

It was then Fera's suitability for work in the foggeras that came under scrutiny.

"You! Move over there!" the guard shouted, indicating that Mwari should move across to where those slaves stood who would be taken to do hard labour in the tunnels. Mwari stubbornly stood his ground. The guard hit Mwari across his face. Mwari's face was jolted to one side with the force of the slap, but his feet remained firmly on the ground.

"What do we have here, a hero? You do not want to make me angry, slave! Your life is worth nothing." The guard leaned in to Mwari. They stood eyeball to eyeball. Mwari smelt his foul breath.

"Go on, fight me. I dare you!" hissed the guard, as he edged for a fight.

The guard knew, without a shadow of a doubt, that he would emerge the victor. If the time were any other and if Fera's very life and limb were not at stake, Mwari would have leapt to attack the hideous slob who stood before him, but it was not the time nor the place for heroics. Mwari reluctantly did as he was told, leaving Fera alone to fend for herself.

The guard then turned his attention to Fera. When the boy had first arrived in Garama, he had appeared to the guards to be weak and puny and it was for that reason that he had escaped their attention. The guard then looked at the boy closely. Perhaps, he thought, he would be suitable for housework; nothing too taxing for his weak frame. He grunted some indecipherable instruction to another guard who stood nearby. Such man reacted immediately and ran in the direction of the outbuildings, which housed a large kitchen. Mwari watched the scene. His heart raced with anticipation. He did not want to allow himself to think that perhaps their ruse had worked after all and that Fera would be taken to work in the kitchens.

Momentarily, an old woman, rather fat and incredibly dirty from head to toe, walked from the kitchen towards them. She stood squarely in front of Fera and eyed her intently and suspiciously. After several minutes, she spoke,

"I thought you said that you had a boy for me. I do not want a girl. The work in the kitchen is hard. The fetching and carrying cannot be done by a girl."

Everyone looked stunned. Mwari looked at Jadon and Gibeon. The thing that they had most feared had happened.

"This is a boy, I assure you." said the guard incredulously.

"Don't be stupid. Are you blind or something? It takes a woman to know such a thing and one thing is certain, this puny creature is a girl. Look here."

The woman pulled Fera's cloak back to reveal only her shirt, through which one could clearly see the outline of her breasts.

"I may be no expert at many things, but I can recognise those in the dark. Some men might have breasts, I have seen a few, but this one, she is all woman."

The vulgar woman laughed, as she pointed to Fera's chest. The guard did not like the fact that he had been duped by a scrawny girl and he most certainly did not like the fact that a fat kitchen maid was mocking him in front of his men. He had to save face and so he slapped Fera violently across the head.

"That serves you right. Who do you think you are, you stupid girl?" shouted the guard.

Fera looked enraged, as if she had been gravely insulted. She took a step closer to the guard, glared into his eyes and shouted,

"I am Fera, daughter of Shoa and Sofala. I hail from the Great City of Catal Huyuk. The ancestors of my people have prophesied that I and my sisters would undertake a mission of great importance. I have dined with Queens and Kings. I have travelled to meet Luna, Goddess of the Moon and I have the guidance and protection of Aten, God of the Sun. That is who I am, you imbecilic oaf. How dare you lay your hands on me!" With those words, Fera leapt at the guard like a crazed wild animal and pressed her dagger to his throat. "Touch me again and you will regret it!"

The other guards instantly ran to their colleague's aide. Fera kicked, bit and screamed as they tried to tear her away from the guard. She was quickly silenced when someone hit her again across the head with their fist and Fera fell to the floor, unconscious. The guard composed himself and then walked over to where Fera's body lay. He kicked her in the ribs.

"Take this delusional cow to the women's camp. She can never be allowed to work the kitchens."

The guard smeared the blood off his neck where Fera's knife had punctured his skin. He decided that it was best that the girl be put to work in the fields or that she look after the animals. At least no knives would be accessible to her there.

Mwari and his men had been helpless to intervene and they had no choice but to stand by as Fera's limp body was dragged off in the opposite direction to where they would soon be taken. Mwari looked to the skies and prayed,

"Look after her Aten." Mwari knew that Fera could be her own worst enemy. She had a big mouth and amongst the Garramantes, a big mouth was a liability. A big mouth got one killed.

"At least they think she is quite mad, spewing all that nonsense about Gods and Goddesses, Kings and Queens. They seemed to not have believed her. Perhaps that's a good thing, Mwari." whispered Jadon, as they walked in the direction of the tunnels.

"I hope that when she wakes up, she will realise the error of her ways and keep quiet, otherwise, she is likely to get a few more beatings." added Gibeon.

"I doubt that. She has not shut up since we left Catal Huyuk. It is unlikely that she will start now." joked Jadon.

"That's what I am afraid of." Mwari's words rang hauntingly true for all the men. They all feared for Fera.

4

BARAKA

The next morning, Fera awoke with a mighty headache and a gash the size of her palm across the back of her head. She was not sure where she was or how long she had been unconscious. All she knew was that she was all alone, since Mwari, Jadon and Gibeon were no-where in sight. She struggled to stand up from the makeshift bed upon which she lay.

"Stay still. I fixed you up as best as I could, but the wound has yet to knit. You must stay calm."

Fera looked up into the kindest eyes that she had seen in a long time. They reminded her of her mother's eyes. The woman was dressed very shabbily and her long, black curly hair ran riot on her head.

"Where am I?"

"You are in the women's camp. All the women slaves are brought here. My name is Zakariya."

The fear shone through Fera's eyes. The events which had rendered her unconscious slowly came back to her. Zakariya sensed the girl's uncertainty.

"What is your name?"

"Fera."

"How did you come to be here, Fera?"

"I", Fera thought it best not to admit to the strange woman that she was alone, "We were taken en route through the Great Desert."

"You said we but you were brought to our camp alone."

"Yes, I was travelling with my guardian and his men. We were all captured."

"That is one thing that all us women here in the camp share in common. We were all taken forcibly and against our will."

Zakariya could sense that talking about her capture was distressing for Fera and so she told Fera to rest and that they would talk more later. And Fera did rest. She slept for a whole day and a night. Zakariya feared that the knock that Fera had taken to her head, had injured her more severely than originally thought, but all the women were extremely relieved when Fera awoke the next morning. Any newcomer to the camp raised interest, but the girl who had stood up to the guard's brutality, earned a special admiration from the women.

"Every part of my body aches." groaned Fera, after she had awoken from her deep sleep.

"It would do. You have two broken ribs and a nasty head wound from that beast, Imouharen. He is the head guard, second in command to Fezzan. He is a brutal and callous man. But never fear, pain subsides and the body heals. That which seems insurmountable now, will be a distant memory tomorrow." said Zakariya.

"You remind me of my mother. I miss her desperately."

"Mothers are gifts of life and love. They must be treasured."

"Do you have children?" Fera noticed that Zakariya looked away. Tears welled up in her eyes. "I am sorry. I did not mean to upset you. You spoke so tenderly of motherhood. I assumed that you are a mother."

"I was one, but I am one no longer. My children died in this camp, starved and brutalised. They were only five and six, you know. My boy was the eldest. His name was Tiziri. His name meant moonlight. My daughter was called Ayyur, after the moon. They were worked like dogs. Their little bodies could not take the gruelling work. Eventually, they left me as silently as they had first entered into this world. I found them both, cold and lifeless in their beds. When they were born, they never cried, you know. Strange, really! My husband and I were worried, since all babies cried as they breathed their first breath. Mine never did. They were angels. There is not a day that goes by that I do not yearn to be their mother again."

Fera watched as Zakariya stared into space. Her story had been relayed with great sadness, but also a tinge of bitterness and anger. Although Zakariya's crying did not make a sound, large tears escaped her big eyes to roll down her cheeks. Fera could not help but to cry as well. Fera's tears may have been for a very different reason, but both women sensed that their tears united their spirits and healed their weary hearts. Fera hugged the strange woman who sat before her. Zakariya soon wiped her eyes. It seemed as though there was no time for self-pity in the camp. The work was hard, but survival was even harder.

"Fera, you will only be allowed to lay here for today. However awful you still feel, you will have to get up and work tomorrow, otherwise the guards will beat you further. You will have to work through the pain. I have arranged for you to do some light work. You will carry the water to and from the fields where the others are planting crops. Keep your head down and forget about that temper of yours. We all heard about what you did. We were glad that you did it. Imouharen deserved it and much worse, but you are now paying the price for such impertinence. In the camp, we protect each other, so it is imperative that you do nothing that could unleash the wrath of the guards. One false move by one of us and all of us will suffer. You understand?" Fera understood.

Over the ensuing days, Fera buckled down and did as she was told. Life in the camp was hard, but bearable. The women and their many children showed warmth and kindness to Fera. Food was minimal, the work hours were long, but the laughter and smiles through it all, were plentiful.

Fera constantly wondered of the whereabouts of Mwari and the men. The women could only tell her that they had most probably been taken to the tunnels, since most healthy workers ended up there.

"My husband was taken there. So was my son. He was sixteen. The boy was injured in a rock fall so they sent him back here. Zakariya nursed him well again, but they sent him back there." told one of the women. Her voice was angry. "After that, I did not hear from him for a long, long time. I feared that he was dead, that both my son and husband were dead, but thankfully Zakariya did not see their death in the spirals." Fera did not understand.

"The spirals, what are they?" asked Fera.

"Zakariya is a jinni, a magic woman. She has the power to see things which others cannot." said the woman.

"Then she would be able to help me. I need to know if my sisters are safe. If Mwari, Jadon and Gibeon are alive?" Fera wasted no time in approaching Zakariya for help.

"Fera, I cannot always see the future. With some, it is only darkness. I cannot see their spirals. With others, I see images. It is a dangerous thing to toy with the spirits."

"Please, I need to know if my sisters are well. I will do anything, give anything. I have money. I will give it to you." Zakariya seemed unconvinced. Fera reached for her amulet, which hung beneath her clothes, hidden from sight.

"This was made for me by my father. You may also have it. It has value. It could be used to buy off the guards. Get some food for the children or some herbs. You said that you needed some to heal the sick in the camp." Fera's eyes beseeched Zakariya.

"I will gladly accept the money, not for myself, but for the children. But, as for your amulet, I would not dream of taking it."

Zakariya reached for her own amulet which hung around her neck. It was a beautifully crafted silver and enamel object in the shape of an open hand. It had the image of an eye designed in the centre of the palm.

"I too have one. It is called a hamsa. It represents an open palm which repels evil. The five fingers represent the pillars of Islam."

Zakariya pointed to each of the fingers as she spoke, "It is important in my faith that we profess our faith, pray, give alms, fast and undertake a pilgrimage to the Holy lands. My amulet was passed to me by my mother. It holds magical powers and represents power, blessings and strength. It protects me from evil spirits. It holds Baraka. Thus, I would never part with mine and I would never ask you to part with yours."

Fera remembered that she had seen a similar symbol hanging on the wall in Joab's house in Axum. It also depicted a hand with five fingers. Fera reflected momentarily on how similar the various faiths were.

"Baraka, what is that?" asked Fera.

"My people refer to Baraka as the positive power of the Saints, a blessing from God. It is a source of inspiration which permeates all things. It can be found in jewellery or talismans or even in plants such as henna. It is also found in myrrh and sandalwood incense."

Fera realised just how significant myrrh was. There had been so many times in her life and during their journey that they had been reminded of its healing and spiritual powers. Zakariya took hold of Fera's hand and turned over her palm. She traced circles on Fera's palm with her graceful forefinger.

"Your amulet will continue to protect you, just as mine has protected me. I see its powers in your past and in your future life." Fera watched as Zakariya traced spirals on her palm. Such action both intrigued and mystified Fera.

"Why do you do that?"

"These spirals are symbolic of a person's life path. Our lives are cyclical in nature. We begin at the end and end at the beginning. Our spiritual and emotional growth, as we pass through our lives, is defined by the outward progression of the spiral. They tell me all that I need to know."

"What else do you see?"

"You have grown and matured much in your recent past, but your spiral is not yet at its end. You have far to go yet. You will cross the paths of many during your life."

Zakariya's feint smile disappeared. Her expression changed. She never liked to reveal any predictions that would bring unhappiness to their recipient. She was reluctant to tell Fera what she saw. Fera pressed her for an answer,

"What do you see now, tell me?"

"I see great heartache, perhaps even death. It will happen more sooner than later." Fera's heart sank,

"My sister? Is it my sister? Will she die? Is she already dead? I could not bear it if that were true."

"I cannot say. My visions are not clear." Zakariya hated lying to Fera, but she believed that she was doing the right thing by not telling Fera what she actually saw.

"I do know that an evil force has attached itself to your life path. It will drain you and all those whom you hold dear.

It will try to kill you. It may even try to kill your loved ones. You need to fight or this evil will consume your goodness."

"How will I do that?"

Zakariya reached for a small leather pouch which was hidden beneath a loose stone in the flagstone floor. She emptied the pouch's contents into Fera's open palm. Thirty or so smooth, round pebbles tumbled out.

"My people believe that if a woman ties rags to trees and stones and then throws away the rags and stones, any evil which is seen in her life path, will be transferred to the stones and rags. I collected these pebbles when my children died."

"But you never threw them away?"

"No. I coveted them as I covet the memories of my children. To me, they represent my hatred and anger. I have never wanted to throw them away because then I would have to release the hatred that has grown for so long in my heart. This anger fuels my need to one day take my revenge on those responsible for taking my life away from me."

"Then why do you give them to me now?

"It is time. The spirits of my children visited me in my dreams last night. They implored me to be happy. Now is as good a time as any other for me to do as they have asked. If I give you my stones and you release them, perhaps we can rid both our lives of evil."

Fera acknowledged Zakariya's great courage and was honoured by the gift that Zakariya was willing to bestow upon her.

"Where will I get the rags?"

"Those you already have. You must rip an item of your clothing into shreds of cloth. Those, you will then tie to a tree."

"I haven't seen any trees around these parts."

"We'll make a plan, fear not."

Fera felt strangely relieved, yet excited by what she had learnt from Zakariya. Later that night, when all the guards were pre-occupied with their nocturnal jaunts, Zakariya and Fera stole away into the cool night air to execute an ancient magical rite. They were not able to find a tree, but decided that a large bush would do just fine.

Fera tore a large portion of her shirt into shreds. She tied the rags around the pebbles which Zakariya had given to her as well as on the branches of the bush.

"Not so tight, Fera. They must be loose enough so that when the desert winds come up, they can blow the rags away. Tie the rags tightly around the stones though."

Fera understood better than before how the magical rite worked. As one tossed the stones, one would then release their evil from one's life. So, Fera released the stones with all the strength that she could muster. As she let each one slip from her grip, she prayed that Boise would be released from the grip of death; that Mwari, Jadon and Gibeon would be safe; that she would be reunited with her sisters and that they would succeed in their mission to defeat Luna and her evil, but most of all, that Zakariya would find peace and be saved from the evil that was forced labour.

Fera thought then how she despised Fezzan and all that he stood for. Perhaps it was good to hold onto some feelings, especially if those feelings drove her to see more clearly the true nature of those with whom she would have to cross paths with in future.

***

Mwari had calculated that in order to free himself and his party, he would have to demand a meeting with Fezzan and remind him that he was not a slave, but rather a once loyal ally to his father, the Sultan Mohammad, for whom he had fought valiantly in many a war waged by the Kingdom of Almohad. Once Fezzan had made known his name to them on that fateful day of their capture, Mwari had instantly remembered that Fezzan was the long-last son of the great Sultan Mohammad. He, without hesitation, had shared such information with Jadon and Gideon.

"I met his father once, you know. Not in person mind you, but as part of a group of mercenaries hired by the Sultan to help protect his territories. He was the ruler of the great and powerful Kingdom of Almohad. For many a year, they dominated the lucrative caravan routes across the Great Desert as well as sea trade over the Great Sea."

"Where is the Sultan now?" asked Jadon.

"He died many moons ago. He left three sons to inherit his kingdom. He bequeathed that the Kingdom of Almohad would be divided into three equal parts amongst his sons upon his death."

"So Fezzan was one of these sons?"

"Yes, he inherited control over the northern territories which remained known as the Almohad Kingdom. His brother, Khaldun was given lands to the west. They were renamed as the Marinid Kingdom and the youngest brother Ashir was left to control lands to the south and east. He named these lands the Zayyanid Kingdom."

"How did Fezzan end up with the Garramantes then?" asked Gibeon.

"I do not know the whole story. I heard through the desert traders that he betrayed his brothers. After the Sultan's death, I no longer fought in the Almohad armies and so I did not keep abreast of events that occurred after that or what happened to the Sultan's heirs."

"Well, whatever happened, Fezzan seems to have turned out the worst of his brothers. Surely, no dutiful son would leave his birth right behind to pillage and maraud the desert plains with a bunch of criminals." added Jadon.

Mwari pondered Jadon's words. Human nature intrigued him, it always had, especially how a good man could slowly turn evil and in some cases, almost overnight. He knew from bitter experience, that it was possible. The good in a man's heart could be wiped away by an endless array of events, be they death, power, loss or vengeance. A childhood filled with teachings of religion and a lifetime devoted to the pursuit of meaning and goodness, would prove no barrier to the encroachment of evil. Evil was an all-pervasive and ultimately all-consuming force.

For weeks, Mwari had planned, down to minute detail, his move to attract Fezzan's attention. Between sunrise and sunset, there was very little else that the slaves could do to while away the hours, but think and Mwari could do little else, but lay awake at night and plan their escape. Jadon and Gibeon chastised him for not taking full advantage of the little time that they had to rest their weary bodies from the hard toil in the Garramantes' tunnels, but Mwari's mind did not stop racing. He had to find a way to meet with Fezzan. Mwari calculated that he would cause some or other commotion on a day when Fezzan made his usual inspection of the tunnels. Perhaps with enough commotion, Fezzan's attention could be drawn. Although Mwari's plans never saw the light of day, his opportunity to eventually meet Fezzan came from a most unexpected quarter. Mwari and the men had just eaten their meagre rations one evening, when the guards brutishly herded them out of the slave encampment and marched them towards an unknown destination.

"Where are you taking us?" enquired Mwari of Imouharen.

"Never you mind, scum! Just walk and be quick about it."

Imouharen was abrupt and evasive. He hit Mwari across the back of his head. Mwari faltered, but did not fall. Mwari feared the worst. Had they been sold again? If they were moved elsewhere by a new slave owner, they might never have seen Fera again. Mwari had replayed in his mind the scene of the reveal of Fera's true identity, many times since it had occurred. It had filled him with fear. The guards were anything, but understanding or compassionate. Day after day, they had brutalised the men working in the tunnels. Whipping was the order of the day. If a slave slackened their efforts or spoke back or spoke at all for that matter, they would be whipped. If the guard's cruelty was not inflicted physically, then it was through incessant verbal abuse. They continually belittled the men. Those weakened by lack of food and water as well as hard labour, soon broke under the weight of the guards' tyranny. Mwari longed for the day that he and his men could escape, even though they were abysmally mindful that escape was near impossible.

Mwari and his men were escorted back to the commercial centre at Garama. Once there, they were taken to a large house called a riad. From the outside it appeared to resemble the many other houses in the neighbourhood. It was a two-storey structure, built of mud brick. There were no visible windows to the exterior of the house. As they walked through the large doors, adorned with the symbol of

Five Snakes, they were ushered into a large interior courtyard. It was obvious that the house's owner was someone of great wealth. Mwari made a mental note of the markings on the door. He had seen such markings many times before. In fact, all the houses in Garama and in Axum were marked in some or other distinguishable manner. The Five Snakes symbolised a Muslim house. A Star of David represented a Jewish home. A Rose with four petals indicated a Christian household. Mwari had not liked the idea of differentiating people in such a way, but he made it a point to never question the cultural and spiritual beliefs of people, for he believed that all religions had an inherent right to exist and pursue their beliefs as they deemed fit. The fragrant hit of lemon and orange brought Mwari's thoughts back to the present.

"Get down!" shouted the guards, "You will wait here until you are summoned."

Mwari, Jadon and Gibeon were forcibly pushed to the floor. They sat and waited. Their surroundings were once again foreign to them. It appeared as though they were sitting in some kind of courtyard. Doors branched out from it in all four directions. The walls were adorned with tadelakt plaster, a lime plaster which was rammed, polished and treated with soap to make it waterproof, and zellige tiles which were made from terra cotta and inlaid with intricate tile work in the varied shapes of stars and crosses. The greens, blues and yellows of the tiles made for a bright and happy contrast to the dark earth of the foggaras. At the centre of the centrally placed interior courtyard, was a large fountain and equidistant from each other in the four corners of the courtyard, grew two lemon and two orange trees. Even Gibeon and Jadon admired their surroundings.

After what seemed like an eternity, the doors to the north side of the courtyard flung open. Several other guards walked briskly past them. They appeared to be carrying a woman, whose head appeared to be covered in a hessian sack. She was kicking and screaming. It was obvious that she did not want to be carried like a sack of grain. She was dressed in filthy, tattered clothes, as though she had come out the other side of a vicious battle with a wild desert animal. Mwari and his men had seen many an inhumane sight since they had arrived in Garama. The most vicious of these, had been the treatment of women at the hands of the guards. It was clear that male slaves had only one purpose and that was to work from dawn until dusk in the tunnels. If they could not work, their value was reduced to nothing and they were whipped to death or worse yet, they were left in the desert to starve. Female slaves, on the other hand, seemed to have more value than their male counterparts, if only, that such value was measured in the sums of money that the trade in human flesh could bring.

Mwari would have thought that any possession that could yield value would be prized and protected, but such was not the case with the Garramantes. Those women not sold, were used and abused by the guards or worked to death on the land. Mwari felt pity for the poor creature that was being dragged past them. He wondered which fate awaited her. Would she be sold or would her body be used and abused that night by whoever sat on the opposite side of the door?

"Take your filthy hands off me, you pigs!" shouted the woman. "You will not get away with this."

Mwari and his men looked at each other. They had heard that particular voice raised in anger before, more times than not, an anger which had been directed squarely at their door.

"Fera!" whispered Jadon.

Mwari looked at Jadon, disbelievingly.

The doors closed behind the guards as they disappeared into the room with Fera. Mwari's heart sank. He and the men listened intently for any sounds emanating from the other side of the door. They could only hear muffled voices.

**

"Let me loose, you swine! How dare you man-handle me! You have no idea who I am. You will see the wrath of Aten for treating me in this vile way." screamed Fera.

Fezzan listened to the rants and ravings of the wild creature who lay writhing on the floor in front of him. Word of her audacious, albeit somewhat deceptive ruse, had quickly reached his ears. The guards would have been highly dissatisfied at the idea of having been duped by a slave, but they were outright livid that the deception had been at the hands of a woman. Fezzan knew that the Garramantes held little regard for women, other than what they contended were their only purposes, namely procreation and recreation.

Fezzan did not agree with all their ways, but over the years he had restrained his own beliefs so as to avoid unnecessary clashes and to secure the abiding loyalty of his men. Theirs was a cruel existence which often demanded even crueller behaviour from him and his men. His men only understood violence and cruelty and thus, much to his own dislike, Fezzan had adapted his nature to accordingly fit in with theirs.

"Leave us! I will interrogate this wild creature."

The sternness of their commander's voice left little doubt in the guards' minds that he meant business. They smiled smugly at Fera as they exited the room. Since she had been unceremoniously dumped in the centre of the room and the hessian sack had been removed from her head, she had stood up and was glaring venomously at Fezzan.

"I see you refused my invitation to be bathed and dressed in new clothes."

Fera just glared into the eyes of the man whom she did not know, but whom she had, nevertheless, grown to detest.

"I can see you harbour much dislike for me. Why would that be, when we have never had the pleasure of having met formally?" Fera rolled her eyes and ignored Fezzan's attempt at civility.

"Oh, so I am getting the silent treatment, am I? You were very verbal with my guards."

Fezzan walked over to a table and poured himself some wine in a shiny silver goblet. He gulped its contents greedily, wiping his mouth with his sleeve when he was done. Fera turned up her nose at his uncouth manners. She expected nothing less from the man who stood so arrogantly in front of her.

"Does something displease you? Would you like some wine?" Fezzan had noticed Fera's reaction. He poured Fera some wine.

"Here, drink this."

Fera looked away. She was determined not to look into his eyes any longer and not to accept any kindness from him whatsoever. She could not get the imagery of Zakariya's children out of her mind. Fezzan pushed the wine goblet into Fera's hands.

"I do not talk to a murderer and a criminal." Fera retorted, defiantly.

Fera threw the goblet at Fezzan. She held her courage and waited for a violent reaction from him, but it did not come. Fezzan simply wiped the wine from his face. He stood silent for a minute and thought about the words that he had just heard spoken. He then replied jokingly,

"You mean me? Am I the murderer and criminal? Who is it that I have presumably murdered? I cannot remember murdering anyone?" Fezzan looked so smug. He had a wide smile on his face, exposing his pure white teeth. Fera was shocked by the fact that he appeared to be so nonchalant.

"You are a slave raider. You have left a trail of misery everywhere you have gone. Over in the women's camp, lie sick and dying women and children. Your guards vilely abuse and work the women slaves to the point that many die miserable deaths every single day and yet, you have the temerity to stand there and pretend to be blameless."

Fera was shouting. Mwari and his men heard her shouting and feared for her safety, since Fezzan was known as a merciless man to many across the Great Desert. Fezzan walked up close to Fera and looked deep into her emerald eyes, which even under the layers of dirt on her face, appeared mesmerising and beguiling. He replied,

"Their suffering is not at my hand. I have never laid a finger on them. I am no murderer."

"Have you forgotten the desert merchant who met his death at the end of your sword? I watched you kill him. The female slaves might not die at your hand, but you sanction the actions of your guards, who treat them brutally and sadistically. They deny them food. They beat and starve their children. You should be ashamed of yourself."

Fezzan did not like the fact that a mere slip of a girl was holding a proverbial mirror to his face, exposing his flaws and making him think about that which he chose to ignore. It had been years since he had been taken in by the Garramantes and he had found it far better to simply stifle any part of his nature that was compassionate and kind. Fezzan did not want to defend his actions to Fera, but for some reason he felt compelled to.

"The merchant's death was necessary. They slither the sands of the Great Desert to ply their trade. They are greedy thieves. They buy goods for far less than their value and sell them for a princely profit. Poor farmers and local merchants suffer greatly at their hands. The merchant's death held more value than his life. Sometimes, the bad must die for the good to live." Fezzan stopped and then added, "I have never lifted my hand to a woman and I never shall. The Garramantes rule by fear and force. It is their way, not mine."

"Yet, you do nothing to stop them. I do not know which is worse, actually hurting someone or standing by and watching others do your dirty work." Fera had never before heard such senseless rationale. She continued her lecture. Her voice became pitched. "What makes you the arbiter of life and death anyway? You should be ashamed of yourself."

Fezzan's patience was running thin. How dare such a young woman challenge or question him? He walked close to Fera again. His body stood merely inches away from her. He sensed that deep emotion and perhaps, even deep passion, ran through her veins. He almost felt her heart, as it beat through her tattered shirt, exposing the fullness of her ample bosom.

She intrigued Fezzan and not because she was physically alluring. No woman had ever piqued his interest as the woman standing defiantly before him, had just done. He felt himself being drawn to her and yet, being angered by her at the same time. There had not been a woman alive whom he had not made submissive to his will, not until then and he became irritated at the thought of someone holding such power over him.

"You were called to me to answer my questions. I am not in the habit of explaining myself, not to you or to anyone else! Now, you will speak when you are spoken to. If not, perhaps your friends might convince you to behave."

"Where are they?"

"Outside this room."

"I do not believe you."

Fezzan took hold of Fera's arm and escorted her to the door. He barely opened it, but Fera was left convinced that Mwari and the men were indeed still alive. Fera's heart leapt as she saw Mwari, Jadon and Gibeon sitting on the floor in the courtyard. Fezzan shut the door again.

"So, you will now behave?"

Fera had seen the cruelty dished out under Fezzan's watch and she was not about to inflict his wrath on Mwari and the men, so she bit her tongue.

"What is it that you want to know?"

"Now that's better. You see, a cordial conversation is possible without the shouting and the fighting." Fezzan watched Fera closely. She looked incredibly uncomfortable, so he elected to approach her carefully, despite his mild irritation.

"What is your name, girl? Where do you come from?

"My name is Fera. I was born in the Great City of Catal Huyuk." Fera spoke with calculated calmness.

"Do you have parents?"

"Everyone has parents..." Fera wanted to continue with a further sarcastic retort, but she stopped herself. "My father, Shoa, is a jewellery craftsman. He made this amulet for me." Fera looked down and took her amulet from beneath her shirt. "My mother's name is Sofala."

"It's a beautiful piece. It would fetch a handsome price."

"Not everything is for sale. I would never part with it."

"I would not dream of asking you to, besides if I wanted something, I would just take it." Fezzan ignored Fera's retaliatory and argumentative jibes. "What brings you to these parts?" Fera looked at Fezzan with a look of utter astonishment and derision as though she was amazed at how Fezzan could ask such a stupid question of her.

"Of course, I know how you got here, but how did you come to be travelling through the Great Desert?"

"Why do you need to know that? You obviously have no interest in me or my life. This small chat is utterly futile."

Fezzan realised that he was getting no-where with the fiery-spirited young woman before him. He was in no mood to fight his way through a conversation. He neither had the time for it nor the patience to endure endless sparring, even though he found Fera enticingly captivating, notwithstanding her filthy appearance. Few people were worth his effort. Inwardly, he felt that Fera was worth the time and effort that it would take to get to know her, but his interest in her quickly changed to boredom, when he grasped the extent of her stubbornness.

"Guards, take this woman to her new quarters."

"Am I no longer to stay in the camp with the other women?"

"Why would you want to? Here in my house, you will be fed and clothed. We will speak again and perhaps by such time, you will have re-evaluated your attitude towards me and realise that I mean you no harm."

Fera did not know which side of Fezzan she feared more; the Fezzan who killed a man, without blinking an eye or the Fezzan who was obviously putting up pretences of kindness. She did not trust him. She did not like him. He should not have mattered to her or even affected her, yet Fera was greatly unbalanced by him. She did not enjoy such a feeling. Fera was grateful that the guard did not cover her head with the filthy old bag as he escorted her from the room, although her blindfold and muzzle still unnerved her. She wished that she could have made eye contact with Mwari and the men as she exited the room, even if it was only for a second and then only to convey that she was doing well.

Upon Fera's exit, Mwari and his men were escorted into the room to meet with their captor. Fezzan calculated that his approach towards them would have to be vastly different from the manner in which he had dealt with Fera. Men recognised and reacted to a firm hand.

When they stood before him, Fezzan looked Mwari squarely in the eyes and said,

"You have had the pleasure of knowing my name. Perhaps you could tell me yours?"

Mwari had met far greater adversaries in his time. Fezzan did not intimidate him. All Mwari could remember was the stubborn young man who had continually questioned his father, the Sultan Mohammad's, every instruction and the boy who had expertly, with his own particular brand of charm, managed to wind his father around his little finger.

It was obvious to Mwari back then, that Fezzan was the Sultan's favourite son. The Sultan had confirmed his great love for Fezzan on many occasions. The thought drew a smile on Mwari's face.

"Have I said something amusing?" asked Fezzan.

"No, but you have not changed a bit. You are still the same; as persistent and charming as ever."

"Have we met before?"

"You will not remember me. I have aged much over the years. You have also, but time has not been that good to my looks." Fezzan looked puzzled. Mwari continued,

"I fought many wars at your father's side. There is no reason that you should remember me. I was simply one of the rank and file of soldiers, too many to mention or recognise. But you, you have grown into a powerful man. I must admit, I was surprised that you landed up amongst these rabble." said Mwari indicating plainly and unapologetically his true feelings about the Garramantes. "I would never have expected you to leave your lands and your family to become a slave raider."

"I had no choice in the matter." Fezzan's words were matter of fact, yet his tone of voice was tinged with the feint trace of bitterness and hurt.

"Every person has a choice in life, but a person must be man enough to own up to that choice. I chose to fight in other men's wars for payment. I have regretted my past actions to this very day, but I chose to atone for my deeds. How did you come to be a trader in human flesh, to take innocent people and sell them for money with no regard for their rights and their feelings?"

Jadon and Gibeon eyed Mwari as though they were silently cautioning him to tread carefully, for all their lives hung in the balance. Mwari continued undeterred,

"You had no right to detain me and my party here. We have done you no harm. We are not slaves. We were simply crossing the Great Sea of Sand en route to the Pearl of the Desert. I am heading an important mission, which your actions in capturing us against our will, have seriously obstructed. I demand that you release me and my party at once."

"And who is travelling with you?"

Mwari brought Gibeon and Jadon forward and introduced them to Fezzan.

"My ward was separated from us. She was the girl that was taken from here a moment ago. I am responsible for her safety."

Fezzan sensed Mwari's deep concern for Fera's well-being.

"She will be fine. I have ordered that she be cared for. She will come to no harm under my roof."

Mwari looked at Fezzan with suspicion.

"I know that you have no reason to believe me, given recent events. I can see that you are a man convinced by deeds rather than words." With that, Fezzan spoke to Imouharen,

"See that Mwari and his men are treated to our finest hospitality." Fezzan then addressed Mwari once again,

"I will see that you are reunited with your ward. You will all join us at tomorrow's festivities. There is to be a wedding in my house and you and your party are invited to celebrate the great day with me. After that, you may continue on your journey. I shall provide you with camels and a suitably skilled guide to assist you to cross the Great Desert."

Mwari was grateful for the fact that they did not have to return to the grime and darkness of the foggaras, but he remained on guard. It seemed too good to believe that Fezzan had agreed to allow them to leave. Fezzan's about face in his attitude, made Mwari feel growingly uneasy.

He questioned whether a slave raider could so easily relinquish control and ownership of a slave. How would such gesture have been received by the other members of the Garramantes tribe? Mwari had often heard the guards speak the word 'Fard' which meant that the individual is nothing without the tribe.' So, would the tribe allow Fezzan to do something which would be so blatantly contrary to the best commercial interests of the Garramantes, even if he was their leader? Mwari doubted it, but he was, however, relieved by the fact that he and his men were once again reunited with Fera later that day,

"We missed you." expressed Jadon to Fera as they saw her for the first time, since they had been taken to the tunnels. Fera showed a rare display of affection towards him by giving him a warm hug.

"I thought you were all dead. Zakariya could not tell me if you were alive or dead. She could not see my sisters either."

"Who is Zakariya?" asked Gibeon.

Fera did not know where to begin, since Zakariya had impacted so greatly on her life in such a short space of time, but she recounted her days at the women's camp with such emotion and interest that the men were enthralled to listen to her. Mwari was glad to see the beginnings of enlightenment and maturity in Fera. The Fera he had met so many days ago, was so self-absorbed, so pre-occupied with her own existence and her own desires. He could see a change in her, a change which was seemingly for the better. When Fera had finished speaking, Mwari said,

"Well perhaps we can get out of here soon. Let's just indulge Fezzan and attend his wedding tomorrow and then we shall leave for the Pearl of the Desert."

Mwari's words hit Fera like a ton of clay bricks. She felt feint. She could not wrap her mind around the fact that Fezzan was to be married. Many questions swirled in her thoughts, chief amongst them being, why she should even remotely care whether he was to be married or not. For some inexplicable reason, it did seem to matter to her. She tried to appear unaffected by the news,

"That sounds wonderful. A celebration will be most welcome. We haven't eaten properly in days and we all could use a bath, that's for sure!" The latter fact was true enough. Mwari and his party looked worse for wear and there would be nothing like a warm, fragrant bath to cure what ailed them.

Even after her luxurious bath later that afternoon, although Fera's body was refreshed, she still felt mentally fatigued. Her mother had always told her that she worried too much; that she turned over every little detail of what she heard and saw to the point that it drove, not only Fera mad, but all those around her. Once again, Fera knew that her mother's words rang true.

Fera was bathed and dressed by a kind woman, dressed modestly in a mulhafa, a long kaftan of sorts, and a hijab, a traditional head scarf, which was elegantly wound around her head and neck. The woman patiently explained the garment that Fera had been sent to wear to the wedding as well as the traditions associated with the wedding.

"This is a kaftan. It is somewhat similar to what you were wearing except that it has no qob. It was specially chosen for you to wear. It is beautiful, is it not?"

Fera nodded in agreement since the robe's red fabric, adorned with silver beads, was a rare sight. Fera had always hated dresses, but for some reason the dress which she wore, as she glanced at herself in the large ornate mirror, was different. It was perhaps, for the first time in her life that she felt truly feminine. The old woman then presented her with a pair of leather slippers, called balgha. Fera's were in the same red as her kaftan.

"These come in black or white, any colour really." added the woman, as she slipped the shoes onto Fera's feet. The slippers felt like satin against Fera's skin.

"These are good dancing shoes and a wedding is a good place to dance, is it not?"

The woman then presented Fera with a necklace pouch. Fera had never seen such an object before. It was an ornately decorated leather pouch, long and narrow at its top and then wider at its base. It was meant to be suspended from one's neck by the silver chains attached on either side of the pouch. Three silver talismans hung from the base of the pouch.

"These hold significant meaning." said the woman pointing to the silver charms. "They come in different shapes and sizes. Some are pure silver, whilst others are decorated with enamelling and gemstones. Your talismans are particularly valuable. Look, the silver is decorated with red enamel and rubies. The silver is a work of art. It must have been crafted by the Maghrebim. They are the Jewish silversmiths here in town. They are extremely skilled."

Fera looked closely at the talismans. They were intricately carved in the form of a diamond. The woman explained further,

"A diamond-shaped talisman represents femininity, womanhood and fertility. It is a significant symbol. You must be proud to wear it. It is usually given to a woman when she is held in high regard. As with all talismans that offer protection against evil, this one will protect your femininity and your womanhood." The woman blushed as though she knew something which Fera did not.

"It is beautiful." Fera ran her fingers admiringly over the object as the afternoon sunlight, which beamed into her room, danced off the rubies embedded in the silver diamond-shaped talismans. "But, who would give such a valuable gift. I am a stranger here?"

"My people are very generous by nature. Perhaps you have a secret admirer?"

Fera could not imagine who that person could have been. It suddenly dawned on her that it must have been Mwari and the men. They knew that she had gone through a tough time of late. Perhaps it was a gesture on their part to make her feel better. She felt touched by their kindness. Once the woman had placed the necklace pouch around Fera's neck, she took a few steps back and admired the product of her hard work.

"You look like one of us. You will fit in nicely at the bride's Beberiska party tonight."

"Beberiska party? What is that?" asked Fera. The many new words spoken in the foreign tongue of the woman, had left Fera baffled, yet intrigued, but she relished the opportunity to learn about new cultures.

"The bride and the women from her family meet and henna tattoos are drawn on the bride's hands and feet. It is a wonderful evening. You will see for yourself. The tattoos are drawn in beautiful floral and geometrical designs. They are intended to protect and nurture the bride."

True to the woman's word, the Beberiska was a most social and jovial party. Women of all ages attended, all clad in hand-crafted kaftans. The bride was an extremely young girl, timid yet beautiful. Fera greeted her warmly and extended her good wishes for her upcoming nuptials. Fera had no cause to dislike the bride or to bear her ill will, for after all, she was a complete stranger entering into a union, the notion of which Fera had abhorred her entire life, yet Fera felt strangely confused by her ambivalence towards her. The bride was neither a friend nor a foe to Fera. If anything, Fera should have felt pity for the bride, since she was obviously very young for marriage, but Fera felt the subtle pangs of resentment.

Fera wondered if the bride's parents had chosen Fezzan as her groom or whether the bride had had any say in the choice of him being her husband to be. The tradition of family and more particularly of the parents of the bride choosing a husband for a young girl was commonplace in Catal Huyuk as well. Fera always considered such tradition as an archaic institution and contrary to her freedom of choice, but she, like many young woman, felt torn between respect for her culture, her traditions and love for her parents and the need to express her own voice. Fera decided to set aside her own feelings for the evening and to simply enjoy the banter amongst the women.

Soon, the bride's hands and feet were intricately decorated with the red-orange dye of the henna plant. The woman artist who applied the tattoos even extended an invitation to Fera to participate in the ritual. Fera was eager to accept. While her hands were being decorated, Fera had the chance to listen to the women speak about the wedding. Everyone sat drinking tea, eating cakes made from marzipan and listening to traditional music. It reminded Fera of the times that she and her sisters had spent together in front of the hearth, talking with their mother.

"This wedding is going to be the most beautiful wedding that we have seen in years. No expense has been spared." said one woman.

"You should have seen the presents that the bride has received. Oh, the gold jewellery, the clothes and the perfume! The bride is very fortunate to be marrying someone so highly esteemed. He will always be in a position to look after her well." said another. Fera looked confused, so another woman explained,

"It is custom to present the bride with lavish gifts. This particular bride is luckier than most for the groom has great wealth."

"Oh!" replied Fera. She did not want to appear disinterested or rude so she asked, "Are there other traditions that form part of the wedding ceremony?"

"Of course! It is a big event. Sometimes the pre-wedding ceremonies can last almost seven days. After the bride gets her gifts, a furnishing party is held. We got together five days ago for that. The women in the bride's family delivered all manner of household goods, such as blankets, bedding, carpets and pottery to the bride's future home. Of course, our groom paid for everything. He is very wealthy you know." said one of the guests.

"I have heard that said." replied Fera. If she had to hear a further comment on how wealthy Fezzan was, Fera thought that she would pull her hair out in exasperation.

"We then all attended another pre-wedding ceremony where the bride took a milk bath. The milk is intended to purify the bride. The oldest women amongst us, called the Negassa, helped her bathe and then we dressed her in a beautiful white wedding kaftan, which the groom also bought, because he is very wealthy, you know." said yet another woman.

Fera hid her mild irritation, by taking a big gulp of tea and stuffing a traditional cake in her mouth. It was probably not the most elegant move on her part, but she was beyond the point of caring. The women were then excited to do the bride's make-up for her wedding. Kohl, which Fera learnt was a mixture of soot and other herbs, was generously applied to the bride's eyebrows, eyelids and eyelashes. It gave the bride a sensual and sultry appearance, thought Fera. Rouge was rubbed onto her cheeks. Fera thought that the bride's cheeks appeared somewhat overdone, since the red substance was smeared from the middle of her cheeks to her jawline but it was not Fera's place to comment on that which she did not understand, so she bit her lip and did not express her opinion on the matter. She could, however, not help but enquire after the distinct tattoos on the bride's chin and nose. The markings were not large, but had been clearly noticeable to Fera the instant that she had met the bride.

"What do those symbolise? Does the bride get tattoed as part of her wedding preparation?" asked Fera of the woman who had dressed her earlier in the day.

"They represent a rite of passage for a young girl into womanhood. In our culture, when a girl reaches puberty, her mother, aunts and female family friends tattoo her face and wrists."

Fera watched intently as the bride's neck and head were adorned with numerous necklaces made from amber beads and silver.

When the women had finished dressing the bride, they all took turns to admire her and to wish her well.

They all talked well into the early hours of the wedding day. The bride was given much unsolicited advice from her older relatives on the secrets of marriage, such as what she could expect on her wedding night and how she should not be shocked by the strange event which she would soon experience. The timid bride blushed at some of the things that she heard. Fera surmised that she must have been a virgin. Much of what the women divulged in conversation was known to Fera. Her mother had always been open with Fera and her sisters and Fera had seen enough of the farm animals in springtime to understand what could possibly take place on a person's wedding night.

Fera hoped that the wedding night of the bride that she had just met, would be gentler and more romantic than what she had seen in the barn back in Catal Huyuk. Thinking about romance and the private interactions between the young bride and her strong, muscular groom, with his pure white teeth and jet-black hair, made Fera feel awkward and uncomfortable, so she pushed all thoughts of it out of her mind.

The wedding day went off as seamless as the Beberiska had. Family and friends from both sides of the isle filled the courtyard of Fezzan's house. There were many faces which Fera had not seen before. She thought nothing of it at the time, for it was quite acceptable for many unexpected guests to arrive at a wedding. The smell of many exotic and delicious foods wafted through the air. The tables were sumptuously laid with fruits such as dates, figs and grapes. Couscous prepared with veal, mutton, beef, tomatoes, turnips and pimentos, as well as harira soup looked generously appetising. Wine, which had been imported from the west of Ka, flowed abundantly.

The wedding was to take place that day in the perfumed courtyard. Fera sat next to Mwari and the men as they waited for the ceremony to begin. They appeared clean shaven and wore djellabas of blue and white. Fera, used to seeing them looking dirty and untidy, was pleasantly surprised at how well they had scrubbed up and how handsome they looked in their fezzes.

Everyone waited with baited breath for the appearance of the bride. Fera, particularly wanted to catch a glimpse of her wedding kaftan. The women had spoken non-stop of how intricately embellished it was and how breathtakingly beautiful the bride looked in it. Fera had barely got any sleep the night before and she sat in silence, filled with anxious emotion waiting for the bride's arrival. She could not understand the reason for feeling so on edge, for it was not her wedding after all. There was no reason for her to feel uneasy.

The bride seemed to be taking much longer than expected to make her entrance. Fera's heart raced and her thoughts jumbled incoherently in her mind. She eventually broke under the strain of her feelings. She leaned over and whispered to Mwari,

"I need some fresh air. I'll return."

With that, she quickly made her way upstairs to the refuge of her room. She flung herself on the bed. She could not stop the tears from escaping her eyes. She heard the sounds of drumming and singing. She realised that the wedding must have started, but she did not feel inclined to return to the festivities. Her sobs masked the sound of the door as it was gently opened. Fezzan stood in the doorway. His voice startled Fera. She stood up.

"It is bad luck to cry at a wedding. Do you not wish great happiness for the bride and groom on their special day?"

Fera stopped crying. She had not expected to see Fezzan standing in front of her. Was he not supposed to be downstairs marrying the virginal bride? Fera was tongue-tied.

"So, I see we are back to that again. Not speaking. What have I done this time to displease you?" Fera thought for a moment and then said,

"Should you not be with your bride?"

"My what?"

"Your bride? The one who is waiting for you in the courtyard?"

Fera had once thought Fezzan to be the cruellest man that she had ever met, but his continued play at ignorance was beyond belief. Fezzan felt confused.

"I have no idea what you are talking about. I am not getting married."

"But I thought...."

Fera questioned herself as to whether she had been mistaken. Had Mwari not told her that Fezzan was to be married? Had the women at the Beberiska not as much as confirmed that the wealthy patron behind the lavish gifts and clothing given to the bride, had been Fezzan himself? Fera doubted everything that she had heard and seen. She felt confused.

"You thought that I was to be married. Fortunately, not! The wedding is that of Imouharen's eldest daughter. He has been a most trusted and loyal companion and friend since I came to Garama. It was only right for me to pay for the wedding. It is my way of repaying his loyalty and friendship."

Fera felt weak in the knees. She felt herself falling. Fezzan rushed to her side and caught her before she hit the ground.

"I am sure that you think that many women have fallen at my feet, but this is the first time that anyone has truly done so." said Fezzan jokingly.

Fezzan held Fera in his strong, warm embrace. Fera said nothing. His face rested inches away from hers. His penetratingly deep gaze into her wide eyes, was only broken when his attention was drawn down her neck towards her necklace.

"Do you like it?" he asked. It all became clear to Fera.

"This was from you?"

"It was my mother's. It was given to her by my father. It is very precious to me. My mother told me to give it to the woman that I would one day marry."

Fera was too shocked by Fezzan's declaration to respond to his words. She could not put together a coherent sentence. Fortunately for Fera, the need to exchange any words with Fezzan passed when he gently leaned down and passionately kissed her quivering, yet welcoming lips.

***

Fera had fallen asleep that night with the memory of Fezzan's eyes etched on her mind and the passionate kisses which they had shared, still lingering on her lips.

They had both missed the actual wedding ceremony, which by all accounts, was a most joyous event, if one judged by the loud singing and dancing that could be heard way into the night. Fezzan and Fera had instead talked for hours that night about their childhoods and their families. It felt so wonderful for Fera to be able to confide in him her fears and anxieties about the mission and of course, about her sisters.

"We separated at Abydos. Boise was extremely ill when I last saw her. My only prayer is that they reached Dendera safely. I trust that Aten will watch over them until we see each other again at the Pearl of the Desert." said Fera in an emotional and teary voice.

Fezzan put his strong arms around Fera to console her. His embrace felt reassuring and made Fera feel hopeful. Fezzan admired Fera's fierce protective nature towards her sisters. He shared with Fera that he remembered a time, many years back in his youth, when he too had shared a close bond with his own siblings.

"But that is now at an end. I can never trust them ever again. There are some things that one can never forget, much less forgive." said Fezzan.

Fera sensed that Fezzan had more to say and so she just listened. She knew that sometimes all anyone ever needed was a sympathetic ear.

"After my father's death it all turned so sour between my brothers and me. I thought that his death would have brought us closer. I never really suspected, in my wildest dreams, that they harboured utter contempt and dislike, no dislike is an underestimation, my brothers hated me. I lived the values that my father had preached his whole life; love, tolerance, forgiveness. I welcomed everyone into my kingdom, Muslims, Jews and Christians alike. There was total religious tolerance under my rule. I know that this contributed to the growth and commercial success of my kingdom. Mine, was a beautiful kingdom, Fera. The commercial centre was a beautiful city with great art and culture. This was in part due to the influx of Jewish and Christian refugees who came there, having fled from religious persecution. They brought with them vast wealth, which was invested in building new houses, new temples and new mosques."

Fezzan stared into the candle flame which flickered on the table next to where he and Fera sat. It was as though he saw his beloved city rise up in its flame. The vivid pictures he painted of the Almohad Kingdom, as he told Fera about it, made her feel as though she was actually there.

"My brother Khaldun bitterly resented this prosperity. He hated the concept of religious tolerance. For him, the supreme religion was Islam. He had adopted a totally different leadership style to me. His cruelty inspired a legacy of disloyalty and hatred amongst his people, so much so, that his large army eventually refused to fight for him. At one point, he commanded a forty thousand strong cavalry and archers. His personal guard alone had numbered seven thousand men. All of them turned their back on him."

"What did he do?"

"He found those who would give him undying and blind allegiance. He relied on the Beja tribes to fight in his army. Under his command, they raided and pillaged the kingdoms and villages which bordered the Great Sky River. It was not long before they were at odds with the Kingdoms of Axum and Kush. You know well how Ezana and his brother Ta-Seti had long dreamt of expanding their trade across the Great Desert. The Great Desert is a vast expanse. One would think that there would be enough trade for all, but even the Sea of Sand was never big enough to accommodate the greed and ambition of my brother and those who sought to snatch control of the lucrative trade routes across the Great Desert."

"Did they attack your kingdom?"

"No, Khaldun had other, more sinister plans for me. He plotted to get control over the Almohad Kingdom through treachery and deception. One day, he and my youngest brother Ashir came to see me. They begged me to work with them to unify our father's kingdom. They proposed that we unite our three kingdoms under our joint rule and that we would honour the memory of our father if we succeeded in doing so. Fera, I idolised my father. We were extremely close, perhaps closer than my brothers and my father ever were, so to say the least, the idea of reuniting the three kingdoms intrigued me."

"What did you say to their proposal? Did you agree?"

"I did, much to my own downfall. You see, all the time, that Khaldun was preaching love and brotherhood, he was actually scheming behind my back. He never had any intention to jointly rule a unified kingdom. His sole intention was to rid himself of the two obstacles which stood in the way of his plans for total domination. He accused me of being a traitor, for giving refuge to the Jewish and

Christian refugees from the Marinid Kingdom, especially after he had professed that Islam was to be the sole religion for a unified Almohad Kingdom. I was put on trial, if that is what one would call that sham of a process. I never stood a chance. I was charged, convicted and sentenced for a crime that I did not commit. I was banished from the lands of my birth and sold as a slave to the Garramantes."

Fera gasped. She tenderly and empathetically stroked Fezzan's hand and forearm.

"The other day when you told me of the hardships faced by the women in the slave camp, it was the first time in a long time, that I thought about the day when I had arrived as a slave, here in Garama. I too was beaten by the guards, but at least I could defend myself. I felt ashamed that I had forgotten how I had felt to be treated so cruelly. I had lost the ability to show compassion for my fellow men and women."

"But you are now the leader of the Garramantes. How was that even possible? One thing I have learnt since I arrived here in Garama and from my time spent at the camp, is that the Garramantes are fiercely tribal. If you were a slave and moreover not one of them, how did you accede to such a position of power?"

"Through sheer brute force, I suppose. I was a hard worker in the tunnels, but it was my fighting abilities that shone through. I showed them that I was fearless and that I could be ruthless when called to be. I was the best of the best when it came to slave raiding. I was asked to do things that I shall never speak of, but I came out on the other side as a much admired warrior. My predecessor recognised my talents and abilities and on his death, I was installed as the leader of the Garramantes."

"What about your own kingdom? Did you not yearn for home?"

"The home that I had known as a boy and the kingdom that I had built as a man, no longer exists. My brother Ashir now rules over the Almohad Kingdom. Over the years, I have made my peace with my lot in life. Life with the Garramantes has been hard. God knows that I have had to make many sacrifices. It is not a perfect life, but I am someone important here."

"You are someone important without the cruelty and brutality that comes with being a member of the Garramantes." Fezzan kissed Fera's forehead.

"You are young, my love. You do not understand the ways of the world." Fera reacted sharply,

"That may be true, but I stand up for what I believe in. No matter whether I am accepted by others or have position and wealth, I would never compromise my integrity. At the end of the day, that is all a person has."

Feelings of anger and annoyance rose within Fera. Fezzan read her mood. He had experienced the backlash that came with getting on Fera's wrong side, so he decided to tread carefully.

"You are right, of course. I cannot change what is done, but I can look to the future and examine whether this way of life that I have come to know and accept, is the only way of life for me in the future." Fera looked unconvinced.

"I cannot change the ways of the Garramantes, Fera, you understand that, do you not? I must decide whether my future lies here? I must decide to leave them, for they will never leave me."

"Does your future lie here?"

"I do not know."

Fera rolled her eyes at Fezzan. The love that had shone from them a moment before, was replaced with disappointment. It was obvious what Fera wanted to hear. Fezzan did not have all the answers for her at that moment. He sidestepped the issue,

"There is one thing that I am sure of though." Fezzan paused for a moment and stopped to kiss Fera once more. He found her kisses intoxicating.

"Destiny has brought you to me. Wherever you are, is my home, my true home."

***

Fezzan would soon be haunted by those last words that he had whispered lovingly into Fera's ear, for as the sun peeped over the horizon the next morning, Fezzan, was abruptly awoken by Mwari and his men, who stood over his bed, tugging and shouting for him to wake up. Looks of fear and disbelief drained their faces of colour. Mwari's words were like a knife to Fezzan's heart,

"She is gone. Fera has been taken!"

Mwari stood motionless, unable to comprehend what had happened overnight. The world around him suddenly became a darker place. He felt lost, overwhelmed and hopeless. The prophecy of the Holy Prophet engulfed his mind and played over and over again in his thoughts.

'A feud between the Moon and the Sun will cast a shadow towards Ka. Darkness will bring fear...... the survival of a Great City and the path to bring back light will be found in a journey led by four daughters....'

Mwari realised that he had failed in his mission and betrayed the trust of the Holy Prophet and Shoa. Without the Daughters of Ka, they could not succeed in their mission. Luna would be victorious. He sank to his knees and wept bitter tears, for everything that seemed forever lost.

5

THE BEAUTIFUL ONES

Mwari, his men and Fezzan rode through the great Sea of Sand like mad men. The route to the Pearl of the Desert was well frequented, since Aten's home was an important stop for traders and merchants crossing the Great Desert to ply their wares across Ka. The vegetation, being sparse grassland and desert shrub, was no obstacle to Fezzan's finest steeds.

They had left Garama in extreme haste. Barely an hour after Fezzan had been woken up by Mwari and his men, he had ordered Imouharen to saddle his fastest mounts. They had no idea where Fera was or who had taken her or where she had been taken to, for that matter. So, when Mwari had suggested that they travel to meet with Aten, Fezzan had willingly agreed that they should seek out the answers they needed there.

Mwari had assured Fezzan that Aten was the best person to assist them and rather than run off half-cocked into the desert, looking for shadows and ghosts, Fezzan had concluded that Mwari's rationale was sound. Few could question the all-powerful abilities of Aten. The kitchen staff had prepared food parcels, mostly leftovers from the wedding feast of the night before and so Fezzan and the men had departed his home at sunrise.

For Fezzan, he was leaving behind far more than just the luxurious comfort which he had come to know as the leader of the Garramantes. In fact, deep down, he knew that he leaving a way of life and that thought filled him with mixed feelings. He felt torn. His new-found love for Fera willed his heart forward, but his mind stood ambivalent at the thought of leaving a life of position and privilege. As he rode through the desert, Fezzan recalled his last conversation with Imouharen before he had left,

"You do not have to go, you know. Women come and go. Is this one so special that you will leave all this for her?"

Imouharen hinted at the fact that Fezzan would be sacrificing a home, great riches, but most of all, the esteem of the tribe.

"The tribe must always come first, before any woman, at any rate." said Imouharen.

Fezzan understood, that to the Garramantes, tribal loyalty was supreme, above all else.

"I understand what you are saying, old friend, I think we have been together long enough for me to speak candidly. You were well aware that my transition to the Garramantes' way of life did not come easy."

"That's an understatement!" laughed Imouharen.

"Well, there has always been a part of me that has needed something more, something different. Meeting this woman has opened my eyes to the possibility that I can be more; that I can be the man that my father demanded of me."

Fezzan stopped himself saying that he regretted not being better and not having behaved better, for that would have been an insult to Imouharen and the tribes' way of life. He could not bring himself to say that he had for years resented the fact that he had had to live to the standards and values of others. He could not be so blunt then as to hurt his one true friend.

"I cannot pretend to understand your meaning, friend. I have not known any other existence than the one I live. I, unlike you, have no comparisons to make. I respect the fact that a man must be true to himself. When we face death, we cannot pass into the next life with nothing but regret at not having lived life authentically. You must therefore go and be happy with this troublesome creature that you say you love. At least you found a beautiful one. Not like me, ten wives and not a beauty amongst them. I tell you now, as I have told you often before, women are nothing but trouble. They lead us men by the noses. They are always our downfall when it comes to matters of the heart."

"Well, if that is true, then you are like one of those mules that carry water to the foggeras, well and truly licked." said Fezzan. Imouharen laughed heartily.

"I would ask a favour before I depart. Call it a kindness for an old friend." asked Fezzan cautiously.

"Anything!"

"There is a woman in the slave camp called Zakariya. Her husband worked in the tunnels. I believe he died years ago. I would ask that you free her or find her some employment in your house. Do what you can for her, it is important to me."

"You mean that it is important to that burnished copper-haired woman of yours. You see, women are indeed trouble. Next, you'll be asking that I free all the slaves."

"It is not my place to do so, but I would add that the Garramantes have built up a reputation as shrewd traders of camels, foodstuffs and gold. Perhaps, if they diverted their attention to such activities, they would find it more lucrative than slaving."

"Now you are pushing your luck!"

"I know, but I see the potential for greatness for the tribe. With the water from the tunnels, agriculture can thrive and if the tribe puts the same effort into trade as they do into other things, their success will grow even further. And with you at the helm, old friend, there is only one way and that's up."

Imouharen was not angered by Fezzan's honesty, for if the truth be told, he himself had big plans for his tribe, which he hoped he could now set in motion as their leader. Fezzan and Imouharen then parted on a good footing, as good friends should.

Thus, Fezzan found himself in the uncomfortable position of riding away from a familiar world into the unknown, his only thought was that he had to find Fera before she came to harm. He was determined not to lose her. He had given up everything to be with her and he was never one to regret a decision once made, so there would be no going back, he had to catch up with Fera. He had decided that she would be found and then he would make her his bride. He smiled to himself at the thought of how his mother would have received Fera. She had unfortunately, died too soon for him to ever know, but Fezzan hoped that she would have approved of his choice.

En route to the Pearl of the Desert, Mwari was afforded the opportunity to get to know Fezzan. He strongly suspected that he and Fera shared feelings, which ran stronger than mere friendship. Jadon and Gibeon had both commented that it would had to have taken something very powerful for a man such as Fezzan to up and leave his life. They concluded that it could only have been love that would have prompted Fezzan to leave with them in search of Fera, for there was no greater human emotion than love, except perhaps hate, but Mwari was astute and perceptive enough to realise that Fera did not hate Fezzan. She may have at one point thought him to be a rogue and not fit to be in the same room with her, but of late, her feelings towards him had softened.

Admittedly, Mwari did not outright expect that Fera loved Fezzan, but the mere fact that he had dropped everything to look for her, said all that needed to be said. His actions spoke loudly and confirmed that he held very strong feelings for Fera. Whether Fera reciprocated such feelings, was still a mystery to Mwari, but he knew Fera well enough to know that she was not the type of woman to lead a man on. Fera was as straight as an arrow; what you saw is what you got with her.

Strangely, Mwari felt that it was his duty to watch over Fera and explore Fezzan's true feelings. Fera was not the easiest of people to become overly emotional about. Mwari had a closer connection with Boise and Feur. Nena remained an enigma, but that was not unusual since she had always been a hard one to read, but Mwari had always thought of Fera as fearlessly independent. He saw his role as her minder, without the need to have to protect her every minute of every day because she could take care of herself, unlike Boise and Feur who were infinitely more vulnerable. All he needed to do was ensure that Fera was kept on a short lease, so to speak. That way, he could prevent her from making needless mistakes when she rushed headlong into life.

So, in an attempt to prevent Fera from falling into an ill-conceived relationship with Fezzan, Mwari took it upon himself to speak with Fezzan one night as they rested at one of the Garramantes' encampments on their way to Aten.

"She is quite a handful. She is wilful, stubborn and impatient. Those are all admirable character traits. I would not like to see her lose herself." said Mwari. Fezzan knew exactly what Mwari was hinting at.

"I was entrusted by her father to look after her and I shall do that until, well.... until I am no longer required to."

"I have no need to change the woman that she is. It is those traits which endeared me to her in the first place." replied Fezzan.

"It is not the fact that you may or may not want her to change. I fear that she will feel a certain pressure to conform. Society, religion and culture often dictate that women, especially married women, must be submissive to their husbands. My culture and religion is no different. My wife sacrificed her desires and needs in life for me. She changed herself, for me. Of course, she probably did not realise she had done so. If you'd asked her, she probably could not have owned up to it, because the changes were that imperceptible. Everything just crept up on her. I did not realise she'd changed. I was too wrapped up in myself to notice or even to care. I see a rare quality in Fera. She is like a beautiful wild bird. It would be tragic if life and love clipped her wings."

"I never thought about it like that."

"Men never do." Fezzan gave Mwari a quizzical look.

"Do I sound like a traitor to my gender? I am not, I assure you, but call it the wisdom of growing old. I have had much time to reflect on my life, what I did, what I should not have done. Life and experience is a great teacher. It is often only in the lives and experiences of others that a mirror is held up to oneself. I do not make it my business these days to preach religion, but there was a time that I lived my life strictly by religious teachings and moral cultural traditions. I learnt the hard way; that even those are sometimes cruel and harsh on the plight of women. Some men use religion as a way to subjugate women, to render their role as lesser to that of men." Mwari paused contemplatively for a moment but then continued,

My own life has taught me to question everything now and not to simply accept religious and cultural doctrines at face value."

"I can assure you, Mwari, I have no ill intentions towards Fera. After we find her safe and well, I shall ask her to marry me, that is, if she will have me. I cannot predict what life has in store for us, but I believe that a husband and wife, a man and woman are equals in every way."

Mwari felt slightly relieved that he had a better sense of Fezzan and his motivations, although he still silently noted that he would keep an eye on Fezzan for as long as Fera was in his care and even after such time as Fera's care had devolved back to her father, and even then Mwari had decided that he would still express any reservations which he had at that time to Shoa and to Fera personally, if the need arose.

With the awkward part of the conversation out of the way, Mwari and Fezzan turned their attention to their most pressing problem, being Fera's whereabouts. Jadon and Gibeon weighed in on the matter.

"My hunch is that she was taken by the Beja. Their defeat at Meroe must have left them vengeful. It must have been a bitter pill for them to swallow, being forced back into the Sea Hills." said Jadon.

"Don't forget the treaty. Without revenues from their trade routes, the huge amounts of land tax alone would have drained their wealth." added Gibeon.

"It could very well have been the rich merchants of Kush. They also have an axe to grind. We stopped them and Ta-Seti from gaining control over the natural wealth of Meroe and free trade in Kush." said Mwari.

"I do not believe that Candace, Queen of Meroe, would allow them to get above themselves, ever again. With Ta-Seti being banished to the Danakil, who would lead them? No, they are probably cow-towing to Candace, in the hope that they can rescue some of their lands and wealth from Queen Candace's plan to bring them to their knees, financially speaking of course." said Jadon. Jadon was right in his calculations, thought the men. With Ta-Seti and the merchants and nobles of Kush eliminated from the list of possible suspects, the only logical culprit would be Al Aziz and his Beja.

"But, could there be a person closer to home that could be complicit in the crime? Who did you tell of your feelings for Fera?" asked Mwari of Fezzan.

"Only Imouharen, but I trust him with my life. I cannot believe that he would knowingly betray me. I won't believe it."

"The Garramantes tribe are a tight knit group. Your leaving could have been seen as a threat. I know you said that Imouharen was happy to become tribal leader, but it is conceivable that he was happy to do so to your face, but in reality, he was really unhappy about your leaving. Your reputation as a ruthless slave trader precedes you. Perhaps the fear of losing your skills could have driven him to plot against you." surmised Mwari.

"What would kidnapping Fera achieve, since he knew I would have left the tribe anyway to search for her. They would still have lost my slave raiding skills."

"But if Fera disappears, perhaps they think that you would return to them. Slaves disappear easily enough if they are killed or if they are sold off in some foreign land. He had so readily accepted the fact that you wanted to search for Fera. Why? Well, I say that it was because he would become the leader of the Garramantes. By plotting that you would never find Fera ever again, he would ensure that you would eventually return to the only home that you have known for many years after you could not find her. Returning to the tribe, not as a leader, but as a skilled slave raider, would have fulfilled two evil ends."

Fezzan did not know how to react to Mwari's words. They sounded rational, but Fezzan could not bring himself to believe that Imouharen could be so calculating. He knew him to be a violent, sometimes ruthless man when he wanted to be, but could he have acted that way towards an old friend?

The conversation that Fezzan had with the men that night only left him feeling even more conflicted and more confused. They all agreed that the quicker they reached Aten the better, since he might have the answers that they so dearly needed. Unanswered questions and fear for Fera's life hastened their journey across the Great Desert towards Aten.

***

The bluest of skies and the iridescent light of the first rays of the morning sun as it broke upon the horizon, marked Daniel, Boise and Feur's arrival at Dendera.

Daniel and Feur were awestruck by the Temple of Hathor as it rose monastically from the banks of the Great Sky River. They were even more surprised at the attendance of the great number of people, who stood along the river bank; shouting excitedly as they pointed up river,

"The power of Hathor is to be reunited with the power of the Sun God this day. The sky rejoices, the earth dances, the sacred musicians shout in praise." were just some of the chants that Nena and the others heard that morning.

Initially, Nena could not understand what all the commotion was about and then one of the onlookers had told her to look to the river at the long river boats that were approaching them. Muscular men rowed several boats up river, in unison and in time to the beat of the drums which were being played at the water's edge. Nena felt as though the drum beats echoed the rhythm of her own heartbeat.

The mood was exhilarating and infectious. Women's voices carried across the air in song and chants. Nena did not know what everyone was waiting for, but she suddenly found herself getting swept up in the crowd's excitement as well. As the boats drew nearer, the sounds of many sistrums rattled through the air. Nena saw that the lead boat carried a veiled altar. The second and third boats carried a bevy of beautiful women. They were dressed in long, flowing white linen robes with beaded collars. Some wore distinctive beaded menyets which consisted of coloured beads that hung down their backs; with amulets counterpoised at the nape of their necks, while others carried their menyets in their hands. Nena greatly admired their shoulder length pitch-black hair.

As the boats touched the shoreline, the air filled with the fragrant smell of incense. Nena recognised the smell. It reminded her of the Great Temple back home. Another familiar sight followed. An elderly priest walked towards the Temple. He carried a large bowl of incense. Then, one by one, the priestesses disembarked the boats and formed a processional guard of honour from the river to the Temple. Throngs of people pushed and shoved their way towards them, everyone eager to see and touch the priestesses. In unison, the priestesses chanted,

"We are now in the presence of The Great One of Many Names. To some she is known as the Lady of the Stars. To others, she is the Mistress of Life. To us, the Hathors, the Guardians of Hathor, she is our Mother of Mothers."

Their words ushered in a woman who appeared from behind the veiled altar of the lead boat. When she was unveiled, her beauty was revealed for all to see. She had milky-white skin. Her eyelids were painted turquoise and her hair which was jet-black, long and adorned with a lotus flower, fell to beneath her buttocks. Her golden robe; decorated with translucent stars, shimmered in the morning sunlight. A gold disk, symbolic of the sun, sat atop her head and her divine collar or menat and sacred sistrum completed her awe-inspiring look. As Nena stood in awe of the scene before her, Feur joined her at the water's edge.

"How is Boise?" The appearance of Feur drew Nena's attention firmly back to reality.

"Daniel is with her. He thought it best to let her rest in the shade." Feur pointed to where Daniel sat with Boise, in the shade of a nearby bush.

"We need to see Hathor. Boise is still asleep." replied Feur.

Feur was grateful for the herbs provided by Kheri-Heb. She had administered them religiously as they had travelled. Boise's condition had not worsened since they had left Abydos. It was as though she was in a deep sleep. Only her pale, waxen-like skin, which was deathly cold to the touch, belied the fact that she was seriously ill. As Hathor made her way up to the Temple, the priestesses sang, chanted and danced. It was as though their actions held great significance, for the more they celebrated Hathor, the more feelings of abundant joy, love, bliss and beauty filled the air. It was clear to all that their actions embodied the joys of life and everyone wanted to share in such joy. The crowds reached out to touch the body of Hathor. Feur and Nena were pushed and shoved in the fray.

"I want to be healed by your beauty and renewed by your power!" shouted desperate strangers.

Some people appeared afflicted with physical ailments, whilst others looked perfectly normal. Feur observed the scene and realised that they too needed to get Boise as close to Hathor as they possibly could.

"Quick, Nena, tell Daniel carry Boise here. Hathor must see and touch her."

Nena wasted no time in running back to where Daniel waited, but to their great disappointment, they could not navigate their way back through the large crowds. Nena prided herself on being lady-like, but even she pushed and shoved worshippers, all in a desperate bid to bring Boise before Hathor, who was moving through the crowds, touching pleading faces and outstretched hands.

"We are never going to get to her." uttered Daniel in desperation. "These people are too frenzied and swept up in the excitement to see and touch Hathor. I will not put Boise in further danger. This could go terribly wrong if a fight were to break out. I am going back. We will find another way."

Nena and Feur were desolate. They had got so close to Hathor that they could smell her fragrant perfume, but the crowds proved an impenetrable barrier which they could not break. They returned to sit with Daniel and Boise, exhausted and despondent.

Once Hathor had entered the Temple, the frenzy of the faithful followers of Hathor dissipated. People left the Temple precinct, most likely to go about the rest of their day, thought Feur. Those who had been fortunate enough to greet Hathor would carry out their daily chores with zest and happiness, whilst some would plan and plot their steps for the next time Hathor's beautiful ones made their way to the Temple. Tiredness and disappointment washed over Feur and Nena and they soon fell asleep in the cool shade of the bush. Their brief nap did not last long.

"Wake up, girls!" Feur heard Daniel's voice. She nudged Nena. She surmised that they had dozed off for at least an hour or so, but in reality, it had been merely for an instant. Standing before them was one of the beautiful ones, a young priestess. She smiled at them and said,

"The Lady of the Stars would like to meet the one who wears a willow amulet."

Feur, Nena and Daniel looked shocked. They knew that Boise wore such an amulet, but they questioned how Hathor would have known it. It was as though the priestess silenced their doubts,

"The Mother of Mothers knows all. Please, come with me into the Temple. The Goddess Hathor is eager to meet you."

Daniel carried Boise into the Temple, which appeared to be constructed of huge blocks of stone. Feur and Nena walked cautiously behind him, for they did not know what to expect. They watched their beautiful guide observe a strict purification process. She washed her hands and feet in a shallow bath at the entrance of the Temple. Daniel was struck by the similarities of religious rituals. Cleanliness was also practised in the Great Temple back home. The priests washed themselves at least four times a day. They also ate as purely and healthily as they could and so, foods like garlic, pigeon, cow's meat and fish were strictly forbidden. They were also not allowed to wear wool from animals that were regarded as unclean.

The priestess suddenly stopped in front of a large door to the left side of the Temple and ushered her followers to an outside precinct of the Temple. A perfectly oval and most likely man-made lake, was surrounded by red mud-brick walls and the walkway to the lake was lined with fountains. On the other side of the lake stood a brick sanatorium where the priestesses cared for the sick and the dying. Pointing to the lake the priestess instructed,

"You must all wash your hands and feet in the holy waters. As you do so, repeat the words 'I am clean' before returning to the Temple."

Daniel, Feur and Nena did as they were asked. Daniel cupped water over Boise's hands and feet. Even the cool waters could not revive her from her sleep-like state. When they were finished, the priestess instructed further,

"Follow me into the Hall of Offerings."

As they entered the Temple, their jaws dropped at the magnificence of their surroundings. The Temple walls depicted pictures of Hathor, various amulets and the materials from which they were made, as well as pictures of things that were offered up to Hathor, such as food and flowers.

They stood beneath a roof which was constructed of a sandstone slab and upheld by four pillars. It appeared to be a sundial with a circular map of the stars painted on it in green and gold. Various images brought the ceiling to life. The sky was divided into northern and southern halves. Winged creatures, such as vultures and falcons flew overhead. Northern stars, a bull's leg and a hippopotamus came to life in the northern half, while the southern stars twinkled in the southern half of the sky. The paths of the sun and the moon, as they moved through the skies and the contrast between day and night, were clearly distinguishable, as was the image of a lunar eclipse and a solar eclipse.

Daniel stood looking up into the heavens. He was mesmerised. He had heard from the priests back in Catal Huyuk that pilgrims, who had regularly visited the Temple of Hathor, had reported to them that it was a place of healing and magic for the sick and the dying; a place where ancient magical therapies were practiced and a place where ancient processions and festivals took place, all dictated by the movements of the sun and the moon, but none of those reports as conveyed to Daniel by the priests, had done the Temple of Hathor justice. Daniel was enthralled by its sacred beauty, as were Feur and Nena.

They were then led into the Hall of Appearances. For a split second, Daniel and the sisters experienced a déjà vu moment. They had experienced a similar setting once before in Abydos. Daniel was not surprised that the layout of the Temple of Seti at Abydos and the House of Hathor would be so similarly constructed. The Hall consisted of six rooms. Room one was used to store holy objects; room two was used as an exit point to retrieve water from the Great Sky River; room three acted as a thoroughfare room used by the priestesses to move between rooms; room four was used to make the perfumes and incense used at the Temple, room five was a storage room and lastly, room six exited to the outside sanctuary. Daniel admired the exceptional organisation within the Temple confines.

Once again the priestess took the lead and then she was joined by many others of her kind in a holy anointment ritual in which they anointed their hands in a purification ceremony using waters from the Great Sky River and holy oils. Daniel knew that it was widely known that priests and priestesses from any sacred Temple, such as the one in which they found themselves, followed the anointment ritual with dedication and reverence, with some then fasting for up to ten days and spending time in the most sacred part of the Temple to contemplate the powers of the Great Spirit or the powers of the Gods and Goddesses.

"You may now enter our Mother's sanctuary." said the priestess to Daniel, Feur and Nena. Once they had entered the sanctuary, she announced their presence.

"Hail. Lady of the West, Mistress of Life. Those whom you have commanded are here in your gracious and beautiful presence." Hathor reacted immediately,

"I am Hathor. I am the Sky Goddess and the Mistress of the Nocturnal Stars, Ruler over Sirius. I exist in the living tree, in the land where trees do not exist. Bring the Lady of the Willow before me."

Daniel stepped forward with Boise. He laid her down gently on the altar. Hathor touched Boise's forehead. She could see many images just as they had once been seen through the eyes of Boise.

"The Seven Hathors guide my visions through the past, present, future, before-life, after life and in the dream-world, so that I may see the life of this child from the day that she was born. We see her dreams. She is a child of nature. She has a great capacity to love." Hathor's attention was drawn to Boise's amulet.

"I see that she has the protection of the willow tree. I too have the magical protection of the willow earth. I will guide her passage as she travels into the Realm of Light, where my brother Khnemu will meet her and lead her into his House of Eternity."

Feur was devastated by Hathor's words, for she was under the impression that Hathor was their only hope to heal Boise, but instead Hathor seemed to have concluded that Boise would soon die. Suddenly, Hathor's expression turned to one of alarm and concern.

"This child's sickness was at the hands of great evil. She stood between the one who covets the power of Everlastingness and his obsession with the eye of wedjat."

Hathor closed her eyes. She grimaced as she saw images of the flesh of the avatar of the skies being savagely ripped from its bones. She continued,

"The Goddess of the Moon has struck an evil pact with Sirius. They will stop at nothing to get their hands on the eyes of wedjat.

"Who is this Sirius?" asked Daniel.

"Sirius is a formidable foe. He was once Lord Khnemu's protégé. He learnt many magical funerary spells, as well as how to yield great power, but he became greedy and coveted the power of the Great God of Everlastingness, Lord Khnemu. His insatiable lust for power resulted in his banishment from Abydos. In his great mercy, Lord Khnemu left Sirius with only the power to announce the coming of the first morning star, which arrives with the onset of the summer solstice and the start of the great rains, which turn the Holy River from dryness to great abundance. Sirius, naturally, was greatly insulted by this benevolent gesture since he demanded greater powers. Luna has promised Sirius that she will grant him the power of Everlastingness. She already has possession of the eye of wedjat from Aten's falcon, known to all as the moon wedjat and she now relies on Sirius to do her evil bidding for her and get her the other eye." Daniel tried to make sense of the information that he was hearing."

"The other eye? Are there two eyes of wedjat? I was not aware that there was even one." asked Nena.

"Legend has told that there are two wedjats. One is a lapis lazuli stone, with its deep blue colour representing the moon. The other, a red jasper crystal symbolises the sun. We refer to this stone as the sun wedjat. If a person holds both stones in their hand at the same time and says a magic spell asking to be made a God, then such person would receive everlasting life and live out an eternity with the Gods and have almost insurmountable powers. Because the wedjats are so powerful together, years ago when the Turquoise Figurine was destroyed, the Sky Father and the Sky Mother left the stones in the safe-keeping of two people whom they trusted most."

"Who?" asked Nena, totally captivated by the tale.

"I was given the jasper stone and Aten was sent the lapis lazuli stone. He magically transformed the moon wedjat into the eye of his falcon, since no-one would ever think to look there. I would be the protector of the sun's powers and Aten, in turn would keep the moon wedjat. That way, neither the powers of the sun nor the moon would ever be supreme."

"So Aten's powers, without the sun wedjat, are tempered." added Nena. It may have taken her a while to understand, but in the end she did.

"Correct. The two wedjats would remain apart until such time as the Turquoise Figurine is once again whole."

Feur suddenly realised that the magnitude of their mission had moved far beyond just saving the Great City. The need to reunite the pieces of the Turquoise Figurine had become even more imperative.

"So, Sirius hunts the eye of wedjat, which he will in turn give to Luna. She has promised to give him the power of Everlastingness in exchange for the eyes. Is it within Luna's power to do this? " clarified Daniel.

"I am afraid that she has already made an evil pact with Sirius. Luna has promised Sirius that her dark moon magic will secure him this power. Fortunately for us, such promise was not hers to make, because the power of Everlastingness lies entirely in Lord Khnemu's hands."

"Has Sirius found what he most desires, the eye of wedjat?" asked Feur.

"He failed in his first attempt to locate it, but he left pain and destruction in his wake. This ailing girl laying here is proof of this."

Everyone looked down at Boise's silent figure. Her breathing was becoming slower and more laboured.

"You mean to say that he was searching for one of the eyes when we were attacked by the rabid dogs?" added Feur.

"Yes. He attacked your camp."

"We have never had possession of the Eye of wedjat. Not then and not now, so why would he have attacked us? I do not understand." said Daniel.

"The Seven Hathors have shown me the image of a scarab. Which one of you has it?"

Feur was shocked again by the powers of Hathor to see the unseen. Feur rummaged through her belongings. She pulled out the parting gift which Fera had given to her. She held it out to Hathor.

"My sister, Fera said that this will protect us on our journey to Dendera. She was given it by Candace, Queen of Meroe. But what has this got to do with Sirius?"

"It has everything to do with it, my child! It is quite clear to me now that Sirius must have seen this scarab in Fera's possession on the night that he attacked your camp. He obviously mistook the scarab for the sun wedjat. His obsession to find it has driven him mad. He is quite unable to see things for what they really are."

"So, without the eyes of wedjat, Sirius and Luna's evil plot is thwarted?" asked Daniel.

Hathor would have relished the idea of telling Daniel otherwise, but if she had answered him affirmatively, she would knowingly have misled the poor souls who stood before her.

"Unfortunately, not. Luna does still have the moon wedjat. She captured Aten's falcon and ripped its eye from its socket. Sirius is still desperate to get his hands on the sun wedjat. He has now seized who he thinks is its bearer, albeit that person, in reality, does not have the sun wedjat at all. She may have had an object which looked like the sun wedjat, but such object is now in your possession. He still has not realised that, of course, but he soon will." It took a moment for Nena's muddled thoughts to become clear,

"He has Fera? Oh no! When did he track her down? Is she in danger? Will he kill her? What will happen when he finds out that she does not have the sun wedjat?" Feur tightly clasped Nena's hand to calm her down.

"Where is the sun wedjat then?" asked Daniel.

"The Seven Hathors have told that your sister is well for the time being. She was taken, but a day ago. She was stolen from the very bed in which she lay. She will be taken to Bandiagara. Every sixty years, a great Sigui celebration takes place there. Sirius hopes to be at his most powerful at such time. He intends to present Luna with the sun wedjat at the ceremony. Luna will then invoke the powers of both the sun and the moon wedjats and grant him the power of Everlastingness."

It was as though Hathor's words reached Boise's mind in her sleep-like state. Her breathing became increasingly laboured and very shallow. Hathor turned her attention to Boise.

"The time draws near for this child of the earth to pass into the netherworld."

"No!" cried Feur and Nena simultaneously.

"I beg you Goddess Hathor, please, that cannot be correct. Lord Khnemu refused her entry into his world."

Hathor turned to speak with one of her priestesses.

"Bring me the Book of Life and Death."

After consulting the entries for several minutes, Hathor responded,

"The Seven Hathors have not seen the name of Boise written in the Book of Life and Death, as yet, but they say that it will be written there soon. This child has lived and thus she must die. We do not have much time before she passes into the Realm of Light."

Nena burst into tears. Both sisters crouched over the deathly silent body of their sister. Feur tenderly held Boise's face and whispered of the extent to which she and Nena both loved their sister. Hathor's heart broke at the sight of the two pitiful figures as they prayed and cried over their beloved sister. She was deeply touched by the love and affection which they so patently held for their sister. Sisterhood was a significant bond shared by Hathor and all her priestesses. She fiercely guarded and cherished it and thus, she understood the pain that Nena and Feur would experience at the loss of Boise. She could not bear their suffering. The Seven Hathors had shown her visions of these Daughters of Ka. She knew that their existence was significant. She knew that they had a destiny to fulfil. She realised that it was within her powers to save the child who still had much life to live and that by doing so, she would save their mission to reunite the pieces of the Turquoise Figurine. Hathor had long since wished and prayed for a world in which the forces of nature were balanced. She decided to call her High Priestess Seshper forward.

"We must do everything in our power to bring this child back to life. As the Magician of Medicines, is this possible?"

Seshper nodded and smiled. Instinctively and without further instruction, Seshper began performing the ancient healing spell on Boise. She placed her hands on Boise's wound and repeated the words,

"Hail Great Khnemu, do not take away the years and bring the days of this innocent soul to an end. Heal this girl of the poison and venom which courses through her veins. When this holy water passes over her lips, may she be healed and rise again to walk the sands and swim the waters across the length and breadth of Ka."

As Seshper said her words, she lifted a bowl which contained water sourced from the Great Sky River, to Boise's lips. She cupped water in her hand and allowed it to trickle onto Boise's lips. She then gently removed the willow tree amulet from around Boise's neck. She placed the amulet together with a bunch of dried sage in a ceramic bowl and lit the healing herb. She fanned the smoke which it emitted in her direction and on the amulet.

The entire time that Seshper was busy performing her ritual, the other priestesses beat the holy Temple drums in the background. Every beat mimicked the heartbeat of the Mother of all Mothers and the Sky Mother, as they willed Boise to life. As the drums grew louder, their hearts beat stronger, and so did Boise's heart beat faster, as she fought her way back from her journey to the afterlife. Seshper then took some tobacco and threw it over one of the sacred drums. She said,

"I honour you Great God Khnemu and ask for your presence." Seshper then replaced the amulet with a stone from the Great Sky River.

"Lord Khnemu, clear the negative energies from the body of this girl." Seshper then threw more tobacco in all four directions; first to the north, then to the east, the south and the west.

"I call upon the Guardians of the Watchtowers to blow from the four corners of Ka so that the poison in this girl can be blown away and that she may be healed. I thank you Lord Khnemu."

With a final expression of thanks, the healing ritual was at an end. Feur, Nena and Daniel were unsure whether it had worked, but they believed in the power of healing possessed by Hathor. They soon saw signs that Boise was returning to the world of the living. She slowly regained consciousness. Little by little, her body, mind and soul seemed to revive.

After a few days, Boise had miraculously awoken and was able to take some refreshment, the first nourishment that she had taken in many a day. Feur and Nena were so relieved. In the days after Boise's attack, they had seen Daniel slowly lose his mind to worry and desperation. They had feared that he too would be lost to them in a pit of despair, if they had not been able to seek out the healing powers of Hathor.

Fortunately, and to their great relief, the revival of Boise had given Daniel a new lease on life. Feur and Nena were impressed by Daniel's dogged devotion to Boise. They looked at him through new eyes and wondered how they could ever have doubted the depth of love shared between him and their sister. They were pleased for Boise, that she had found a committed life partner, one who would care for her through thick and thin, through sickness and in health. They had only ever witnessed such a love before between their own parents and they were reassured that love could still conquer all.

When Boise was properly on the mend, after having spent several days in the sanatorium under the watchful care of the priestesses, Daniel and the sisters were once again summoned to speak with Hathor.

"I am eager to see you on your way again." said Hathor.

"Want to be rid of us that much?" joked Daniel.

"No, dear man, but I do want you all to complete the mission that you have been tasked to fulfil."

"I forgot about that for a moment. It seems like so many other things happen to detract us from our path. We have only found one piece of the Turquoise Figurine and that's with Fera. Now that she has been taken by Sirius, who knows whether she will be able to keep it safe and in her possession." said Nena.

"You have accomplished far more than you realise."

Hathor summoned one of her priestesses, who handed her a small round object. For a mere instant, Feur thought that she glimpsed the colour turquoise. Hathor opened her palm to expose the object.

"This was found, clasped tightly in your hand, Boise. My priestesses thought it was a possession of yours. They too, did not fully understand its value."

"Why? What is it? I do not recognise it. It is not mine." said Boise as she inspected the object.

"Oh, but it does belong to you. It was given to you by Lord Khnemu. It was his gift to you, but more importantly his gift to all humanity. This is a piece of the Turquoise Figurine." Everyone gasped at the news.

"I cannot believe this. It was under our noses the whole time. You laid so still, with your arms folded and hands clasped, that no-one thought to disturb you, Boise." said Daniel, in amazement.

"Well, that only leaves us with two pieces. We still have a fair way to go in order to lay our hands on all seven pieces." added Nena.

"Perhaps, I can be of assistance as well. I am not one to allow my brother, Lord Khnemu to outshine me in the act of giving gifts. What you may not know is that amongst my many names, I am also known as the Mistress of Turquoise, since my powers originate from the Turquoise Goddess. She created beauty and balance in the world by ensuring that the forces of nature are protected and that good prospers over evil. I have devoted my life to such purpose as well. Many years ago, we found a strange looking object here in the Temple. It was made of turquoise and so I treasured it all these years. I locked it away in my sanctuary. The night before your arrival, which the Seven Hathors had foretold before it had happened, I dreamt of the Turquoise Goddess. In my dream, she and I walked through the Temple confines. We bathed in the holy lake. She then guided me to my sanctuary and reminded me of the strange object which we found so many years ago. In my dream, she told me to give it to you and that you would know what to do with it."

Hathor then handed the object to Feur and sure enough, it was indeed the third piece of the Turquoise Figurine.

"Return this to the Turquoise Goddess."

"We are most grateful for all your help, Goddess Hathor." exclaimed Nena with great excitement in her voice.

"But wait. That is not all that I must do for you."

Everyone looked startled. They considered the help provided by Hathor as having been more than sufficient.

"Come with me."

Hathor led them back into the Hall of Offerings. They once again were afforded the opportunity to admire the vaulted ceilings with its celestial depictions.

"Daniel, you asked me once before, where the sun wedjat was?" Daniel nodded. "Just like Aten, I had it hidden all these years in the one place that few might find it. Aten's ingenuity was regrettably outsmarted by the wiles and tenacity of Luna, but she has no power here and so the sun wedjat has remained safe in my realm."

Nena looked around anxiously. She had always loved games, especially hide and seek.

"Where did you hide it?" asked Daniel.

"Where many looked and yet few would see the tiny jasper stone amongst all the other magnificent imagery."

Hathor hinted with her eyes for Daniel and the sisters to look upwards.

"It's up there. Look carefully. Do you see the image of the baboon being held by its tail? That signifies a solar eclipse, when the moon casts a shadow over Ka and blocks out the sun.

"I do, I do!" shouted Nena. "It's in the eye of the baboon. That's really clever."

"I thought so." said Hathor, with a note of satisfaction and pride in her voice. "Close your eyes. We need to make a wish for the stone to fall; like a star falling from the nocturnal sky."

After a moment, with their eyes open again, Nena said,

"It did not fall. Perhaps we did not wish hard enough. Let's do it again."

"No need dear child. Open your hand." Nena opened her hand and in her palm lay the shiny red jasper stone.

"The sun wedjat." whispered Nena incredulously.

"Now you must look after that with your life. It must be taken to Aten without delay. You do not have a moment to lose. When Sirius finds out that he has been duped, he will be livid. He will want to get his hands on the eye. Luna has great powers of second sight. She may already have seen that I have given you the sun wedjat, but the Seven Hathors have told me that we have time. They have helped me to shield the events here in Dendera from prying eyes."

Hathor paused for a moment and reached for piece of papyrus which lay on a nearby table. She rolled it up and tied it with a piece of string. She handed it to Daniel. He was inquisitive as to the nature of the words written on it.

"I want you, Daniel, to give this to Aten. He will know what to do with it. Keep it well hidden." Daniel promised that he would do as Hathor had asked.

Hathor stood looking at the sisters and Daniel. She was astonished and proud of what they had already accomplished, but slightly apprehensive for what they would still have to face. She knew that they would in the end succeed, provided that they stood together. She wanted to ensure that they left Dendera with a little extra confidence and courage. She said,

"I and my priestesses shall continue to pray to the Sky Father and Sky Mother to bless your efforts as you journey on towards the Pearl of the Desert. Before you depart in the morning, we shall perform a spell to empower you and to remove all obstacles in your path."

Daniel and the sisters were sad yet, happy and confident to set out to find Aten the next day. Dendera and the beautiful ones had not only restored their health, but also their spirits.

As they left the House of Hathor in the distance, Feur thought again about the ritual that the priestesses had performed on the eve of their departure. She had freely given her ancient manuscript which Gebremekel had given to her at the Dibre Bizen Monastery, but she somewhat regretted that she would never have been able to decipher its hidden meanings with the priests back home. Then again, she reminded herself that, perhaps leaving it with Hathor and her priestesses, would give her a reason to return there in the future. Boise looked at Feur. It was as if she had read her thoughts,

"I was just thinking about last night. I hope our gifts to the Sky Mother will bring success to our mission." said Feur.

Both sisters thought back to the previous night. Hathor had invited them into the Temple for the ritual. She had asked each of them to present a gift to the Sky Mother. She had told them that it had to be something of sentimental value to each of them. Feur had given her book. Boise had given the glass vial filled with cool waters from the Bet Maryam Church at Lalibela. Nena had given the ivory and gold jewellery which Ezana had given to her and Daniel had placed a dried flower, which he had pressed between the pages of the book that he had been reading when Boise had first walked past him on the day of their first meeting.

Hathor had asked each of them to sit facing north inside a circle of salt. They had left their objects inside the circle as gifts for the Sky Mother and once they had thanked the Sky Mother for her gift of protection, wisdom and courage for their journey, they had blown the salt away and broken the ring. Hathor had said that the brushing away of the salt symbolised the fact that their troubles and perhaps any new obstacles that they had yet to encounter, would all be scattered to the four corners of Ka. Boise remembered that Feur had asked her a question before she had become lost in thought.

"Me too! Heaven knows, we need all the help that we can get. A little magic from a few Gods and Goddesses will go a long way to getting us to our destination." smiled Boise.

Both sisters hoped that Hathor's spell to empower them would result in their troubles being left behind them, but they knew better. Fortunately, they had fought their way through hardship and even defeated death, with the help of Khnemu and Hathor, but they wondered whether Fera had been equally fortunate. The unknown factors which lay before them and the unanswered question of whether Fera, Mwari, Jadon and Gibeon were even still alive, drained their recently renewed spirit and confidence.

6

THE WRATH OF THE SUN GOD

It was Feur who had spotted them first. She had been standing on the rooftop of Aten's house, admiring the desert surroundings, when she had spied some movement on the horizon.

Ever since she, her sisters and Daniel had arrived from Dendera, Feur had found herself trapped in a melancholy mood. She had felt physically exhausted. Although the trip on camel-back to Aten's desert hideaway had not been as long or as arduous as she had first thought, Feur had felt the emotional impact of the past few weeks.

The aftermath of almost losing Boise and being attacked and of course, the ever present fears for the well-being of Fera and the men, had seemed to drain Feur of all energy, which even Hathor's magic or the warm welcome into Aten's safe embrace had not seemed to revive. Feur had thus taken to seeking out the solitude of Aten's rooftop. It was a place where she could sit and think, since her thoughts had proven to be a drain on her spirits as well, but mostly, it was a place where she could pray to her parents, particularly her mother, for her guidance and her strength.

At midday on the second day after their arrival, Feur surveyed the large fortified wall around the city, with its many two-storied, white-painted houses, tightly arranged in clusters within its confines. She understood the reason for the women having the most enviable outposts on the rooftops, for the views from there stretched for as far as the eye could see. Feur looked towards the horizon. The sky was clear and there was no wind to speak of. It was as though the force of the winds had been silenced.

Travelling from Dendera through the desert had exposed them to the harshest of nature's elements. The winds, in particular, had blown relentlessly during the day and at night. At times, they had felt as though the winds were battling against them, trying to impede their progress, with every step that they took. Luckily, they had braved the elements to reach Aten's house, wind-swept and tired, but relieved to have made it there in one piece.

Feur had, as always, kept a vigilant eye on her sisters, especially Boise. She had not yet fully recovered her strength, but she had fought her way through the Sea of Sand like a seasoned warrior, without one complaint. Nena, on the other hand, had as usual, complained incessantly. Feur longed to simply get to their destination, if only to get Nena to stop moaning. Thoughts of Nena's erratic nature always made Feur think about Fera and the more that she did, the more she worried about Fera's safety.

Feur constantly thought about Fera. Even her dreams were filled with wild imaginings of the day when Fera would miraculously reappear or when they would meet up with her. Sofala had always taught her daughters to believe in the power of dreams, so when Feur had awoken that morning with the lingering image of Fera's face in her dreams, she had felt dejected and disappointed that Fera was not there with her, as she had dreamt that she was. Disappointed by reality, Feur had then stolen away to the quiet and safety of the rooftop, to pray that her mother would guide and protect Fera wherever she was.

Feur looked out into the distance. She thought she saw movement. Initially, she dismissed it as being insignificant, for the Pearl of the Desert was an important stop for merchants as they crossed the Great Desert. It was not an uncommon sight to see camel trains entering the town one day and then leaving the next, after having refreshed themselves and their camels in one of the only water sources for miles and miles.

Feur kept her eyes firmly fixed on the mysterious objects as they moved at a swift pace, leaving a trail of dust bellowing behind them. She could make out that the cloak-clad figures were riding horses. That in itself was an unusual sight, for Feur had only seen camels used as a mode of transport over the day and a half since she had arrived in the Pearl of the Desert. The sandy whirlwind of motion drew closer and closer to the city's gates. Within minutes, the riders had reached the fortified walls. Feur watched as they dismounted to speak to the guards who kept watch at the large fortified gates which marked the entry to the Old Quarters, that part of the town that the many homes of the residents of Aten's fortress could be found. One of the riders seemed to speak the tongue of the locals. He laughed heartily with the guards. Feur thought that perhaps, they knew each other. He removed his blue head scarf to reveal a rugged-looking face and long black hair. His skin was tanned, but not as dark as the skin of the man standing next to him. That man was tall and wore a long black cloak. The other two men were equally large-framed.

Feur felt a tinge of the familiar as she stared intently at the men. They were still a fair way from her and so she could not see their features clearly. She squinted, as though doing so would make the picture of their faces appear clearer. It was not until the other three men also un-wrapped their headscarves, that the penny dropped for her. Her heart leapt. She could not keep herself from screaming out to them at the top of her voice,

"Mwari, Jadon, Gibeon, it's me, Feur."

It was obvious that they did not hear her. The hustle and bustle of the merchants and their animals in the town below and obviously their friendly banter with the guards, made it impossible for them to hear her. Feur wasted no time. She stumbled clumsily down the stairs and out the front door. Boise, Daniel and Nena sat in the kitchen. She shouted something at them as she ran past, but it was indecipherable to their ears.

"I don't know what has got into that girl. I thought that she was tired. Didn't she go to the rooftop to rest or something?" remarked Nena. Daniel and Boise looked perplexed. They wondered if the weight of worry and tiredness had finally got the better of Feur.

"She is going to meet up with Mwari." said Aten. All the commotion in his usually quiet house drew Aten out from his quarters.

"Mwari? Is he here?" asked Boise surprised.

"But I thought he would have gone after Fera? Didn't he? What is he doing here? You mean to tell me that she is all alone out there?" added Boise, with fear in her voice and in her eyes.

"Fear not, precious one. We will find her. Let's welcome him and together we can come up with a plan." Aten's voice reassured Boise.

Feur ran and ran as fast as she could, until she reached the men. She bounded into Mwari's arms like a long last daughter.

"Oh, Mwari, I am so relieved to see you." She looked over to the men. Jadon and Gibeon smiled warmly. "You too, it is good to see you both as well." Feur looked in the eyes of the other stranger. His face, she did not recognise.

"Feur, this is Fezzan. He is helping us to find Fera." replied Mwari.

Feur looked somewhat confused. She was grateful for any person's help to find Fera, but she did not understand how the handsome stranger fitted into the picture. Jadon read her thoughts,

"We'll explain everything later." winked Jadon. Feur was intrigued by the innuendo in his gesture.

"For now, take us to Aten." said Mwari.

They left their horses to be cared for by the guards, while they followed Feur to meet Aten. They were all warmly welcomed into Aten's abode. Old friends and new acquaintances, then enjoyed Aten's hospitality. The food and wine flowed and Mwari was genuinely glad for the rest. He was however, shocked by the humbleness of Aten's home, for he had heard so much about the power and might of Aten, that he naturally expected the surroundings to match his preconceived notions. He was not disappointed by Aten's power of astuteness and observation though. The more Mwari spoke to Aten, the more intrigued he became.

"So you knew that we were coming here?" asked Mwari, still amazed by the fact that Aten had known of their arrival.

"There is not much that passes by me unnoticed" smiled Aten. "Fortunately I have been able to keep watch over you all. I had to, since there are forces much too evil at play trying to keep these girls from succeeding in their mission." Aten looked at Feur, Nena and Boise as he spoke.

"We know who you mean. We never like to mention her name." whispered Nena.

"No-one does anymore." smiled Aten. "But it has become harder for me to see her evil. She captured my falcon and stole the moon wedjat. It became even more difficult then for me to see her movements. She may have turned the Elementals against us, but I have those who are still loyal to me. You met the Goddess of the Dunes, I believe?"

"She was sent at your request to protect us?" asked Mwari. Aten nodded.

"How can we express our gratitude? That night was truly frightful. We would never have survived if it had not been for her protective embrace." expressed Mwari.

"The Goddess of the Wind, Oya and the Goddess of the River, Imanje, continue to be incited to carry out Luna's evil ends." Nena gasped at the mention of Luna's name.

"There is no reason to fear her here, child. She has no power in my domain. But she still poses a threat. She has the moon wedjat. It has extreme powers, even on its own. Over the years, my hatred for Luna has taken me to the brink of using the stones' powers to serve my desperate need for revenge. I caused needless suffering to countless people all across the kingdoms of Ka. Thankfully, my powers were kept in check, for if I had possessed the sun wedjat, I could easily have been consumed by my hatred for Luna. To this day, I shudder at the thought of what could have happened...." Before Aten could finish his sentence, Feur remarked.

"If it were not for Hathor." added Feur.

"I see that she has told you the story of the two wedjats."

Mwari and the men then looked bewildered, as though they were missing a piece of the puzzle. So, Aten retold the story of the sun and moon wedjats to them all.

"So, you now see how important it is that your mission to save the Turquoise Goddess succeeds."

Aten's words jolted Daniel's memory. He reached for the inner pocket of his cloak and took out the amuletic papyrus which Hathor had asked that he give to Aten.

"Goddess Hathor said that you would know what to do with this."

"What is it?" asked Boise.

"It contains the ancient words of a mystical spell which only a person with mystical powers can read." replied Aten.

"Like you?" enquired Feur.

"Yes. Only a God or Goddess has the powers to invoke and release the magic in the words of the spell."

Aten took the rolled parchment, still bound with Hathor's seal and hid it in his cloak. He then turned to address Nena,

"I believe you also have something from Hathor?"

"You're right. Silly me! I would forget my head if it wasn't attached to my neck!" giggled Nena.

Everyone standing near to Nena simply exchanged smiles. No-one commented on the notion, for of course Nena was absolutely right. She was always an ethereal creature, lost in a dream world. Despite the solid doses of reality she had been given on their mission thus far, she was still as forgetful as ever. As Nena handed the sun wedjat to Aten, she commented,

"Are you sure that this will be safe in your hands. Hathor mentioned specifically that she was entrusted with the sun wedjats' safekeeping so that your power could remain tempered?"

"Fear not, for my years' have taught me that revenge and lust for power is futile. Man can never dominate the great powers of nature for their own selfish ends. The universe will always seek out its own reckoning. I see now that there is a place for both the powers of Luna and my own powers. We must co-exist. We can both remain distinctly powerful in our own right, as long as we never glut on power to the detriment of others. But, if it will make you feel more reassured, then you hold onto it Nena, but be sure not to lose it."

"Oh, she won't." said Feur, as she snatched it from Nena. "I think that it will be best all round if I hold onto this, don't you think?" She grinned at Nena, who initially did not look pleased, but nevertheless capitulated. Feur's actions were not intended to be malicious and Nena silently acknowledged her own limitations.

"It is a pity that Luna has not made that same realisation." added Mwari.

"Both the sun wedjat and the amuletic papyrus will remain safe and hidden. The time will come for us to use them, but now is not such a time. We must first find Fera. These daughters of Ka will be reunited, for if they are not together, it will be nigh impossible to reunite the pieces of the Turquoise Figurine." said Aten, looking at the sisters.

"Do you have any idea where Fera is?" asked Fezzan. It was the first time that he had spoken since Mwari had introduced him to everyone.

"Goddess Hathor said that she has been taken to Bandiagara for the Sigui ceremony." added Daniel.

Fezzan's reaction at the mention of Bandiagara drew a worried look on his face. Mwari instantly noticed Fezzan's uneasiness.

"That is true enough. Bandiagara is the home of the Tellem people. They are known to many across Ka as the white dwarves. They have a great spiritual leader called Hogon." added Aten.

"I know Bandiagara well. We must leave at once if we are to make it there for the start of the ceremony." explained Fezzan.

Mwari felt heartened at Fezzan's enthusiasm to save Fera, but he could not shake the suspicion he felt at noticing Fezzan's initial reaction at hearing where Fera had been taken.

"We shall all leave in the morning. A good night's rest will do you all good. We will find Fera." said Aten reassuringly as he looked at the worried faces around him.

With those last words, everyone turned in for the evening, although getting some sleep was far from everyone's minds, especially Fezzan, who lay awake, haunted by the beautiful green eyes and fiery, copper hair of the woman he loved.

***

Fera could not for the life of her remember being taken or by whom. She assumed that she must have been hit over the head whilst she had slept, since the evidence of her apparent attack; a large, round bump, could be felt at the nape of her neck. Her last memory was that she had turned

159

in for the night, after having spent a blissful few hours with Fezzan and then she had awoken to chaos. She did not know where she was. Her hands were tied, her eyes were blindfolded and her head throbbed painfully. Loud voices rang out all around her; shouting commands in a language which she did not understand. She felt like one of the slaves that she and her sisters had seen, boarding the boats in the Port of Adolos. She imagined then how they must have felt; alone, scared and forced into slavery for unknown masters. She felt then as they must have felt. She felt as though she was walking into an abyss.

Besides the immense fear, Fera was also exhausted, perhaps to a point beyond her own understanding, for she could not remember a time when she had been as tired. Not even her journey through the Great Desert or the hard labour in the camp of the Garramantes could compare to the measure of exhaustion which she had then experienced. Her captors had made her walk and walk. She did not know how long she had done so, but her bare feet were raw and burning. The extreme heat of the desert sand literally cooked the soles of her feet. She had stumbled to her knees a couple of times, only to be shouted at and whipped by some unknown, savage and cruel master. She had begged for mercy and asked for some shoes or at the very least, some rags to bind her raw feet, only to be jeered at and insulted by her captors.

She sensed that there were other people being treated as abominably as she was being treated, for the cries of pain and anguish of others rang out intermittently across the great expanse of the desert. It seemed as though every time someone slowed down or fell to the ground from exhaustion, the captors would attack them viciously, for Fera often heard the sounds of cracking whips and the pitiful wailing of women and painful cries of men.

Her captors were relentless in their pace. They allowed no-one to rest, not even at night, when the unforgiving heat of the day was replaced with the icy cold winds of the night. Fera was exhausted; so much so that she just wanted to collapse, but since she feared being beaten, she trudged on.

She willed her mind to be stronger than her fears and her emotions.

Eventually, after they had walked for some time, they were unceremoniously stopped. Fera's blindfold was removed. The sharp light of day hurt her eyes and made her squint in its glare. When her vision was restored, she was horrified at the sight before her. She and several other slaves were standing at the precipice of a series of steep cliffs. They were surrounded by their captors, vicious men of small stature, their only distinguishing feature being their unusual white faces. They were not white in colour, but rather painted white. In fact, every part of their bodies, not covered by clothes, was painted white.

The men continued to shout loudly and continuously. It soon dawned on Fera that they expected the men and women whom they had captured to walk down the steep cliffs. Fera had never been scared of heights, but the sheer drop to the sandy valley below, made her feel anxious and scared. She had never scaled anything as steep as the cliffs, which descended before her. She watched the reactions of those around her. It was obvious that many of those near her, were scared of heights. Some women fainted at the prospect of what they were expected to do, whilst others tried to escape their captors, only to be hunted down and viciously beaten.

One of the men tried to defend a woman, probably his wife or sister from being beaten, but he met a worse fate when he was thrown from the cliff by the leader of their captors. The man's body bounced from one rocky outcrop to another, like a piece of rag being beaten against a rock on washing day. The screams of his woman reverberated through the sandstone cliffs.

Fera could not stand to witness such brutality any longer. She was not sure why she did it or where she managed to find the courage, but she shouted at her captors to stop their abuse and to show some mercy. Her father had told her to look fear in the face and that was what she intended to do, even if it meant risking her own life to achieve it. Her shouts were met with little compassion from her white-faced captors. Instead, she was slapped across the face and then kicked in the ribs, when she fell to the ground. She coughed and choked. As she tried to get up off the ground, she heard a voice speak to her in a language that she understood,

"I would stay down if I were you. If you get up now, they will only beat you again. You are nothing to them. They will sooner throw you from the cliff."

A small man, with a painted face, stared at Fera. She glared at him, for he was after all one of her captors, but she then realised that he was showing her some measure of kindness. He had large black eyes, which appeared kind. When Fera's aggressors were satisfied that she had been put in her place, they continued with their immediate task at hand, which was to herd the other slaves down the steep trails which ran down the cliffs. With their attention elsewhere, Fera could exchange a few words with one of her captors.

"My name is Umar. You have been taken as a slave of my Master, Sirius. Down those cliffs is the land of my people, the Tellem." whispered Umar, careful not to alert the prying eyes of his Master.

"Where am I?" asked Fera.

"You are in the land of my birth. It is called Bandiagara? Have you heard of it?"

Fera shook her head slowly, for the residual headache left from the bump on her head and then most recently, the pain from her assault, remained with her. She deliberately remained evasive about her knowledge of Bandiagara. The truth was, that she really knew very little about it, other than the fact that she had recognised the name as a location where one of the pieces of the Turquoise Figurine could be found. At least the hope of finding it, was the one bright spark at the end of one very long and painful ordeal which Fera had to experience.

"Yes. So you have heard of my home." Umar appeared genuinely happy by such revelation as though he was relieved that his land and his people had not disappeared into oblivion.

"I have only heard the name. I know nothing else about it."

"The kingdom of Bandiagara was formed many moons ago by a great man named Nangabanu. He was a Tellem Hunter. He built a town in the cliffs of the sandstone hills in Bandiagara. This scared sandstone chain of cliffs extends for some two hundred kilometres. The highest peak stretches over a thousand metres."

Fera did not care to hear the topographical details of her surroundings. She knew that it was fortuitous that she had come to Bandiagara, but she had hoped to make her way there on her own steam, not being pulled along and abused as she walked.

"Why am I here? I do not understand why I was taken by this Sirius? Can you tell me, please?"

"It is not my place. You will soon know the reason. Now, watch your step as we descend the steep trails. One misstep and you will meet a similar fate to that poor soul down there."

Fera could not rid her mind of the brutal image of the man being thrown off the cliff. She did as she was told. The trail perilously snaked its way down the cliffs. As they descended, Umar pointed out the many distinct features of the landscape, such as the sandstone tombs which were carved into the cliffs.

"We bury our dead in those. It is high up enough to protect their bodies from the flooding of the river which runs through the valley, except for the last five years, that is. It has not rained in these parts and so the valley has remained a dry pit." Umar looked sad as he spoke of an obvious intense drought.

When they eventually reached the bottom of the cliffs, Fera saw what appeared to be a large village. Houses, shaped in circular design, were built next to the cliff face. Some had grass roofs, whilst others were constructed of sandstone only. Fera took time to marvel at her surroundings, for the ingenuity of the Tellem people was clearly evident by their architecture. The steep cliffs of Bandiagara rose on either side of the valley and a once mighty river, but then barely a trickle, ran through it, thus protecting the Tellem people from unsuspecting attacks from desert nomads. The slaves were taken to the centre of the village to the largest sandstone dwelling. Umar stayed close to Fera.

"Our fearless leader, Hogon, will now appear and make his choice?"

"Of what?" Umar did not respond. "Choice of what?" reiterated Fera anxiously.

"He will choose one from amongst the women. Our people believe that the moon is dry and dead and thus it can bring no water. This is the result of the feud between the sun and the moon. We have suffered greatly. Our cattle have perished and our crops barely yield a harvest any more. We need water desperately. The only way to reverse this vicious evil drought is to perform a rain ceremony. We shall pray for the rain to come. We shall ask the Goddess Luna to be merciful."

"Well, that is impossible, isn't it? Good luck with that." quipped Fera.

Uma gave her a quizzical look, but once again did not respond. There were many things which irritated Fera, chief amongst which, was when people did not answer her when she spoke to them.

"The Goddess of the Moon will answer our prayers, if we do as she commands."

"What does she want you to do?" asked Fera again. Umar still remained silent.

Suddenly, a commotion erupted, as a man, similarly white-faced, but adorned with animal pelts, ivory and gold jewels, exited the large house. A large crowd of villagers had by then collected near to where Fera was standing. They cheered and shouted as the man stood before them. Fera surmised that he must have been the leader whom Umar had spoken of. Hogon addressed the crowd.

"My people, I had a dream that rain would come to our lands, but we must honour the Goddess Luna with a gift before she will make it rain." Everyone cheered even louder. "We must make a sacrifice to our generous benefactor." Hogon lifted his hand to summon Sirius before him. Fera watched intently.

"Our brave warriors, under the leadership of Sirius, have captured these slaves. Their efforts do our people proud. The men will be put to work building homes and tombs for the next generation of the living and the dead." The crowds grew more and more exited. "From amongst the women, I will choose a virgin. She will be sacrificed to the Goddess Luna."

Hogon's last statement drove the villagers into a frenzy. Hogon walked through the group of captives. Sirius walked loyally at his side. He stopped before each one of their captives and examined them closely. One after the other was deemed unsuitable by Hogon. At last, he reached Fera. She stared into his dark eyes, which were highlighted by his painted face. She had feared the worst when she had discovered the identity of her captors, but even in her wildest nightmares, she had never contemplated that she would find herself in the predicament in which she then found herself.

Hogon looked at her and then at Sirius, as though needing his confirmation. Sirius nodded. Hogon smiled as though he had eventually, somehow reached an elusive victory which had been cruelly denied to him. Fera closed her eyes. Her worst fear had been realised. She was alone in a strange land and about to be sacrificed. Her knees felt unstable. Her heart raced. She felt like a caged animal. She could not run, nor hide. Her fate was sealed.

"We have found the one." shouted Hogon to his people. He lifted Fera's hand in the air as though she was a victor, but in reality she had won nothing.

"At tonight's festivities, she will be sacrificed and tomorrow we shall sing, dance and rejoice under the swollen grey skies."

Fera was abruptly pulled away from the other women by Sirius and then dragged towards the entrance of the large sandstone house. Fera decided in that moment, that she would not die without fighting. She resisted Sirius' vice-like grip. She dug her heels into the sandy earth and did everything in her power to prevent Sirius from taking her inside. He once again slapped her across the head. She felt momentarily light-headed. She wanted to shout a response and tell her brutal captor that she refused to be sacrificed, but all energy drained from her body. She slumped to the ground, unable to move an inch further. Sirius remained undeterred by her shenanigan and simply continued to drag her roughly by her one arm. Fera felt as though she was on the verge of unconsciousness. Whilst fighting for her life, she heard a voice call out from the crowd. It seemed familiar to her.

"Take your filthy hands off that woman! She will not be sacrificed by you or by anyone."

Fera mustered up the energy to lift her head. She looked into the face of Fezzan as he moved through the crowds towards her. Her heart leapt with joy. Fezzan came face to face with Sirius.

"You will take your hands off her or your blood will stain the earth of your birth land this very day." threatened Fezzan, in a venomous tone.

Mwari, Jadon and Gibeon had by then also emerged from the crowd to stand alongside Fezzan. They had all drawn their swords. Fera did not see her sisters anywhere.

"On whose authority do you command me to release this slave? You have no standing here. I own this woman." Sirius laughed. "You honestly think that you can take on all my men."

Fezzan realised that they were miserably outnumbered. He racked his brain to find a solution to their dilemma. His plan to rescue Fera had not been fully thought through. He, Mwari, Jadon, Gibeon and the sisters had left the Pearl of the Desert and moved towards Bandiagara as swiftly as they could. Even the steep cliffs of Bandiagara had not lessened their pace. They had arrived in the Tellem village to witness Sirius' brutality towards Fera. Fezzan had thought of nothing else, other than rescuing his love. He had given no thought to the large numbers of Tellem hunters or the protected position of the village itself, which offered little opportunity for a quick escape.

As Fezzan stood eyeball to eyeball with Sirius, the only solution appeared to be that they would have to physically fight their way out of the situation, irrespective of the consequences. Sirius was not one to turn down a fight and so, he abruptly and violently threw Fera to one side to devote his sole attention to the brazen stranger before him.

Fera cried out in pain as Sirius hurled her against the wall of the large sandstone dwelling. Fezzan felt as though his heart would break at seeing Fera being harmed, but instead of succumbing to his anger, he channelled all his energies to face the cruel little man who stood arrogantly before him, with his sword in one hand and a malevolent scowl on his white face. Before they could engage in hand to hand combat, another voice rang out through the crowd. It was so loud that all who heard it felt the earth shudder beneath their feet. Fezzan surveyed the crowds. He saw Aten ride forward on his large copper-coloured steed. The crowds gasped in awe of the sight and moved aside immediately. They all knew that they stood in the presence of greatness, in the presence of a God, whom they feared, for they had felt his wrath of late. The dry wind-swept earth was a testimony to his great power.

"On my authority! I command that you leave this girl be." bellowed Aten. "If this girl comes to any further harm, I shall see this village destroyed. I shall bake the cliffs and the valley under the heat of a scalding sun, for an eternity." Hogon stood defiant.

"We are not afraid of your evil. We have sought the protection from the Goddess of the Moon. She has promised me that my people will suffer no more if we sacrifice a virgin in her name. She has chosen this girl." said Hogon to Aten, whilst pointing at Fera.

"Luna has promised to grant me the power of Everlastingness if I present her with the sun wedjat." added Sirius. "And I will not allow you, nor anyone else to stand in my way."

"Greed and hunger for power has clouded your judgement, Sirius. Luna has deceived you. She has deceived you all. She has no power to grant you what you most desire. Only Lord Khnemu has that power. As his protégé for so many years, I would have thought you would have known better than to trust the lies and manipulations of Luna."

"She already has the moon wedjat. Once I give her the sun wedjat, she will have all that she needs to fulfil her promise."

"I know that she brutally ripped the moon wedjat from my falcon, but she will never lay her hands on the sun wedjat, for as long as I live and breathe."

"That can easily be remedied here and now." threatened Sirius.

"Your threats are as futile as your existence. For your insufferable arrogance and disloyalty, you should have been more severely punished, but Lord Khnemu acted mercifully towards you and still granted you the power to herald the morning star. You are not fit for even that power. You fail to realise the full consequences of your actions. By allying yourself with Luna and doing her evil bidding, you have not only disgraced yourself, but you have put survival of our beloved Ka at risk."

"You have the temerity to call me a disgrace, when you turn against the peoples of Ka. You bring drought to their lands. Countless souls have died as a consequence of your feud with Luna. She has promised these people respite from your vengeance. She will bring rain to their sun-scorched lands. She offers them hope and life. What do you offer?" scoffed Sirius.

"It is true that I have acted unjustly towards many nations across Ka." Aten then turned to address the Tellem crowds. "I am the first to admit my shame and disgust at my behaviour. There is no justification for the wrongs I have done. For many years, I was a broken man, with a broken heart. My reason for living was simply to avenge the wrongs committed by Luna towards my precious daughter and her husband. But, the time for revenge has passed. Balance will be brought to the powers of the sun and the moon when the Turquoise Goddess returns."

"That is not your decision to make. Goddess Luna will never allow that to happen. She will command the sole powers over the sun and moon when she has the power of the wedjats under her control. I will give her the sun wedjat."

Aten removed the red jasper stone from a pouch which hung at his waist.

"You mean this?"

Sirius looked confused for an instant.

"The sun wedjat has always been in the safekeeping of Goddess Hathor. She has now given it to me, so you see, your plan is seriously flawed." said Aten.

"You are lying. I saw the sun wedjat with my own eyes. This girl kept it hidden in the folds of her cloak."

"You saw what looked like the wedjat. Fera was given a sacred faience scarab as a gift by the Queen of Meroe."

"No, that cannot be."

Sirius took a few steps back to where Fera lay. He pulled at her cloak in an attempt to remove it from her body. Fera fought back. She mustered all her strength to thwart Sirius' attempts. Fezzan ran over to Fera's aid. Sirius held a knife to Fera's throat.

"Come any closer and she will die. She has the wedjat. I saw it that night when I attacked your camp with my rabid dogs. I know that for a fact since I saw it with my own eyes."

Sirius tugged at Fera's clothing, desperately searching for the mythical item that he had seen before in Fera's possession.

"Whatever you believe you saw, know this, I have the sun wedjat in my possession. With its powers under my control, I will bring its powers to bear down on you, Sirius and on the Tellem people. It pains me to do it, but I will ensure that nothing, but cracked earth plagues your people for every generation to come."

"My people have suffered enough with the drying of our lands. We will not survive more of the same." added Hogon. "But, sacrificing her would have brought us rain. Without appeasing Luna, how will my people survive?"

"Do you honestly believe that Luna will save your people? If she had to get her hands on the wedjats, she will yield their powers for her own evil ends."

"But, you have threatened us with a worse fate? We are doomed either way." said Hogon.

"I have warned of the consequences if you fail to heed my advice. I seek the return of the Turquoise Goddess. For that to come about, the wedjats must be returned to their rightful owner. It is only through returning the sun and moon wedjats to the Turquoise Goddess that we can all be saved; that your people and all the nations across Ka can be saved. Luna seeks neither peace nor the continued success and survival of your people. She will use the power of the wedjats against us all. The suffering of your people in the past and at present, will pale in comparison to the suffering that Luna will bring." replied Aten.

Hogon looked torn. As a leader, he felt his primary obligation was to protect his people. To achieve that, he had to bring rain. Luna offered him that outcome. But if he chose to ally himself with Luna, he would bring the eternal wrath of Aten upon his people for generations to come. Hogon looked at his many sons. He could not bear to enslave them and their children to a life of struggle and drudgery. But, on the other hand, did Luna not yield as much power as Aten? Did she not also possess the power of the moon wedjat? Did it not grant her the ability to be as powerful as Aten? Hogon felt confused. The decision that he faced was momentous.

Feur, Boise and Nena had watched the scene play out in front of their eyes. They had remained cloaked and silently inconspicuous amongst the crowds of Tellem villagers. Mwari had warned them to keep out of the way, as far as possible. They had stood helplessly by as Fera had been assaulted, but they could stand back no longer. If there was ever a time that Aten and the men needed their support, albeit only moral support, it was then.

The sisters, hand in hand, walked forward and stood defiant next to Mwari and the men. Fera, for the first time in a long time, saw her sisters, all of her sisters, standing in front of her. She could see Boise was alive and well. Her mother had answered her prayers. Nena and Feur looked their usual selves. Fera was so relieved that she started to cry. They all smiled at Fera as a sign for her not to worry, for all would be fine since they were together again. Hogon looked from Sirius to Aten, unsure of where the salvation of his people lay.

"Do not believe him. He is lying." shouted Sirius. "You must do as Luna has commanded." Sirius realised that if Hogon did not sacrifice Fera, Luna would be most unpleased. Sirius was unconcerned with the fate of the Tellem people if Hogon chose to disobey her commands, but he was concerned about his own fate. He had promised Luna the sun wedjat. Given that Aten held it firmly in his possession, Sirius knew that he could not fulfil his promise to Luna. He had suffered the dissatisfaction of an immortal God before in his life, when he had displeased Lord Khnemu. He had managed to live another day then, but he knew that Luna lacked the mercy of Khnemu. His failure to get her the sun wedjat would be unforgivable in her eyes. The little powers he had, would invariably be taken away from him. Sirius knew that for certain. He could not bear the idea of being banished to Luna's underground prisons, for an eternity and even if he managed to evade her capture, he would be hunted by her evil fiends forever. She had eyes and ears everywhere. Her adze were everywhere. There would be no corner of Ka that would offer him protection against Luna's wrath.

"I would never mislead you in a matter as deeply important as this. Your choice is simple. Choose life and turn against Luna or choose death for you and your people."

Aten's final words hit Hogon like a deathly blow. Feur watched Hogon's reaction to Aten's words. She could see that he was a torn man. He appeared unconvinced that releasing Fera was the only way forward for his people. Aten's dire predictions and words of caution did not seem to resonate with Hogon. Mwari saw his chance to capitalise on Hogon's uncertainty and he stepped forward and addressed Hogon.

"Great King Hogon, I am Mwari of the Kingdom of Monomotapa. I would like to offer a gift to you and your people."

Mwari asked Feur to give him the faience scarab which Queen Candace had gifted to Fera. Feur did not understand the reason for Mwari wanting it and so she was initially reluctant to hand it over to him.

"You trust me, don't you? This is the only way." Feur looked hesitant.

"Give it to him. He will not put us in harm's way. I trust him." said Boise.

Feur handed Mwari the object which she had protectively looked after since they had left Dendera. Mwari walked to stand in front of Hogon. He knelt before Hogon to show deference to a king, albeit a flawed one in Mwari's eyes. Mwari knew that men like Hogon, were deeply traditional, even perhaps a little superstitious and thus if Mwari appealed to Hogon on that level, he might succeed in convincing Hogon to release Fera.

"I have a proposition for you, great King. I shall hand you this sacred scarab in exchange for the life of that young girl."

Jadon and Gibeon both looked at each other in total amazement. They thought that Mwari had lost his mind. Why on earth would he have chosen such a time to pay homage to some forgotten leader of the Tellem people? Hogon moved closer to Mwari to inspect the object that he held in his hand. His eyes grew wider as he saw a beautiful beetle with its intense blue-green glazed ceramic body. His reaction was exactly what Mwari had anticipated.

Mwari smiled inwardly and thought back to when he and Gebremekel had spent the afternoon paging through the ancient manuscripts of the monastery library and they had eventually found an entry in the ancient writings of Abune Libanos. Gebremekel had said then that the information which they had discovered might have the power to destroy Luna and unravel her evil plan. Mwari understood that Luna would not yet be destroyed, but he knew that it was time to use the information in his possession to save Fera and to save their mission.

"Where did you get this?" asked Hogon.

"It was a gift from a powerful Queen. Do you recognise it?" asked Mwari meekly. He knew the answer before it was spoken.

"My people have always believed in the power of nature. We have always believed in the power of the beetle. We believe that it holds mystical powers. The beetle deposits its eggs in a piece of dung and rolls it in a ball, which is buried in the earth for twenty-nine days. When the eggs hatch, the beetle pushes the ball in water and the new-born beetles then have a constant food supply. It is on that day, that the sun and the moon align and the rains are brought with it. The beetle is an all-powerful creature. It creates life without procreation, for it does not need a female partner. It creates life for our people and brings nourishment to our lands." Hogon paused speaking, as though the immensity of the moment became too much for him to bear.

"This sacred beetle was stolen from my people many moons ago. How did you come by it?"

"How I found it is irrelevant in light of its great importance to you and your people." said Mwari. "The ancient writings of the monks at the Dibre Bizen Monastery told of a gift which a great and inspirational teacher once gave to your people. This scarab is that gift."

"Tatyos gave it to his pupil, our great leader, Nangabanu?" mouthed Hogon.

"Yes. Did he not visit your kingdom on his magical cloak?" Hogon nodded and recalled,

"The tale of Tatyos and his magical beetle is known far and wide to all the village children, through every generation of my people. My parents told me about it and I have told the tale to my children. Tatyos gave it as a gift to my people. It was intended to protect our realm. As long as it was safely in our care, the rains would always come and our world would always be generated afresh. But it was stolen more than five years ago. The rains then stopped." Hogon gave a look of complete desolation.

"And who do you think stole it? Have you ever thought that it was no coincidence that it was stolen at a time when the suffering of your people began? Perhaps the demise of your crops and cattle was not at the hands of Aten after all?" asked Mwari. Hogon shrugged his shoulders.

"What do you mean?"

"I believe that Luna stole the beetle, but more than that, she stole the hope, faith and ultimately the free will of your people. She knew that your people had been blessed with the gift of rain, for as long as you possessed the power of the beetle. She also knew that your people believed so fervently in the powers of the beetle to bring rains, that when it was gone, you would be desperate enough to reach out to anyone who would help your people, anyone who promised to bring rains to your sun-parched lands. Can you not see that Luna has engineered your people's demise and their dependence on her all along? She has made you need her. She has made you all desperate for the help that she has purported to offer. You have the chance now to be free from her control. Agree to my proposal. Set your people free."

Mwari hoped that he had said enough to convince Hogon. After some moments of intense thought, Hogon replied,

"I will do as you ask. The girl is free to go. Our great leader Nangabanu will be honoured with the gift of the beetle. You shall take it to him. He will be pleased and the rains will come."

The villagers, who had stood by silently, suddenly erupted into loud singing and dancing when they realised that the beetle had been returned to its rightful home. Fezzan did not waste a moment and rushed to Fera's side.

"I am here. No harm will ever come to you again, my love, for as long as I live and breathe."

He kissed Fera's forehead. Feur, Nena and Boise watched the show of affection between Fera and Fezzan. They were happy for their sister, yet extremely surprised, for the behaviour was so uncharacteristically Fera.

"I am sure you never expected to see that in our lifetime?" teased Nena to her sisters.

"And she always made fun of us for gushing about love and romance?" added Boise, as she smiled warmly at Daniel. Even the men were surprised by the sight of Fera and Fezzan.

"Where's Sirius?" asked Daniel, as he scanned the jubilant crowds.

"He must have slipped into the crowds when we were not looking." said Jadon.

"He obviously realised that he could not defeat the power of good. Evil never wins. It may take time, we can all attest to that, but in the end, good always conquers evil." Aten's wise words gave everyone food for thought.

"I shall now escort you to the tomb of our great leader. You can pay your respects then and lay the beetle at the feet of our most revered leader." said Hogon to Mwari.

"Thank you Hogon, it takes a wise and great spiritual leader to put the well-being of his people before himself. You are a leader whom your people can be proud of."

Hogon was a man who showed little visible emotions, but he nodded in appreciation of Aten's kind words.

Later that night, Hogon, Mwari and Aten weaved their way through secret tunnels, which lay deep within the Bandiagara escarpment, to the final resting place of Nangabanu. His tomb was a dark and sombre place.

"I shall leave you to pay your respects." whispered Hogon to Mwari and Aten.

"That will be appreciated."

When Hogon had left, Mwari placed the faience scarab on the ground near the entrance of the burial sanctuary of the Tellem's once-great leader. Mwari spoke to the spirit of Nagabanu as though he was still alive,

"This sacred object is now in your care once more." said Mwari.

"With it, we bring the blessing of rain and continued prosperity for your lands and your people." added Aten.

Suddenly, the scarab appeared to transform into a living beetle. Mwari and Aten watched as it scurried down a hole in the ground at the feet of Nangabanu. Minutes later it returned, pushing a ball out of the hole with its hind legs. The ball was not made of dung. It appeared to be constructed of sand and earth found in the tomb. It rolled and rolled the ball until it came to rest at Aten's feet. It then disappeared.

Both Aten and Mwari looked at each other, feeling totally bewildered. Aten reached down for the ball. As his fingers touched it, its sandy encasing crumbled to reveal an object hidden at its centre. Aten rubbed the object to free it from dirt and dust to reveal a dazzling and translucent blue stone.

"Is this what I think it is?" asked Mwari.

"Nature has returned the kindness of your gift. Nature will always renew itself and bestow blessings on those who care for and protect it. Today, you gave the sacred beetle life and with that life, the rebirth of nature has been heralded and restored."

Both Mwari and Aten knew that the mission of the Daughters of Ka was one step closer to finality. They had found another piece of the Turquoise Figurine. Soon, the figurine would be whole again and the return of the Turquoise Goddess to the realm of Ka, would bring an end to evil and death. Mwari could not wait to share the news with his men and the four sisters, whom he considered as dear to him as his own daughter had once been.

7

THE RECKONING

The outline of the cone-shaped minarets of the Friday Mosque, which stood at least thirty-six feet high, rose on the horizon before them. It was the first peak for Mwari and his party at the wonders which lay ahead in the great city of Jenne in the Land of Gold and Knowledge.

It was also Feur's first glimpse of a place that she had learnt much about from the priests in the Great Temple, back in Catal Huyuk. She could barely contain her excitement at the thought of actually being able to explore the Great Mosque and its great libraries. For anyone who had an intense love of learning, the many libraries of Jenne represented one of the most important centres of learning anywhere in Ka. Sonni-Ali, the ruler over the Land of Gold and Knowledge, showed great respect for men of learning. In fact, he paid handsome salaries to many learned people, such as religious clerics and doctors to both study and write manuscripts relating to many varied subjects, such as botany, medicine, chemistry, mathematics and climatology.

Aten, Mwari and his party had arrived in the city on a Friday, a day marked as a holy day, when all the inhabitants of the city were called to prayers. Throngs of worshippers, most dressed in white, streamed in and out of the Friday Mosque.

The Mosque was a truly imposing sight as it stood high on a three metre platform, so that it could remain untouched by the flooding of the river. Sun-baked earth bricks called ferey, made from sand and earth mortar over which a smooth coat of plaster was applied, gave the mosque walls a strong, yet smooth appearance. Bundles of protruding wooden sticks called toron, decorated its walls as well.

In her excitement, Feur wanted to simply run up the six stairs which led to the Mosque's grand entrance, but Aten stopped her.

"This is a holy place Feur. We need permission to enter and when we do, men and women use different entrances.

We will make enquiries from the local clerics. While we are gone, stay out of trouble. The city is swarming with possible dangers." instructed Mwari to everyone.

Jadon and Gibeon had once again reverted to their old military habits. They remained continually alert as they knew that the large Songhai military were an ever-present force, guarding the city against invasion from the Berbers. They had come up against the brave soldiers which made up the Songhai army, on more than one occasion in their lives. The bulk of its thirty thousand strong infantry and ten thousand strong cavalry were stationed at Gao, the seat of power of the King Sonni-Ali or Dali as he was referred to by his subjects.

Gao was also the kingdom's main seat of trade and business. The chief military commander, known as the Dina-Koi, ran the military operations from Gao and then delegated functions to his Generals, who were based in various locations around the Songhai empire. The military general in Jenne was called the Jenne-Koi. Jadon and Gibeon had never met him before, but they knew him only by reputation, which was one of fierce and merciless rigour. The defeated armies of Songhai enemies had often said that the Songhai army was so quick and merciless that when they attacked, they stole daylight from under their enemies' noses and reduced their existence to nothing but darkness. The soldiers of their enemies, who were strong and who managed to survive a Songhai onslaught, would be taken as slaves by the Generals to fight for Dali.

Jadon and Gibeon had thankfully evaded capture by the Songhai armies and had sworn never to fight in an ill-fated war initiated by any leader against the Songhai, whose warriors were always armed to the teeth. Their foot soldiers had spears, arrows and copper or leather shields, whilst the elite cavalry wore iron breastplates under their battle tunics. It was not only the army that Sonni-Ali had re-organised, he had also trained and equipped mighty fleets which patrolled the river. Under their leader, the Master of the Water, Jenne's fleets were yet other impenetrable defence against any foreign invaders to the great wealth and abundance of the Songhai kingdom.

"We'll keep a lookout for everyone, Mwari, don't you worry about that." said Jadon confidently, in reply to Mwari's instruction.

Having satisfied themselves of everyone's safety, Aten and Mwari decided to visit the Mosque. They walked up the stairs, removed their shoes and solemnly entered, leaving the rest of their party behind them. Fezzan was invited to join them, but declined, much to Fera's surprise. Instead of opting to join Mwari or to explore the city with the others, Fezzan had decided to stay out of sight and look after the horses. Fera had also elected to remain by his side.

"You all go ahead. I am still tired and sore. I prefer to rest. We'll get some food from a nearby merchant and wait for you here." said Fera to her sisters.

Later, Fera and Fezzan approached a local Songhai merchant who was dressed in a customary blue tunic and head turban. He was obviously a wealthy man, for he sported various ornamental chains around his neck. He received Fera, in his business establishment, with a warm yet, traditional greeting.

Songhai merchants were known for their hospitality and generosity. Perhaps it was a matter of survival, since they had to house and feed so many travellers, who stopped to visit the city on their way through the Great Desert and thus, they soon realised that if they were generous and kind to all their customers, they would attract more customers and thereby greatly enhance the financial success of their businesses.

The merchant enquired after Fera's health. Fera smiled inwardly when she considered whether she should burden the poor stranger with a true account of her health status. She knew that he may have regretted asking her that question if she had answered him fully. She was momentarily unsure whether she should respond to his polite enquiries in the traditional manner, by stating that she was well, but she knew that response would be far from the truth, since she did not feel well at all. If she had been honest and told the merchant about how she had lived through an haboob, been taken by Sirius and physically abused by the white dwarves; not to mention, how she had crossed the Great Sea, the Gulf of Zula and the Dead Lands, he would probably have regarded her response as the far-fetched ravings of a mad woman. Even Fera could not believe what she and her sisters had gone through since they had left home. Instead, Fera simply smiled politely and reciprocated his greeting.

There must have been a close relationship between the city's merchants and the nobility, noticed Fera, for several nobles, wearing izars or the traditional head wrap, had also exchanged greetings with the merchant, as Fera had walked into the shop.

Fezzan had opted to stand outside the shop. Fera was slightly perturbed by his reticent behaviour and it was almost as though he was wary of being recognised, for he raised his qob over his head. Fera just assumed that he was shielding his skin from the sun and the wind. They had been at the mercy of the elements of late and thus, on closer consideration, his behaviour came as no surprise to Fera.

As Fera walked around the merchant's shop, she was enthralled to see the variety of goods that were on sale. The merchant was eager to show off the terabeba or elaborately designed cotton mats as well as the beautiful terracotta pottery, which were the handicrafts of the local women. Fera wished that she could have bought a piece for her mother since she knew that her mother would have loved to receive a mat or a jug, but Fera had no idea what the rest of their journey had in store for them. She would have hated to have bought something and then seen it broken.

Fera enquired whether the merchant sold food. He offered her some howru, a millet paste topped with okra and peanuts. He also asked Fera if she would like to try some of his own brewed white wine made from fermented palmeta leaves. He gave her a sample to taste. Fera enjoyed its sweet and pleasant taste.

With her pleasant excursion at an end, Fera paid the merchant in salt, which was the local Songhai currency, and left the shop. The salt currency reminded Fera of Nakta and his many wives, who collected salt from the Emerald Lake. She thought again how lucky they had all been to have met him and how, strangely, all the nations of Ka were interconnected through trade and commerce. The Afar people traded their salt with Songhai merchants, the merchants in Catal Huyuk sent their goods south to Axum and Meroe which, in turn, sent their goods to the west. Camel caravans and the Beja acted as conduits for all the trade across Ka. On her journey, thus far, Fera had found learning about the various commercial activities of the various kingdoms of Ka, very interesting. Thoughts of Nakta, invariably led Fera to also wonder what had happened to Harim and Hasshub. She prayed that they were safe and unharmed.

Unlike Fera and Fezzan, the others in their party, had elected to explore the city of Jenne. As they had walked, Feur expressed her dissatisfaction.

"Well, isn't that just a little unfair?" said an exasperated Feur, "I have waited my whole life to see the Mosque and its libraries and now that I am here, I cannot go inside."

"Be patient!" replied Boise. "Perhaps we can explore the outside? Daniel, can you tell us about the history of the Mosque?"

Boise purposefully tried to address Feur's disappointment by diverting her attention elsewhere.

"I know the history of the Mosque, so Daniel needn't bother." retorted Feur, slightly annoyed. "I have read about it for years. The Mosque was built by the great King Sonni Ali of the Songhai, on the floodplains of the river. Islam is the dominant religion of the city. The Songhai Royal Palace is also on this site. The King has a palace in Gao as well. I think he keeps his wives and concubines there and he lives here. "

"A wise man." joked Jadon.

"Did you know that King Sonni-Ali acceded to the throne by patrilineal succession." added Daniel.

"What does that mean?" asked Nena.

"Only the son of the King's sister can inherit the throne. A King has many wives and so cannot trust the genuineness of the origin of the birth of a son from one of his wives."

"Why? Surely one knows if one's wife is faithful?" asked Feur.

"It is possible that a man, other than the King could father a child, isn't it?" asked Daniel. Nena could not conceive of the notion of a wife being unfaithful.

"Not only husbands can be unfaithful. Wives can also be unfaithful to their husbands." volunteered Gibeon.

"Either way, infidelity is sinful and disrespectful to both a husband and a wife. Marriage is a solemn commitment, which should not be taken lightly." replied Daniel. Boise was glad that she and Daniel shared the same values.

"I think it takes all the intimacy and romance out of marriage if one party is unfaithful." said Boise. Daniel turned to Boise,

"You'd be happy to know, my love, romance is alive and well here. Songhai women serenade their husbands before they seduce them. After dinner, a wife will burn incense and then either sing or play music for her husband until he falls asleep."

"Well that's more like it. It's high time that we got wooed, but does the singing and playing of music come before or after the seduction?" asked Jadon to Gibeon, looking rather confused.

"I agree. Why should men always romance women?" replied Gibeon.

"Because that's the way it is supposed to be. It totally disrupts the order of things any other way. I and all other women want to be wooed and that's that." exclaimed Nena.

Their conversation had brought them to the outer perimeters of the Great Mosque. They could not help but stare at the tall minarets once again.

"I never noticed that before. They are topped with ostrich eggs. How remarkable!" said Nena, "I wonder what the significance of that is?"

"Ostrich eggs symbolise creation and life." said Feur.

They walked around the city, admiring its wealth and its architecture. Jenne was obviously a rich city, which did brisk trade. Its physical location on the flood plains of the river provided fertile soil for growing millet, rice and wild grains and for rearing sheep and goats. All manner of goods appeared to be coming into and leaving the city on the trade caravans. Copper from Catal Huyuk and salt from the

Emerald Lake was imported into the city and gold, ivory, kola nuts and of course, slaves were exported.

"The city has plentiful resources of iron-ore and stone, which it trades with surrounding communities. The city's blacksmiths then smelt iron ore to make tools, ornaments and weapons." said Jadon. "King Sonni-Ali was a clever man to plunder and besiege this place. He tried for seven years to take control of Jenne and now that his power is firmly entrenched, he can just sit back and enjoy his wealth."

"With great wealth comes a great responsibility to one's people and the land." said Feur.

"Yes, yes, all that, of course, but it would be nice not to have to work for a living." said Jadon.

"You should know!" joked Gibeon.

Jadon would have been more offended by such comment, if Gibeon hadn't hit the nail on the head. Jadon knew it to be true. He had always made his living as a soldier, but he had never really considered such activity to be work, it was more a calling. So in future, if he could not be a soldier, then he honestly, would not have wanted to do anything else which could be considered to be work."

"Perhaps, there is a rich wife for you here in the city?" joked Daniel, "When we see the King, we'll ask him for the hand of one of his daughters, shall we?"

Everyone laughed, but Jadon was not amused at being the butt of everyone's joke.

Aten and Mwari returned within the hour. The religious clerics had refused to give them an audience. They were told that they would had to wait until the next day, when the King would be holding a public audience in the large walled courtyard of the Songhai Palace. Aten was none too pleased at their treatment at the hands of the clerics.

As they exited the Mosque, Aten and Mwari were suddenly apprehended by a group of fierce Songhai warriors, whose presence did not surprise Mwari, for he strongly suspected that the clerics did not like nor trust any strangers in their city.

Nena and the others, who had seen Mwari and Aten exit the Mosque, were not immediately alerted to the imminent danger, which they would all soon face.

"That's hospitable! The King has sent a royal guard to escort us into the Mosque." commented Nena, as she saw Mwari and Aten in the distance.

"Those fellows do not look as though they are friendly." observed Jadon. "And they are most definitely not escorting Aten and Mwari. They appear to be arresting them!"

The warriors were tall and muscular and yielded long spears. Mwari and Aten were abruptly pushed down the steps of the Mosque. Jadon and Gibeon leapt to their feet, but before they could advance to aid Mwari and Aten, another equally fierce group of warriors surrounded them, their sharp spears at the ready to swiftly deal with any person who resisted their control.

"Stay calm girls. Do as they say. I am sure we will get to the bottom of this soon." advised Daniel. They could always count on Daniel to be the voice of reason and calm. They were all arrested and taken to a local building. It appeared to be someone's home. It was neither opulent nor shabby. The soldiers locked the doors behind them.

"Do you have any idea why we are being detained?" asked Daniel of Mwari and Aten.

"King Sonni-Ali is very mistrustful of strangers. We tried to explain who we were to the religious leaders in the Mosque, but it is obvious that they deemed us to be a threat. They probably consider us to be invaders of some sort." said Mwari. "They will no doubt keep us here until tomorrow when we will be taken before the King."

"Are they afraid we will escape? Everything is locked." remarked Daniel.

Unusually, all the furniture inside the rooms, such as cupboards and internal doors were locked and there was a vast array of goods stored in the rooms, such as salt and grains. The house seemed to double as a home and a storage facility.

"My presence here does not help your cause either. Perhaps my reputation has preceded me to this kingdom as well." said Aten sadly.

Of late, it had really dawned on Aten, just how feared and disliked he had become throughout the kingdoms of Ka. Everyone seemed to hold him responsible for the suffering which had been inflicted on them by the feud between himself and Luna. No-one in Mwari's party blamed Aten. He was a man, an immortal man, but a man nonetheless, not infallible and most certainly flawed. They all knew that he had genuinely atoned for his past conduct and they were immensely grateful for his continued support and help.

"The King will see that none of us mean any harm to him or his rule. All we want is the piece of the Turquoise Figurine and once we get it, we will be on our way. When we explain this to him tomorrow, surely he will see reason." added Daniel.

The next morning Aten, Mwari and the others, except Fera and Fezzan, were escorted under armed guard towards an open courtyard of the Songhai Royal Palace. They entered the courtyard through a public gate, which was similarly used by the throngs of people who made their way to seek an audience with their Dali.

The wealth of the city was reflected in the gardens of the palace. As Boise surveyed the greenery around her, she was unsurprised at the beauty of the flora, since the city was built on rich and fertile floodplains. The rains which had fallen overnight, had obviously added to the natural abundance of their surroundings. Aten and the others were instructed to remove their shoes as a sign of respect, which all visitors had to show to the King and then they were told to stand in a row in the middle of the courtyard, which itself was relatively crowded with many people.

The Songhai cavalry, armed foot soldiers, advisors, stewards and lastly nobles, who were dressed in robes and turbans of blue or black cotton and adorned with gold jewels were present, as were ordinary villagers, who had invariably travelled long distances to seek the King's counsel. There were also many slaves gathered on the edges of the crowd. Some were sumptuously dressed and obviously the slaves of the nobles, whilst others were called arbi slaves, for they worked in the palace as craftsmen, potters, woodworkers and musicians.

Mwari and Aten recognised those dressed in white robes to be the religious leaders with whom they had tried to engage in the Great Mosque. They had appeared highly sceptical and mistrusting of Aten and Mwari during their first encounter and it was obvious that such feelings still persisted, since they looked at both Mwari and Aten through leering eyes.

The presence of the women did nothing to change the opinions of the clerics either. Feur noticed that the men and women in the crowds, stood apart, much the same as had been witnessed the day before. It was clear that men and women in the city led separate lives in public. Feur was not sure whether she liked the notion of separation between the sexes in work and in daily life, but despite her own misgivings, she respected the religious and cultural ways of the Songhai.

The arrival of the King was preceded by the sound of loud drums called doba, which appeared to have been fashioned from long hollowed-out logs. Their music was distinctive for each occasion. When the King ate his meals, they would play one type of tune and when the King stepped out into the public domain, another tune would be played. That day, the music was jovial and extremely loud and made the crowds cheer. The noise of the drum beats was soon joined by the raucous voices of the sorko, the praise singers, which filled the air above the courtyard. The sorkos were descendants of the Jengu, the magical water spirits who protected the domain of Imanje, the Goddess of the River. The sorkos believed that their songs, praise-poems and music protected the King from evil spirits.

Ten personal pages, all holding large shields and long swords, elaborately decorated with gold, entered the courtyard. They stood to attention, completely motionless, with only their eyes moving left and right as they scanned the perimeters for possible intruders to the King's arrival. The Kings' pedigree dogs, adorned in gold collars, entered the courtyard next. They too stood on guard, panting in the heat of the morning sun.

It was obvious to Mwari that either the Songhai warriors held their King in very high regard and considered it their most important role to protect his being and entrench his power through their presence, or that they had a pervading fear that the King's power was somehow at risk and their presence was to prevent him from being removed from power.

The air carried a feeling of nervous anxiousness. The sorkos' voices suddenly grew even louder, when a large man stepped into the courtyard. The crowds shouted for their Dali. It was the first time that the sisters had set eyes on King Sonni-Ali and they were mildly amused at how similar in looks he appeared to their own Holy Mother Goddess. He too, was adorned with many gold necklaces, which totally hid his thick neck from view. His forearms were also covered in gold bracelets. He appeared very effeminate. Even his voice, which was very soft, could not be considered to be the voice of a powerful king, since it sounded very much like that of a young boy. It was widely known that a Songhai King did not raise his voice in public. He spoke through his herald, a fat man, who stood stalwartly by his side, taking his instructions and then conveying same to Aten, Mwari and the others.

"Our King does not like strangers in his kingdom. Explain your presence here?

Aten addressed the King on behalf of the group. He began by bending down and taking a handful of earth and throwing it over his head, as was customary when approaching the King. He then introduced himself and the others.

"That is all good and well. Our King welcomes you Lord Aten. It is an honour to have you visit our humble city. But, why are you here? It is not often that a great one such as you, ventures this far west of Ka." said the herald.

"These women and these men," said Aten pointing to Mwari and his party, "They are on a mission for the Holy Mother Goddess from the Great City of Catal Huyuk to locate the pieces of the Turquoise Figurine and reunite them so that the Turquoise Goddess may return to our beloved Ka."

The herald wanted to answer Aten but was summarily stopped when the King raised his bulbous forefinger, which was adorned with several gold rings. Uncharacteristically, the King responded to Aten personally,

"It has been too long that my kingdom and the kingdoms of my friends and enemies alike, all throughout Ka, have been plagued by chaos. This feud between you, Lord Aten and the Goddess Luna, has brought devastation to my people. Her hate for you has elicited a violent reaction from Luna. Her torrential rains, which fall indiscriminately over my city, swell the river. This, in turn places the Great Mosque and my palace at risk. Over the years we have taken precautions and raised the height of the platform on which the mosque is built, but there has not been much that my people could do to prevent their crops from washing away or their livestock from drowning or falling sick. Am I to believe that you now mean no harm to me and my people?"

"I have seen the error of my ways and seek to help these people in their quest. I no longer desire being at odds with Luna, but my change of heart has not been enough to convince Luna to end the feud. She is determined to make their mission fail. She has done everything to stop them. Their success will bring an end to Luna's malicious ways. We need your help to achieve this."

King Sonni-Ali looked intrigued by the notion that the great Lord Aten needed his help.

"What is it that I can do?"

"We have it on good authority that the Great Mosque houses many great treasures. One of those is the Khatim."

"Yes, the eight pointed star. It represents the seal of the Prophets and has mythical powers." Aten nodded his head.

"At its centre is a lapis lazuli stone. When the Turquoise Figurine was shattered many moons ago, a piece of the figurine found its way here, to the great spiritual and educational centre of Ka. The stone in the Khatim is a piece of the Turquoise Figurine."

"And you want me to give this valuable artefact to you, one which has been in the care of my people for thousands of years?"

"Your kingdom will cease to exist if we fail in our mission. Life as we know it, hangs in the balance. You hold the power to bring back the Turquoise Goddess. Your kingdom and your people will be even more prosperous and stronger if you help us."

"And if I choose not to?"

"You know the wrath of Luna and the devastation that her vengeance creates. How often has the river flooded its banks under the weight of continuous rains and ferocious winds? You know that Luna directs the wrath of the Goddess of the Winds and if we fail to bring the Elementals into balance, she will completely destroy your kingdom. The Great Mosque, which has stood for thousands of years, will be reduced to mud and all the villages, for miles and miles, will know hardship when their crops rot and their livestock drown." cautioned Aten.

King Sonni-Ali paused for a moment and appeared to be giving Aten's words some serious thought. Minutes dragged by. The silence was then punctuated by a loud commotion emanating from the back of the crowds. The King and his entourage looked annoyed by the intrusion. After some minutes, the King's Jenne-Koi made his way forward through the crowds. He whispered some news in the ear of the herald, who in turn relayed the message to the King, who did not appear pleased by what he heard, for the veins on his thick neck started to bulge.

"You must think me a fool, Lord Aten. I almost believed your fervent pleas for help, but recent events have, sadly for you, revealed the true reason for your unexpected appearance in my kingdom." Aten looked at the others. He did not understand the King's meaning.

"Let's not play games, shall we?"

"I assure you, we have no ulterior motives for being here?"

"Well, why then are you travelling with a traitor and a criminal?"

The King nodded to his military commander, who wasted no time in bringing forward Fezzan and Fera. Nena gasped. Feur's worst fears had been realised. She had hoped that Fera and Fezzan would have stayed out of sight, but obviously one of the many inhabitants of the city had reported their presence to the authorities. The locals owed complete and utter loyalty to the King and no doubt had ratted on the presence of strangers in their city.

"They are not traitors or criminals. The girl is the ward of Mwari here. She is sister to these girls." said Aten, as he pointed to Mwari and then the other sisters.

"I do not mean the girl. I could not care less about her. I mean him. His name is Fezzan and he is of the Garramantes tribe, the arch enemy of my people. They have for centuries pillaged and raided their way through the Great Desert. They have robbed my people of their wealth and stolen my slaves. This man is guilty of treachery and if it is the last thing that I shall ever do, I will bring him to justice. Seize him. Throw him in prison. He will stand trial for his deeds and if found guilty, he will die by his sword. A fitting death really, for a man who lived life by his sword."

As the soldiers took Fezzan away, Fera grabbed onto Fezzan and would not let him go.

"You cannot do this! He is no longer the leader of the Garramantes. Please, great King, I beg you to show mercy."

Neither the King nor the soldiers took any notice of Fera's cries. She was dismissively pushed aside and left sobbing in a heap on the floor. Her sisters ran to her aid. Before the King left the courtyard, he whispered something into his herald's ear, which the herald made known to them all,

"Dali, will mercifully release you all. You will not face any charges, but you will be kept for the night under armed guard in case you attempt some ill-fated heroic act. You are however, summoned to attend the trial of the traitor, Fezzan of the Garramantes, in the morning."

With those words, the entire royal entourage left the courtyard and the crowds dispersed. The Songhai people always enjoyed attending the King's public audiences, but that day they had got more of a show than usual. As they left the courtyard, they whispered excitedly to each other that they would be returning the next day to learn the fate of the accused. Mwari and the others were left behind to console Fera,

"We will save him, Fera." said Mwari sympathetically.

"You can't be sure of that. The Songhai obviously hate the Garramantes. As long as they consider him to be one of them, his fate is sealed."

Aten and Mwari exchanged worried looks. They would have to think long and hard about the best strategy going forward. They knew that if anything happened to Fezzan, it would break Fera and without her fighting spirit, their chances of success at finding the remaining pieces of the Turquoise Figurine and reaching Ife would soon fade away into oblivion.

They were all told to return to the house that they had first been detained in during their first night in Jenne. It took a while to encourage Fera to stop crying, but when she did, she sat with the others, as they anticipated the occurrence of events the next day.

"Can Fezzan be assured of a fair trial?" asked Daniel.

"The Songhai kingdom is widely regarded as having a strong justice system. They have two forms of justice. One is Royal justice and the other is Islamic justice. Fezzan has been charged with treachery, their highest form of wrongdoing. King Sonni-Ali will most probably hear the matter and dispense his punishment if Fezzan is found guilty." said Aten.

"But the King obviously hates him. He has already tried him. You heard him. He said Fezzan was guilty and he would do everything in his power to see him punished. There can be no justice tomorrow." said Jadon.

He did not like saying so and regretted being so brutally honest, especially when he saw Fera's reaction. She looked truly devastated. Their heated conversation was interrupted with a loud bang on their door. A Songhai soldier explained dutifully that they had a visitor. As a tall, skinny man, who wore a white robe and carried a bundle of large manuscripts, was ushered into the room, the soldier abruptly closed the door behind him. Aten stood up and walked towards the man.

"Everyone, this is Al-Sadi. He is a scholar and a jurist. He will assist us to understand the finer points of Songhai criminal law. He will represent Fezzan at his trial." The man nodded and enquired after everyone's health, as was customary. He sat down and started paging through the dusty old manuscripts. The room was silent. Everyone waited with baited breath for him to speak. After several minutes, he spoke in a firm, yet calm voice,

"I have met with the accused and I have consulted the ancient manuscripts. Our best course of action is to secure a hearing before the Qadi. I believe that we stand a good chance to petition the King to recuse himself from hearing this matter. If we are successful in doing so, we can then ask the Qadi to pardon Fezzan."

"I don't understand. Who is the Qadi?" asked Fera.

"He is a judge responsible for administering law according to our faith."

"Would the King allow this to happen?" asked Mwari.

"He may not have a choice in the matter. The King can only hear cases involving treachery by Songhai citizens. Fezzan is not from this land."

Fera's spirits had somewhat revived with the appearance of Al-Sadi. He offered her a reason to hope.

"Will this tactic work?" asked Aten.

"I believe that we shall be successful in our petition before the King." said Al-Sadi. Everyone sighed with relief.

"I thought that this latest incident would permanently derail our mission. I am so relieved to hear otherwise." said Daniel.

"Yes, it is good news, but we must not be too hasty to assume that things will go off as we have discussed. My years' of legal practice have taught me to be cautiously optimistic." added Al-Sadi.

"Even if we manage to have the matter heard before the Qadi, it will still leave Fezzan to face a trial under Islamic law. That is another matter all in of itself."

"One hurdle at a time, I say. Let's all get some rest tonight so we can face tomorrow with renewed strength." said Jadon.

Fera knew that she would never rest, not until Fezzan was a free man and most definitely, not a moment before the trial was over.

The dawn of the next day approached quickly and before the sisters knew it, they found themselves in the Songhai

Palace courtyard once again. The fanfare associated with the King's entry the day before was notably absent. There were no drums and no sorkos. The mood was serious and contemplative. The crowds, which were even larger than the day before, watched silently as Al-Sadi addressed the King and expounded the same reasoning which he had explained to Aten, Mwari and the others the night before, which was that the King lacked the power to oversee Fezzan's hearing because it was a matter to be handled by religious law not royal law.

The King listened intently to Al-Sadi's argument and then consulted his most trusted advisors. Those watching could clearly observe that the King was extremely displeased by what he was being advised. It was clear that he had had his mind set on prosecuting and punishing Fezzan. One might even have argued that he had already seen no other outcome other than Fezzan's guilt and subsequent death. Begrudgingly, the King had no choice but to capitulate when his advisers told him that Al-Sadi's legal argument was indeed correct. The King then communicated his decision through his herald,

"The King has taken counsel from his learned advisors. Your petition is hereby granted. This matter shall be heard before the Qadi. He shall determine whether to proceed with any charges against the accused. These proceedings shall adjourn until noon, whereafter the accused shall answer to the charges of treachery and slave raiding."

The idea of a trial under religious law, which in the case of the Songhai kingdom was Islamic law, filled Mwari with fear. He had seen both sides of a religious trial. He had stood in both the shoes of the accuser and the accused. He put on a brave face for the sisters, especially Fera, but he was all too aware of what could go wrong.

Al-Sadi had advised that a hearing before the Qadi offered Fezzan the best chance of having the charges against him dismissed. That was due to several reasons; one being that the Qadi was a man of honour who had to be free, Muslim, sane, not convicted of any crime and educated in the law. He would thus apply the principles and rules according to the law, the Qur'an and his own unbiased sense of equity. Secondly, although appointed by the King, the only duty that the Qadi owed to the King was to apply the law as dictated by the Holy Scriptures. He did not have to apply the law as demanded by the King or by the King's will.

Al-Sadi reassured Mwari that the Qadi was thus objective and trustworthy. The fact that the Qadi's judgement was final, made Mwari feel slightly uneasy, but he decided to reserve his evaluation of whether a trial in such a manner was the best choice, until after the proceedings.

A couple of hours later, everyone sat silently in the courtyard waiting for the trial to begin. Nobles, villagers and merchants alike, watched patiently for the arrival of the Qadi. Fera wanted to sit as close to Fezzan as she could, but the dictates of the proceedings meant that he had to sit alone on the far end of the courtyard with only Al-Sadi to keep him company. Distance did not stop Fera from making eye contact with Fezzan. The once strong and seemingly invincible man, whom she had come to know, had been slightly tamed by the experience of being arrested and put on trial. Fezzan, nevertheless, smiled and winked at her. Her presence gave him strength and hope that everything would work out in the end, as long as they were together. Fezzan was also grateful to see the faces of Aten, Mwari and the others. They all barely knew him, yet they were putting themselves and their mission in jeopardy to save him. He appreciated such selflessness.

At precisely noon, the Qadi, dressed in a white robe and carrying a copy of the Qur'an covered in green binding, entered the courtyard and took his place at the centre of a large table. Feur noticed that he was rather old, just like Joab had been. Joab had also been a religious man, albeit a devotee to the Jewish faith.

After the Qadi had introduced himself to everyone, explained the order of proceedings and the nature of his role and had given a stern warning to all those spectators present at the trial, that he would not tolerate unacceptable outbursts of any kind, he instructed the Plaintiff to lead their evidence against the Defendant, who was Fezzan. One of the King's own military generals, the Jenne-Koi, stood up to lead evidence against Fezzan.

"Learned Qadi, this man, the Defendant, goes by the name of Fezzan. He is one of the Garramantes tribe. In fact, he is their leader." Al-Sadi jumped up to object,

"The leader of the Garramantes is a man called Imouharen, not the Defendant."

"You will get your chance to lead evidence." instructed the Qadi, "For now, I will allow the Plaintiff to speak fully. You will be granted the same right."

Al-Sadi returned to his seat. It was obvious that the Plaintiff's strategy was to twist evidence and facts in their favour. The Jenne-Koi continued,

"Be that as it may, under the Defendant's leadership, the Garramantes tribe has embarked on many raids against our King, our Kingdom and our people. On the Defendant's particular command and instruction, the Garramantes have pillaged our lands, our crops and they have stolen countless numbers of our slaves. Numerous merchants are here to testify that they have fallen victim to the brutality and treachery of the Garramantes. Many seated here today, will testify that they saw Fezzan personally lead and participate in the raids and pillaging against them. It is an inescapable truth that this man seated here, is an enemy to our people and for his crimes, he must be found guilty and punished accordingly. His acts are an insult to our beloved Dali and all our hard-working people, who struggle to make a living, which the Garramantes have on so many occasions robbed us of."

As the Jenne-Koi spoke and pointed to the merchants and the Songhai villagers, their eyes followed his every word and gesture and they gave him their uninterrupted attention. They gasped, nodded their heads, looked sad and then appeared betrayed, as if on cue. Their reactions appeared totally convincing. Fera and her sisters looked around them. Even their presence drew sharp looks of disapproval from the villagers, for they were seen as enemies of the Songhai nation.

After the Jenne-Koi had spoken, he led the evidence of several merchants, all of whom had in one way or another fallen prey, as he asserted, to the Garramantes' greed and brutality. It was the testimony of one particular merchant which captivated the full scope of the shock and horror of the crowd.

"Our camel train was stopped. The exports from Jenne were pillaged. Our Master was brutally stabbed to death. The men and our slaves were then taken to Garama to work in the tunnels." said the merchant.

"Did you see the man who killed your master?" The merchant pointed to Fezzan.

"And did you see the Defendant instruct his tribe to take the slaves and men of your master?"

The merchant nodded. Mutterings and whispers echoed through the crowds. It was seemingly an open and shut case. Fezzan was obviously guilty of treachery and slave raiding. The Jenne-Koi then sat down, smugly confident that there was no evidence that could possibly be led to rebut such testimony. The Qadi looked to Al-Sadi,

"Learned Qadi, the Defendant admits that he killed the Master of this man and that he then took his men and slaves." Everyone gasped, including Mwari and the others.

"What is he doing? Is he mad? You cannot admit to the very crimes that you are accused of doing." whispered Gibeon to Jadon.

"Fezzan is done for?" replied Jadon. Feur overheard them. She grabbed Fera's hand tightly to reassure her. Al-Sadi continued,

"It is a well-known fact that Fezzan is the first born son of the Great Sultan Muhammed of the Almohad Kingdom. It is a lesser known fact that Fezzan was cruelly sold into slavery by his own brother, Khaldun. Fezzan was sold as a slave to the Garramantes. He was beaten and humiliated and forced into slave raiding. Everyone who reads the holy word knows that a slave is not equal to his master. A Master can exercise free will, a slave cannot. Fezzan was forced for years to execute the instructions of his Garramantes' Masters. Thus, any wrongdoing committed by Fezzan, whilst he was a slave, cannot be imputed to him. His Master is the one who should be held to account. It would be right and just to show mercy on one who had no mercy shown to him, one who was sold into slavery by his own kin; one who was forced to do unspeakable acts against others at the behest of his slave Masters. I ask, learned Qadi, that this court show mercy on this poor man." The Jenne-Koi stood up once again,

"Mercy, to a man who became the leader of the Garramantes! The Defendant was no mere slave of their tribe. He rose to a position of significant power. The holy word only permits lawful enslavement when a slave is captured in war or is born into slavery. The Defendant was neither captured in war nor was he born a slave. Thus, the accused cannot be considered to be a slave in the legal sense. I would further argue that even if the Defendant was initially sold into slavery, he did not remain in that state. It is obvious that the Garramantes tribe allowed the Defendant to become their most prized fighter and then their most feared slave raider, so valuable he became to them, that when their leader died, the Defendant was chosen to be their leader. The Holy word states that slave Masters can allow their slaves to earn their freedom and I submit that the Defendant earned his freedom. Thus, as a free man, he can and he must be held to account for the wrongs which he has committed against our people."

It was clear that in the Jenne-Koi, Al-Sadi faced a ruthless and skilled opponent, who was well versed in both the legal and religious principles. His argument seemed to have resonated with the Qadi, for he stared intently and nodded repeatedly, as though he agreed with the arguments of the Jenne-Koi.

The first-hand account of the merchant and his murdered master had been convincing. The Qadi seemed convinced that Fezzan was not a slave, both in the legal and the religious sense. Al-Sadi, for a split second, regretted the strategy which he had decided upon. He wondered to himself whether it had been too risky to admit Fezzan's guilt outright? He wondered whether, despite such the explosive admissions of his client, he could turn things around? In all his years as a jurist and scholar, Al-Sadi had never admitted defeat and so he decided then and there that he would not give up the fight to save Fezzan. He would simply have to appeal to the Qadi's profound respect for religion. It was Fezzan's only salvation.

"Learned Qadi, I would like to call forward a witness who will testify to the great kindness and benevolence of the Defendant."

"Bring this person forward then."

Everyone looked around to see the identity of the mysterious witness. A woman stepped forward. She was dressed in a blue djellaba and a qob covered her head. As she removed it, her long, black curly hair glistened in the sunlight. Fera instantly recognised the kind face and even kinder eyes of her dear friend, Zakariya. They made eye contact. Zakariya smiled. Fera's initial joy at seeing her was quickly replaced with fear. Fera felt sick to her stomach, for was Zakariya after all not taken as a slave by the Garramantes? How could her presence possibly help Fezzan in any way? Al-Sadi addressed Zakariya,

"Do you know this man, the Defendant?"

"Yes."

"How do you know him?"

"My husband and I were taken as slaves to the foggaras of the Garramantes."

"How is it that you are no longer there, working in their slave camps?"

"I was removed from the work camp by their leader, Imouharen. I was offered work in his home. I did work for him for a while, but I longed to see my own kin and so he allowed me to return to Jenne, the place of my birth."

"Did this Imouharen decide to free you out of his own accord?"

"No, he was instructed to do so. Well, perhaps instructed is not the correct word. He said that he was encouraged to behave more mercifully towards the slaves."

"Who encouraged him?"

"That man over there." Zakariya pointed to Fezzan.

"What happened to the other slaves that were in the camp with you?"

"Most of the women were freed. I do not know whether the men were also freed."

"You mean to tell me that Imouharen, a known Garramantes tribal leader, freed all the women slaves. Why would he do such a thing?"

"Imouharen told me that his friend, Fezzan, asked him to free me and then encouraged him to stop the trade in slaves and turn the Garramantes' attention to other commercial activities such as agriculture."

"Thank you, Zakariya, your testimony has been most helpful." Al-Sadi then addressed the Qadi directly,

"Learned Qadi, as you know, although our laws permit slavery, a practice which we also condone here in our kingdom, the holy word teaches us that slaves are not mere chattel. They must be treated with kindness and mercy. The Defendant has, without a shadow of a doubt, indulged in this practice, albeit that he was forced into carrying out the will and beliefs of others. I would argue that if a man who was sold into slavery and then, despite his own circumstances was able to act with great kindness and mercy by freeing a slave woman and then by speaking up against slavery and was able to convince a Garramantes' leader to grant the freedom to countless more women slaves, such a man and such kind acts should earn a man great blessings in the hereafter. The Defendant inspired the Garramantes to change their ways and he defied their traditions by giving up his position as their leader. Such a man should be rewarded for his benevolent acts. Learned Qadi, you have the power to pardon the Defendant for his crimes and I would humbly ask that you forgive his past misdeeds."

Before the Qadi could respond, another voice shouted from the crowds. It was only Fezzan who recognised it. He looked up to see his brother Khaldun standing before the Qadi. Fezzan was shocked by the reappearance of Khaldun. They had not seen each other in many years; in fact, not since Khaldun had tricked Fezzan and sold him into slavery. The Qadi reacted harshly,

"You have no standing at this trial. If you are not called as a witness by either side, it would not be proper for me to hear what you have to say. Who are you?"

"My name is Khaldun. The Defendant is my brother." The crowds buzzed with incredulity. The trial had certainly taken an exciting turn.

"Do you object to this man addressing the court?" asked the Qadi to the Jenne-Koi. He said that he did not. Al-Sadi was caught off guard. He did not know whether he should object to Khaldun's presence or not. He looked at Fezzan for instruction. Fezzan simply shook his head as though he had reconciled his mind to the inevitable.

"Since there are no objections, I shall entertain your presence. You may speak." said the Qadi.

"I can only imagine the pitiful tale that this man, my brother, has woven. But, I caution you against believing anything that he has to say. None of what you have been told about him is the truth. This man killed our beloved father, the Sultan Muhammed."

Khaldun wiped a make-believe tear from his eye. It was obvious to all, that he was playing the role of the victim for all that it was worth. The crowds gasped and sighed in disgust at such news. Khaldun continued,

"My brother, the manipulator and conniver, spread lies about me and my younger brother to our father. He turned my father against us. He was so convincing in his manipulations that my father, upon his death, bequeathed him the most fertile piece of land in my father's kingdom. My other brother, Ashir and I, were left to struggle, whilst the Defendant grew richer and richer."

"That is a lie." shouted Fezzan, "I worked the soil and built up my kingdom with my own bare hands and side by side with my people! Instead of improving and building your kingdom, which Father left you, you chose to roam Ka. You joined bandits who burnt and massacred towns and villages. Father would disinherit you, if he were still alive and heard you mouth such lies!"

"This court will not tolerate such outbursts. I would ask that you control your client." demanded the Qadi of Al-Sadi.

Fezzan was extremely angry and it took everything in his power for Al-Sadi to calm him down. Khaldun just smirked at his brother's reaction and continued,

"If those crimes against his own father and his own brothers were not enough, then perhaps this man's crimes against our beloved faith will be? This man committed the worst sin imaginable. He took in Christian refugees who refused to submit to the teachings of our faith. He gave them shelter, but worst of all, he took their money. He sold out our beliefs and the principles of our holy faith. He made a mockery of the valiant acts of great supporters of our faith, such as the courageous Amed Grag. For that, he must be punished and the only punishment fit for such an egregious act, is death."

The crowds roared in support of Khaldun's devotion to his religious beliefs, which were shared by the vast majority of the people who lived in Jenne.

"I will have silence in my court." demanded the Qadi. The crowds immediately subdued.

"The Defendant's response to such allegations?" intimated the Qadi. Fezzan whispered to Al-Sadi.

"Learned Qadi, the Defendant begs leave to address the court directly."

The Qadi nodded in agreement. Fezzan stood up and staring directly at the Qadi and the crowds, he spoke,

"I will not apologise for taking in countless victims persecuted for their religion. I see no wrong in people practising a faith of their own choosing. No-one deserves to be persecuted for believing in a different faith. The peoples of the Great City of Catal Huyuk pray to the Great Spirit. Many of the peoples of Axum follow Judaism. The priests at Lalibela practice the Christian faith. The people at Dendera and Abydos pray to the immortal Gods and Goddesses. Ka is home to many religions. The wisdom of the ages is found in the teachings of many religions and faiths. The holy books, messages, symbols, religious rituals and rites may differ from one faith to the next, but at their very core, they are the same. They all focus on the need to build spirituality based on principles of human kindness, respect and love."

The crowds grew silent. As Fezzan spoke, one could hear a pin drop. Fera felt immensely proud of Fezzan at that precise moment. He was no longer the man who she had first met, feared and despised. He had become the man who she had always hoped he would be. Fezzan knew that he was not a man to cry easily, but he found it hard to hold back a tear after he had finished addressing the court. He looked at Fera's face. She was crying. He saw the love in her eyes. Inwardly, he had the realisation that saying the words which he had, had allowed him, for the first time in many years, to actually become who he had wanted to become, to be the principled and courageous man that his father had always expected him to be. Fezzan felt proud to stand up for that which he believed in.

Khaldun's reaction was the polar opposite of Fezzan's. He appeared incensed by the age-old hatred he held for Fezzan. It was clear that he would die fighting. He attempted to stand up and respond to Fezzan's words, but the Qadi held up his hand.

"Enough! I will not allow this court to be the personal weapon used by one brother against another. I can see that there are many unresolved issues between these brothers, but they do not concern me. I am only concerned with the evidence brought before me. My task is to separate fact from fiction and emotion. If neither the Plaintiff nor the Defendant have anything further to advance," the Qadi looked at the Jenne-Koi and then Al-Sadi, who both shook their heads, "Then I shall adjourn today's proceedingto consider the evidence and render my decision. We shall resume in two hours."

As the Qadi stood to exit the courtyard, all who sat before him, similarly arose, for the Qadi commanded great respect, not only for his knowledge of the legal principles, but also given his mastery of the principles of the Islamic faith.

Two hours proved to be the longest wait for Fera and the others. They all remained behind in the courtyard awaiting the Qadi's final decision. The wait gave them time to digest and discuss the sudden appearance of Khaldun.

"I thought that Khaldun was dead?" asked Fera of Fezzan.

"So did I. I have no idea where he's been all this time. I lost contact with my family when I was sold to the Garramantes."

"Your brother has allied himself with Amed Grag. He has opted to do the evil bidding of Luna." added Aten.

Fezzan wanted to ask how Aten would know such information, but then knew better of it. His train of thought was further interrupted when Aten continued,

"He led the Almohad armies joined by the Beja, Amed Grag and their armies to attack the Bar Nagish."

The sisters did not know who the man called Amed Grag was and they found it difficult to follow the conversation, but when Aten mentioned the name of the Bar Nagish, their interest was piqued.

"Who is this Amed Grag?" asked Fera.

"He is known far and wide by the name Amed, the Left-handed. He hailed from the ancient city of Adal in Kush. It is believed that his father was a very rich and powerful merchant. He led several minor skirmishes and minor raids on Axum. Like his father, Amed Grag was also motivated by wealth and religion. He wanted to stop Axum's constant attacks on Kush lands as well as end King Ezana's insatiable demands for land taxes and tributes from the Kush merchants. He also wanted control over the rich pasturelands in the mountainous highlands of Axum. Amed Grag's father and later he himself refused to pay tribute to Ezana."

"But why would my brother ally himself with Amed Grag? I know my brother to be many things, but I cannot imagine him joining forces with such men."

"The answer is rather simple. Your brother wanted power as much as Amed Grag did. It was expedient for them to join forces, birds of a feather flock together, so they say. If Amed Grag and his allies had succeeded in snatching control of the Port of Adolos from the Bar Nagish, they could easily have turned their sights on Axum and its wealth. Control of the sea trade for goods such as salt, gold, ivory and slaves had proved too irresistible for such greedy war-mongers."

"So, the wealth of Axum and the port of Adolos was the ultimate prize?" asked Mwari. Aten nodded.

"When Khaldun had obviously run his kingdom into the ground and turned his people against him, he had found

himself left with little or no political and economic might."
Fezzan was trying to understand his brother's motivations.

"Exactly! And that is where Amed Grag came in. Once his power was firmly entrenched in Axum, your brother would have had the full support of Axum's armies and wealth. He would then have been in an excellent position to demand total loyalty from his subjects. " said Aten.

"Which, knowing him, he would have turned such power against his own people."

Fezzan's words were tinged with deep sadness. He could not understand how a man could be so easily turned by hatred, especially one who had been raised with such love.

"Since we know that King Ezana is still firmly at the helm in Axum and the Bar Nagish still controls the Port of Adolos, what became of Amed Grag then? Did he even launch such an attack?" asked Jadon.

"He most certainly did attack the Port of Adolos, but when he realised that his armies alone could not defeat the nine thousand strong infantry of the Bar Nagish, he sought the help of a higher power."

"Who?" asked Feur, thoroughly engrossed in Aten's tale.

"Someone we are all familiar with."

"Don't tell me? It can't be Luna, can it?" asked Daniel sarcastically.

"Of course, wherever there is mischief to be made, she is never far away. She caused the winds to blow ferociously over the port city. The soldiers could barely stand upright, much less guard their positions, the winds were so forceful. It became truly unbearable for the Bar Nagish's soldiers to fend off the attack from Amed Grag's forces. You have all probably heard it said that the Bar Nagish is a really fearless warrior. Well, it is true. He is one of the most fearless men that I have had the privilege of knowing, but he is also the most sensible. He wanted to continue fighting, but knew that his soldiers were grossly outnumbered and outmanoeuvred by the combined forces of Amed Grag and Luna's evil magic."

"So what did he do?" asked Nena.

"The only thing possible; he prayed for my help."

"That makes total sense. How did you help them?" asked Fera, recalling how Aten had come to her aid once before.

"I matched her power with mine, wind against fire. I instructed the soldiers to light fires around the perimeters of the Bar Nagish's castle. They did not want to at first, since they thought that the fires would rage uncontrollably in the winds and set the city ablaze. But I would never have let that happen. I gave Luna a little bit of her own medicine."

"What did you do?" asked Feur. "Whatever it was, I am sure Luna deserved it." Aten smiled naughtily.

"I caused the summer temperatures to rise under a scorching sun. This heat mixed with the turbulent wind, caused whirling eddies of air and fire to sweep towards Amed Grag and his army. Their horses were spooked and ran off in the opposite direction, with their riders hanging on for dear life. Their infantry was caught in the path of the fire; most were burnt alive. The ones that lived were finished off by the Bar Nagish, who swooped in and killed the lot."

"And Amed Grag?" asked Daniel.

"He came face to face with the Bar Nagish. With his energies spent and his body impaired by the blaze which swept through his army, he was no match for the Bar Nagish, who pounced on him with an unbridled ferocity. The Amed Grag's right hand was severed from his body by the sword of the Bar Nagish. He kept the hand as a memento of his great victory." Nena and Boise grimaced at the idea of a hand being severed so brutally.

"And that gave us a defeated left-handed man. Did he die?" asked Mwari.

"No-one knew for certain. He simply vanished off the face of Ka. It took me quite a while to track his movements. I suspect Luna gave him and Khaldun safe haven. Who knows, perhaps that is where they have remained hidden all these years."

"I thought that I knew the worst of my brother's ill-fated deeds. Selling his own flesh and blood into slavery was unforgivable, but such crime was committed against only me. These evil alliances with Amed Grag and Luna have caused thousands to die. Such acts will never be forgiven. I had always hoped that Khaldun would atone for his evil acts against others and against me. I might have even forgiven him had he done so, but what I have heard said here today, has shut both my mind and my heart to my brother. To me, he is now truly dead."

Fera embraced Fezzan. His powerful arms wrapped around her protectively. Little did she realise then, that embracing her, gave him greater solace and strength than she would ever know.

The Qadi returned later that afternoon with an unequivocal decision, Fezzan was not guilty of the crimes that he had been charged with. More than just an acquittal, Fezzan was pardoned for the wrongs that he had committed whilst with the Garramantes, based on the strength of his compassion shown towards Zakariya and the many women slaves whom he helped to free. The Qadi believed that his acts were a symbol of great benevolence and that his sins should be expiated.

Fezzan was relieved when the decision was read out. He had feared for so long that he would one day be punished by man or by Allah, for his evil acts. He had been given a reprieve, a second chance at living and he silently vowed, in the presence of the woman he loved, that he would not take such blessings for granted. He would live each day devoted to the pursuit of good and happiness. He had dreams of one day returning home with his bride. He was determined to resurrect his kingdom and make it great and prosperous once again. He did not know when or how he would accomplish such dream, but he had every faith that it would become a reality. He felt invincible with the love of his life at his side and the promise of a new day to look forward to.

Later that night, everyone was unexpectedly summoned before Sonni-Ali. For Mwari, such appearance felt like an unnecessary delay. He wanted to leave Jenne as quickly as they possibly could, but there was still one piece of outstanding business which they all had with the King which had to be resolved, one way or the other. They had expected some resistance on the part of the King in handing over the piece of the Turquoise Figurine, simply because it was somewhat of a religious artefact, but they had not expected that they would have to face yet another onslaught of accusations and threats, that time from an unexpected arrival in Jenne.

Fezzan was once more surprised when he saw not only his brother, Khaldun, standing with Sonni-Ali as they entered the King's chambers, but Amed Grag himself. His misshapen figure, with his missing right hand and large scar across the length of his face, could be recognised anywhere.

Amed Grag, in turn, was unperturbed by Fezzan's presence. It was the sight of Aten which seemed to elicit his strongest reaction. Once Mwari, the men and the sisters all stood before the King, it was Aten who spoke first,

"Great King, before we depart from your kingdom, we ask once more that you return the piece of the Turquoise Figurine to these women so that they may succeed in their mission." The King looked at both Khaldun and then at Amed Grag. He then spoke,

"It is a matter which I have had many sleepless nights thinking about. You are asking that I relinquish a valuable piece of my people's history. I am not sure whether it would be fair to do so."

"The legend and destiny of the Turquoise Goddess belongs to all the peoples of Ka, not only the people of Jenne." exclaimed Daniel.

Mwari took hold of Daniel's arm as though to suggest that he remain calm and allow Aten to handle the situation.

"That may be, but why should I hand it over to you all. You, who keep company with individuals whom I regard to be morally corrupt." It was obvious that Sonni-Ali was referring to Fezzan.

"The Qadi has pardoned Fezzan of all wrongdoing. Surely that leaves the matter there. Besides the mission to reunite the pieces of the Turquoise Figurine rests on the courageous shoulders of these young women. They have travelled long and fought hard to accomplish their mission. They have risked their lives to save all of us, including you and your people. They need all our help to succeed." added Aten.

"It has come to my attention that it is not simply a question of giving you what you want. I have other factors which must be considered and other allegiances which must be honoured. I cannot make a decision that will place my kingdom and my people in harm's way."

"We are not asking you to put your people in harm's way. If you help us, you will ultimately help your kingdom and your people." said Aten.

"Who are these other allegiances of whom you speak?" asked Mwari. King Sonni-Ali looked to Amed Grag and Khaldun.

"Oh, I see, you mean them, but how can helping us affect your relationship with your allies?" asked Mwari.

Amed Grag and Khaldun had been silent until then, but they stepped forward,

"We have been loyal trading partners to the Songhai King and have respected his kingdom's borders when we could so easily have pillaged them and taken all the gold and riches of this land for ourselves." said Amed Grag, who spoke directly to the King. Khaldun echoed Amed Grag's sentiments.

"We have shown you our loyalty and now it is time for you to reciprocate, by refusing these people's request. They do not have you and your kingdom's best interests at heart. You know the kind of man Fezzan is. I do not care what transpired before the Qadi. He is as guilty as he ever was of stealing from your people. If you help them now, they will see you as nothing more than a weak man; a weak and feeble king who can bend to the will of the mighty Aten. These lands have suffered because of Aten's wrath and now you are considering helping the very man who has been the source of so much grief and devastation for your kingdom." shouted Khaldun.

It was obvious that Khaldun intended to intimidate King Sonni-Ali with his manipulations. Amed Grag opted for a harsher and less subtle approach to convince the King not to help Aten.

"If you side with them, you must consider our alliance dead. You will become our enemy and so will your kingdom and its people. With the help of our new allies, who are considerable in number, we shall make it our mission to bring your rule to an end. It will give us great pleasure to take control of the riches of Jenne."

Amed Grag scowled and hissed as he spoke. Fera thought that he looked like a man possessed. Hatred and anger seemed to consume his entire being. Aten could not allow Amed Grag and Khaldun to malign Fezzan or anyone else for that matter.

"King Sonni-Ali, before you side with these two, I hope you will allow me the opportunity to defend our position."

The King waved his hand in the air to indicate his assent to Aten's proposal. Mwari was not sure if the King's half-hearted gesture meant that he was angry or that he was just plain irritated.

"These two men," began Aten, referring to Amed Grag and Khaldun, "They are guilty of the very thing that they accuse Fezzan of. They too have roamed and pillaged the kingdoms bordering the Great Sky River. They too have allied themselves with individuals whose reputations leave much to be desired. I see very little difference between the Beja tribes and the Garramantes. The difference between Fezzan and his brother is, however, night and day. No self-respecting person would sell his own flesh and blood into slavery, as Khaldun did to Fezzan or falsely imprison his youngest brother, as he did with Ashir. Fezzan did much that was unforgivable, but his atonement has brought him the forgiveness and pardon of the Qadi and that should be enough. Fezzan has proven himself to be a hero. He did not have to come to the aid of these women in order to help them to achieve their mission, but he did. He chose to accompany them to Jenne, when he knew full well that his own personal safety would be jeopardised by doing so, but he did it anyway. Khaldun and Amed Grag have never been held to account for their egregious actions, nor have they shown themselves worthy of your esteem and respect, great King. They should be locked away." Aten's voice had become more pitched, as his level of emotion had increased. He had the King's complete attention and so continued,

"I believe that a man is judged by the company that he keeps. If you, King Sonni-Ali, are to be judged by your people and by future generations, as a great man and an even greater King, then you must think twice about keeping the company of these two. They are traitors and thieves, who themselves are outcasts in their own kingdoms. They have no genuine motives here. Amed Grag only covets the riches of others, be they the riches from the sea trade of the Bar Nagish or the wealth of the Songhai kingdom. He will do anything and say anything to get his hands on the ill-gotten gains of decent people. It will only be a matter of time before they will manipulate and connive you out of your birthright. Their greedy eyes see only the Songhai riches to plunder. You and your people matter not. I implore you to see them for who they really are."

The room filled with an uncomfortable silence. It was obvious, once again, that the indecision of King Sonni-Ali was his achilles heel. Mwari thought then that he despised weak men; men who knew that they should take the path to righteousness, but chose the complete opposite. The right decision was staring the King squarely in the eyes and yet he remained oblivious. After a few tentative moments, he instructed,

"I need some time to consider my decision. I will not be rushed nor cajoled into making a hasty decision that will not benefit me or my people."

The King marched from the room with his many attendants rushing after him. The King had spoken and thus no amount of pleading or convincing from either side, would have done any further good. Aten reconciled himself to the fact that their fate lay in the hands of a man whose mind had been easily corrupted by lies. Aten's only hope was that the dark rot of cowardice, greed and fear had not yet reached the inner vestiges of King Sonni-Ali's heart.

Mwari had a similar thought, only he had no hope that the King would see reason and live the values of kindness and decency. Mwari had long since abandoned the notion that men could be trusted to do the right thing. His experiences thus far on their mission and with the sisters, had given him a glimmer of hope, but such light burnt very dimly indeed, it was nothing more than the mere flicker of a candle, burning in the vast expanse of the Great Desert.

Such light would be impossible to see and would be barely enough to light one's way through the darkness.

***

That night, King Sonni-Ali experienced a sleepless night. He tossed and turned in the folds of his sumptuous bed. His dreams were filled with distressing images. He dreamt that he stood before a beautiful silver lake, which shimmered under a radiant full moon. The image of a beautiful young girl reflected on the water's surface. He did not recognise her face. Initially, she appeared calm and then quite suddenly, she began to flail in the water, as though she was drowning. He dove in to rescue her, but as he reached the centre of the lake, to his great shock and surprise, the girl was no longer there. He felt bewildered and confused, as though the moon's reflections on the water's surface, were playing tricks on him. He swam back to shore. He grew more and more tired as he swam. His legs felt like lead weight and he struggled to keep his head above water. When tiredness overwhelmed him, he found himself sinking deeper and deeper into the water, until he lost the will power and the strength to fight for survival. As his lungs filled with water and he sank into the dark depths below, he awoke in terror, with large beads of sweat running down his forehead. His bedding was damp and smelt of salty sweat.

Sonni-Ali was not a particularly learned man. He had always relied upon the wisdom of his scholars or clerics, but even he understood the poignant significance of his dream. He was a man burdened by an enormously difficult decision, one which would determine his future and that of his kingdom and his people. Should he believe the words of Aten and trust that Aten was not lying about Luna or should he continue to ally himself with Luna? He rationalised that if he sided with Luna, Aten's wrath could be greater than it had been for many years? The Songhai had suffered for years under sweltering heat conditions. Aten's feud with Luna had left death and starvation in its wake.

Who was Aten to accuse Luna of evil, when he himself had been complicit in the crimes committed against the Songhai people?

On the other hand, if he betrayed the alliance with Amed Grag and Khaldun, would his people survive continual attacks by a once loyal ally, turned mortal foe? If the riches of his kingdom were pillaged and plundered, his rule would not survive under such an onslaught. He knew for a fact that Khaldun and Amed Grag had allied themselves with Al Aziz. He knew that Al Aziz and Amed Grag were kindred spirits when it came to their mutual hatred of Axum and of course Aten, given the role that Aten had always played in allying himself against all those who had attacked Axum, Meroe and the Port of Adolos. Sonni-Ali knew that if he now sided against them, Amed Grag would consider such betrayal to be grossly unforgivable. He would stop at nothing to destroy the Songhai Kingdom and its ruler.

Sonni-Ali felt the immense pressure and the even greater weight of the consequences of the decision that he had to make. His jumbled thoughts kept him tossing and turning that night, until the cold light of day began to peep over the horizon. When he could stand his indecision no longer, he jumped out of bed and decided to face the biggest decision of his life, in the only way in which he knew how. He would turn to his faith and the age-old traditions of his people for the answers. He quickly dressed, so that he could visit the Great Mosque at dawn.

The small figure of a powerful king, saying his prayers before the qibla or prayer wall, would be a stark contrast from the three huge box-like minarets of the prayer wall. In the morning sky, high above the Great Mosque, hung a moon in its last quarter. King Sonni-Ali was relieved that the power of moon magic was fading. Soon, its power would have totally dissipated and with it, Luna's power to influence the nations of Ka and the Songhai people. Sonni-Ali saw the moon's transition to an old moon as a sign from above, that perhaps the repercussions of his decision might not be so grave and inauspicious for himself and his people.

Elsewhere on the eastern side of the Mosque, Mwari too, knelt on the sandy earth floors of the prayer hall to offer his prayers. The loud, yet melodic voices of the holy clerics, as they said their morning prayers, were the only external sounds that penetrated the mud walls of the hall. Mwari was grateful for the solitude, since it gave him time to think. His strong devotion to his faith had always steered him in the right direction when life's tough decisions and obstacles had threatened to derail the course of his life, his sanity and his happiness.

Mwari realised then, just how important his faith had been in his life. He had strayed from it for a short time, but he had paid a bitter price for such arrogance. If there was one thing which Mwari had become blatantly aware of since he had embarked on the mission with the sisters, it was that his faith had to be in the forefront of his life. It was his reason for being. It grounded him. Because of it and through it, he became a better and stronger person.

Later that morning, King Sonni-Ali's decision surprised and shocked everyone who stood in his royal chambers. With eager faces and bated breath, everyone waited for the King's pronouncements, which were made once again by the King directly and not by his herald. Fera surmised that such direct communication had to be the result of the great importance of his words. It was also a much more expedient form of communication, thought Fera, since using middle-men to converse, was totally impractical. The King wasted no time in sharing his long-awaited decision.

"I have thought long and hard about this. In fact, I have wrestled with this decision, like no other decision before it. I believe in the power of justice and the rule of law. I also believe in the power of tradition. I see only one clear path before me. My strong faith in the traditions and customs of my people, which have been passed down from one generation to the next, for hundreds of years, will guide me, will guide us all to the truth."

The King's words were baffling to Mwari and his party. No-one understood his exact meaning. The King continued,

"I have decided to follow an age-old Songhai custom to determine guilt and innocence. Admittedly, I am torn between the two versions which have been brought before me. I do not fully believe you, Lord Aten and yet, I also have my doubts about your motives, Amed Grag and Khaldun. To alleviate my doubts, you shall all be required to perform the same ritual."

"This is just plain ludicrous. Our alliance was brokered many moons ago. If our actions have not shown our loyalty and goodwill to your kingdom, then I am not sure what will. I find this most unacceptable. How dare you question our motives in this manner?" shouted Amed Grag.

It was obvious that Amed Grag's words had totally incensed King Sonni-Ali, for he stood up from his highly ornate hand-carved chair and roared uncharacteristically,

"I do not care how my decisions may affect you, Amed Grag. You forget your place. You remain in my kingdom at my pleasure. I have allowed our alliance to continue because it suits me and my kingdom. As easily as I have indulged your presence here, it would be as easy to see you removed!"

Khaldun reached out and touched Amed Grag's one good arm in an attempt to calm him. He knew that any further outbreaks by Amed Grag could permanently scupper their very tenuous relations with the Songhai and if there was one thing which Khaldun feared, it was losing the patronage of his powerful allies. Without Amed Grag and Sonni-Ali's military support, he would never be able to take back control over the Almohad kingdom from his brother Ashir. It was a prize which he coveted above all else, even more than his revenge against Fezzan. Amed Grag realised that it would not be wise to push Sonni-Ali too far, so he remained silent. It was better to indulge the King for the moment. With emotions temporarily under control, Sonni-Ali continued,

"Very well, you shall all drink from the chalice which my herald will present to you. I assure you, it is not poison. It contains water in which a piece of wood from one of our holy trees has been soaked. The bark is bitter and sour to the taste, so you may find that the water is extremely distasteful. You will each take a generous gulp."

One by one, Aten, then Amed Grag and lastly Khaldun were handed the gold chalice and instructed to drink from it. Their contorted facial expressions clearly showed that the water indeed, tasted foul. Almost as instantly as Aten had ingested the liquid, he become violently ill. He vomited the vile-tasting liquid on the floor at his feet. Everyone then turned their attention to Khaldun and Amed Grag. Surprisingly, they seemed to be able to hold down the liquid.

"So, pray tell, what does this little trick prove?" asked Khaldun of King Sonni-Ali, as he wiped his mouth with his sleeve.

"Much, if you must know. My people revere this custom for getting at the truth in a man's words. If a person who partakes of the liquid vomits after drinking it, we believe that he is a man who speaks the truth. If, on the other hand, a man does not vomit up the liquid, his words must not be believed."

"That is complete and utter nonsense! You mean to tell me that you will willingly elect to abandon our alliance on the strength of an old wives' tale. You cannot be serious!" shouted Amed Grag.

"I have never been more serious in my life. If a man cannot believe in the teachings of his own life and his own people, then who must he believe? Perhaps if the two of you had owed more allegiance and shown more respect for your own people and your own customs, you would not be outcasts today." replied Sonni-Ali.

Khaldun and Amed Grag realised that their fate was sealed. They tried to rush towards the door, but their escape was met with resistance from the Songhai warriors, who stood in constant attendance of King Sonni-Ali.

"You are both under arrest. You will have your day in court and should you be found guilty of any crimes against the peoples of Ka, not too mention against me, my rule and my people, I shall be glad to see you both locked away for a very long time."

"You will regret this! You have made a grave error and soon you will be held to account for this miscarriage of justice. You may be able to dispose of us, but it will not be that easy to destroy Luna. I pity you and your pathetic kingdom!"

As Amed Grag was carried away, kicking and screaming, the years of pent up rage and anger spewed in his words.

Khaldun was no less venomous, except his words were directed at Fezzan,

"You will never rule our father's kingdom ever again. You will be doomed to roam the Great Desert, like the murderer that you are!"

There was a time when such words would have struck at the very core of Fezzan's being, but as he stood side by side and hand in hand with Fera, he felt unaffected by his brother's rage and hatred. Only feelings of pity for the promise of a life lost and relief that his father was not there to witness Khaldun's evil demise, filled Fezzan's thoughts. After Amed Grag and Khaldun were dragged from the room, King Sonni-Ali addressed Aten,

"I trust that I shall not rue the day that I decided to ally my kingdom with you and help your mission to reunite the Turquoise Figurine, Lord Aten?" remarked the King.

"Today, you have shown yourself to be a most wise man. It will be a decision that neither you nor anyone who has helped us achieve our ends, will ever come to regret. That is my solemn vow to you. Peace will soon endure all throughout Ka and your people, the Songhai will once again prosper and thrive." replied Aten.

The next day, with the sacred stone in hand, which had remained embedded in the Khatim or eight pointed star and been secretly housed in the Great Mosque for many hundreds of years, Aten, Mwari and their party set out for Ife. As they travelled, Fera was reminded of what Luna had said, 'We are going to Ife, we face Ife, we are returning from Ife'. Her words had proved strangely prophetic. Luna had known then already that they would end up in Ife. She had probably also known of all the holy destinations where they would find the pieces of the Turquoise Figurine, although she had deliberately hidden such information from them. If it had not been for Aten's divine powers and the kindness and assistance of strangers, they would never have made their way across the length and breadth of Ka; across turbulent seas, across vast deserts and over seemingly insurmountably high mountains and deep ravines.

Thankfully, they were finally moving towards their final destination, the Shadow Kingdom of Ife. A world so steeped in mystery and awe that few outsiders had ever ventured into its mythical realm. Fera and her sisters did not know what to expect. Daniel and the other men, however, knew exactly what lay ahead of them. Whether such knowledge had been acquired through real-life experience of having been there before or simply from the pages of dusty old books, which had remained hidden in the recesses of the library of the Great City's Temple in Catal Huyuk, the men agreed that they would remain alert and vigilant. Anything that could happen, was bound to happen in Ife, thoughts which they all tried to push aside, for fear that they could completely derail their mission. There was no turning back. Their mission was almost complete. The destiny of the Daughters of Ka would soon be realised.

8

ABSOLUTION

They all stared into the bright red flames of their campfire. Mwari had instructed his party to camp overnight a short way outside Ife, so that the next day they could ride into Ife, refreshed and ready for what destiny had in store for them. Everyone felt as though they were on the precipice of something great. Excitement and anxiousness permeated the atmosphere in the camp. The group's conversation was frank, yet earnest.

"I can't believe that we have come this far, can you?" asked Feur of her sisters. "I feel as though this journey has profoundly changed me, perhaps forever."

"I feel the same way." replied Nena. "Who would ever have believed that I, who thought this mission to be nothing more than a trip to find a long lost statue, would have climbed mountains and walked through deserts? I always hated walking to the market back home."

Nena laughed, but then was momentarily silent before she continued, "You know, when we left Catal Huyuk, I really did not comprehend just how serious and complex this mission would be."

"How you have changed, Nena. Have you realised, that since we left Dendera, you have not moaned once?"

"I have never moaned?"

Everyone rolled their eyes at Nena as a sign that they totally dismissed her denial as complete fiction.

"No, truly, have I really been so much of a moaner?" Without needing their replies as confirmation of their true feelings, Nena laughed, "I have, haven't I? Well, at least, I had the chance to grow up a little." Aten words brought Nena to consider more serious realisations,

"I believe that life changes and teaches us many things, but we must be open to such change and willing to learn. What have you learned about yourself on your journey, Nena?" asked Aten.

"I have learnt that I am stronger and more confident than people think I am. I have learnt that I am not willing to accept other people's choices for my life. I am the author of my own story. I choose the characters in my story and I choose the storyline. I think that the concept of destiny is difficult to grasp for most women. In Catal Huyuk and every place we have been to since, I have seen with my own eyes, that women seem to accept, often without hesitation or proper consideration, that they must get married, have children and obey their husbands; that certain decisions for their lives have somehow already been made for them, simply because they were born female. I believe that the Gods or the Great Spirit or whichever other deity a person believes in, do not really plan our lives for us or map out our life's path in the stars. They set us on a course, but we are given the power to choose the direction of our lives. I now see that the power to make one's own decisions is the best gift of all. I never did. I saw it as a burden and thought it was far easier just to conform to what society expected of me."

Mwari and his party, with mouths agape, sat incredulous that such profound and insightful words had come out of Nena's mouth.

"Goodness me, you learnt all that! I can't say that we have discovered such deep truths about ourselves." said Jadon, taking the liberty to speak on behalf of himself and Gibeon.

"But, we have learnt not to judge people so quickly. We were quick to underestimate Asaph; God rest his soul. We saw him as an imbecilic oaf, but he proved us wrong. His love, loyalty and support to us all will never be forgotten."

Gibeon took hold of Fera's hand. She reciprocated his warm gesture and was grateful for Jadon's kind words about Asaph. Fera considered whether her impression of Jadon and Gibeon had changed at all.

"My first impression of you two was that you were over-confident and brazen. It was strangely comforting that my sisters and I had such strong protectors. If you think that your roles in our mission have been insignificant, believe me, they haven't." said Fera to Jadon and Gibeon.

"Some of my darkest days were spent trudging through the Al Suud. If it were not for both of you and your relentless strength and courage, I would never have made it. I almost became crippled by my fears of the Ninki Nanka. I must thank you both for keeping me afloat, both literally and figuratively."

"Don't forget, they also found the first piece of the Turquoise Figurine." added Feur.

"That's right, even if they failed to follow my express instructions." said Mwari with the playful look of a father, chiding his naughty children. Jadon and Gibeon just chuckled in response, for they knew Mwari was only joking.

"You've become a lot less serious, Mwari. I speak for everyone when I say that you were very intimidating when we first met. Jadon and I have seen many seasoned soldiers in our time, but you take the prize for being the toughest task master. We knew that you had our backs on and off the battlefield though." said Jadon.

Gibeon thought then how he admired Mwari. He was a deft hand at fighting and a keen military strategist. Such skills had come to the fore many times, including the time when Mwari had designed plans to protect Meroe.

"I was dreadfully scared of you, Mwari." said Boise.

"It did not seem like that. You were the first to approach and talk to me. I did not mean to scare anyone. It has been my way for many years to keep to myself. Such remoteness has often been interpreted by many as uncaring and brusque. But that is not me."

"I know. We are firm friends now. I think of you as a father figure and I am not scared of you anymore. You're just a big old bear in my eyes, with a soft and warm heart, which is well and truly hidden by that less than approachable exterior of yours." said Boise.

She was grateful that their friendship had grown in leaps and bounds. Daniel quietly agreed with Boise's opinion of Mwari, but he could not help but wonder whether there was so much more about Mwari that remained an enigma to them all.

"I am grateful for that friendship, Boise. You have truly evolved from that timid young girl that I first met. I know you were not a girl then. Of course, you were a young woman; you are a young woman still, but to me you have evolved from a girl to a strong and courageous woman. Few others would have survived a bite from a rabid dog and few others would have fought and succeeded in escaping the clutches of an Eloko. You should be very proud of all that you have accomplished."

Boise smiled. Mwari thought then how much that smile reminded him of his own daughter. At least, he had not disappointed Boise, but her smiling face brought home painful memories of just how much he had lost through his own folly. Fera saw a glimmer of sadness move across Mwari's face and she decided that she would have none of it.

"Mwari, I liked you the moment we met in the woods by the Charshamba River. I was enraptured by the exciting lands which you spoke of. Do you remember meeting me?" asked Fera.

"I do. Your excitement to leave Catal Huyuk and go on adventures into Ka was something I understood. There was a time that I myself wanted to run away from home and leave everything behind me in search of the great unknown."

"But?" I sense there's a but in there somewhere."

"No but." Mwari hesitated for a moment, "Has it met your expectations, the mission, the adventure, the journey to foreign lands? Has it been as exciting as you thought it would be?" asked Mwari.

Fera would have lied if she had said that such thoughts had never crossed her mind. They had and often.

"There are parts of our journey that I would sooner forget, but I believe that my destiny has led me to this point. My father always called me his wild child and my whole life I have lived up to that reputation. I am grateful for my adventurous streak, for without it, I would never have met this man seated beside me."

Fera looked into Fezzan's eyes. As she spoke, it was as though the outside world was completely shut out and that she and Fezzan were the only two people around,

"I found my kindred spirit, someone with all the qualities that I wanted in a person whom I would one day consider being more than just my friend. He is kind, patient, respects me as a woman and as a person. He values my independence and my mind. He sees me as more than just a simple woman, who must be cosseted and patronised, like many men see their women, weak and senseless objects that can to be bought and sold at will, whether such transactions are the result of slavery or marriage. He sees me as his equal." Fezzan kissed Fera's cheek.

"He knows what's good for him if he did not. We have all seen the wrath of Fera's temper during this journey. And you all thought Mwari was scary? Well, Fera, you were initially very intimidating to me. But I have come to love and accept your quirks." said Daniel.

"My quirks? Speak for yourself. There were many times that your quirks, your continual talking about tombs and mummies and well too many dull things to mention, have driven us all mad. We all know you are very clever, but perhaps at times, you have thought yourself to be far cleverer than you actually are?

"You're right, Fera, no-one knows everything. We all have our limitations. I have learnt that. I must endeavour to be more humble and to hold my tongue at times." said Daniel.

He and Fera had reached a civil, yet slowly warming relationship and he hoped that one day, when he married Boise, Fera would come to see him as a beloved brother.

"As long as you do right by Boise, you are alright in my books?" said Fera.

"And speaking of sisters, you three have tested my patience, sometimes to breaking point, but it has been through your own unique quirks and peculiarities that I have learnt temperance and understanding. You have taught me the true meaning of love and sisterhood and for that I shall be forever grateful." said Fera to her sisters. They hugged each other warmly.

"Aten, what have you learnt? Can a great man such as you, who obviously knows everything, find out something new about himself?" asked Mwari.

"I have rediscovered my humanity. The eyes of the many people whom I have met, some admittedly very hostile and resentful of my past behaviour, have been mirrors to my own soul. They have brought home to me that my actions had terrible consequences; that revenge eats away at a man's soul and renders him blind to all the good that is around him. Forgiving Luna has been the biggest challenge of my life, but it is in forgiving her that I shall find true redemption."

"Do you think that we have heard the last of her?" asked Mwari of Aten.

"I doubt that. Her powers are waning fast, but she still has the moon wedjat. Its powers can sustain her for a short while. My fear is that she has convinced someone else to execute her evil plans. If one thing is for sure, Luna no longer conducts her evil deeds herself, she gets others to act in her name. Ife is an unknown world, even to me and with Luna still out there, able to weave even the slightest bit of evil in the hearts and minds of others, we must remain on our guard, ever vigilant as we depart tomorrow." Aten's words were so hauntingly true, that they sent shivers down everyone's spines.

Later that night, when all those around her were silent and most likely asleep, Feur looked upwards into the night sky. She realised that there were more stars in the sky than there had been for very a long time. The stars made her think of the Goddess Hathor. They had met so many wonderful people, many of whom Feur would ordinarily never have had the opportunity to meet. Fera lay awake beside her.

"Are you awake, Feur?"

"Yes. I feel slightly apprehensive. Perhaps it is for tomorrow. We really do not know what to expect. I feel sad in a way that our journey will soon be at an end."

"But also relieved, I'm sure. I look forward to seeing Mother and Father again, don't you?" asked Fera.

She received no response and assumed that Feur must have fallen asleep to the sooth sounds of her voice. It had often happened to Fera before, when she and her sisters had lain awake at night, talking about everything and anything. Naturally, Fera had always dominated their conversations, with wild imaginings about the exciting adventures which she planned to go on when she was older.

Her sisters had been silently lulled to sleep then by the sooth sounds of Fera's voice. Fera thought back on their campsite conversation earlier that evening and was reminded that there were two people whom she personally had to thank, for they had contributed to her own emotional and spiritual growth more than any other and they were her parents. She had always looked at her mother and known that she did not want to be like her, married and settled, but since meeting Fezzan,

Fera had realised that her mother's world would not be so abhorrent to her after all. She did not have to choose between her own dreams and societies' norms. There was a place for both and she could mould and shape her life as she needed it to be. Fera realised that her mother's values and her teachings had been the one true constant in her life and on her journey. Her mother's best qualities were embedded deep within her soul and Fera was grateful for that. She would thank her mother when she returned home.

Fera's thoughts then drifted to her Father, Shoa. He had always been a rock in her life. From an early age, she had aspired to emulate his strength and his courage. His morals and his life lessons had informed all her decisions. She missed his wisdom and looked forward to seeing him again. It was with the faces of her mother and father, which shone brightly in her mind and in her memory, that Fera nodded off to sleep.

The next day at dawn, as they entered the rain forests which bordered the Shadow Kingdom of Ife, the mists, which had initially hidden the forests from view, crawled ominously towards them, like invisible sentries; who somehow needed to inspect the strangers that had the courage to venture into their mysterious world.

It was only after they had travelled a short distance through the thick translucent barrier of mist that they saw a world that was beyond any that they had ever imagined before. The rain forests surrounding Ife were unlike any place that Boise had ever seen in her life. Her mother had always said that as a child, Boise had shown a special affinity for all creatures, both great and small and that she had always loved nature.

Boise greatly admired her subtropical surroundings as they moved on horseback towards Ife, the capital city of the Shadow Kingdom. The shady canopy of trees created a cool and moist respite from the dry heat of the Great Desert beyond, even though the humidity was energy sapping.

The trees were greener and more verdant than she had ever seen in her life. Not even the forests along the Charshamba River back home or the forests of Meroe, held a candle to the rain forests surrounding Ife. The coniferous forests back home with their tall, evergreen conifers contrasted sharply with the tall, broad-leafed trees, ferns, mosses, palms and orchids which Boise found herself surrounded by, in the rain forests of Ife.

The forest's birdlife also appeared prolific, with the sounds of tropical, multi-coloured birds and acrobatic monkeys, that moved busily through the trees. The forest was very dense, but fortunately a path had been opened through the vegetation by the many travellers and merchants who had constantly streamed towards the city.

Ife attracted much trade, especially in agricultural products, since cocoa farms were plentiful. Boise rode with Daniel. She found that it was a very pleasant way to travel, saddled behind him, with her arms tightly wound around his waist. They spoke as their horse obediently followed the other riders towards Ife.

"I don't know very much about Ife. Do you?" she asked Daniel.

"The Yoruba people believe that Ife was formed when the Gods ordered that a handful of earth be thrown in the ocean to form land. A cockerel was then left on the land to scatter the earth. It did and thus Ife came into being."

"The image of a cockerel doing that is quite endearing. It reminds me of home and my animals. I had lots of chickens, you know. I gave them all names. Fera said I was mad, but I didn't care. I think that every living creature has a place in this world and should be respected." Boise had always thought that naming something gave it respect and acknowledgement.

"I also named my chickens for another equally important reason. If they had names, it was less likely that they would be eaten. Fera thinks that farm animals, such as chickens, are there to sustain humans, but she would never eat a chicken with a sweet name."

"I heard that. You make me out to be some ravenous carnivore! I never once harmed or ate any one of your silly chickens." replied Fera.

"Yes, that's only because they had names."

"No, it was because they were your pets and I respected them as being creatures that you loved. Besides, who wants to eat chickens that wear ribbons and bows around their necks. It is just plain unnatural, I say. In any event, I respected your property. It had nothing to do with those ridiculous names." Everyone laughed at the mental image of Boise's pampered chickens.

"Mwari, who rules the Shadow Kingdom?" asked Feur.

"I am not sure who sits on the Oyo Kingdom's throne. Do you, Aten?" asked Mwari.

Mwari had travelled to many kingdoms in Ka, but he had never travelled so far west before to know enough information about Ife and its rulers.

"I believe the great grandson of Alaafin of Oyo should now be Ife's ruler. I have not had the pleasure of meeting him yet, but they say he is a decent man, like his great grandfather was. I do believe that he was afflicted with a rare ailment, however. His grandfather, Alaafin was the first ruler of the Oya Kingdom. His name means 'owner of the palace'. He was the first man to find the land and create a vibrant kingdom. It was always told that as a young man Alaafin and his brother were great warriors. During a raid on one of their warring neighbours, Alaafin and his brother got into a huge fight. No-one knew why they had fought, but it was so serious a matter that it divided the brothers as well as their armies. Alaafin, who was left with a much smaller army than his brother, could not wage war against his kin and so he was forced to roam the lush rain forests and fertile lands of the Shadow Kingdom to find his own piece of land upon which to settle. As luck had it, he came upon an old chief from a neighbouring village, who was saddened by Alaafin's predicament and so had decided to help him by giving him a large snake. It was no ordinary snake. It had a magical chain around its neck. The old chief told Alaafin to release the snake, but to follow it closely for seven days. When the snake eventually stopped, Alaafin would know that he had arrived at the exact spot where he was destined to build his new home."

"So he stopped just beyond the rain forest, at the very place that we are now heading for?" asked Nena. Aten nodded.

"Yes, Ife became the capital of his new Oyo kingdom. From those humble beginnings, it has grown over the years to become a vibrant kingdom with abundant trade. Over one hundred thousand Yoruba people call Ife their home." added Aten.

When they finally reached the city of Ife, it presented a most unusual sight. It was vastly different from the great metropoli of Axum and Meroe. There were no great monuments or stelae to be seen anywhere, but its imposing earth banks, surrounded by deep ditches, made a strong impression on Mwari and his party. It was clear that the King made the security of his city a priority. Jadon surveyed the area.

"No-one will easily enter or exit this city. It appears as though we have to cross the bridge to enter through those large wooden gates over there." said Jadon.

As they drew up close to the gates, Gibeon tried to see what lay beyond the first ring of earth.

"Beyond that, there seems to be a second embankment. You're right, once in this place, it will be almost impossible to get out, without our movements being detected." said Gibeon.

"We must then always be on guard. Should one of us stay outside in case we get into trouble in the city?" asked Fezzan.

Before anyone had a chance to analyse Fezzan's reasoning, the large wooden gates were opened and a group of fierce looking warriors rode out towards them.

"Do not be afraid of them. It is customary for all strangers who venture into the city to be escorted to meet the King. I see they have wasted no time in spotting our approach. Everyone, just stay calm! We mean them no harm and they will see that. Let me do all the talking." instructed Aten.

"Girls, do not be afraid." reassured Mwari.

It was obvious how serious Mwari took his role as their protector in the strange place in which they then found themselves.

They were escorted through the city's gates, amidst what appeared to be preparations for a great celebration of some sort, since the locals were busy making garlands and masks.

The bright colours of the red and orange flowers, which were being woven with green vine leaves into garlands and the equally colourful dresses of the women executing such tasks, were a pleasant assault on the senses, especially for the sisters who thought how beautiful, proud and regal the women looked, with their plaited hair, beaded headdresses and gold and copper rings around their necks.

Aten exchanged words with the warriors. It did not appear that they regarded him or those with him as a threat of any kind, for they instructed that the riders dismount and follow them towards a large building which stood at the centre of the city.

"They are taking us to see the King. They say he is called Onis." said Aten, who himself seemed surprised by such declaration, since he did not recognise the name of Onis.

As soon as Aten had said the name of the King, Fera noticed a sudden and immediate reaction from Mwari. His face seemed to drain of colour and one could hear the panic in his voice as he spoke,

"I'll stay out here. Perhaps Fezzan can stay with me. It will be wise to keep watch over the horses. We can also keep tabs on the goings-on outside. One never knows what surprises could be in store for us." said Mwari. Fezzan supported Mwari's plan.

"I agree. We'll keep watch out here!" replied Fezzan confidently.

Aten exchanged more words with the Yoruba warriors, that time the tone of the communications sounded slightly more aggressive and at one point, one of the warriors even shouted at Aten. It was clear that they were not in favour of anyone remaining behind.

"They say that it will not be acceptable for you to stay here. We must all go in to meet the King." said Aten. "It would not be wise to stoke a fire where there is none to be had. If we make these men angry, they will become suspicious of our motives for being in their kingdom."

Mwari did not like hearing Aten's words. Everyone was overtly aware of his extreme opposition to see the King. Fera wondered why Mwari was behaving in such a manner. He had always appeared fearless, in fact, he had ventured where no-one else had dared to go, whilst on their journey. His behaviour was very puzzling to all who witnessed it. Eventually, Mwari relented, begrudgingly.

They all dutifully followed their minders into the royal palace. Unusually, Mwari stayed well behind the others, almost as though he was deliberately trying to obscure his presence behind the bulky frames of Jadon and Gibeon. Fera thought that he shouldn't have bothered doing so, for few men were tall enough to totally hide Mwari from view.

The building was nothing spectacular, both internally and externally. There were no distinctive adornments on the red-earth walls and the furniture was rudimentary, to say the least.

There was a large pit fire in the centre of the great room and what appeared to be animal skins, from a wide variety of animals, on the floors. It was obvious that the Yoruba were ardent hunters. The skins evidenced that they had a particular penchant for lion and zebra, for their skins seemed to dominate those in the room.

Boise took a mental note of what she saw and concluded that she disapproved strongly of such activity. She would keep her opinion to herself though, for the Yoruba warriors looked very fierce and she would not want to get on their wrong side, for any reason whatsoever.

"For a King's quarter's, this room is not very luxurious, is it?" whispered Nena to her sisters. Fera shushed Nena. It was an inopportune moment for any of them to talk.

The presence of a great number of members in the royal court, was the first sign that they were standing in a royal palace. It was, of course, not unusual for any King to surround himself with a large, devoted and fiercely loyal entourage. They had all witnessed that in Jenne, with King Sonni-Ali; but the size of the Yoruba King's royal court greatly surpassed anything that they had seen before.

It was not only their numbers which could intimidate any newcomers to the city, but their striking painted faces. Nena was slightly taken aback by their appearance and her face showed it. She loved all manner of adornments for the face and skin, but she had never seen the likes of the faces that stared intently at her.

"Don't worry, it is traditional face paint, made from the blister beetle. It causes raised welts on the skin. Highly decorative in these parts." whispered Daniel.

A man dressed in animal pelt regalia approached them and introduced himself. He was stick thin, which in itself was another unusual sight, for all the members of the royal entourage were not. It was obvious that he was a learned man, for he spoke to Aten in a tongue which they could all understand. Fera was grateful not to have to continue listening to Daniel as he translated Aten's conversations.

"Welcome Lord Aten to the Shadow Kingdom of King Onis. I am Uzama. I am the King's aide. It is my responsibility to welcome guests to our kingdom. I also perform state rituals."

Uzama took Aten around the room to greet other members of the royal court. Mwari and the others stayed huddled in one spot and watched the scene play out before them. One person at a time greeted Aten. Their eyes were wide and they appeared equally as respectful of Aten as he was of them.

"I think they recognise Aten. Who wouldn't, I suppose?" said Daniel.

"I wonder if they like or dislike him?" said Boise.

She watched each Yoruba royal member's reaction as they greeted Aten. None showed an immediate dislike towards him. Boise was grateful for that. At least poor Aten would not have to apologise again or explain away his past behaviour. She thought that he had shown sufficient penitence for his past deeds. He had shown deep remorse and for her, that was enough. Boise suspected that the

Shadow Kingdom was too far west to be negatively affected by the feud between Aten and Luna. The lush forests and abundant fauna and flora evidenced that the manipulations of the sun, wind and rain, hardly seemed to have touched the earth in the Oya kingdom.

"These are our Palace Chiefs. They are responsible to look after the King's wives and children, of which there are many." said Uzama. Aten smiled politely at each one.

"And lastly, these are our City Chiefs. They manage the affairs of the city and oversee the royal warriors. Our city is quite developed, as I am sure you saw when you first entered our gates, but such development requires constant maintenance and upkeep, not too mention expansion. In our Yoruba tongue, the word 'Ife' means 'expansion'. Our city is expanding at an alarming rate. Our numbers swell with the fertility of our men and women and we also have quite a few people from other kingdoms, who have made Ife their home." Uzama realised that he was prattling on too much. "Well, enough of that, I shall take you to meet our beloved ruler, Onis."

Aten was taken to stand before a man seated in a large chair. It was not really a throne in the truest sense of the word; it was more a large wooden seat, made luxurious by the animal pelts draped over it. The man who sat in the chair was far more interesting to behold. He was a large man. His arms and his legs were extremely muscular. His had high cheek bones and blistered cheeks. The large, sharp, white teeth of some wild creature, probably a lion, adorned his neck and waist and he wore a headdress of ivory beads. To many, he would have been considered quite handsome, but the sisters looked at each other, with looks that seemed to suggest that they did not approve of his looks. They were startled when Onis rose from his seat to walk towards them. Feur's heart dropped to her feet. She prayed that he did not have mystical powers that allowed him to hear people's thoughts, for then he would have heard her harsh judgements of his appearance. But, Onis brushed right past her and walked towards Mwari, his eyes staring fixedly before him, as though he had seen a ghost. He pushed Jadon and Gibeon aside and stopped squarely in front of Mwari.

"I knew the Gods would allow our paths to cross once more. I never would have imagined that you would have the audacity to stand before me. Your presence is an insult to me and to her memory."

Onis spat into Mwari's face and at his feet. Mwari continued to stare into Onis' eyes, even as he wiped away the thick, white spit.

"I did not know that you would be here. If I had known that you ruled this kingdom, I would never have come here. I have always taken great pains to ensure that our paths never crossed again. I stayed away from Monomotapa for that very reason."

Mwari's voice was soft, but his tone was unsettling and mysterious. Daniel and the others were shocked by what they saw. Mwari, a man of great calm, looked visibly frazzled. Daniel sensed some confirmation in his previous suspicions that Mwari was hiding something. It was plain for all to see, that Mwari and Onis had a history, which was clearly not a pleasant one. Onis addressed one of his City Chiefs,

"Seize this man. He is a traitor."

"I don't understand, Onis. Please allow us to sort out this issue. There must a mistake. This man is one of my travel party. I assure you, he has done no harm. He is the most harmless soul that I have ever met." pleaded Aten.

"And that is where you are mistaken. This man is a killer." replied Onis.

"You are wrong. Mwari would never deliberately hurt anyone. He has been our constant guide and protector during our mission." added Boise. "He has become like family to my sisters and I."

"You should be very afraid to have this man as a member of your family. He will betray you; he may even harm you. I should know. He killed my beloved Shona."

"She was never yours. She was my wife." said Mwari. His voice was neither raised nor angry. It sounded distressed and wounded.

233

"She should have been. You never deserved her. She would be alive today had it not been for you. I don't care who these people think you are. As far as I am concerned, a leopard never changes its spots. You were a killer and in my eyes you shall remain so."

"Onis, is it not conceivable that a man can change? Life has an uncanny way of righting wrongs and teaching us harsh lessons. Whatever Mwari has done, I am sure that he has atoned for his past deeds. In fact, I know he has. He bravely, without consideration for his own safety, took on our mission to reunite the Turquoise Figurine. He has stood by these girls through thick and thin. He has shown true friendship and loyalty to all of us."

Aten looked into the eyes of his party as he spoke. He saw nothing, but fear and confusion in their stares.

"I believe you when you say that this man is your friend. He was my friend once. We grew up together. Some said, we were closer than brothers. I thought of him as my brother. Did you know that we were born on the same day? Our tribe was elated at the news of our births. We were inseparable as children. Our fathers raised us to assume the same destiny. We were intended to enter into religious life with the cult of Mhondoro."

Onis no longer addressed Aten, but rather stood before Mwari and looked him straight in his eyes as he spoke,

"You became obsessed with your own self-importance. I rue the day when you became blinded by power and hate. You changed into someone that I and Shona could not recognise." Onis looked at Aten again.

"He told everyone in the village that the ancestor spirits had told him that he was born to lead our people; that he would rise to greatness and become a living God on earth and our people's representative in Monomotapa. He became drunk on the notion of power and control. A beast stirred within him, one which not even Shona or myself, could tame." Onis looked at the shocked faces of the sisters.

"That is not the worst of it. Our village was hit by a crippling drought. Our herds were decimated. Many children from my village died. Mwari told the village elders that the ancestors had spoken to him and told him exactly when to perform a rain ceremony. Everyone laughed at him and mocked him, but he was right. His prediction of the exact time and place to hold the ceremony, brought the rain. Our parched lands were given a second lease on life, as were our people. The elders were so grateful that they made him a living God, a great religious man and since our people respect and revere the Mhondoro cult, Mwari, as its new leader, became a God in everyone's eyes."

"Onis, forgive me, but I fail to see what Mwari did that could have been so bad. He saved your people." said Daniel. "He may have conspired with the ancestor spirits to bring rain, but that was all."

"His true self was only revealed after that. With the support and blind allegiance of the tribal elders, Mwari's obsession with power and control grew undeterred. His influence and power over the tribal elders became insurmountable. Anyone who stood against him or defied his wishes, either disappeared or was killed. He did not tolerate insurrection. Anyone who dared express an opinion in opposition to his own opinion, was deemed a traitor. His lust for absolute control drove him to be suspicious of everyone around him, including myself, his best friend and Shona, his own beloved wife. His jealous and suspicious nature killed the best human being that I had ever known and loved."

As Onis spoke, Mwari remained silent, his head bent forward, his shoulders slumped. Fera felt concerned for him. She had never seen him look so dejected. He looked like a broken man. Onis' revelations were indeed shocking to her and everyone in their party, but Fera's father had impressed upon her to always seek out the truth and since they had yet to hear Mwari's side of the story, Fera was determined not to judge Mwari harshly, until she was in full possession of all the facts.

"You look ashamed for your conduct, but I doubt that you really are." said Onis to Mwari, who then slowly raised his head and responded to Onis' cruel words,

"I am tormented every day by my actions towards Shona and you, my first true friend. I should have believed her when she told me that the child was mine." It was now Mwari's turn to try and explain his actions to everyone.

"Onis speaks the truth about me. My mind and my soul became corrupted by power. I became invincible, so I thought. The need for power became a toxic drug. I needed more and more to sustain myself. Onis and Shona tried to show me the error of my ways. They tried, but I refused to listen. Instead, I became threatened by their efforts and their close bond."

"We were never lovers. I loved her, yes, with all my being, but I respected you and the sanctity of your marriage too much to ever do anything to jeopardise my friendship with you or to disrespect her." shouted Onis.

"I know that now, but I could not believe that back then. The spirit ancestors told me that I should be vigilant, for someone close to me would betray me. I got it in my head that you and Shona had a romantic relationship. When she became with child, I jumped to conclusions. When you both ran away, for me, all my suspicions were confirmed. If only you and Shona had stayed."

"We had no choice. Do you not remember how you acted when you thought that Shona was carrying my child? You went on a revenge filled rampage. Anyone who dared commit any act which you considered morally offensive, was killed. Do you even know how many innocent people were slaughtered in the name of your morality? It was your unforgiving heart that chased us away. It was at your behest that the tribal elders charged us with immorality. They said that our conduct had brought shame on our people. If we had stayed, they would have sentenced us to death and you would have done nothing to stop them. Shona wanted to stay. She thought that she could somehow get through to you. I am glad that I convinced her to leave."

"Did you come to Ife then? I looked for you and Shona. In fact, I spent many years of my life wandering around Ka searching for you; looking for salvation and forgiveness. I never found you or it. Instead, I fought my way through other men's wars to forget the pain of my past."

"You mean to appease your conscience. Well, you won't find forgiveness here. I am glad that you never found us. At least Shona lived out her last days in peace. She never stopped loving you. She never stopped praying for your soul."

"Did she forgive me?" asked Mwari.

Onis stared into the eyes of his old foe with a dismissive and angry look. He refused to answer Mwari, since he wanted to prolong Mwari's suffering.

"Take this man to prison. I am Onis here. I am the highest and most divine ruler in this kingdom. My word is law."

Onis stared into the eyes of his old foe. His look was angry and the tone of his voice was dismissive and bitter.

"It is time that you feel the consequences of your actions. I will show you the same degree of compassion and love which you showed to Shona and myself, which was nothing. Shona died of a broken heart. You will die a death equally as painful. I condemn you to die. Before tomorrow is at an end, you will be sacrificed. At least, your death will not be as much of a waste as your life has been."

With those last words, Onis walked hastily from the room. Mwari was seized, his hands bound, and he was taken from the room. He never uttered a sound.

"Mwari!" shouted Boise. "We'll fight to keep you alive."

"Aten, can you not do something to save Mwari? Please, go and talk to the King. He will listen to you. He must listen to you." begged Feur.

"Each of us has a destiny to fulfil. Mwari does not know it yet, but every day of his life, every good and bad deed has brought him to this very moment. His fate was sealed before he was even born. There comes a time for us all to find absolution from those whom we have wronged by our life's choices and decisions. There is nothing that can be done."

"That cannot be true. You are a great and powerful God. You possess the wedjat. Can you not invoke some spell or something?" asked Daniel. He felt a sense of urgency to save Mwari, which he did not fully comprehend.

"Jadon, Gibeon, let's see whether we can put our heads together. Perhaps we can free Mwari from his prison cell. Let's survey the city. Perhaps we can find a weak point in the city's defences that will allow us to escape across its banks and trenches. I'll find out where they are holding Mwari. You two, find us a way out of here." instructed Fezzan to Jadon and Gibeon.

"If you do this, you could endanger our mission. With you and the men captured, what chance will these women have in accomplishing what they set out to do. Think carefully and wisely before you attempt anything rash." suggested Aten.

"Do you expect us to do nothing then, surely that isn't what you are saying? Why are you choosing to do nothing? You heard Onis. His mind is made up, Mwari will die, as sure as you and I stand here." said Daniel.

Aten understood that they faced a life and death situation. He wished that he could be of more help, but he felt his powers draining. He chose not to disclose such fact to the sisters or the men, for fear that they would become scared and worried. After a few moments, Aten had collected his thoughts,

"We shall wait until the celebrations tomorrow. I must believe, as must you all, that an opportunity will avail itself to save Mwari. Tomorrow, I will appeal once more to Onis' sense of forgiveness. There must be some part of him that would rather not see his beloved childhood friend sacrificed. I shall endeavour to find it. I will not stop until I do."

No-one was convinced that Aten's way was best, but he had never steered them in the wrong direction before and they trusted his judgement.

"I hope you're right." remarked Daniel. "A man's life depends on this gamble."

The sobs coming from Feur and Nena made Aten feel acutely aware of the enormity of the obligation which he had undertaken to fulfil. It was the first time in a long time that Aten felt uneasy about anything, much less about the decision which he had just made. There was nothing that any of them could do except to wait; to wait for the commencement of festivities of the following day.

Fera and her sisters did nothing, but watch the frenetic activity which took place around them. The city was buzzing with the obvious excitement of the locals for the coming of age of the local maidens.

Fera and her sisters could not share in such excitement, since the seizure and imminent execution of Mwari had brought nothing but feelings of fear, sadness and great anxiety for them.

Fera had felt the same way when Fezzan had stood trial for crimes which he had not committed, but the two situations were starkly different. At least, Fezzan was treated fairly and afforded a trial in which he could defend himself against the charges levelled against him. Mwari was not that fortunate.

Onis stood as his judge and executioner. There would be no trials, no fairness and certainly no justice to be had by him. Fera felt sickened to her stomach at the thought of poor Mwari languishing in a prison cell without any hope of freedom and only the knowledge that his death was inevitable.

Nena and Feur had taken Mwari's arrest quite badly, for they cried and cried. Boise was no-where to be seen. No amount of soothing from Fera could allay Nena and Feur's concerns or calm their emotions. The men, other than Aten, could not offer any help in that regard either and it was obvious that the men chose to devote their efforts to finding a way to rescue Mwari and to planning a route for everyone's escape out of the city, if they succeeded in doing so.

Fezzan had told Fera that it was no use just sitting around and waiting. If there was a way to resolve their problems, he would find it. She loved his spirit of determination and his endless hope. On the otherhand, Fera did not feel hopeful at all. In fact, for the first time in a long while, despite all the trials and tribulations during their mission, which had driven her to the brink of despair, she felt totally vulnerable. Aten was their only hope. Fera decided to visit a local church. Perhaps her prayers would be answered, one last time.

Boise had only one thought the next morning when she awoke and that was to visit Mwari. The things which Onis had accused Mwari of, had greatly disturbed her. Onis had told them of a man whom Boise did not recognise. She could not reconcile the harsh account by Onis of the Mwari he knew, with the man that she had come to know. She found Mwari pacing up and down his prison cell.

"How did you get in? I thought that they would not allow anyone to see me?" said Mwari with a faint smile on his face. The sight of Boise was a most welcome sight.

"Who would refuse a father a visit from his daughter?" Boise smiled and winked at Mwari, who held out his hands through the bars of his cell. Boise grasped them warmly. Mwari thought that what Boise had told his guards was not far from the truth. He was very fond of Boise. In fact, he could not be fonder, if she was his daughter.

"I had to see you. My thoughts are .." Before Boise could continue, Mwari interjected,

"I feel so ashamed. I can see disappointment in your eyes. I cannot blame you for being angry with me. The things you now know about me, make me so embarrassed."

"What makes you think that I am angry? I am not angry. I am just sad and a little confused by it all. I don't believe everything that Onis told us about you. That is why I am here. I needed to speak with you, to know the truth. It is not my place to judge you. I am your friend and I shall listen to whatever you wish to say. I believe that there are certain times in our life that we simply need a shoulder to cry or a kind, sympathetic ear. Listening to myself, it sounds as though I have given up on you. That is not the case. I will never do that. We all will never give up on you. Aten has vowed to speak with Onis again. The men are racking their brains for a way to get you out of here. They are determined for us all to escape the city."

"I am grateful for their efforts and for your faith in me. I have run away from myself since I was a young man. I hid my true self from even my own eyes, but a man can never escape his own conscience. My actions haunt me. There is no place in Ka that I could escape to that would hide the shame that I carry with me all the time. Believe me, I have looked for such place, but I have never found it. I shall tell you everything in the confidence that should today be my last day, I will have unburdened my soul."

Boise sat down on the floor next to the prison bars. Mwari, still holding Boise's hand, faced his worst fears and shared his story with Boise.

"Everything that Onis said about my lust for power was the truth. As a young man, I was consumed with power. It did not start out the same way as it ended up, though. My powers were never intended to be used for evil. I was an ordinary boy. I helped my father with his crops and livestock. One day, I was stricken with a high fever. No-one knew what had caused it. I almost died. My father called the local N'anga, our village healer, to examine me. He said that I was possessed by the spirits. He performed a ritual to induce the spirits inside me to reveal their identity and they did. The N'anga told my father that my illness was caused by the Mhondoro spirits, that they had called me, since I was a Mhondoro medium. I was sent my Mutape, who was my ritual assistant. He taught me much about the secrets of the Mhondoro spirits. These spirits were my people's royal ancestors, the great rulers of the past. As a Mhondoro medium, I would be responsible for communicating with the Mhondoro spirits when my village experienced problems, such as droughts, locust infestations or diseases. The Mhondoro spirits were also consulted in all decisions affecting land, since they own all the tribal land. When a Chief dies, the Mhondoro spirits must be consulted and the Chief's successor must be presented to the spirits before he is appointed. So, you see, as a person who could communicate with the powerful Mhondoro spirits, I was given a great deal of power."

"And Onis, was he also a Mohondoro medium?" asked Boise.

"No, although our fortuitous births had been believed to be signs that we were both destined for greatness, the spirits never spoke to Onis."

"Perhaps that is the reason for his hatred towards you. He was obviously jealous that you were chosen and that he wasn't."

"We had been raised to share a common destiny. He took it very badly when he was not able to go away with me to the Spirit Province to learn about the Mhondoro cult. We lost touch for a time and when I returned, I found a very different friend to the one that I had left behind. He was bitter and sullen. He was a changed man. Things got worse when I married Shona. She had been our mutual childhood friend. I always knew that we both had feelings for her. The only thing we were both not sure of, was which one of the two of us, she loved."

"That would not have been a mystery when she chose you."

"I think that Onis had secretly held out hope that she would choose him, but when she had agreed to become my wife, he had hated me even more."

"And Shona, did he hate her for choosing you?"

"I do not think that Onis could ever have hated Shona. He had loved her to his very core. I believe that he loves her still, or the memory of her, at any rate. He honestly believed that it was I who used my powers, my communications with the Mhondoro spirits to convince her to marry me. I think he thought that I had somehow corrupted her mind with my evil."

"Did you love her?" asked Boise.

"More than life itself! Our love was beyond compare. I have never loved any other woman as I loved her, not even my second wife." Boise was taken aback.

"I didn't know that you married again?"

"It was many years later. I met her whilst travelling through Ka. She was a wonderful woman. She gave me a beautiful daughter. I was not a good husband to her or any kind of a father to my daughter. I could never stop running from my past."

"Where is she now, your daughter?"

"I do not know. I left them behind and never looked back. My wife married another and that man raised my precious girl as his own daughter." Mwari saw the look of utter disgust on Boise's face.

"I know what you must be thinking. How could a father do such a thing? You are right. I regretted it the moment that I had done it. Years later, I went back to find them, but they had already moved. I was told that my wife's new husband was a travelling merchant. I searched for them wherever I went, but I never found them. It was as though they had simply vanished."

Mwari became consumed with emotion. He broke down and sobbed. Boise had never before seen a grown man weep so bitterly. Her heart broke for Mwari.

"Is what Onis said about Shona also true?"

"I incited the village elders to charge Shona and Onis with immorality. One day, when I saw Shona and Onis kissing each other, I truly believed the warnings of the Mhondoro spirits, that someone close to me would betray me. It was also at that time that Shona had told me that she was pregnant with our first child. I did not believe her when she had told me that nothing had happened between her and Onis, that he had kissed her, that she had not invited nor encouraged him in any way. It is unacceptable in my culture to step outside the bounds of marriage and become close to another. I had worked long and hard to build my reputation as a moral, Mhondoro medium. The people looked up to me. Our Chief respected me. If everyone believed that my own wife had acted so immorally and betrayed her marriage vows, I believed that my moral authority would have been severely tainted, perhaps even obliterated. My whole identity was built around my spiritual powers. If I had lost that, who would I have been? I could not tolerate deception and lies, especially from those nearest and dearest to me. I had only one choice and that was to expose Onis and Shona's deception and betrayal. When all the village elders and the Chief himself, agreed with me that Onis and Shona had behaved abominably and that they should be punished, I felt vindicated. I knew that I was in the right and that they had wronged me. Of course, when Shona and Onis ran away and I could not find them, my mind filled with darkness and my heart turned black."

"And you took out that anger on others?"

"Many innocent people died in the aftermath of Shona and Onis' disappearance. Every crime committed against the Chief, however small, was evil in my eyes and the perpetrators had to be punished. In life, I had the support of the Chief and village elders and in the spirit world, the Mhondoro spirits guided me and sanctioned my actions. I became invincible, infallible. The Mhondoro spirits gave me power to do as I pleased and sadly, I did just that. One day, I looked into the eyes of a young man, perhaps a boy really, who had been accused of stealing food. He had been orphaned and scrounged around the village for food to survive. He begged and pleaded for mercy, but he would not apologise for what he had done. I could not see innocence in his eyes or the fact that he had been abandoned by his parents. He was the victim but all I saw was the sin of his crime, his obstinacy and his unwillingness to be held accountable for his wrongdoings. I never really saw the boy at all. It was Onis' face and eyes that stared back at me, not the boy's; it was Onis' sin and stubbornness that drove me to administer lash after lash as punishment for his crimes. I was consumed by anger and frustration at never having had the opportunity to resolve my past with Onis and Shona. That boy, died by my hand. I beat him so severely. He died in my arms. I was the last person to stare into his eyes, those eyes which haunt me every day, those eyes that were filled with so much physical pain and mental anguish."

Mwari could not speak any further. The tears streamed down his cheeks. He held out his arms, as though reaching for something which he could not quite grasp. He stared blankly into the darkness of his cell, as though he was reliving that dreadful moment in his past; as though the boy whose life he had cruelly taken, stood right next to him. Boise could not stop herself from crying as well, when she saw Mwari's heartache. After some minutes, Mwari continued,

"When I looked into the boy's dead eyes and saw what I had done, I suddenly thought of Shona and the child that she had been carrying when she had run away. For years, the doubts of whether the child was mine had plagued me. I knew Shona to be a good and honest woman, yet I could not quite shake the image of her kissing Onis or the nagging doubts that Onis had fathered her child. That boy's big eyes made me think differently, more clearly. I wondered what had become of my own child. I panicked at the thought that perhaps the boy could have been my child. I was not thinking coherent and rational thoughts. I was confused, but through my extreme guilt and remorse at what I had done, I knew that I had walked down a dark path in my life, one which I could travel no longer. I knew that I had to change, that I had to allow love and forgiveness in my heart and mind, if I was ever going to forgive myself for taking a life, so cruelly from an innocent boy. It was as though the veil of doubt and suspicion over my eyes, had suddenly lifted. I knew that I believed Shona. I finally believed that the child she had been carrying was mine. I don't know what made me believe that, but I did. It was an epiphany, as though the Mhondoro spirits had cleared my vision. I felt relieved, yet highly ashamed. It was too late to know if such visions were true. All I could do was to try and make amends for the many wrongs that I had perpetrated against my own people."

"What did you do then?"

"I left my home, my village and my people. I wandered for several years through Ka and fought in other men's wars. The irony of that was, of course, that I thought helping them in their causes would free me from my own demons, but those men were exactly as I had once been, drunk with the lust for power. I then found salvation in the kindness of a complete stranger. It was Gebremekel, who had offered a broken man solitude and sanctuary in his monastery at Dibre Bizen. The monks opened their world and their friendship to me. It was there that I met the Holy Prophet. For the first time, since I had lost my friendship with Onis and Shona, I felt the kindness and comfort of having friends. I had their forgiveness and understanding for my past life, but I still could not forgive myself. I felt like a hypocrite living amongst such good and pure souls and so, I left the monastery. I told myself that it was to look for Shona and my child, but when I could not find them, I settled for marriage once again. Even that, could not calm my restless soul. My whole life has been doomed to an eternal search for something, first for self-meaning and identity; then for love and then for forgiveness. When the Holy Prophet had asked me to lead the mission, I accepted without hesitation. It presented yet another opportunity to search for something. I was determined not to fail, but I have failed. I have failed you all, Boise!"

"No, you have not. We would never have come this far had it not been for you. I cannot tell you that I condone your past actions, but they are just that, your past. Everyone has a past. Some may not be proud of the people that they once were, but it is not my place, it is no-one's place to judge you or what you did or didn't do. That is for a higher power. All I know is that you were given a second chance at life when you were asked to protect and lead us on our mission. Succeeding at that is how you can begin to make up for some of the things that you feel that you should not have done. Any child would be proud to have you as their father and you must believe that if you had been given the chance to know your children, they would have thought the same. They would be proud of who you have become, even if they may not have approved of who you were many years ago."

Mwari reached through the prison bars to hug Boise, whom he considered a daughter, even if they were not related by blood. Her support and kindness gave him the strength that he needed to face the events that would take place at the celebrations that day.

After their visit had ended and Boise had left his cell, Mwari thought again about their conversation. It had been the first time, ever, that he had confided in another human being. He did not find it strange that it should have been Boise, to whom he would unburden his mind and his soul, since, after all, she had been the first to courageously reach out to him. She had never judged him; instead she had shown him understanding and compassion, but most of all, she had given him the gift of forgiveness, not her forgiveness, but his own.

Mwari no longer feared the wrath of the Mhondoro spirits. He knew that he could face his destiny with courage. If that day was to be his last, he had accepted the inevitability of his death and the fact that he would be held to account for the way in which he had lived his life. The only thing Mwari could pray for, was that he would be shown mercy, when he finally met his Maker, for he understood that the sins of his life had been numerous, perhaps too many to be forgotten or forgiven.

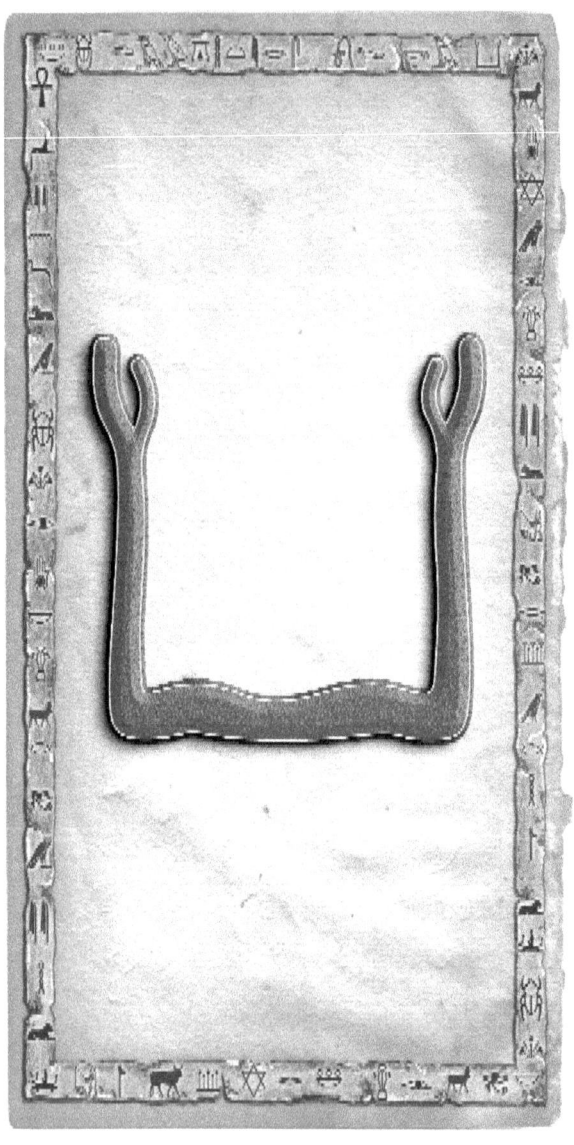

9

WHERE THERE IS LOVE, THERE CAN BE NO DARKNESS

The coming of age of the city of Ife's virginal maidens was a significant milestone and was marked during a great celebration, for it symbolised the ritual of praising the Jengu, the water spirits who dwelt within the depths of the river.

Feur learnt from the local women that young virginal maidens were removed from their homes and taken to secret places to prepare for the celebration. They had to live in seclusion for many days, follow strict rituals and learn the language of the Jengu. It was a singular privilege to participate in the celebration to praise the Jengu for their role in calming the Goddess of the River, for if they did not, the village would soon have known the wrath of the Goddess of the River's anger. She would swell the river in a violent temper and cause the waters to flood the village. Such event would have had serious consequences for the villagers, who stood to lose their homes, but it would also have spelt disaster for the farmers, who were the lifeblood of the city's agricultural backbone.

When Fera, her sisters and the men arrived at the river that day, the location where the celebrations would take place, it was almost dusk. The air was warm, for it was still summer. Fera's love of summer and her desire that its days should drag on endlessly, had not been on the forefront of her mind that day. She was filled with gut-wrenching anxiety for Mwari and for the fate of their mission. The start of the celebration could not come quick enough, even if it meant that a perfectly splendid summer's day had to come to an end.

The entire royal entourage arrived in full royal regalia. Even Onis' many wives and children made an appearance. Nena could not count the number of wives and children, but they appeared to be many. Their presence made Nena think that Onis must have found some measure of happiness in his life after all, for despite the fact that his love for Shona had been so short-lived and never fully realised, he had still found love elsewhere. Onis' hatred for Mwari had been laid bare for all to see and Nena wondered whether his entire life had been consumed by such hate and if so, had that robbed him of the opportunity of truly loving the wives and children whom she saw at the celebration.

The locals lined the water's edge and all, including the family of the virginal maidens, sang for the return of the maidens. Offerings of baskets of flowers and fruits would soon be set adrift by the maidens as gifts to the water spirits. If, after they were pushed into the water, they sank beneath the waves, it would be considered as a sign that the gifts had been accepted by the Jengu.

After a short time, the maidens arrived, to much fanfare. They were dressed in capes, skirts and raffia headdresses and they carried palm fronds. The crowds erupted in applause and chanted at their reappearance after so many days in seclusion. A medicine man called an Ekale, who wore an unusual looking mask, said prayers in a loud voice and then led the maidens to the water's edge. The Ekale waded through the water to a depth of waist height. Once he had steadied himself in the water, he invited the maidens to join him. One by one, each entered the water to be plunged quickly, but reverently by the Ekale into the water. The act of doing that was symbolic of the people's faith and belief in the Jengu, who were seen as their protectors.

Fera and her sisters were thoroughly captivated by the sights around them. The sun had set and a thin veil of darkness had fallen over Ife. Sunlight was quickly replaced by artificial light. The locals held torches made from cocoa palm fronds and the maidens, who had returned to stand along the shoreline, held small candles, which they then set adrift on the water's surface. The water became luminescent, as the lights flickered and jumped off its surface.

Aten had been standing next to the sisters. They had noticed all day that he had looked particularly frail, as though, his life force was slowly being drained from him.

As all vestiges of the sun and daylight disappeared, Aten felt extremely weak. It was Fezzan and Daniel who caught him before he fell to the ground.

"Aten, are you unwell?" asked Fera.

"Let me just sit for a while and catch my breath. I will be fine." replied Aten.

He knew that he was being less than forthright with Fera. He was well aware that during night hours his energy source became depleted. Fera had probably surmised as much, but Aten did not want to share with her or anyone else, the extent to which his powers had been diminishing of late. That was the reason that he had always avoided appearances in public after the sun set. It was a harsh reality of his fate, that his powers would wane as Luna's grew stronger.

He had attempted to prolong the inevitable that day by saying prayers and chanting to the sun in the hope that he could retain his strength just long enough so that he could attend the evening's celebrations, where he could attempt one last time to convince Onis to free Mwari, but the universe had other plans in store for him. Aten was reminded at that moment of how insignificant he was in the great scheme of things. He and his powers existed by the grace and benevolence of nature, as did Luna's powers. He accepted his weakened state, but prayed that it would not compromise their attempts to free Mwari or negatively influence the outcome of their mission to reunite the pieces of the Turquoise Figurine.

The arrival of Onis surrounded by his royal guards and then the arrival of Mwari, who appeared thoroughly dejected and forlorn, diverted everyone's attention from Aten's affliction, much to Aten's relief. He believed that if he reserved the little energy that he still had, he would be able to fulfil his obligations.

Mwari, hands bound, was taken to the water's edge. He was abruptly told to get down on a makeshift wooden raft of sorts and told to lie there in silence.

Aten watched as Onis signalled the Ekale, who then motioned to the maidens to set their baskets of flowers and fruits adrift, as a sign of their devotion and their lifetime commitment to the Jengu. As soon as their gifts touched the water's surface, the gentle waters engulfed them greedily. The locals watched intently and when they saw the offerings sink below the surface, they cheered ecstatically. The people who stood near to Fera, shouted and screamed,

"The Jengu have accepted our gifts." shouted one woman.

"Our city is blessed!" said one old man, with a look of great appreciation on his face.

"Imanje, Goddess of the River is happy now, for the Jengu have appeased and calmed her anger." said yet another local woman.

Fera and her sisters had never before witnessed a celebration such as the one that they were watching, but they understood how the people could find strength in the practise of their traditions and in particular, the reverence shown to River Goddess and her watery domain.

The Charshamba River had always been a symbol of mysticism and renewal for everyone back home. Gifts and offerings were regularly given up to both celebrate and quell the anger of Imanje. The one thing that Fera and her sisters could not understand was how Goddess Imanje could demand so much more than the eternal devotion and respect of the locals. When it was announced that Mwari, seen as a criminal in the eyes of Onis, Ife' Supreme Ruler, would be sacrificed as well, to appease Imanje, the news had come as a great shock to the sisters and to the men. The crowds, however, roared with apparent delight. Supposedly, it was a tradition for criminals to be sacrificed on the eve of the celebration of the Jengu.

"Onis, I am sure that the gifts of flowers and fruits presented to the Goddess Imanje are more than adequate to show the locals' admiration and to ensure that both she and the Jengu remain content and satisfied? Why is there a need to sacrifice Mwari's life as well?" pleaded Aten.

"The ancestors have commanded that all who dwell in the watery realm are honoured this day."

"Who could possibly demand such a price?" asked Aten.

"Mami Watta, the Goddess of the Waters, naturally!"

"I do not believe that one as powerful as Mami Watta, one who is a mother herself, could want such a thing. It cannot be." replied Aten.

Aten knew Mami Watta extremely well. She might have raged the battle to keep her only daughter, Goddess Imanje, from siding with Luna, but Aten knew that there was no possible way that she herself would have turned against the light. She had always supported the Turquoise Goddess, especially in her own troubles with her daughters, Spring, Summer, Autumn and Winter.

"The ancestors have foretold that a religious man must be sacrificed. Given that Mwari, by his own admission, has committed many evil acts which have caused countless deaths, I feel no compunction in echoing the call of the ancestors. You have no power here, Lord Aten. Mwari will die and there is nothing that you can do about it." shouted Onis.

Boise had listened patiently to the venomous and untruthful words that Onis was spewing to a gullible crowd. She decided that she could listen to it no longer. She stepped forward, oblivious of any protocols that might have existed when appearing in the presence of a King and oblivious to the risk that she might be placing herself and her sisters in. She had one thought in mind and that was to expose Onis for the fraud that he was. At the top of her lungs, so as to ensure that the large crowds heard her clearly, she shouted;

"Your King is a fraud."

At first the crowds dismissed her words, for they did not completely understand her meaning. Boise continued, despite Aten's ardent requests for her to remain silent.

"Your beloved and revered King possesses no magical powers that enable him to speak with the Mhondoro spirits. He came to this land many moons ago and he lied to you all. He is not and has never been one of the Mhondoro cult. His entire rule is based on lies. He rose to be your King through deception and treachery. I know that your faith and your traditions are important to you all, but the man whose death you are calling for now, is not only a holy man with the ability to speak to the Mhondoro Spirits, he is also a man who has been gravely wronged by your King." Pointing at Onis, Boise continued,

"Your beloved King ran away with Mwari's wife and his unborn child. Mwari searched for years to find them, without success. Mwari may have committed many acts in his past, acts for which he remains deeply remorseful and repentant, but he has found forgiveness. My sisters and I left our home in search of the Turquoise Figurine. Mwari has not only risked everything for us, but also for all of you as well."

Boise was well aware that she might have been stretching the truth just a little by omitting to relay all that she had learnt from Mwari, but she reckoned that desperate times most certainly had called for desperate measures. The crowds fell silent, incredulous at Boise's revelations. Fera looked around her. Several people stood with their mouths agape. Others asked, in hushed tones, whether the young stranger was telling the truth about their Onis. Despite their varied reactions, they all stood hypnotised by Boise's every word.

"Mwari's death will be too high a price to pay for the continued prosperity of your lands. I beg you to find it in your hearts to forgive this gentle soul. If you cannot show him mercy, then I fear for you all. I fear for your descendants who will always be plagued with the knowledge that their mothers, fathers and their grandparents before them could have saved a truly good man, but who instead chose to do nothing. How will the Mhondoro spirits see such an act? Will they reckon that a wrong was done against one of their own? Will they seek revenge against all of you and your descendants for many moons to come? Only time will tell whether they too, will demand their own price for such a betrayal? Will drought and infestation of your crops be their response? I would hope not, but no-one knows for sure?"

As Feur listened to Boise, the beginnings of a smile touched her lips. Nothing about what Boise had said was remotely humorous, but Feur was amazed at the courage of the sister with whom she had always shared a penchant for books and storytelling. How Boise had put her vivid imagination to good use? They had all heard much about Mwari's past, but the things Boise was saying were truly quite outrageous, perhaps too incredible to be believed.

When Boise had finished with her monologue, she was panting, almost out of breath. Daniel winked at her. Fera and Nena smiled warmly, both proud that Boise had defended Mwari so vehemently. They understood that she shared a close friendship with Mwari and her speaking up in defence of that, was further proof of her deep feelings for him. Boise still questioned whether she had said enough or said the right things to stop the sacrifice of Mwari, for she received no reaction from the crowds, since she had stopped talking. It was Onis who reacted first. He looked out over his subjects and spoke in a humbled tone.

"My people, I have wronged you, but not in the way that you would think. I left my home in Monomutapa, a desperately tortured soul. I was jealous of my best friend; jealous of his life path; jealous that the Mhondoro spirits had spoken to him and not to me; jealous that he married the woman that I adored; jealous that he lived the life that I was meant to live, the life that my own beloved father had always promised that I would have. In Ife, I found salvation and peace. I was accepted for the man that I was and not the man that everyone wanted me to be. I admit that I was not honest about my religious background or my training and for that I am truly repentant, but I gave my entire mind and soul to building this kingdom. I devoted my life to our beloved dead ruler, may his soul rest in peace. I carried out his last wishes to succeed him to the throne, since he had no heirs and to lead his people to prosperity. I led our soldiers to many victories. I bled with my fellow soldiers of Ife. I worked my hands to the bone, when our lands were devastated with floods and droughts. I found love with my many wives, all daughters of this land, and I celebrated the births of my many children, all born on this land. I have devoted my life to the peace and prosperity of this kingdom. If that does not make me one of you, I am not sure what will? If my fate is to step down as your ruler, for one who is more worthy in your eyes, then I shall gladly do it. All I ask is that you forgive my weakness and accept that my acts were never intended to cause any harm to you, the people of Ife. I can live, if I am not your King, but I could not live if I did not receive your forgiveness or if I were banished from the only home that I have ever known."

The silence at the water's edge was deafening. It was as though, even the sounds of nature, had stopped to listen to Onis' words. Onis then walked to the raft to which Mwari had been tied. He instructed the royal warriors to untie the prisoner. Onis then helped Mwari to his feet.

"You, my friend, my brother, above all, I owe you an apology. I hope that you will be able to forgive me for the wrongs that I have done to you?"

"It is I who must apologise. You took Shona and ran away in fear for your lives. You thought that your lives were in danger and after all, they were. Back then, I was a man possessed. My heart was too filled with hatred and with greed for power and position. I saw no reason. I saw only suspicion and doubt. No matter what you and Shona would have said or how you would have explained your conduct, I had already found you guilty. If you had not run, you would both have inevitably been killed. But, I am a changed man. I saw the evil in myself and I have spent my life fighting against it." said Mwari.

"So, we are in agreement then, we have both been in the wrong? I think it is time that we wipe the slates of our questionable pasts clean and start afresh, but before I can do that Mwari, I must unburden my soul. I must tell you what became of Shona and her child." said Onis.

Mwari was surprised by Onis' words, for he had assumed that Shona and the child had died in childbirth.

"Perhaps it is best to bury the ghosts of yesterday and not re-open old wounds." said Mwari.

The unusually calm evening air suddenly stirred. Aten felt a shiver run up his spine. Thankfully, there were few times in his life when he had stood in the presence of pure evil, but he knew when it was around, since the very core of his being became alert to its appearance. It was as though a feeling of pure malice and vindictiveness was strangling the fresh night air and the newly found spirit of reconciliation that had been achieved between Mwari and

Onis. Aten found it hard to breathe. The sisters stood by his side, at the ready to assist him, but Aten knew that there was no amount of care that could remove the life-draining force that had joined them all at the water's edge.

The silence that had overtaken the crowds a moment earlier was suddenly pierced with the sound of a woman's voice. To Daniel's ears, it sounded like a mature women's voice, although he could not decipher her exact words. It appeared that the voice was moving closer and closer to the royal podium. An old crone draped from head to toe in a black cape, seemingly aged, since she walked with the aid of a large walking stick, pushed her way through the crowds to stand before Onis. He did not recognise her. There was only one person there who sensed her presence. The woman spoke,

"The ghosts of yesterday will never remain buried. The memories of the past are a curse on our future."

As the woman threw off her cloak, with one violent pull, the face of the Luna was made visible to all present. The old woman was not old after all. Her face was middle aged, yet hauntingly beautiful. Her hair was not grey as it should have been, but rather jet-black. Her eyes were terrifyingly captivating, like pools of the darkest and deepest waters that few would venture into for fear of the evil lurking within their depths.

Fera looked at her sisters. Boise clung to Daniel, Nena and Feur stood close together. The sight before their eyes, was not unlike that day in Luna's underground grotto. Fera had not known what to expect then and she ominously found herself in the same spiral of doubt and fear as before. They had initially run to Luna in the belief that she was their hope, their salvation and since then they had continued to spend countless days running from Luna's evil. In a split second, looking at Luna, Fera felt as though she was experiencing all the hurt, pain, anguish, tiredness and sorrow that their journey had brought. Luna had been unquestioningly responsible for all the bad things that had happened to her, her sisters and the men. As her mind raced through the places and faces that they had encountered on their journey, Fera felt a hand touch hers. It was warm and large. It enveloped her hand, like a calming, comforting embrace. She looked down and recognised the hand's owner. It was Fezzan. Her fear was suddenly given a jolt of courage. They may have run away from Luna in the past, but the time for running was over. The time to face Luna head on had arrived and Fera felt up to the challenge.

Aten struggled to get to his feet. It was obvious to all who saw him, that he had become almost frail. The strong man that Fera had seen ride towards her in the Al Suud was a distant memory.

"Don't tire yourself." encouraged Boise.

"All the paths in my life have led to this one moment. I shall face my nemesis, if it is the last thing I do. I must do it for my daughter."

It was as though Aten's thoughts of his only child gave him the strength that he needed at that moment. He walked towards Luna. As he approached her, she laughed in his face. Her laugh was hollow and menacing, so much so, that the crowds grew even more silent than they had been.

Faces, filled with fear, watched as Aten strode towards Luna. Their age-old feud had been the subject of legend and myth. Everyone across Ka had been affected by the hatred that had passed between them for ages. Every child had, at one time or another, awoken in a cold sweat with nightmares filled with stories of Luna and Aten. Every farmer had prayed that their lands would not be devastated by the feud which existed between Luna and Aten. No person or kingdom had remained untouched by the consequences of the Sun God and the Moon Goddess' mutual hatred and venom for each other. The crowds in Ife were no different. They had always feared the power of the Gods, none more so, than the two who stood before them, face to face, eyeball to eyeball.

"You dare challenge me. We both know that in your weakened state, you are no match for my powers." spouted Luna.

She pushed Aten with an elegant, graceful hand. He was unsteady on his feet, but did not fall over. With a gesture that was intended to show off her power, she pushed Aten again, but merely with a hard jab of her index finger. That time, he fell to the ground. Luna laughed. She looked around at the astonished, yet fearful faces around her that watched her every move.

"How dare you all judge me! How dare you pity him! If it were not for Aten's blindness to the whims of his daughter, my son would be here with me now. He deprived me of a life spent with my only son."

Luna seemed to be momentarily distracted by the faces in the crowd, as though looking into their eyes as they stared at her, had caused her to suddenly reconsider her behaviour. But, her moment of consternation was fleeting. From his position on the ground, Aten mustered up the strength to respond,

"You are the maker of your own doom. You had a choice. You could have opened your eyes to the beauty of the love that our children shared, yet you chose to stay blinded by your hatred for me. You deprived yourself of a lifetime of happiness and you took everyone with you into that dark abyss in which you hid all these years." Aten was out of breath as he finished his sentence.

"Look at you! You have no powers over me. When I possess the wedjats, I will destroy you and I will destroy all those who have sided against me."

Luna stared across the terrified faces of the bystanders as she uttered her threat. Some stifled screams could be discerned from the locals, but mostly the silence continued.

"Have you forgotten, Luna, you need both wedjats for your power to be complete and that is the one thing that you will never lay your hands on." responded Aten, as he took the sun wedjat from his cloak and held it up for all to see.

Luna stared at the red jasper stone. The candle and torchlight which surrounded them, illuminated the stone for all to see. Light danced off its perfectly crafted surface, to mesmerise all those who looked at it.

"Aten, watch out!" shouted Jadon.

Before Aten could react to Jadon's warning, a small figure had jumped out from no-where to snatch the stone from Aten's hand.

"Oh no!" mouthed Fera, as she looked in the eyes of the mysterious thief. She still saw his piercing little, beady eyes in her nightmares. The face of Sirius was unmistakeable. Jadon and Gibeon, driven to react quickly by their military training, attempted to stop Sirius in the act, but his size and agility made their task difficult. Sirius jumped and scurried beyond their reach. It was Luna who brought Sirius to order.

"Stop, Sirius. Hand me the wedjat. We have a bargain, do we not?"

"Do we? Do we really? I am not so sure that I can trust you anymore to keep your word."

"Of course you can trust me. Just give me the wedjat and I will give you the one thing that you desire most."

"No. You give me what you promised first. I will then hand over the wedjat."

Luna's tone became laboured, as though her irritation with Sirius had reached breaking point. Sirius refused. He felt trapped. He was so close to getting that which he had always desired; a victory he could almost taste and yet, he was no further to getting the power of Everlastingness than he had ever been. He had hoped to take possession of the sun wedjat at Bandiagara, but fate had let it slip through his hands. The rising of the morning star had passed and so had his chance to obtain the power of Everlastingness on his own. If only he could have taken the wedjat from Fera, he would not have had to bargain with Luna. He chided himself for chasing false dreams. If only he had taken a harder look at the object in the girl's possession? Sirius decided that there was no time to feel sorry for himself. He had made a deal with Luna and if it meant honouring that deal to get the power of Everlastingness, then he would just have to do that.

"Do I have your word that you will do as you have promised?" he asked Luna one last time.

"Of course I will! You know that there is no conceivable reason for me to turn against my friends and you have been a loyal friend." replied Luna.

Fera silently prayed that Sirius would see through Luna's lies. She questioned how it could be that a person could be so oblivious to the world around them. Could Sirius not see the deception in Luna's eyes? It was clear that she was saying one thing to him, but that one thing would never be realised. Luna held out her hand and smiled misleadingly at Sirius. He reluctantly handed her the wedjat.

"No!" cried out Aten, "You naive little man. You do not know what you have done. You have single-handedly given Luna the power to destroy us all. There will be no stopping her with the power of both wedjats under her control." Aten's head sank into his hands, as though he had finally realised defeat.

As the wedjat was placed into Luna's hand, the winds began to blow violently from all four directions and the waters in the river became turbulent. Sirius, who stood waiting for Luna to make good on their pact, lost his footing and was swept towards the water. Everyone held onto the person next to them so as to keep themselves from falling over in the strong winds. As Sirius tumbled into the water, he struggled and gurgled. He shouted for help, for it was obvious that he was unable to swim. The water around him swirled and swirled. He disappeared under the water and then reappeared, gasping for air.

His battle to live lasted for a few minutes, but ended unceremoniously when he was devoured by a large creature. The only glimpse that anyone saw of his attacker was the image of a large fish head and a long snake-like tail. Fera, Jadon and Gibeon's worst fears had been realised when they recognised the creature to be the much feared Ninki Nanka. Locals screamed at the sight of Sirius being dragged under the water. Luna undeterred, turned around and around as though inciting the winds to blow more and more. As she spun, she chanted,

"I call upon the Mistresses of the dominions of the air and the water to join forces with me. Together, we shall be invincible. Anyone who dares challenge our powers will feel the wrath of our revenge. Aten's power is no more. The moon will pass its dark shadow of power over the sun and all the nations of Ka will be covered in darkness; a darkness in which I shall assume complete domination over nature and all mankind." cried out Luna.

Luna relied upon the fact that the presence of the Ninki Nanka and its attack on Sirius had disturbed the usually calm and serene domain of the Goddess of the River. Such disturbances would not have placated the Jengu as the trusted guardians of Imaje, for they too, would abruptly have been awoken by all the commotion.

The waters in the river seemed to swell as though their very depths intended to rise to the surface and cause the river to flood. Those people at the water's edge quickly realised that they stood in harm's way. They began to run for their lives, for if Imanje and the Jengu appeared from beneath the water, the river would burst its banks and the whole city would be engulfed in a watery grave. Aten knew that he had few cards left to play. His powers were insignificant and futile. Luna had finally got the better of him, but perhaps he could muster up the strength to prevent the city from being swept away.

There was only one force greater than the powers of Imanje and the Jengu combined and that was the life-force that was Mami Watta, the Goddess of the Waters. She would never side with Luna. She despised what Luna stood for; what Luna had become and what Luna had accomplished in corrupting her daughter Imanje. Aten was confident that she would bring an end to the threat that Imanje posed. At the top of his voice, Aten shouted once more,

"Mami Watta, powerful and revered Goddess of the Waters, I call upon you to calm your daughter's rage. Help me to convince her that the path that she has taken will lead to nothing but misery. She will forever be a slave to Luna's will and she will be complicit in the evil that Luna will visit upon the peoples of Ka. For years, I have been feared and hated for the part that I have played in my feud with Luna. I have only recently come to understand the true repercussions of my evil deeds. I shall always carry the guilt of knowing that I caused such pain and suffering, for so many people. I would not want that same fate thrust upon your daughter, especially when she has the opportunity to avoid falling from grace as I have. When the peoples of Ka eventually lose all respect for her, as they most surely will, they will no longer show their devotion and respect to her. Her domain will become a place of death, rather than a place of life. Her waters will become contaminated and polluted with all manner of foul things. In turning against Luna now, Imanje will save herself and she will continue to be revered by all."

For a moment or two after Aten had pleaded with Mami Watta, the only sound that could be heard was that of the winds, as it whirled through the air. The crowds that remained near the river, all looked upwards into the skies as if they searched for the elusive Mami Watta there. Since none of them had ever seen her in their lives or known how she looked, the crowds simply scanned the skies for any unfamiliar sight. Mami Watta's existence would have been introduced to every child in Ife on the day of their birth, when she would have whispered in their ears as they were baptised. From then on, every person in Ka would have grown up to love and respect the mighty Goddess of the Waters, who was the Supreme Mistress over all the rivers, lakes and seas which flowed through Ka. Mami Watta had the reputation of being kind and benevolent. She was deeply motherly and protective of all who sought her protection. She had always received the dead, as well as the living into her comforting embrace. She was the source of wealth and life for many. She never became easily angered, unless she lost her temper and on the rare occasions that she did, she could become quite destructive and violent.

After several more minutes of waiting for an appearance by Mami Watta, the scene at the river became more and more bleak. No-one could withstand the violent onslaught of water and wind brought by Luna and her minions.

Then, as utterly hopeless as everyone felt, the atmosphere changed, almost instantly and with it a calm serenity fell over the city. The winds grew silent. The waters on the river grew calm. The sudden change also created thoughts of fear and confusion in the crowds. If they had known better, the deathly silence could easily have been interpreted by the people to be a sign that great evil was afoot, but they all believed and trusted that Mami Watta would appear. Thoughts of Mami Watta had always left her admirers feeling great serenity and peace. The presence of the Goddess of the Waters could never invoke evil, at all. Soon, a translucent mist floated off the surface of the river and rose to form the figure of a woman. She had pearly white eyes, which were bright and happy. She was dressed in an iridescent gown with seven skirts of blue and green, each layer representing the rivers, lakes and seas of Ka and each layer shining more brightly than the one before it. Nena was mesmerised by her beauty, as was everyone who had waited patiently for her arrival. She smiled warmly at everyone who stood at the river's edge. Her smile reminded Fera of her mother's smile. Her voice was soft-toned and sweet,

"I have heard your call for help, great Sun God. I offer my support to you. I will ensure that my daughter and her guardians know the truth in your words and that they heed your advice, for if they do not, they will understand the measure of my discontent. I have always advocated peace and harmony between the realms of mankind and all those who dwell within my watery domain and as long as I control the watery realms, it will remain so."

"Thank-you, our Mother of the Waters! Your presence and your support is a great blessing to us all." Mami Watta smiled at Aten.

"I shall always stand on the side of good and fight evil where it occurs. Speaking of evil, I am aware of your plight to save the mission of the Daughters of Ka." Mami Watta then looked at the sisters. "You are a credit to yourselves, Daughters of Ka and to all women across Ka. You show us that women have much to contribute across Ka and that, is your true legacy to us all. I shall see that you have safe passage back home. Please accept a token of my esteem and appreciation."

Mami Watta beckoned Fera and her sisters forward to the river's edge. They stepped forward and stood, each with one arm outstretched, their palms placed one on top of the other, as Mami Watta spoke to them. It was a symbolic gesture of unification and strength, but most of all sisterhood. Mami Watta whispered soft words into their ears, the likes of which none of them had heard before. The crowds looked on, eager and inquisitive to learn what words Mami Watta was imparting to the four beautiful strangers to their city, but Mami Watta's words could only be heard by Fera and her sisters.

"Daughters of Ka, I give to you a gift, sourced from the hidden depths of my domain." The sisters felt soft wisps of air caress their bodies. They looked down to see that two tiny, sparkling pearls of vivid florescent colour had been delicately placed in Fera's palm. Mami Watta continued,

"Some say that these pearls are made from dew drops that fall in the night, but in reality, they are formed from my tears. I have cried bitterly for the demise of Ka and for the fall of my daughter from grace. I shall cry no more. It is time that all in Ka cease their tears. A time of great happiness and love is within our grasp. It is a time which you, the Daughters of Ka, have made possible. I thus entrust you with the task of wiping away the tears of my past and creating a bright and tearless future for us all. I also impart the great wisdom that I have acquired through the ages to you and your sisters, so that you may bring innocence, beauty, purity and a new beginning to our great empire, Ka."

"Thank-you, beloved Mother of the Waters." replied Fera and her sisters, individually.

They all felt truly privileged that they had been singled out for such an honour. They knew that Mami Watta rarely, if ever, appeared outside her realm. Her belief in them kindled a fire in their hearts and minds, as never before.

With those words, the form of Mami Watta drifted effortlessly away into the river, as it flowed downstream. The tranquillity that Mami Watta had brought to Ife could be felt by all. Aten felt intensely relieved. At times, it had seemed as though all the forces of nature had turned against him and the power of good. At least, there were many in Ka who still refused to side with Luna.

The appearance of Mami Watta had totally derailed Luna's evil plans. Luna's once beautiful face, then took on an evil scowl. Her eyes sneered at Aten. Fera could see that Luna was infuriated by Aten's act of calling upon Mami Watta.

"I underestimated you, Aten. Even with diminished powers, you must still harbour intense hatred for me, to take such desperate measures to stop me. Your powers will not last much longer and your allies are sadly few in number. Who will you call on next to help you?" challenged Luna sarcastically.

"I do not hate you, Luna. I pity you, but know this, there are many who will stand against you. It will only be a matter of time, before your evil is destroyed. Why can you not see the consequences of the evil that you invoke? You can change. It is not too late. We are all capable of change. We are all capable of being good. You can turn against evil before it is too late, before your soul is lost forever to the darkness."

"Your pity is wasted on me, old man."

Luna wished fervently that she could somehow rid herself of Aten's presence. There was no time to cast a spell over him. She had to think of a way to stop his incessant meddling in her plans. It was clear that he was physically a broken man, or soon would be, since her powers were growing stronger, but he was relentless in his steadfastness to protect the peoples of Ka. It appeared, that despite his weakened state, he would risk his own life to save others and most importantly to save the mission of the sisters to reunite the missing pieces of the Turquoise Figurine. Luna vowed to never allow Aten to succeed on that score.

She thought quickly of possible strategies that she could explore. She reckoned that she had capitalised on the evil of men's hearts before to do her evil bidding and perhaps she could use such strategy again. She had one last card to play. Perhaps if she turned Mwari against Onis, who despite their newfound and tentative peace, would then hate each other or even kill each other after she had she revealed to all what she knew, she could ensure Mwari's death and the failure of his mission to help the Daughters of Ka. Luna no longer saw Aten as any threat whatsoever. Mwari's death would cause the sisters to lose all hope and perhaps that would be the advantage that Luna desperately sought. Luna walked to stand before Mwari and Onis.

"Is man really capable of change? I doubt it. Take these two here." Luna pointed at Onis and Mwari. "Are they true friends now? Do their explanations and faint-hearted apologies mean that they have now changed?" Luna stared Onis directly in the eyes.

"Would your friend Mwari really have forgiven you if he knew the secret that you have hidden from him all these years? Can there be secrets between true friends? Perhaps man is not that capable of change or of good, after all?" Luna's words were tinged with sarcasm and malice.

"What is she talking about, Onis?" asked Mwari of Onis.

"I cannot say." Onis struggled to make eye contact with Mwari, which made Mwari feel uneasy and suspicious.

"Really Onis, do you think playing ignorant is the best way to handle this? Perhaps you should try to live up to Aten's high ideals for mankind? You can change. You can be good and turn against evil before your soul is lost forever to darkness. Is it not time to tell the truth about Shona's child?" said Luna venomously. She laughed hysterically at the irony of Aten's words.

"What child? I thought that Shona and the child died in childbirth. Is that true?" asked Mwari, "Answer me?"

Onis looked away. He had sworn that he would never reveal the truth to Mwari. The thought of keeping the existence of Mwari's son from him, was Onis' way of exacting a measure of revenge against Mwari for what he had done to Shona. Onis believed that if he had to live his life without Shona, then it was only fair that Mwari would never get to know the son that Shona bore him. Mwari walked up to Onis.

"Tell me the truth." shouted Mwari. Onis remained stubbornly silent. "I thought we had turned a corner and buried the past, but I see now that you are still capable of deception. If you value the bonds that we have shared since birth, you will come out with it, whatever you are hiding from me." Onis broke under the weight of his conscience, he shouted out,

"I kept the truth hidden for the child's sake. On her deathbed, Shona begged me never to tell you that you had a son. She feared that you would seek revenge against him, since you believed that he was mine. Your belief that the child was mine was never true, of course. He might have been your biological child, but I raised him as my own, for as long as I could."

"A son!" said Mwari incredulous. "What do you mean you raised him for as long as you could?"

"I tried. God knows, I tried to love him, for he was after all Shona's child, but all I saw when I looked into his eyes, was the memory of Shona staring back at me. I did the best that I could for the boy. It was not fair of me to raise the son of a man whom I had hated for so long. It was not fair to the child."

"Where is he now?"

"I gave him up. I sent him away to be raised with a friend in a place where he would never have to face the unhappy circumstances of his birth."

"Where is he now?"

"I tried to keep in touch with the people who cared for him, if not for his sake, for Shona's. She would have wanted me to ensure that he was well looked after."

"And was he?"

"Yes, that is, until his adopted parents died. After that, I lost all contact with him. I believe the child was left in an orphanage. I tried to look for him, but I never found him."

Mwari seemed to explode with anger.

"A moment ago you apologised for all the wrongs that you had done to me and yet you withheld the news that I have a son that lives, but most importantly, one which you neglected to tell me, had been given away. How could you do such a thing? How could you separate a child from the only parent that he had and leave him with strangers?"

"He was not left with strangers, like I told you, he was left with a friend. Besides, you wouldn't have wanted him with the state you were in. You probably would have had him killed."

"How dare you suggest that I would have killed my own child! If I had known he was my son, I would never have abandoned him."

Mwari could not withhold his anger. It coursed through his veins with fire-like speed. All the old feelings towards

Onis resurfaced once again. Mwari could not help himself. He lunged forward and grabbed Onis by the throat and began to strangle him. The only thought on his mind was that Onis deserved to die for what he had done.

"Mwari, get off, he is not worth it!" shouted Jadon as he, Gibeon and Daniel tried feverishly to pull Mwari off from Onis. Luna stood silently and watched the scene of revenge play out before her. She smugly said,

"You see; it never takes much to see the true nature of man revealed. Man will always turn to the dark side. A moment ago, these men's hearts were filled with love and forgiveness, but now their minds are fixated on revenge and murder." said Luna, with a satisfied sneer on her face.

"You instigated this Luna! Can you not see the harm you do! You must be stopped, even if I have to do it myself." shouted Aten as he stood to his feet and moved towards Luna.

He was unsure of exactly how he would stop her, but he was not averse to physical force if he needed to. There had only ever been one person who could make his blood boil and bring the thought of murder to his mind and that had been Luna. It was time that he acted on such thoughts, irrespective of the consequences. Aten staggered towards Luna and tried to grab her. He was not sure what he hoped to achieve by his actions, but he forged ahead. Unfortunately, Luna's strength far outmatched his. She pushed him to the ground, violently. Aten felt physically defeated. Aten realised that Luna's powers had become so powerful and that he could no longer stop her evil on his own.

"You now have what you have always wanted. I lay at your feet, a destroyed man, but I beg you Luna, if there is a shred of mercy and decency within your soul, please do not carry out your threat. Exact your revenge against me, but please, show mercy on the many innocent people of Ka. If you fulfil your threats to plunge the world into darkness, only wars, starvation and devastation will follow. You have known the hurt and grief of death. You have loved before and you have known the pain of loss before, a loss which almost killed you. Please, I beseech you to show mercy."

"Shut up, old man. I no longer have to listen to your rantings. You are mistaken if you think that I care about Ka or about any of the poor wretches that will suffer. I could not care whether they lived or died. Are you so stupid as to think that anything will change if I decide to show mercy as you request? Nothing will change, I tell you, nothing! Mankind will still wage wars instigated by greed and lust for power. Nature will still be destroyed. Wars and devastation has not been and never will be the result of my actions. Evil thrives in the hearts of mankind, whether I intervene or not. Was it I who caused Ta-Seti to hate his brother? Was it I who only married Meroe with a greater lust for the wealth and riches of the city of Meroe, than love and affection for my wife? Was it I who took the pride and heritage away from the Beja so as to plant the seeds of hate within their hearts? Was it I who drove the slave raiders of the Great Desert to trade in human flesh and care nothing for their cargo? Was it I who caused Winter to be jealous of her sisters, resulting in the Turquoise Goddess ending her life? No, I think not." Luna's voice had reached fever pitch. The years of anger and hatred had boiled to the surface.

"But it was you who preyed on the vulnerabilities, doubts and vices of countless numbers of people, so that they would do your bidding. Their evil may not have been by your hand, but their evil most certainly was by your design. You plotted and planned mankind's fall from grace and those whom you manipulated were too blinded by hatred to know that they were merely puppets on your string. It is obvious that my words and pleas have fallen on deaf ears, but if you choose to ignore my pleas for mercy, then there are those whose powers you will not be able to dismiss so easily."

"Aten, you surprise me. Perhaps you have forgotten the powers of the wedjats, which I now possess? Do I have to end your life to finally be rid of you?" Luna's laugh sent shivers down the spines of those who watched her.

"I do not fear death, even death at your hands, but it will not come to that." said Aten.

"Who is going to stop me? I have repeatedly told you that you are no match for me. The truth be told; you never were?"

As Aten listened to Luna spew hatred and malice, he reminded himself that he wanted to avoid using the amuletic papyrus if he could prevent doing so, but he was at his wits end. He had exhausted all other avenues. Luna had not been stopped. Luna would never be stopped, unless he invoked the powers of the Gods. He had always dreaded the thought that it would take more than his powers alone to stop Luna. He had given her every opportunity to repent and cease her evil ways, but she had remained resolute in her hatred of him and her plans to destroy Ka. His only hope was to call on the Gods, so that they could convince Luna of the evil of her ways. They would bring her to her knees if she refused to yield and refused to give up her lust for revenge.

Aten removed the sacred amuletic papyrus which Hathor had sent to him. Its appearance immediately elicited a reaction from Luna, although she tried to maintain her bravado. Even Luna's powers paled in insignificance to the powers of Hathor, Khnemu and Sekmet combined and deep down Luna knew that, although she remained defiant.

"I call upon the powers of the Great Gods and Goddesses to break the evil powers of Luna, Goddess of the Moon." Aten took the papyrus and held it to the sky, "Stand with me mighty ones, stand with all the peoples of Ka against Luna. Help us defeat her evil."

"Do you honestly think that I am afraid of you all? Well, think again. I have the wedjats and my powers are unassailable."

"Not against the powers of all the Gods. Look, they have all committed themselves to helping me invoke a powerful magic against you. This time, I will not fail. With their help, you will be destroyed once and for all." shouted Aten.

Luna looked at the papyrus shown to her then by Aten. She saw the pictures symbolic of the great Gods, displayed thereon in ancient writing; pictures of the funery scarab which represented the power of the everlasting light and peace of Khnemu, God of the Underworld; the lotus flower of Hathor which represented her enduring love and beauty and the lioness, symbolic of Sekmet, the Goddess of War and

Fire. Luna remained unyielding and stubborn in her belief that she was all-powerful, even more so than Ka's most powerful Gods and Goddesses put together.

"I see that you still refuse to stop your evil. I have begged and pleaded with you to abandon your reckless and senseless lust for revenge, but you will not listen. I have no other choice but to invoke the powerful magic of the Gods and Goddesses. Once I invoke the ancient spell of the amuletic papyrus, the retaliation of the Gods and Goddesses towards you for your evil ways and for your disrespect shown, not only to the Gods and Goddesses, but to all the peoples of Ka, will prove impossible to thwart. Mistress Sekmet will ignite a fire in your soul, an eternal fire that will burn away all the hatred and revenge that fills your heart and mind, until nothing within you remains. Lord Khnemu will erase your name from the Book of Life and Death. Your life will be erased and with it, the life of your son, for if you were never born, then neither could your son have lived. Mistress Hathor will wipe any traces of love that you may once have felt for another, as well as any possibility of love that you may ever feel for anyone in the future. All that will remain, after the spell is said and done, is an empty, burnt-out shell of a person with no capacity to feel joy and love. You will rot and wither away for all eternity. This I swear will be your fate, even if it takes the last breath in my body to achieve."

Aten's voice was no longer a loud shout. He delivered his final vow to Luna calmly and methodically and with complete solemnity, in every word he spoke.

"Once I burn this papyrus, the ancient spell will be cast and your fate will be sealed forever."

Aten asked Fezzan to hand him one of the torches which burnt bright on a nearby stand. Luna watched as Aten's hand drew closer and closer to lighting the papyrus. Her mind became frenzied. What retaliation did she have of her own in response to Aten? Luna struggled to order her thoughts. She knew that the wedjats were no match for the ancient spell of all the Gods and Goddesses, whose symbols were as clear as daylight on the papyrus. She knew that Aten was telling her the truth. There were few things that

Luna feared and Aten had found the one thing that could destroy her.

But, it was not the thought of Sekmet's or Hathor's wrath, but rather that of Lord Khnemu, which sent shivers of absolute fear and horror through Luna's veins. The thought of the life of her precious boy being obliterated, so that all traces of him were erased from her life, was the one thing that she could not allow to happen. His birth had given her life. It had given her a reason to live, a reason to love. She had loved him desperately. She still loved him desperately. It was her anger and her fixation on revenge which had hurt that love, but she hoped that it was not dead; that she had not killed it forever. She prayed that, perhaps one day, she could rekindle it; that perhaps one day, her beloved boy would forgive her.

Aten's hand carrying the torch flame came within inches of the papyrus. The corner of the amuletic papyrus lit. Luna panicked. She realised at last that her continued devotion to her lust for revenge would cause her own son's death and that would be too high a price to pay. Luna would not risk that.

"Stop! I relent. I relent. Please, you cannot harm my child! I ask forgiveness from all those whom I have harmed. I see now the chaos and destruction that my hatred has brought on Ka and on myself and on my child. It has destroyed the love which I shared with my son. It has destroyed the woman that I once was, the woman whom everyone loved and revered, but soon came to despise. I have only myself to blame."

Luna collapsed on the floor, with tears flowing freely down her cheeks. Aten doused the flame which could have seen Luna's whole existence go up in smoke. Everyone watched her. They could not believe that the once mighty and much feared Goddess of the Moon had been reduced to a whimpering mess and a broken woman.

Fera and her sisters watched the demise of the woman who had been the bane of their existence. She had wanted them dead. She had caused so many people across Ka to die and suffer and she had never shown genuine remorse for her actions. She had taken her gamble on revenge and hatred too far and had lost, miserably. Fera thought then that love truly did conquer all, for it had even brought Luna to her knees, since in reality, it was only Luna's love for her beloved son that had forced her to stop her evil ways.

Nena looked at Luna, dejected and all alone on the floor. She was not sure if she should feel pity for the woman that Luna had become, since wasn't Luna after all, a woman who had known the pain of a broken heart? She had lost the two most precious people in her life. She had probably never recovered from their deaths. Her grief and sorrow had soured all vestiges of love and goodness in her heart, until there was nothing left but bitterness and blackness. Nena remembered how her mother had always taught her and her sisters to forgive each other when they had fought.

'It does not pay to keep the anger inside. It does not pay to hold a grudge.' she had told them. She was right, but Nena wondered whether the peoples of Ka would ever be able to forgive Luna. Nena hoped that as time passed and the memories had faded, of the hurt that Luna had caused, that those whose lives she had irrevocably changed, would find it in their hearts and minds to forgive Luna. She probably deserved a second chance more than most, since she had great powers, which if used in the pursuit of goodness, could bring many blessings upon the peoples of Ka.

Mwari was similarly overcome by Luna's ability to ask for forgiveness. It inspired him to reach out to Onis once again. He had wondered through Ka for so many years with nothing but malice in his heart. He knew that it was time to forgive Onis. He turned to Onis who stood beside him,

"After what you hid from me all these years, I should by all rights, never forgive you, but I shall, but not for you. I'll forgive you for myself. Should I not do so, the rest of my days will be plagued with regret and I choose to live my life without regret. The only thing I ask, is that you tell me where I might find my son? Do you have any idea where he might be?"

"Unfortunately, I do not, but I must tell you that it was Shona's dying wish that I tell you that she forgave you whole-heartedly. She held no ill feelings towards you. I deprived you of the joy of knowing your son and for that I am eternally sorry. When I sent your son away, I left him with a token, an amulet on a bracelet, to remind him of his mother and that he was once loved. I hoped that when he was old enough, that he would use the amulet to find his people and perhaps reunite with his father."

The discussion between Onis and Mwari, piqued Boise's attention.

"What amulet? How did it look?" asked Boise.

"It was an amulet which depicted a fish eagle, a powerful symbol of the Monomutapa kingdom." said Onis. Boise removed the amulet which hung around her neck.

"Like this one?" Boise showed it to Onis.

"Yes, but how did you get this?"

"It was given to me by Daniel." Boise looked at Daniel as she answered Onis.

Daniel's face looked deathly pale, as though he had awoken from a nightmare or seen an apparition. For a split second, he neither heard a sound nor could speak. He was tongue-tied. Onis viewed the amulet. It looked very familiar. Daniel also seemed utterly thrown by Onis' revelations.

"Daniel, can you hear me?" asked Boise. Daniel did not answer.

"Daniel, where did you get this amulet?" asked Onis. Daniel found it hard to talk.

"I have always had it. Since my childhood, I always carried it with me."

"Where were you raised?"

"In an orphanage"

"Where"

"With the priests in Catal Huyuk."

Daniel's words sounded like a bolt of lightning out of the blue and caught everyone by surprise, but most especially Onis. It dawned on him that the boy that he had wilfully abandoned, so many years back, had miraculously returned.

"Oh, my God!" mouthed Mwari.

He too realised the truth. Was it fate or luck that had reunited him with his son? Mwari felt his legs give way underneath him. He fell to his knees. Daniel struggled for a moment, uncertain of what to do. He felt lost. He did not know how he should react. Should he accept Mwari as his father and give no thought to the years and distance that had existed between them? As father and son, they had no bond. They were strangers, but yet they were not.

They had got to know each other on their journey. They had become friends. He liked and trusted Mwari. Did he still feel the same way now that he knew Mwari was his father? Should he be angry with Mwari for his behaviour towards Shona, the mother he had never known or should he ignore the past and accept Mwari for the man that he had become, for the man who had risked his own life to save Boise, his beloved? Daniel's mind raced with confused thoughts. His indecision was finally removed when he found himself involuntarily bending down to help Mwari to his feet. Mwari looked into Daniel's eyes.

"Do you forgive me, my son? Do you forgive the man who acted so abominably towards your mother? How I have prayed over the years to find your mother and make things right with her? I know now that it can never be, but I can make things right with you, if you will give me that chance."

"I have always wondered why your opinion of me mattered so much, why I desperately sought your approval. I suppose it is only natural for a son to stand tall in his father's estimations of him. I searched many moons for my parents. It saddens me greatly to know that I will never meet my mother. By all accounts, she was a loving person." Mwari nodded. Daniel continued,

"If there is one thing that I have learnt since I embarked on this mission with you all and since I met Boise, is that life is very unpredictable and far too short. One must live life to the fullest. Boise has taught me to love again and to be courageous. So, today I am choosing my own destiny, one filled with love and forgiveness. I cannot judge the man who my father used to be, the one seen though his own eyes and those of Onis or the many people whom he has wronged. I can only judge the man, who has guided and protected us all through our journey and the one who has behaved with integrity, courage and trust. I am proud to know that man and proud to call such a man my father."

Daniel and Mwari exchanged a warm embrace. Jadon, Gibeon and the sisters saw the tears well up in Mwari's eyes. In his father's arms, it was the second time in his life that Daniel had felt safe and loved. The first time had been when he had met a beautiful, but shy girl along a dusty road under the sunny skies in Catal Huyuk.

Luna looked on with sadness and regret at the warmth shared between father and son. She hoped that one day she too could see forgiveness shining in her own beloved son's eyes. Luna interjected,

"Before, I return to Mountain Island, I must say a few words to you," Luna turned to address Fera and her sisters. "When I first met the four of you, you all reminded me of myself, when I was a young girl, fearlessly independent and courageous. I was right then to believe that about you all, however, I still grossly underestimated you. I thought that my spells and magic would outwit you. On that score, I could not have been more wrong. Your love and loyalty towards each other proved far more powerful than any moon magic that I could ever conjure up. I did everything in my power to put obstacles in your way, to prevent you from succeeding in your mission, but the power of love and friendship overpowered my evil and for that, I am strangely grateful. It is because of you that I have learnt the real meaning of sisterhood and the real value of womanhood. Women all across Ka have always revered my moon magic. They have lived their lives happily with my guidance and protection. I lost my path along the way. I forgot my true purpose in life. My moon magic was always a source of great beauty, imagination and mystery. It guided fertility and thus was a source of life. It was always the cause of much celebration and dedication by all women. I had forgotten how good it always made me feel to be an inspiration to the women of Ka. I am determined that it shall be that way again. You, Daughters of Ka, have given me a second chance at life and for that I shall always be thankful." The sisters were touched by Luna's words.

Luna then handed Aten the sun wedjat. Its red jasper stone burned brightly in the torchlight.

"I believe that this belongs to an infinitely more important person than I will ever be. Would you return this to its rightful owner?" said Luna.

Aten had never relished the idea of bringing Luna to a place of such broken despair, but he was relieved and glad that she had seen the light. He hoped that their tentative truce could one day become something more. It might never be possible that they could become friends or even allies, but at least, they were no longer enemies and he would mercifully accept that gift. Aten took the sun wedjat from Luna.

He then turned his attention to the task that had been the focus of so much dedication and devotion by so many; the reunification of the pieces of the Turquoise Figurine. He smiled at Fera and her sisters. As he watched them standing silently, yet resolutely beside each other, he took a moment to consider how the destinies of the four Daughters of Ka had been inextricably interwoven with the destiny of the Turquoise Goddess and of Ka itself. He was impressed by their courage, their tenacity and their great bond of friendship and sisterhood. They had accepted the challenge set by the Holy Mother Goddess, without truly knowing and understanding the full impart of the immense undertaking and risk that they would have to face, but despite great danger, they had risen to such challenge, nobly and respectfully. All the peoples of Ka owed them a debt of gratitude. Aten turned his mind to one last piece of business.

"Daughters of Ka, bring me the pieces of the Turquoise Figurine that you have in your keep."

Aten looked at Fera and her sisters as he spoke to them. They all felt the enormity of the moment that they faced. Everything that they had gone through, all the trials and tribulations that they had faced, had all been for one great cause, to reunite the pieces of the Turquoise Figurine and return the Turquoise Goddess to Ka. Nena felt emotional and on the verge of crying, but she was unconcerned since her tears were the result of great happiness and relief.

Fera was the first to react to Aten's request. She took out the 'Little Light' which she, Jadon and Gibeon had found at Lalibela. She gave it to Aten. Boise handed Aten the shining blue object which Khnemu, God of the Underworld had placed in her dying hand, as well as the blue stone which Hathor had presented to her in Abydos. Feur gave him the blue stone which had been nature's gift to Mwari and Aten from the depths of the burial tomb of the great King of the Tellem people at Bandiagara. Lastly, Nena placed the stone from the eight-pointed star, which King Sonni-Ali had begrudgingly at first, but later willingly, given to them in Jenne. To Mwari, it appeared only proper that the sisters were the custodians of the precious pieces of the Turquoise Figurine. If it were not for their efforts and those of their own protectors, success in their mission would have remained elusive.

"But that's only five pieces." exclaimed Nena, with a note of shock in her voice at such realisation. She looked at her sisters, who showed similar signs of concern. Had they come so close to their goal, only to be disappointed at the last conceivable moment?

"Don't forget these!" added Fera, as she handed Aten the pearls which Mami Watta had given to her and her sisters.

"So, it seems as if we have all the pieces of the Turquoise Figurine." said Aten. He placed all seven objects on the earth at his feet. It was only fitting that when, the Turquoise Goddess, as the first and original Daughter of Ka, returned to the realm of mankind, that her feet should touch the ancient soil of Ka. Aten then stepped back and watched the objects.

Instantaneously and miraculously the dark night sky lit up with a cornucopia of blue lights, which frenetically danced and swirled around the heads of the crowds. The seven missing pieces of the Turquoise Figurine magically ascended into the air and formed a blue haze and in front of the eyes of all those present, the blue haze then transformed into the image of a beautiful woman, her face was majestically serene, her dark tresses blew luxuriously in the warm night air and her flowing turquoise gown rippled as she moved. The woman wore turquoise beads draped over her breasts and a turquoise pendant, which shone luminescent as it hung around her neck.

The crowds at the river's edge stared at the vision which seemed to float effortlessly above the ground. For many moons, perhaps even longer than that, not a single person, whether man or God, had laid eyes on the face of the Turquoise Goddess. Her name and her face had become elusive, an enigma, something which everyone in Ka had only heard of, but which few had actually seen. Many had lost hope that she would ever return. Like religion and custom, knowledge of the Turquoise Goddess had passed into the realm of myth and mystery. No-one dared imagine the day when she would return, since such thought seemed impossible, but everyone silently prayed that one day, when she did return to Ka that she would restore peace and order to a realm fraught with war and devastation.

Aten stepped forward. He bowed in the presence of the Turquoise Goddess. She smiled at him. A great warmth and motherly love shone through her clear eyes. Aten returned her smile, unable to utter a word and thoroughly bowled over by her great beauty and benevolent power. Aten handed her the sun and moon wedjats. She gently took one and then the other. She held the red jasper sun wedjat over her right breast. As she did so, it magically formed part of the beads which draped across her body. She then took the lapis lazuli moon wedjat. As she held it next to her body, it too became part of the shell which covered her left breast. With each move, everyone stared, totally mesmerised.

Fera thought to herself then, that the sights and sounds which they all beheld in the Turquoise Goddess' return, should at the very least have elicited some verbal reactions from the crowds, but the silence that had descended upon them all since the appearance of Mami Watta, had simply continued. Wide eyes and open mouths evidenced the wonderment and captivation of all. Fera hardly wanted to breathe for fear that the sound of her breathing would interrupt the scene of great beauty and splendour which she saw.

During many nights of their journey across Ka, Fera had lain awake thinking and dreaming of the moment when they would get to see the return of the Turquoise Goddess. She was not disappointed when the moment had eventually arrived. The Turquoise Goddess was far more beautiful and ethereal than she had ever imagined she would be, but she was after all more than just a beautiful woman. She was a mother, a friend and a protector to all across Ka. The age of peace and beauty had at last arrived with the return of the Turquoise Goddess and all in Ka could breathe a sigh of relief.

The Turquoise Goddess looked over the faces before her. She smiled again. Warmth radiated around her. Her voice, warm and gentle, did not cause alarm as she spoke for the first time in many moons, to all those who looked up at her,

"Things are now as they should be. Thank you all for your courage and strength. Your combined efforts have ushered in a new beginning for us all. Unity is strength and division is weakness. The time is upon us for all the kingdoms of Ka to unite and for all the peoples of Ka to celebrate their diversity and to find peace, harmony and balance between mankind and nature. Where there is love, there can be no darkness." The Turquoise Goddess smiled at Fera and her sisters.

"Return home, Daughters of Ka to reunite with your beloved parents. I too shall see my Mother, Father and my Daughters of the Four Seasons. Never forget, a family tie is like a tree, it can bend, but it cannot break. Your work is at an end. Mine is simply beginning."

The Turquoise Goddess' words lingered on everyone's minds long after the image of her had disappeared into the night sky. The only trace of her having returned to Ka, was a bright band of silvery stars, a welcome gift from the Goddess Hathor, which had been painted across the evening sky, to envelop Ka in its protective embrace.

Fera and her sisters looked up into the night sky, mesmerised and transfixed by the abundant stars. Soon, the hazy band of starlight opened up to reveal a staircase, which stretched from one side of the heavens to the other. A young woman with lustrous golden hair ran across the arc of starlight towards the outstretched arms of a handsome young man. They embraced tenderly, yet passionately, the eternal divide which had existed between them for many moons, having miraculously disappeared and the cruel spell which had kept them apart, having at last been broken. Tears of joy washed over the cheeks of Luna and Aten as they witnessed the joy of their beloved children, being reunited in love.

Fera could not hold back her emotions. She wanted to break down in tears at the sheer joy and happiness which she felt, but she found comfort in the presence of her sisters, who came to her aid as they had countless times before and as they would continue to do, for as long as they lived.

Daniel joined the woman he loved and kissed Boise's cheek. Fezzan firmly took hold of Fera's hand and they exchanged a glance of mutual love and respect for each other, a glance which held the promise of an exciting tomorrow. Mwari, Jadon and Gibeon then joined them as well. Mwari broke their silent contemplations,

"My father once told me that however long the night, the dawn will break. I never quite understood his words, until now that is."

Hand in hand, they all stood looking at Ife. The festivities of the people in the city could be seen and heard, as they merrily and joyously danced and sang, not only in celebration of their great city, Ife, which had been saved, but also in celebration of their beloved Ka. Mwari's wise words rang true for everyone that night, but most especially in the hearts and minds of the Daughters of Ka.

ABOUT THE AUTHOR

Debangelique Thompson was born in South Africa in 1974 and is an attorney, lecturer and academic writer. Her writing is inspired by Africa; a beautiful and mysterious continent, whose beauty is often lost in the darkness of war and despair, but whose light will always shine bright through its rich history, its interesting peoples and its unforgettable stories.

www.ingramcontent.com/pod-product-compliance
Lightning Source LLC
Chambersburg PA
CBHW071307170626
46809CB00001B/359